Praise for

The Gentle Order of Girls and Boys

"The book is informed by the Vietnamese immigrations of the nineteen-seventies but is filled with social observation of contemporary middle-class culture and indie sensibility . . . Quietly beautiful, Strom's stories are hip without being ironic."   —*The New Yorker*

"With precise, lyrical language, Dao Strom takes on motherhood, music, and lust. After spending an afternoon with the four women in *The Gentle Order of Girls and Boys*, I see the world around me differently: every quiet passerby full of yearning, each gesture important and strange."

—AMANDA EYRE WARD, author of *How to Be Lost*

"There is an underlying emotional current running through these stories that pulls you into a world populated by strong, wise, and displaced women. Dao Strom has a rare talent—the ability to capture feelings and thoughts you don't think can be described, and convey them in elegant prose."

—VENDELA VIDA, author of *And Now You Can Go*

"Dao Strom's characters explore a new territory of cultural awareness, of the selves that we seem arbitrarily forced to inhabit. Although uncomfortably fresh in their observation, these stories address old truths. *The Gentle Order of Girls and Boys* is an important and quietly powerful contribution to contemporary fiction."

—SABINA MURRAY, author of *The Caprices*

"*The Gentle Order of Girls and Boys* cuts to the quick of what it means to be alive and burdened with a human heart. With exquisite brushstrokes and piercing accuracy, Dao Strom brings us face to face with the parts of our intimate selves we are so often running up against and at the same time, truly wish to forget."

—HOLIDAY REINHORN, author of *Big Cats*

"Small moments carry enormous weight in these four loosely linked novellas about young Vietnamese women living in present-day California and Texas." —*Publishers Weekly*

The Gentle Order
of Girls and Boys

ALSO BY DAO STROM

Grass Roof, Tin Roof
We Were Meant to Be a Gentle People
You Will Always Be Someone from Somewhere Else

The Gentle Order of Girls and Boys

four stories

DAO STROM

With an introduction by Isabelle Thuy Pelaud
With a new preface by the author

COUNTERPOINT

BERKELEY, CALIFORNIA

For Lincoln, my little angel

Won't soul music change now that our
souls have turned strange?

—*Silver Jews*

The goal of the Lemurians was the development
of the will, of the faculty of imagination. The
education of children was wholly directed
toward this. The boys were hardened in the
strongest manner. They had to learn to undergo
dangers, to overcome pain, to accomplish daring
deeds . . . The raising of girls was different.
While the female child was also hardened,
everything was directed toward her developing
a strong imagination. For example, she was
exposed to the storm in order calmly to feel its
dreadful beauty; she had to witness the combats
of the men fearlessly . . . Thereby propensities
for dreaming and for fantasy developed in the
girl . . .

—*Rudolf Steiner*

Contents

Introduction

by Isabelle Thuy Pelaud

Dao Strom's *The Gentle Order of Girls and Boys* goes against the grain. Its careful attention to language and close examination of subtleties that emerge from the conflicts between inner world and outer world extend the corpus of Vietnamese American literature. Ethnic markers and memories of Vietnam do not infuse the four novellas. As the book ends, readers are left with the impression, "What just happened?" We close our eyes and take a deep breath: "Nothing and Everything." Disquiet phrases begin to surface from consciousness: *careful truth*, *curse of beauty*, *cool calculated honesty*, *murky boundaries*, and more. They linger and resonate.

Conflicting desires and wants pervade these stories. The characters move in the realms of daily life as a student, waitress, musician, daughter, wife, lover, and mother. They are women who experience their worlds in large part through their senses while maintaining a certain degree of detachment from everything. Their bodies, spirits, and minds are pulled in different directions. The Vietnamese American female characters are not excessively good or bad as those we often see in movies—they are ordinarily good *and* bad. They seem trapped in a culture that fails to see them for who they are. And yet the characters don't regard themselves as victims nor as fighters. Instead, they express emotions and thoughts, and take actions that complicate predetermined notions of female wisdom and naïveté. Pointing obliquely to the psychological cost derived from the dissonances between awareness, emotions, and actions is an "Interlude" situated in between the novellas, told from a privileged perspective of a younger brother who, in contrast, appears too pure and too kind.

The courageous exploration of the four heroines' complex interiors evokes the contradictions seen in Maxine Hong Kingston's *The Woman Warrior*, where the narrator admits her struggle between the desire for independence and the longing to be taken care of by a man. Forty years later, Strom's narrators share similar concerns, while excavating directly the excesses of "lightness" and "darkness" that can emanate from such tensions.

Characters in *The Gentle Order of Girls and Boys* search for the meaning of life, while also appearing blind to external racial and gender biases that shape their lives. They don't quite fit in their respective worlds, and yet they're not different enough to stand out as misfits. Their subsequent ambivalence vis-à-vis those who are near them transpires to readers, as we are simultaneously pulled in and pushed out from easy identification with them.

The book is also reminiscent of Monique Truong's *Bitter in the Mouth*, in which the protagonist's ethnicity is revealed only at the end of the novel in order to bypass stereotypes and center the humanity of the Vietnamese American woman's narrator. Literary texts such as these pave the way for other writers to explore the complexities of Vietnamese American characters devoid of memories of the Vietnam War and journeys of escape, without fear of being judged as not "ethnic enough" or as not "refugee enough."

Dao Strom does not write for an audience in search of exoticism or in search of a resolution of the Vietnam War. She asks rather in beautiful prose that the vacillation of her characters between lightness and darkness, their anxieties and joys, be understood on their own terms without having to carry, represent, or measure up to those who came before her.

Preface

This book almost wasn't published. I was a writer at the beginning of my career, in the mid-2000s, whose first novel had been released as a paperback original on an imprint of a major New York publishing house. The expectation was that my second manuscript (a two-book contract) would be a novel, to be published as part of the publisher's main catalog, as a hardcover release and at a higher profile than my first. However, when I turned in the second manuscript I'd written, four novellas about four women, they decided against publishing it. I was asked to repay a percentage of the advance money, and my agent and I took back the manuscript and restarted the search for a new publisher. It was summer 2004 when we began this search. The book in its final form, as *The Gentle Order of Girls and Boys*, eventually found its home with Counterpoint Press in early 2005.

While I wholly accept the reasons why the first publisher decided this manuscript didn't fit in their catalog—among those (as cited) the interiority of the writing and its absence of plot—I also believe another reason this manuscript may've struck editors (especially more than a decade ago) as having too obscure a potential for readership may've had something to do with narrative scarcity.[1]

I might here mention that I am a woman writer of Vietnamese descent. I was born in Vietnam and fled as a refugee (as an infant, with my mother) in 1975, at the Fall of Saigon. I grew up—with no memories whatsoever of Vietnam—in a small northern California town, in a family of mixed-cultural makeup: my mother remarried a Danish American immigrant, and we spent our family years in a rural, mostly white and conservative, community. The generational label given to people like me is an in-between moniker: the "1.5 generation." Our bodies have experienced the physical passage and potential trauma of displacement, yet we are not identified, as strongly as our elders, with the originating culture or geography. For many of us who landed in the West as young children, we are likely to have grown up more influenced by (and trying to assimilate into) the diasporic land's culture and customs, while also conscious of our not fully belonging—in either direction. Needless to say, growing up

---

1. The term "narrative scarcity" and its adverse "narrative plenitude" are ideas I take from Viet Thanh Nguyen, which he mentions in various articles and talks and which he coined in his nonfiction book on war and memory, *Nothing Ever Dies* (Harvard University Press, 2016).

I encountered no literature or media that portrayed lives like my own. At the same time I inhabited the same cultural landscape recognizable to many Americans.

In graduate school at the Iowa Writers' Workshop, I recall one instructor theorizing about "ethnic" American literature. She said the first generation of published writers from any marginalized group would be tasked with the work of laying out the context of that group's history; that it would not be until a historical context was established that subsequent generations of writers could be more free to experiment with form (and, in effect, to write as they pleased—which could also then include not addressing said historical context at all). I might agree with this theory, to an extent, at the same time wishing to push against it.

In the mid-1990s to early 2000s, when I was first beginning my writing career aspirations, it's true there were only a handful of diasporic Vietnamese authors' names circulating. I had encountered Lan Cao, Linh Dinh, Le Ly Hayslip, translations of Nguyen Huy Thiep (this last technically not diasporic). In 1998 an anthology, *Watermark: Vietnamese American Poetry & Prose*, was published by the then-nascent Asian American Writers' Workshop, edited by Barbara Tran, Monique Truong, and Luu Truong Khoi. This anthology (which included two of my short stories) was one of my first exposures to diasporic voices closer to my own age group and "1.5 generation" experience. But it was not until Andrew X. Pham's memoir *Catfish and Mandala* (2000) that I first saw a Vietnamese diasporic voice appear in long-book form, backed by a major publisher. It felt momentous (at least to me), in 2003, when three Vietnamese

American women authors' debut books came out all in the
same year: Monique Truong's *The Book of Salt*, lê thi diem
thúy's *The Gangster We Are All Looking For*, and my own
first book, *Grass Roof, Tin Roof*. My mother, as a writer
in Saigon pre-1975, had been a "pioneer" of sorts in her
own milieu, and I felt like I was following in her footsteps,
maybe, just a little. But I must acknowledge that of course
there were always others before us.

In numbers, this still amounted to relatively few diasporic
Vietnamese writers tasked with—or granted opportunity
to participate in—the so-called setting of historical context
or defining our cultural experience, as of the early 2000s.
And, as Chimamanda Adichie has since so eloquently put
it, there is danger in having only "a single story" about any
group of people. This single-story status is arrived at largely
due to the question of power—who decides which and how
many stories are let through the gates, into a field of public
visibility—and white Americans in the publishing industry
have long been the ones responsible for opening those gates
or not. For Vietnamese Americans, I would argue the single
story so far defining us has to do with war, refugeehood, our
debt to America (or America's debt to us), and is limited, at
times, by being able to perceive us only insofar as we also
define ourselves by those circumstances: our displacement,
entry, and assimilation narratives—which are also, and yet,
war/colonialism/imperialism-consequent narratives. By this I
mean that, although concerned with consequences suffered
by emigrant/immigrant/refugee populations (affected by
world-political events America has played part in), these are
narratives still hinged—especially in the case of Vietnam—on

the centralizing subject of American power and conscience, both its capacities and its perils. While this is all undoubtedly crucial territory to engage, in a world where there exists narrative plenitude, there would also exist permission for many, and any, types of stories, a multiplicity of perspectives to portray a given group of people. We would (and should) be able to define (and un-define) ourselves on our own terms. In narrative plenitude there would exist space for our war and refugee stories, alongside our postwar, pre-war, beyond-war, aside-from-war, and war-irrelevant/irreverent stories, our direct and oblique approaches to subject matter, our aesthetic experiments and our conventional narratives, our loud stories and our quieter ones.

The Gentle Order of Girls and Boys was published for the first time in 2006. It had a small reception at best, some praise, some criticism, and went largely unnoticed. I was still pleased with this, and with the book itself, grateful just to have it in the world especially after its rocky start. I would not publish another book until 2015. This was not for lack of trying but was also in line with my creative development in that period, which was leading me—beyond fiction— toward a more hybrid literary expression, to integrate poetic, musical, and visual instincts, as well as the collaborative, the multi-voiced.

I want to digress, just slightly here, to talk a little about the influence of my mother.

My mother, especially by traditional Vietnamese standards, was and is a fairly radical woman. A "different" kind of mother and woman than most others, as asserted by aunts and my mother's friends over the years. Although I've not been able to read her stories in their original form, in Vietamese language, growing up I always knew the story of her as a writer and journalist. So I understood this about her, or had at least this lens to apply when trying to understand her. I understood this was why she pushed intellect forward as the aspect she wished to be both judged and loved by; I also understood, at fourteen, when she first told me I shouldn't have children if I wanted a career (even suggesting hysterectomy as a form of birth control), not to take it too personally. That she was just trying to tell me, or warn me, the possible way of the world for women like us. Inadvertently, she was my first writing mentor.

And, while the most visible representation of Vietnamese womanhood—for white mainstream America, that is, and especially in the eighties and nineties (the era of my coming-of-age in America)—may've resembled something more like the "fallen" yet virtuous, self-sacrificing, tragic bar girl character in *Miss Saigon* (not to mention other victimized and hyper-sexualized depictions of Asian female bodies in American cinema), for myself the probable "story" of Vietnamese womanhood, as conveyed first through my mother, then through many other Vietnamese women I've since met, is a much more complicated, thorny, heady, contradictory, and un-frameable portrait, and one also still marked, to degrees, by [her] sexuality—the consequences, violations, empowerments, entrapments, and portrayals of it. The feminine—on both shores—appears as something others—male-dominated power structures, that is—feel the need to control or condemn. As just one example: after 1975, my mother's books were banned by the Vietnamese communist government, due to their "decadent" nature. To give some explanation of what "decadent" means in this context, I turn to the two (in English) sources I've encountered that mention my mother's work as a writer. One is from an essay in a journal out of Yale University, *Vietnam Forum*,[2] from 1987, in which the essayist describes my mother's fiction as bearing a "cool description of woman's very human sexuality," and this sexual content being "a slap in the face of an ethical system that has attached a strong stigma to such sexuality and has relied on a narrow concept of chastity to evaluate women and hinder their total development as human beings." My mother shared this essay with me when I was an MFA student at the Iowa Writers' Workshop, where in the Iowa City public library I also found—for the first time ever—one of my mother's books. (I still recall the strangeness of recognizing her pen name—Trùng Dương—on the spine in the foreign-language section of a library in the middle of Iowa.) I quote the term "decadent" from the second source, an *Encyclopedia of Censorship*,[3] which lists censorship parameters for South Vietnamese literature (among other countries' literatures). The term "decadent" appears in

2. Công-Huyền Tôn-Nữ Nha-Trang, "Women Writers of South Vietnam (1954–1975)," *The Vietnam Forum, No. 9* (Southeast Asian Studies Publication Series, Yale University, 1987).
3. Jonathan Green, *Encyclopedia of Censorship* (New York: Facts On File, Inc., 1990).

Category B: works considered as decadent by the
authorities. Vietnamese authors, often women such as
Tuy Hong and Trung Duong, whose works featured
reasonably explicit sex or dealt with otherwise taboo
sexual topics and were as such judged indecent and
immoral.

I venture that my mother may not have considered her "sexual topics" to be "taboo" so much as rooted, rather, in the
realistic: fiction based on the experiences of real women
whose so-called decadence was, perhaps more truthfully, a
(self-)possession of will, that some will always have, to push
against bounds set by a patriarchal culture. My mother was
writing her stories in the late 1960s to early '70s, a time
when feminism was making its waves in western countries
too. From this viewpoint, it is easy to understand how Vietnam's patriarchal traditions chafed her.

From her pictures and recollections, I glean the type
of feminism my mother embodied: cutting her hair short,
claiming her right to education, taking liberties in sexual,
social, and professional arenas—in short, doing things as she
perceived men were free to do. She may've been an outlier,
but she was not unreasonable. At the same age I was beginning my own writing career, she was a recognized writer,
a publisher of an independent Saigon daily newspaper, and
mother of two small children. Later, by the time of our flee-
ing, she was also a war widow. Had we stayed in Vietnam
after 1975, she would've been persecuted for her literary
activities.

I was never trying to imitate my mother's stories.

But the license she had given herself, she had also given me. Whether I was conscious of it or not, I carried something of her lineage—that of Vietnamese women writing the lives of modern Vietnamese women—into my own literary ventures. Though of course the consequences for my mother of writing her women in their contemporary landscape in her time in Saigon were significantly different than my own context.

I was in my late twenties to early thirties when I wrote the stories in *The Gentle Order of Girls and Boys*. I was, as a person, not unlike some of the women protagonists of those stories. I had gone to college, had moved a little nomadically between different U.S. cities, had had numerous romantic relationships (was still sorting through this area of my life), as well as numerous odd jobs; I had artistic ambitions and was the mother of a young child, also a single mother. There were ways that being Vietnamese and a refugee/immigrant from war figured into the experiences of my first decade or so of womanhood, and also many ways it did not. I was writing from both of those places in these stories. I had few articulable goals in my process. I knew it would be four stories—four portraits, so to speak (and then this parameter, even, was interrupted by a fifth "interlude" story arising, the only piece that centers a male—a brother's—perspective). I knew the characters would each have elements of their backstory connecting them to Vietnam, but their ethnicity wouldn't permeate the stories, nor offer explanation or foundation for their current persons. I knew also that I wanted an emotional current to run through (this meant I would follow that rhythm in writing), and this intuitive and liminally associative logic, more so than any plot-driven details or applied narrative architecture, is what would ultimately draw the stories together into a whole work.

It was also, and still is, of greater interest to me to read and write prose that maps characters from their interiors looking out, and that [re]presents—in my opinion, at least—the truer ambiguities and multi-texturality of human experience by *not* neatly tying all the pieces together.

I am a different woman today, and certainly a different kind of writer, than I was when I first wrote these stories. More than a decade ago now. Looking back and reentering their terrain, I encounter a mixture of feelings and impressions. First, there is the surreal sense-memory of remembering writing them, or (in some moments of re-reading) realizing I do not remember the writing at all: I cannot really remember being [her] or tracing [her], that younger female perception enacting the lives of [her] young women characters. For the sometimes-missteps of their desires I feel some tenderness, some chagrin, for these young women; I feel also admiration for the tenacity of their sensitivities, for their affectionate perceptions of the small. And I am compelled to stand out of the way of their proclivities for scrutiny, of nearly everything coming at them, their determination to turn everything external into something of use or meaning on an internal level. I see them, the young women of these stories, working so hard to see, yet also refusing to see, themselves in the (white) American context that engulfs them. They are Vietnamese characters, but also of mixed-Vietnamese and estranged

Vietnamese identities, which—in reality—is just one more way one may abide in relation to one's cultural makeup. As I sit down to write this author's note, intellectually I want to be able to contextualize the stories (and my intent through them) according to what I know, now, about our diasporic literature; but I think, much like myself at the time, these stories are mostly concerned with perceiving—with insisting on their simple *being* through *sensing*—the materials of experience and body that were then present.

As a facile image, I think of the pea beneath the stack of mattresses that imperceptibly intrudes on the princess's sleep. Or I think of mist seeping into a landscape and deceptively soaking it in precipitation, belying the straightforwardness of rain: issues of past / culture / racialization / the feminine / marginalization are in ways always present, like undercurrent or undercutting. Tenuous; indelible. As both a person and writer, for as many years as I can remember, I have walked about within this negotiation that comes with inhabiting a perceptibly brown and female body in a Western land.

*

I am at a reading at the SF Public Library and it is 2018. The lineup for this reading consists of six writers spanning a range of genres—poetry, fiction, interdisciplinary art, comics, photography, music—all of us women and of Vietnamese background. This reading falls under the banner of a collective art/literary project, She Who Has No Master(s). In the audience are a number of younger Vietnamese Americans, one of whom pointedly asks what advice would we give to beginning writers like herself who are also Vietnamese and female. We talk about being women writers and working in and beyond dominant literary contexts, we talk about racial pressures and stereotypes, about inherited trauma and motherhood, about not heeding feedback from our (white, male) colleagues, among other things. Our collective project has been in motion since 2015 and by now it's common for us to encounter audience members struck by the group of us—the visual and physical representation of a Vietnamese diasporic collectivity that is also female—and by the realization that seeing/hearing a multiple number of Vietnamese women's voices sounding their stories together is rare. At this particular October reading in downtown San Francisco, we noted upon entering that just across the street (on the marquee of the SHN Orpheum Theatre), another art event featuring (or titularly claiming to feature) a Vietnamese woman as subject matter is simultaneously occurring: it is a production of *Miss Saigon*. We go into our reading at the SF Public Library marveling and disgusted at the irony of this juxtaposition. Later, I will google "miss saigon sf 2018" to research its reception. I don't want to go too far down this rabbit hole. I glance through a few reviews. The *SF Examiner* calls it "slickly produced and soullessly executed" and "emotionally vacant," while the *Mercury News* review opens with the bald assessment: "There's something grotesque about *Miss Saigon* . . ." and goes on to state the most obvious problem, that the production "plays into an insidiously stereotypical narrative, imagining backward Asian people helplessly waiting for white saviors." While this surely states a prejudice just about every Vietnamese American knows to dismiss (and

many non-Vietnamese folks know it too), it is yet hard to
miss the fact—visual and visceral—that this depiction of the
Vietnamese feminine is still, to an absurd degree, our competition. And, surely more robustly funded and attended.

*

My relationship to my Vietnamese-ness, so to speak, has
been its own long slow return. A form of return one must
attempt over and over, I've come to believe, via meetings and
re-meetings and healing processes that seem sometimes to
have no end. In 2003, when my first novel was published,
I knew no other Vietnamese American writers personally.
In 2004, I did my first event for a Vietnamese organization,
the Diasporic Vietnamese Artists Network, and met its co-
founder, writer, artist, and academic Isabelle Thuy Pelaud.
But it was not until 2010 that we really began to share our
personal stories, and then in 2011 I was invited to be a con-
tributing writer to another DVAN project, *diaCRITICS*, a
blog being launched by then-aspiring novelist Viet Thanh
Nguyen. My roles within this community grew gradually,
organically. In 2015, I proposed to Isabelle that we initiate a
collective project, to bring together the voices of Vietnamese
women writers: this began with a dinner party and sharing our work and personal stories in Isabelle's living room
and quickly grew from there. There were five of us at that
first gathering (and I feel it important to name the names)—
Angie Chau, Aimee Phan, Julie Thi Underhill, Isabelle, and
myself—and since then other voices have joined us to varying
degrees—Stacey Tran, Vi Khi Nao, Anh-Hoa Thi Nguyen,

Thao P. Nguyen, Hoa Nguyen, Anna Moï, Lan Duong, Thi Bui, Beth Nguyen—the circle fluctuating and still evolving. Under the heading She Who Has No Master(s)[4] we debuted our first multi-voice poem at a reading in Portland, Oregon, in May 2016, with five of us sitting together on a bench, letting our voices interweave. I still remember the atmosphere of fortification and vulnerability, and the powerful quiet with which we were received, in that space forged by our collectivity, between our bodies and words. There is a different kind of energy our voices and experiences take on in standing *with* one another, that a single story, a solo voice, cannot encapsulate on its own.

The multi-voice space, too, is a form of narrative plenitude.

It has taken us—I recognize—some time to arrive here. It is 2019 now, a far cry from my mother's and my landing date of 1975. I am not as disconnected today from a "Vietnamese American community" of artists and writers as I was in the early 2000s, when I was writing my first two books. And it is no doubt a privilege that I get to look back on the passage of my writing life and see it traceable in terms of manifested creative works. From this vantage, I can observe that from the beginning, whether I understood it or not, the question of the collective experience and the individual voice within it, was always with me—via the multiple perspectives of the novel-in-linked-stories shape of my first book, and in the four-novellas

---

4. The title of our collective project, She Who Has No Master(s), was inspired by Audre Lorde's essay, "The Master's Tools Will Not Dismantle the Master's House."

framework of my second. I can also observe that my initial impulse in *The Gentle Order of Girls and Boys* to make a space (in this case a book) that contained multiple "portraits" of Vietnamese women, was an impetus—both aesthetic and personal—that would continue growing and morphing with me, to push eventually beyond the constructs of a single book or fiction as its genre, to evolve into the hybrid and collaborative formations it now compels me to work in, engaging hybrid media in my solo work, and engaging the collective voices of other Vietnamese women via our She Who Has No Master(s) project: a scope more multi-faceted than I could've even imagined in 2006.

The Vietnamese and diasporic experience has countless facets, like a river sending its many mouths to the sea, and I believe we are still learning how to listen, and heed, these many voices, their many variances and contours of rhythm and flow and shape. I hope that this reception of the multiplicity of our stories will continue. It is within this expanded and reawakened sense of context that I feel fortunate to greet the re-release of *The Gentle Order of Girls and Boys*.

DAO STROM
February 2019

1. Mary

1. *Meetings*

Ping was smiling sheepishly under Mary's porch light when she answered the door. A sheepish, dumbfounded expression was what Mary was accustomed to seeing on Ping's face, though: she had always thought of him as a hapless person.

She hung in the half-open door with her weight on one leg and her hand resting on the doorknob. She raised her other foot to rub against her ankle as she said, "Hey." She was barefoot and did not care that Ping was seeing her in her sweatpants.

"Hey, Mary. Can I come in? It's fucking cold out here."

He was bouncing on his heels on the porch, his hands jammed in the front pockets of his thin tracksuit windbreaker, his knuckles distorting the polyester. Mary's porch was not much of a porch, more like a stoop with a wooden railing, only three stairs' height above the sidewalk. Ping grinned at her. Something in the largeness of his smile (and he smiled often) sometimes made Mary think he looked idiotic. She knew that was unkind. Yet, certain of Ping's gestures and characteristics—his candidness, his physical awkwardness, his eagerness—always caused a familial, shameful feeling to rise in Mary. It had, too, to do with the fact that he was Asian, like her, but still spoke with an accent. He was Korean; she was Vietnamese. On purpose, Mary did not smile back, only lifted an eyebrow and glanced past him, as if looking for evidence of the weather he'd just mentioned. She caught the fuzzy, amberish gleam of porch lights on the houses opposite hers—the night looked grainy, like an underexposed photograph, she thought.

Mary stepped back and let Ping inside.

———

He had called an hour or so earlier, claiming he had something important to ask her and could he come over immediately? Mary had said yes, because secretly she hoped it might have something to do with Kenny.

It had been more than six months since she'd heard anything from or about Kenny.

Kenny. Who, or what, was he? He was not Korean or Vietnamese, like them, but was a small, reticent white person. He was just a person. He was from Los Angeles, but now he was gone. And, as much as she knew it was a cliché to love someone just because they were gone, she couldn't help it. His keen eyes, his shy looks. The way he was always the quiet one in a room. He was kind but could leave without warning. Was it the leaving that did it? He had walked at the back of the group that night in the dorm hallway; he had leaned his shoulder against the wall and kept his hands in his pockets. Still now, she saw his eyes, their slow shift in her direction. Kenny, the king of mellow—according to Ping, who had known him better than Mary had.

———————

"Cool pad," said Ping, sighing. Mary noted, to herself, that there didn't seem to be about him, now, any of the urgency his phone call had suggested. Walking ahead of her, he flung his body into a surfing pose, arms outstretched, knees bent, and hop-scooted like that down the hall, head bobbing. His sneakers squeaked on the wood floors.

Mary waited until they were in the living room to speak, where she resumed her curled-up position in an armchair. She had been writing in her journal. She closed it, pushed it beneath another book on the undershelf of the coffee table. "So, what's up?"

"Man, I fell asleep in film history yesterday. I totally spaced," said Ping, dropping himself onto the facing couch. "Did you take notes? I was gonna ask to borrow them is all, really." He shrugged, glancing around. "Don't you have roommates?"

"Sometimes I do. They go away a lot." Something about Ping's concern over their class notes did not ring true to Mary, but she would let it slide. "Did you see any of it? The movie, I mean."

Ping yawned extravagantly. "Some. I thought Natalie Wood was supposed to be in it."

"Well, she is, but not till the end. She plays the kidnapped girl when they find her, after she's all grown up. If you fell asleep, you probably missed her."

"I can't remember when I fell asleep. I don't remember Natalie Wood getting kidnapped," said Ping.

"That's because she doesn't show up till the end," said Mary, again.

The movie they had watched that week was *The Searchers*, a Western from the fifties directed by John Ford. The so-named searchers were John Wayne and a young male actor whose looks Mary liked, and the search was for a girl in their family who at the beginning of the movie was abducted by Indians. Mary had enjoyed the film (barring and forgiving its crass, stereotypical portrayal of American Indians by an all-white cast in brown makeup) because she was drawn in by the idea of the men having to spend years searching for the missing sister and how one consequence of this quest was that the younger actor's fiancée was forced to spend the majority of the film waiting chastely for his letters and his return. A typical scenario that nevertheless resounded for Mary: she, too, was waiting, or at least hoping, for letters from far-off places. But it was not only that. The scenario alluded to something deeper, a buried web of feeling that was more profound than personal, almost. She felt a sense of desire that was precarious, beautiful, and dubious.

"Natalie Wood," said Ping, blinking in an odd way and not looking directly at Mary. "Man, was she hot."

"You think?" said Mary. As she observed him making this remark, the thought occurred to her that someone like Ping had no place lusting after beauty of that kind. It was a cruel thought. Then it struck her that maybe she was only looking at a distorted mirror. What was wrong with this picture? Ping, like her, it seemed, did not like his own kind: other Asians.

"Too bad she died so young, you know?" said Ping. "Too bad she fell off that boat and drowned."

"I thought she was murdered or something," said Mary.

"No, she drowned. No one knows for sure how she fell off the boat, though. They think she must've been drunk, and wandered off. She was with her husband and another actor. Christopher Walken! But neither of them saw her fall off the boat. It was in the middle of the making of that movie *Brainstorm*, and then they had to finish the movie without her. That's why it makes no sense, I guess. *Brainstorm*, I mean. Have you ever seen it?"

"No."

"It's just weird. It's this science fiction story where the characters get hooked up to this machine that lets them in on other people's brain waves or something. But the storyline just gets lost by the end."

"Huh," said Mary, not even bothering to feign interest. It was not that she didn't like Ping; no, she would not say that. It was just that he gave her nothing she didn't already have or know—he was no one she would've ever been romantically interested in.

Mary and Ping had first met in Acting I, which Ping had taken because his psychiatrist had recommended it to help him overcome his acute shyness. Mary had taken the course because she believed she had a talent for putting herself in others' psychological shoes. She was of an adaptable nature, she'd thought, and she wanted to explore this; she wanted to be capable of thinking as others thought, whether she agreed with them or not. That way, even unforgivable things, like murder, say, or sadism, could be understood—it was just a matter of perception. This was one of Mary's favorite infuriating statements to make in conversation: that everything, even what *she* believed to be true, was discreditable according to some way or another of perceiving it. But flexible viewpoints had not made her a good actress. Both she and Ping were poor actors, in fact, with no future beyond Acting I. Sometimes they had sat near one another in the classroom's theater seats, in this way silently acknowledging what they held in common (or so Mary uncomfortably thought): a polite Asian modesty that made it impossible for either of them to pretend anything.

Ping was more honest than Mary, however. Once, the year before, he had told her about the time he tried to commit suicide back in high school. His parents had to rush him to the hospital to have his stomach pumped. Mary, listening, lying on the dorm bed opposite Ping's and looking up at the black-and-white charcoal sketch of Clint Eastwood's face that hung above Ping's bed, had felt strange upon receiving this information; first, because she had not completely believed it was true, and second, because she had felt no sympathy for him, even if it was true. Some part of her—she'd been realizing lately—had long been sleeping. It awoke only to be met by bouts of ridiculous angst, usually over some boy or another she barely knew, and then it went back to sleep and she went back to saying things like "If you want to" instead of yes or no. Kenny was the only one she'd not been able to drum up either angst or anger toward. He made only a gentle ripple—subtle strikes, it seemed.

Mary got up from her chair. She found her film history notebook in the book bag on the floor by her computer desk on the other side of the living room. Flipping through the pages to the last class session of notes, she handed the note-book to Ping without a word.

"Oh, right," said Ping, and he glanced at her notes. "John Ford," he said, "I guess I don't really like John Ford. He's too, you know, traditional or something. I think those old films are just boring. Not like Scorsese, you know? Weird fucked-up angles going bam, bam in your face. Not like Travis Bickle, you know?" Mary already knew *Taxi Driver* was Ping's favorite movie; he was not the first dis-gruntled, slightly sexually embittered male in his twenties she had met with this opinion. It was usually this preference or the other one, the Jim Jarmusch one—if one were to as-sess people by what kinds of films they identified with. Mary would say she liked those with the latter preference better (Kenny had been one), though she was also aware of the two choices amounting to, perhaps, the same thing. A search for a male identity that was not the obvious one, the outdated one: "John Wayne, he just seems kind of hokey and racist to me," said Ping.

"But I kind of feel sorry for John Wayne," said Mary, rather mildly and almost magnanimously. "He gets such a bad rap. I mean, what's so wrong with cowboys? They're like a dying breed or something, I think. And then came those Sergio Leone spaghetti westerns, which were, like, way more ironic and conscious of the genre. It was like, goodbye to the old type of hero. I think John Wayne totally knew that, too."

Ping sat looking at her again with his dumbfounded expression. "I wouldn't think you'd like that stuff, Mary. That's weird."

"What stuff?" Doubt flickered in her.

"John Wayne. All that cowboy and Indian shit. It just seems hokey to me," replied Ping.

"I'm not saying I buy into the cowboy and Indian shit. I'm just saying I think there's always still another way to look at things," said Mary. She uncrossed her arms so it would not seem like she was being defensive, and then she looked out the window, briefly.

A pause settled. Ping laid the notebook on his lap. Then he placed both hands, palms down, on either sides of his legs. It was an awkward gesture that stood out to Mary for its openness and, too, for the odd way her notebook balanced on his legs. "Hey," he said finally, "so've you heard anything from Kenny?"

"Not really," she replied, slowly. They were two cats in opposing windowsills, eyeing the same bird on a branch that wavered outside both their windows. "Have you?"

Ping still sat with both hands laid flat on the couch cushions on either side of him, looking in a way flayed, and she wished now that he would move, close himself—*save face, please*. "I heard he's working in a shipyard over there, repairing rich Japanese guys' yachts or something. It's so like Kenny, it's obscure. I really miss him, though, y'know? He's really one of the best friends I ever had."

This wasn't the first time Mary had heard Ping speak admiringly about Kenny, but his tone now had an oblivious and sincere—almost embarrassing, she thought—quality of reminiscence to it. There was something else about Ping, it dawned on her then. She could see Kenny in him. The way he puckered his lips before laughing; a playing-dumb kind of shyness in his expressions. Seeing this now about Ping, she felt uncomfortable, though, too: she realized she could not imagine herself, or anyone, wanting to *touch* Ping. She watched him lean back, his hands laced behind his head, elbows raised, his expression thoughtful; then (reaching to set her notebook on the coffee table between them) he swung his legs round and laid himself out over the full length of the couch, as if accepting an invitation. Mary got smaller and frozen in her own seat, her feet curled under her and her knees pressed together.

"Did you know Kenny was a licensed masseuse?" Ping went on. "He would offer to give me massages sometimes, you know, for practice. He didn't have any kind of hang-ups or anything about his masculinity. We even used to walk around on the street sometimes with our arms around each other, just playing. Or with our hands stuck in each other's back pockets, like totally cheesy." Ping laughed.

"Really," said Mary without inflection. But she was mildly shocked.

"Do you know who Angie is?" asked Ping.

"No."

"Oh. Well, she's just this girl. I guess there was this thing between Kenny and Angie, but she was more of a buddy type of girl, you know? He wasn't in love with her or anything, though they slept together sometimes. Anyhow, I ran into her at this party last weekend, and she said Kenny just left without telling anyone. She thought that was kind of cold of him. So did some of their other friends, she said. But Kenny's like that, you know? He'll be really warm, then sometimes distant."

"Did Kenny have a lot of girlfriends?" Mary ventured this casually, making it sound as if she didn't expect so. That she didn't expect much of him in that arena—girls—at all, in fact.

Ping considered her question, his gaze still on the ceiling. He even paused to say, "Hmm." Then he launched into far more than Mary had thought she would get on the subject. It amounted to three women in the last year, none of whom Kenny would've officially called his girlfriend. Mary had to wonder how Ping would've described her, in relation to Kenny, to another acquaintance. Boldly, she admitted, as Ping moved himself back to a sitting position on the couch, "You know Kenny and I got together before he left, didn't you?"

"Yeah?" Ping's eyes were bright and unfocused, his tone distracted. She could not read whether that meant he had known or not.

"I really liked Kenny. I guess I liked him a lot," she said lamely, gravely.

Ping's elbows rested on his spread-apart knees. His head bobbed up and down in a vague, benign expression. Then he lifted his eyebrows toward her, slightly. "Hey, I'm sorry things didn't work out with you two. I guess I was a little curious about it, though. 'Cause you were both so quiet. But maybe introverted people don't go so well with other introverted people, you know? Maybe they need extroverted people, you know what I mean?"

———

Almost always in her mind's eye she sees him standing still, or she sees him about to move, or moving slowly. He had always seemed remarkably still and slow but deliberate—economical. As if this economy of movement signaled that he was saving up for some larger, grander endeavor sometime in his future. The way his eyes shifted to meet hers that first time in the dorm hallway has played back over and over in her mind's eye. She sees him standing at the end of sidewalks in spots on campus, waiting, looking remotely in her direction. She sees him walking over the rise of a hill in a memory that is not a memory of anything she actually witnessed. When she looks into campfires now she feels a looming sadness, at the back of which something like the ghost of her knowledge of him still walks about. Another vision involves looking at the moon with him somewhere quiet, desertlike, and surreal: a dark blue night, a luminous white earth, a place they have never in this life gone to. The thought of ever meeting him again (of being able to live a life actually loving him) involves, inexplicably, a vision of lying curled together on a hillside, like sleeping goats, refusing to ever get up or go back into town.

What is this town? What does the hillside mean? There is still no explaining it for her. Time, she thinks, is unrelenting.

Kenny was twenty-four when Mary first met him, and he had been in college for the previous six years. Attending on his parents' expectations more than his own, he would've said. He did not really seem to have expectations of his own; or, at least, he was the kind of person whose idea of integrity called for appearing this way.

He hardly talked and sat at the back of classrooms dozing off. As Ping characterized it: with his cap pulled down low over his face. This sleepy demeanor was what had first fascinated Ping about Kenny; Mary, too, was familiar with both cap and pose and had been drawn in by whatever was the mystery of Kenny that resided, somehow, in obscure yet close relation to these surface characteristics—though she would've never expostulated on any of this out loud, as Ping did. Most of the time in Ping's company, Mary let him do the talking. Inevitably, something about Kenny would come up. Something he'd done or worn or said, somewhere he planned to go, things he'd liked or not liked. And Mary listened, collecting all these pieces of information without force or stealth, even, but with a knowing passivity: she was like a calm, empty harbor awaiting boats and sailors, who would eventually come ashore and bring her town to life.

Birthday—November. Built the fire, then walked away, was gone a long time, that time they went camping at Mt. Tam. Middle child. Used to steal stuff at night from the grocery store where he worked in high school. She did not write this information down. The record existed in her mind only, not quite in words so much as in images, in flashes of something akin to insight. To try to write these impressions down would've seemed an as-of-yet-unentitled move on her part, she felt; also, what if such a move could jinx her chances of really knowing him? *Dust, concrete floor, electric orange of heater coils, light through a cracked window, slow music.* Memories of objects, even, could become imbued with the meaning of him, as could words. A couch she had never seen that he had sat on for hours one day, the word *mellow.* Ping talked in this way about Kenny because he was impressed by Kenny's ability to calmly do nothing.

"Kenny's like that," Ping would say, "but you know he's got a lot going on in his head."

If Ping noticed Mary's absorption in his anecdotes about Kenny, he never said so. Most of the time when he talked— about anything, really—he was simply cheerful and guileless.

Transparent, as Mary saw it. Inwardly, she cringed at his candor.

Why did Ping's transparency bother her? She noticed it, too, in other Asians she saw around campus. She had, in all honesty, never been around so many of her own kind in her life before, having grown up in a small town (rural, white, largely Mormon) east of Sacramento. A town she would've never gotten to had it not been for her stepfather, Hammond Speak.

Hammond was a native Californian, a volunteer social worker at the refugee camp where Mary had landed, with her mother and sister, in 1978. In his midthirties at the time, Hammond had been eager to prove his helpfulness and his chivalry. Mary's mother, Su Heng, was the perfect portrait of tragedy for such a man: a widow (her husband had drowned in the course of their escape), once beautiful, but now a tired, haggard woman toting two baby girls. A survivor, but one still in need of rescue.

Hammond and Su Heng—she had defaulted to Sue Speak for a time—were not married anymore. Still, theirs had been the only mixed-racial family in their town for many years, and their children had gotten used to being anomalies of a sort. Thus, the idea of inclusion now baffled Mary; anonymity terrified her. She did not want to be just one more of this crowd, with their black-haired sameness and unexpectant flat faces, their social cluelessness. It seemed to Mary that they had formed out of their varied, yet commonly troubled pasts (of narrow escapes, rough seas, loved ones' deaths) an inexplicable, dutiful blandness. Most of the Asians on campus, it was a fact, were business and science majors; few were artists of any kind.

Sometimes she would see one of them, another Asian girl who lived in the dorms, coming out of the elevator late at night, leaning shyly on the arm of some clean-cut white boy who appeared proud and doting—either that or a little bit sleazy. Mary would vow never to be caught in that position herself, with any boy who walked in such a proprietary and assuming manner beside a girl he was about to have sex with. Boys like this, bland in their own racial way, made Asian girls appear like things to be coveted, Mary thought. Was that what her parents had looked like in the beginning? Was there in this some clue as to why their marriage had not lasted? Mary was wary of it all. She had no interest in this kind of boy herself; she had no interest in coupledom, for that matter. Passing by one of these pairs, she would feel gratitude and satisfaction both at her own solitude. How much they *disappointed* her, these other Asians! She did not want to claim membership among them.

Mary believed Kenny was not like these other white boys. He did not seem to want to own or rescue anyone; his kindness was not politically motivated. She saw him, rather, as a reprieve of sorts, and maybe that was why she felt as she did about him. Or, maybe she didn't know at all why she felt for him as she did.

———

Upon first meeting Ping in their Acting I class, Mary was surprised to learn that he, like she, was a film major. She had assumed, however unjustly, that someone who looked like Ping would have no imagination, no vision of his own, or at least would not have had volition enough to declare official pursuit of such a thing as his imagination.

Ping wore clothes that looked like they had been bought or passed down, unselectively, from a donations center. Cheap polo shirts of a ruddy cotton fabric, dull colors, tapered-leg jeans, sneakers with a generic brand appearance, a lot of mesh showing. Mary didn't dwell on these details to be frivolous or cruel; she just couldn't help but notice. Sometimes she even spoke her judgments aloud, as if they came from a standard well of knowledge about which she believed Ping needed to be enlightened.

"Your haircut makes you look guileless," she told him once, "like you could get easily duped by people."

His black hair was parted in the middle and fell in a bowl shape around his head, flopping over his forehead and ears. His hair had the same sleek, unperturbably straight texture as hers did, which riled Mary a little. She needed to find differences.

"It's happened to me before," said Ping with his snorting laugh. (And Mary hated, too, how his eyes disappeared into the roundness of his cheeks when he smiled too hard; the same thing happened to her, which was why she often didn't smile.) "A prostitute got me," he said. "Seventy bucks she got me for. Walked up to my car at a stop sign in the Tenderloin. Seventy bucks. Afterwards she told me she came up to me 'cause I looked like a sucker."

"Why'd you do that?" Mary wanted to know. She was by this time practiced at being unfazed by Ping's confessions—it was not the first time he'd revealed something semi-shocking to her. "Why'd you go with her?"

"Why're you always asking why about everything?" re-
torted Ping. He thrust out his lower lip. "I mean, why *not*?"

———

Sure, Mary could argue that everything was a matter of
perception.

Even if somebody straps you to a chair, lops off all your
limbs, rapes your sister in front of your eyes? Still you would
not be incited to rage? Still you would hold to your belief
that every action, no matter how horrific, is justifiable? So
challenged her philosophy of sexuality professor, holding her
after class one day. Still you would say your human rights
have not been impinged upon by another person's actions,
that we are all responsible to ourselves only?

Initially, Mary had enrolled in this class in hopes of
learning she wasn't sure what, but something more *mysti-
cally* explanatory about sex, perhaps. The course had turned
out to be mostly about moral issues regarding society and
deviance, which, it seemed to Mary, were irrelevant factors
that told nothing about the true nature of sex, or about why
one was compelled toward certain people and not others, or
why (this was what Mary really wanted an answer to) one
could be compelled toward another person even before any
physical connection or history had been created. In short,
she wanted an intellectual explanation of the mystery of
love. Knowledge was supposed to set you free, wasn't it? So
maybe, she believed, a thorough enough understanding of
the thing could make you impervious to its pitfalls, too.

Her philosophy of sexuality professor's main concern,
meanwhile, was in getting his students to define boundaries of
moral and immoral behavior in their pursuits of pleasure; he

believed this was a paradigm the modern world, and modern youth especially, lacked. In the war between genders might lie a microcosm of discord and other types of wars in the world, over boundaries of all kinds. *Consent* was the issue. Didn't they see that? If humans could just recognize, and *respect*, the concept of consent, perhaps then the world could start to be a safer, more decent place. Perhaps, he would say, they could start in the personal sphere. They could start with asking before touching, with defining and respecting their own and others' bodily rights and boundaries. Maybe if people could learn to touch others' bodies with more care, maybe that, on a broader scale, could lead to people also being less likely to inflict violence upon others' bodies.

He was not the type of man, in looks, that Mary would've expected to hear speak like this; he was in his late thirties, of Middle Eastern descent, olive-complexioned and somewhat ugly—in Mary's eyes—too manly, too grownup-looking. At first, she'd feared he was making a pass at her when he kept her after class to continue arguments, but nothing untoward had ever followed, leaving Mary to wonder: what did this really say about what *she* expected of grown men (or Middle Eastern ones)? He had commended her at the beginning of the semester on her sharpness and was often trying to provoke her with arguments that were meant to make her reveal a bias toward compassion, which she was unwilling to admit she had.

You are in the desert with a baby. You have only enough water for one of you to survive. Whom will you give the water to?

Attachment is a matter of the mind, Mary deflected him. It's only the sentimental-minded who get indignant over pain or injustice. Nature is brutal, maybe inherently flawed, too. And freedom does not have to be physical.

Her professor responded, You mean *human* nature is brutal, stroking his shaggy moustache, half-laughing as he shook his curly head. He often laughed at her in this way, she'd noticed.

Well, that too, she agreed, staying serious.

But you have to make a choice now, Mary, about the baby or you.

She was not making an emotional decision, she thought, just a logical one (and why did people think answers had to go one way or the other, not down the middle?) when she replied, Well, I would split the water, of course.

He comes down the carpeted hallway in perpetual slow motion.

Flat, brown carpet. It has been stained by many different substances and stood on by thousands of barefoot girls. She is nothing new. Neither is her first, no, second (she thinks) experience of love.

From her vantage point in someone else's doorway, she had spotted Ping amid the group coming down the hall that night, had placed herself strategically to say hello as they came by, and thus had gotten herself invited along.

The boys were headed to a party they'd heard about in the neighboring ward. That is what the dormitories were called, these places of first freedom for so many (Mary liked to be sarcastic about it): *wards*. Ping introduced her to the other boys, who barely acknowledged her. Probably they were used to an occasional girl tagging along, and probably they were used to disregarding a girl until she'd done something to differentiate herself. In this group were Kenny and Kenny's blond friend, Jim, from Berkeley; Steve and Ian from Santa Cruz, semi-shaved-headed skater types whose hands continually slipped under their own shirts to brush against their stomachs, as if they took their own bodies as casual comfort; Travis, who played guitar and sang in a band and looked dauntingly similar to Johnny Depp; and Hasan the surfer, prototypically golden, slightly curly-haired, with his own indecipherable vocabulary for the ocean. They were the kind of boys who could cause Mary to feel a dull, consuming ache in her mind and gut whenever she gave thought to what capacities their bodies and attitudes and cold laughter and various instruments of pleasure or skill—surfboards, skateboards, guitars, and tanned hands—suggested they might command. Boys like these seemed to Mary impossibly self-satisfied and out of reach, so caught up were they in their no-girls-needed passions. They seemed oblivious to need entirely, in fact.

Nowhere in Mary's imagination was she able to conjure a picture of girls in groups displaying such flippant possession of their own powers.

A couple of the boys Mary had seen around campus or knew by reputation; others, like Kenny and Jim, she had not seen before. She was frankly puzzled as to how Ping fit into the group, but had seized on his presence there as her opportunity to get inside, somehow. And there had not been time to hesitate. Ping had stopped to talk to her, but the others barely slowed. She was standing in someone else's doorway, a girlfriend she was visiting. It wasn't Ping or any single one of the boys she was saying "Okay" in interest of when Ping said to her, "You can come with us, if you want to." She couldn't have said what it was that compelled her. Only that she had positioned herself in that doorway, knowing she had to without knowing quite why, and when the invitation was issued, she took it. She did not even bother to say goodbye to her girlfriend (who was talking on the phone with her back to the doorway, anyway). For Mary not to go would have meant, what? Something less, something missed. She could not risk missing it.

The boys moved as if propelled by a collective energy; she caught their tailwind.

Ping was the one you looked past in the group, and so was Kenny, in a way. She actually had not taken much notice of him at first, though she did notice his friend Jim, whose shoulder-length blond hair made a ponytail at the nape of his neck. Jim wore a red-and-blue flannel shirt and cowboy boots, yet had a sharp-eyed, intellectual air that Mary had not, at that time, ever before encountered in someone wearing cowboy boots. The boots rounded out the group, she thought; they added texture. It didn't occur to her that these boys might not all know, or even like, one another—she was only assessing the essence of them as she had seen it conjured up in their unified walk down the dormitory hallway. In the accumulation of crumpled jeans, untucked T-shirts, swaying ponytails, and almost-famous good looks; in the careless tilt of their shoulders, their nonchalant strides, the restrained ease of their bodies; all these details melded fluidly into a composite of something that Mary found both beautiful and angst-causing. Altogether these aspects made up a vision: they were the ingredients of envy.

The party was (as many in Mary's opinion were) a disappointment. There was a crush of people in the doorway when the R.A. came around saying all doors must be shut. So someone shut the door, leaving those who had lingered at the back of the crowd to stand in the hallway. That included Mary and Kenny and Jim (though not Ping, who had made it into the room—they saw his head bobbing up and down in the crowd—before the door shut). Without knowing anything else about one another, Mary and Kenny and Jim at least knew they had in common the tendency of arriving at the peripheries of parties. Kenny had his hands shoved into the front pockets of his jeans and one shoulder slouched firmly against the wall, his head also tipped to rest against the wall. Mary thought he looked wistful and tired. He wore black rectangular-framed eyeglasses that made his gaze seem strangely fixed. She looked away from him.

Jim offered her a beer from their twelve-pack.

"I don't drink," she told him, the first words she had spoken since she'd latched herself onto the boys' group.

Now Kenny looked at her, though he shifted just his eyes to do so. This moment felt like a recognition—it disarmed her—of a kind that later (when she thought back to it for the ten-thousandth time) she would realize had always been meant to bring her in mind of the ocean.

2. The Ocean

There had been a story about the ocean that night, she remembers, and camping.

Jim had told it. They had eventually moved on from the
overcrowded party back to Ping's room, a group of six or
seven of them lounging about now on the dormitory beds and
the floor. Kenny was by the closet, rummaging through a box
of records, putting on different ones and then taking them off.
The story Jim told had something to do with himself and a
girl named Heather going "toe-to-toe" in the sand and Kenny
lying there and then getting up and walking away. Mary, listening, did not know what going "toe-to-toe" meant. She had
actually never heard the expression before. She was afraid,
she realized, that it might mean they had been having sex,
and if that were so, the ease with which it was being spoken
of was also something foreign to her and made her feel small
and young. What would it take to become a Heather, she
wondered, invited on camping trips, an undeterrable presence in their anecdotes, strong and vivid even as just a fleeting
image told to strangers? She saw Heather as blond, womanly,
earthy but tomboyish, confident in her position among the
boys, smiling kindly but dismissively at other females.

Mary had been camping by the ocean before, too. She
did not tell this to the room that night, however.

The previous three years of high school she had gone
with the honor roll society on their annual camping trip
to the coast. She had stood on the beach and looked at the
waves and felt awed by the viscous, slick, black appearance
they took on at night, how under the pallidness of the moon

the water looked like oil. Wasn't there a term for that? *Black gold.* In her last year of high school she had begun to be interested in astral projection, believing that in leaving her body it might be possible to meet another person or the essence of that other person—*out there*, she called it—in a state of perfect union. The vulgarity of sex, or the few fumblings at it she had experienced, had not so much discomfited or frightened her as it had shattered something—a purity of desire, perhaps. The idea of being able to meet perfectly with another person in some place beyond the physical was a new kind of hope for her, a new definition of need. That there was in each person a singular essence to be met, and if two people could meet there, maybe then they could make nowhere else matter anymore, was as close to an idea of bliss as she could construct.

Standing, looking at the ocean at night, the feeling was brought up in her anew: she realized it was the kind of moment in life she wanted to be sharing.

Her best friend at the time was a boy named Blake. She got along with him on an intellectual level but was not drawn to him on a physical one. He wasn't ugly, but both of his legs were paralyzed. Mary didn't like to think that was what deterred her, but probably it was. Probably, too, it had a little to do with her wish of meeting another person on some plane other than the physical. Blake had to be pulled across the sand in a red wagon that night they went to the beach with the other honor roll students. Close to the water, he rolled out of his wagon and lay on the sand. Mary went alone for a walk down the beach. When she came back with her feet wet and stood over Blake, she saw that he had fallen asleep. From his knees down he was buried in sand, the water was only a few feet from lapping at his toes, and one arm was twisted above his head. He looked to Mary like he was dead, and she felt suddenly, deeply afraid.

———

Kenny was trying on a faded, fraying denim jacket that was hanging in one of the dorm room's closets. He had already tried on a powder blue ski vest and a men's sports coat out of the same closet.

"Oh yeah, you should get a jacket like that one, Kenny, and wear it under a leather vest, then ride around on your motorcycle like that," said Ping enthusiastically. He struck a motorcycle-riding pose, head thrown back, arms out-stretched. "You'd look so cool, man. All scruffy-looking and mellow on your motorbike. That's perfect."

Mary almost expected Kenny, or somebody, to make fun of Ping for his motorcycle-riding impression, but no one did. Kenny pulled his own leather jacket on over the denim one, in what seemed to be a form of agreement. He had to raise his arms to do so, and his T-shirt stretched upward, exposing his stomach. His jeans sagged so low on his hips that Mary could see the skin well below his belly button.

"He's right, Kenny," agreed Jim. "You should get your-self a leather vest and a denim jacket like that. It's totally you, man."

Kenny put his shoulder against the wall, still wearing both jackets, and said, "But my motorcycle's a piece of shit."

"You totally can fix it, man," said Jim.

"Dude, Kenny, you *have* to fix it," exclaimed Ping, al-most emotionally.

Then, soon, Kenny was putting the stranger's jacket away in the closet and shrugging back into his own. He leaned on the wall waiting, it seemed, for Jim to catch on that it was time to leave. When the boys' gazes met, the line of communication that passed between them went through the air right above Mary's head, she noticed, like a beam of light, but pencil-thin, softly electric.

————

"What are you?"

Usually when she was asked this question, Mary replied sarcastically—*a human being?*—but because he had asked with such genuine and unobtrusive curiosity, this time she answered without irony.

The whole room was looking at her as she answered.

"Oh," said Kenny, "I was just curious." It was earlier in the evening and he was sitting to her left on the floor, his back against a desk, a beer can resting lightly against his leg. It was the most he had spoken to her thus far that night.

Jim, also seated on the floor, but across from her, with his legs spread apart and his cowboy boots making the divergent points of a *V* on either side of her own legs, said, quite cheerfully, "I would've guessed Hawaiian."

Feeling then as if she was deflecting everything, the good and the bad, and that this was a strong thing to do, Mary said, "It's a common mistake."

————

Mary did not actually see Kenny again in person until one day about eight months later. At first, she had not even known she wanted to see him again—that was the truth. In the first

weeks following the night of that party, she'd harbored vague
hopes of running into one or another of those boys and
maybe being recognized or something (maybe by Jim; he had
seemed the friendliest). But, as reality would have it, it was
only Ping whom she continued to see. It was Ping who was
her friend, whether she liked it or not. From this, however,
she began to gather her stories of Kenny—those small pieces
of information that over time would take on a certain hue in
her mind, so that by the time she did see him again, the sight
of him was not so much a surprise as it was a signal, like a
recognition of some fact she already knew inside.

He appeared moving toward her in his slow and reluctant manner down a hallway in the Creative Arts building.
(She thinks he might forever be moving toward her down
the hallways of institutions, shoulder brushing a wall, his
figure the solitary recognizable human element—*her* singular differentiating point, anyhow—amid the indifference of
passageways worn with use and the repeating epiphanies of
young people.) He was dressed in gray and black, dark and
contained-looking. A careful person, she thought. Saying
hello was the elucidation of a moment that, in the years to
come, she would find had the capability of telescoping, far,
both backward and forward. At the time, though, she only
knew something felt amiss because of the way she was all of
a sudden trying to find something condemnable about him.

------

*What they were running on was, in fact, if you thought about
it, the edge of a continent.*

*The wet portion of the beach, recently altered by the
tide, sloped slickly toward the dark lapping water. Mary*

imagined a giant magnetic ball at the bottom of the ocean, giving weight to the way the waves moved in and out, in long slow pulls. The moonlight shimmered on the water. The seaweed vines they'd found to play with—they were chasing and hitting each other with them—were mustard-yellow and slimy, with rubbery leaves still attached to some of the vines. When you swung them, they snapped like whips. Girls were chasing boys. There was nothing original in their game, yet it was satisfying and made Mary feel wild, maybe because of the moon, maybe because she had never been to the ocean at night before, maybe because they were far from home, or so it had seemed to her back then.

With the other girls, Mary stood on the dunes and gazed at the ocean and at the sky.

Someone made a philosophical comment, someone she didn't expect it from. A homely blond girl named Carlene who was usually conservative and lighthearted and dull. But Mary was just jealous. She thought she should've been the one to say it: This sand is from another ocean in another age.

This is my indirect, my imprecise interior view of love, said Mary, trying to compete.

Miss Mary quite contrary, said her friend Blake later when Mary recounted the exchange to him. Why don't you turn off your brain sometime? I think you think too much.

3. Sifting

Mary's intermittent roommate, Eric, had left tiny piles of cocaine on a plate on the coffee table next to the $500 phone bill, and the TV was still playing, when she came out of her bedroom in the morning. Eric must've come in late, long after Ping had left and she'd gone to bed, for she hadn't heard him come in and she had lain awake for some time before falling asleep.

She went to the bathroom to wash her face and brush her hair and teeth. In the kitchen she poured herself a bowl of cereal, trying to ignore the trail of mouse droppings that ran across the countertop and dove behind the refrigerator to resume a black dot outline around the perimeter of the stove, as if the stove itself were an object in a crime scene. She moved on tiptoe—the floor was sticky—to the kitchen sink to find a spoon. Then she took her bowl of cereal to the living room, where she curled her feet under her at the far end of the couch and looked out the window as she ate. She left the TV on: a midmorning talk show. Mexican men loitered outside on the opposite street corner as they did every morning. Soon, a large pickup truck pulled up to the curb, and the men began to push one another in their rush to climb into the truck. Their voices rose like stabs at the air.

Then she heard a giggle enter the living room. Dean, her other intermittent roommate. Since they'd first moved in at the beginning of last fall, the three had resided simultaneously in the apartment for, at the longest, a stretch of two or three weeks. It was February now. Mary never went away; it was Dean and Eric who had other places to be. They disappeared for days and weeks at a time but still paid rent, so Mary didn't mind their erratic presences. She had grown used to their cluttered rooms, the glimpses she caught of their interiors every time she walked down the long entrance hall. Both boys' rooms were in disarray, no floor space showing, things scattered atop every surface—clothes, books, half-unpacked boxes, dirty cups, plates, silverware, papers, odds and ends. In Dean's room several two-by-fours leaned on the wall: an unfinished project. In Eric's room there was an empty birdcage, a large one set on a wrought iron stand, with bird droppings and old newspapers on the floor beneath it.

Sometimes Mary felt tempted to borrow things from their rooms—their belongings seemed indefinitely abandoned. From Dean's room she had taken one belt (she knew he wouldn't care, would even be a little flattered that his female roommate coveted something of his). With Eric she had learned to be a bit more cautious.

What Mary knew about Eric, she knew predominantly through Dean. Eric and Dean were both from Concord, a smaller city east of the Bay Area, where they had gone to high school together. Dean was from a first-generation Chinese immigrant family that was thrifty, enterprising, and newly middle class. Eric's family was Japanese and had been in the States for at least two generations. His father was vice president of an international corporation of some kind; his grandfather had been interned in a camp following World War II. The family was extremely well-off, and his parents traveled often. Eric was an only child. He spoke both Japanese and English fluently and, since his childhood, had traveled regularly back and forth between the States and Japan. He had never held a job and scoffed at going to college. He was twenty-one and spent all his spare time painting. Giant, gloomy canvases and empty Jack Daniel's bottles lined the walls of his room; sometimes a neglected plate and razor blade could be spotted on the floor. Eric always wore black—turtlenecks and plain T-shirts and jeans. He had a stark, square face and thinning straight black hair that hung to his shoulders; his eyes were narrow and shrewd. He was one of the most even-keeled people Mary had ever met, or so she had thought, until one evening she came home to find the coffee table, which was hers, smashed in two. When she asked Eric what had happened he told her that he had broken it. Because, he said, she had borrowed his chair from his room—his wheelchair (they each had one, had bought them together at a secondhand store down the street, for the fun of it)—and she hadn't returned it. So now we're even, he said, looking at her with cold triumph before he exited the room. It was true she had borrowed his wheelchair to use as a dolly for a film class project and had left it at a classmate's house, but she'd had every intention of bringing it back.

Despite this incident, Mary liked Eric; she respected his intelligence and creative energy. He fascinated her in ways she'd not encountered before. She had never met anyone, for instance, who was so unbound by money and—it seemed to her—so consequently, unhappily heedless toward it, too. Sometimes his intensity preceded his entry into a room like a faint glow he cast, something magnetic but unsettling. He was the kind of artist who believed only in the impossibility of ever "making it" as an artist. Some afternoons, Mary entered to find Eric and his friends lounging in the living room playing video games on the couch or playing balancing games in the wheelchairs, rolling back and forth on the wood floors. They tossed taunting, blasé comments at Mary about her doggedness and ambition.

"All right, Hector," Eric would address one of his friends, "do you really think you're ever going to be a famous actor? Am I ever going to be a real painter? Are any of us ever really gonna get to do what we think we want to do?" Then he would stop and look Mary's way with a smirk. "Well maybe, Mary, I shouldn't speak for *you*."

Mary didn't quite know what to make of comments like these, whether she should take them as insult or affirmation of a future for which she hoped: one in which she became somebody who left a mark on the world, artistically speaking. A classmate had once called her Machiavellian because of how, during one film project, she had been rather aggressive over securing the better equipment for her group. This comment briefly crushed her, for she didn't want to be thought ill of by anyone. Still, it had also made her feel a little proud.

"So, Mary," said Dean, seating himself in the chair opposite the couch and addressing her with seemingly pleased nervousness, "Uh, what is with the word on the window? It kinda creeped me out when I came home last night." He grinned conspiratorially, as if to show he appreciated the eccentric in his life. "I thought it was, like, my conscience or something hallucinating messages to me."

The word on the window—the transom window above the front door—read TRUST. It had been emblazoned in black electrical tape on the glass over a week ago, for a recent film lighting assignment in which Mary's class had been instructed to employ nighttime lighting techniques. In homage to 1940s film noir visuals, Mary and her classmates had shone a light through a word written on the transom window in order to make the word appear in huge, slanting shadow-letters on the wall inside. When they had finished rigging the lights, they had TRUST stretched across a third of the length of the long entrance hallway wall.

Long hallways—Mary was learning—were a haven of possibility, visually speaking.

Long hallways made for long, bleak lines; a bleak, ominous kind of beauty. A camera shot down a long hallway conveyed tension; there seemed an inherent expectation that the hallway must eventually lead somewhere, be it a literal revelation or a symbolic one. A bare-walled hallway with a doorway at the end. Any place with stark features was aesthetically exciting to Mary; it could make her adrenaline actually rise. And there was, of course, the pleasurable difficulty of mounting and rigging lights. It was a physical and logistical exercise, requiring both ingenuity and a certain degree of abandon. The more precarious a light rigging was, the more pride Mary and her classmates took in it. For the TRUST effect, they had climbed up a ladder and rigged a makeshift stand C-clamped to the eaves of the roof; and for another shot (the bedroom shot, for which Mary had borrowed Dean's room and Eric's bird, as well), she and her classmates had driven a car onto the sidewalk, parked it close to the apartment building's wall, and then roped and sandbagged a light stand onto the car's roof in order to shine a light through the window at a high enough angle to simulate moonlight.

Mary had asked—this time—to borrow Eric's bird, and Eric had agreed. The bird was a raven named Hennessy and it had cost $2,000. He was large and glossy and black, with a blue sheen to his blackness. As for Dean's room, Mary had spoken to Dean over the phone about it. He would not mind at all, he said, if it meant a pretty girl would be lying in his bed.

The actress lay in Dean's bed wearing a satiny slip-dress while the simulated moonlight beamed in through the slats of the window blinds, casting a striped, blue-tinged rhombus (they had covered the windows in blue filter paper) over the hardwood floor. The bird they posed in a corner of the room on its wood-and-iron perch. For the assignment, Mary and her classmates had storyboarded a shot where the camera was to pan from the bird to the woman in the bed, passing slowly over the moonlit floor along the way. The overdramatic panning would not have been Mary's choice, but she was not the director on this assignment; a woman named Andrea was. Mary was the DP, director of photography.

At one point between takes, one of the gaffers tried to adjust Eric's bird. The bird snapped at him, flapped its wings, and fell off its perch. When the gaffer reached to pick it up, the bird bit him. Then it began to panic in the corner, flapping its clipped wings, half-rising and squawking, hitting the walls in its attempt to get away from the film crew. No one could get near it, not even the actress in her bare feet and glossy slip, who was claiming to be good with animals. So Mary had to call Eric in, and they all watched as Eric talked softly to Hennessy and then gently picked him up. He talked to the bird, Mary noticed, in the same laconic, even, soft-spoken tone she had overheard him use with the girl in England, the one he was running up $500 phone bills for. Mary felt a little sorry for having scared his bird but could not get over the idea that it was crucial to the shot, so she

offered nothing in the way of an apology. When Eric asked
whether they were finished yet—it was a tactful address, his
tone cheerfully, flippantly curious—Mary said no.

The actress returned to the bed, propped on one elbow,
the other arm draped comfortably over the curve of her up-
turned hip. She looked Asian but was actually Hawaiian,
she had said. Her looks were the kind Mary hated to envy
but did; the girl was slim and undeniably well-proportioned,
with a kind of femininity that made Mary feel ungraceful
and childish in comparison. The actress said "Oh, poor bird"
with an expression of winning sympathy. But her comment
was more affirmation of the bird's fate—a continued session
under the blue-filtered lights—than it was any sincere show
of sensitivity. Eric let them finish shooting with the bird and
said nothing more about it to Mary, though he left the following day, with the bird, and was gone the remainder of the
week.

So Mary had left TRUST taped on the window. She knew
it was silly, but she considered it to be a small bit of evidence
that somewhere—somehow—she had belonged.

It was not the only odd artifact she had contributed to
the apartment. She also had a broken timing belt in a plastic
bag hanging from a nail on the living room wall; the wheelchairs (since none of them actually needed to use one, and
Mary used hers as a dolly) were odd, too. Vestiges of toil,
Mary thought of them. Things that didn't typically belong
in living rooms and bedrooms. She collected these items
with the idea that she would find creative alternative uses
for them in the future, and she equated her fascination with
these objects to a longing she felt whenever she entered

places that were under construction, or demolition, too, for that matter. She was attracted to places of ruin and partial assemblage. Broken-down things, dismantled machinery, abandoned warehouses, empty parking lots, empty shopping centers especially—these places satisfied a crucial area of her imagination. Shooting film in places like that gave her a sense of sharpness and liberation that went to her core, and it was more than just the excitement of trespass. Perhaps it was the idea of appropriating usually functional and public spaces for purely personal uses; useless uses, in fact: art and loitering.

Now, at night, the natural moonlight coming through the transom window cast TRUST in shadow on the hallway wall in genuine effect, but it came in smaller and higher up. The letters were not quite as sharply defined as before, when she and her classmates had lit the scene themselves.

"Trust," said Mary, acting surreptitious. "What is trust to you, Dean?"

This made Dean giggle, and Mary knew it was the right tactic to have taken with him. "Something girls give to me that I always end up losing?" he asked.

Mary took a slow bite of her cereal and turned her head to look out the window. She couldn't fathom how Dean got so many girls (as he claimed he did) to sleep with him. To her he was not sexually attractive. His face was a little bit clownish-looking, a little bit eager and doglike. He was very thin, he bounced when he walked, and he was only slightly taller than she was. She couldn't imagine going to bed with a boy like that; there would be nothing to hold on to, she thought, or not enough to hold on to her.

She turned her head to look back at him and gave a slight shrug. "It's just a word. It wasn't even my choice. It was this girl, Andrea, the director's idea. It was *my* idea to put a word on the window, but *she* chose the word. If I'd chosen it, I would've chosen something more objective, you know, like 'liquor mart' or something."

"Sure, sure, liquor, that's a *goood* idea," said Dean, grinning and lighting a cigarette. To have said something that someone like Dean could grin in that way about—this wasn't exactly the reaction Mary had wanted, it occurred to her.

"Liquor? Who's talking about liquor?" They heard Eric before they saw him. He entered the living room dressed in his usual black T-shirt and black jeans. He had his shoes on: Doc Martens. Mary wasn't sure if he'd just come out of his room or through the front door.

"Hey, we're all here," exclaimed Dean. "We're a family again!"

"I don't know about that," said Mary. But she was only teasing Dean, really.

Eric seemed to get it. "Yeah, I don't know if I want to be in the same family as you either, Dean," he said. His sarcasm, like his anger, was gentle yet pronounced. Then he noticed the plate on the coffee table. (The broken table had been replaced with another that Eric had wordlessly brought in one day—the broken one was not mentioned again.) "Oops," he said, stepping forward to pick up his plate.

He straightened and carried it with him into the kitchen.

Mary wondered—vaguely—what he planned to do with his leftover cocaine, but she thought it would be uncool to ask.

"He doesn't even care if he wastes his *drugs*, can you believe that?" said Dean in an indignant, loud whisper.

Mary turned her focus to her cereal bowl, went back to eating. Dean was saying something else now. The way his words came to her as if they were emerging through a fog made her realize she had not been paying attention to him. Her thoughts had been elsewhere. Where? She was staring rather intently at splinters of gray wood on the windowsill. A vapor of melancholy feeling filled her gut for a second, and for that second she wished that Dean were gone, that it was only her and Eric in the apartment.

"There was a guy trying to start a motorcycle outside on the sidewalk when I came home last night," said Dean. "He looked at me, and I looked at him, like I was wondering why he was in front of our apartment and he was wondering why I was going into our apartment. Then he said he was a friend of yours."

The word *motorcycle* got her attention again. "That was just Ping; he's in my film history class. He was borrowing my notes from class," said Mary. She shifted around, almost deciding to get up and go into the kitchen. But then Eric returned and dropped himself down at the other end of the couch, and she felt she should stay a little while longer.

"Hey guys, what's up?" he said, rather cheerfully.

"Mary had a guy over here last night," said Dean.

"Oh yeah?" Eric began flipping through the TV channels with the remote control.

"Oh yeah," said Mary flatly. She was trying to dissociate herself from Dean, she was aware. To neither of them in particular she said, "I didn't know Ping had a motorcycle."

"That guy looked like a dork, to be honest," said Dean. "He definitely wasn't attractive enough for you, Mary. But I bet he likes you, huh? I mean, a guy doesn't come over to a girl's apartment in the middle of the night just 'cause he wants to borrow her film history notes."

Mary shrugged. "He's just a friend of a friend of mine." But she was thinking of something else Ping had told her the night before, about having once broken into the family home of a girl he was obsessed with in high school. He was standing in her bedroom smelling a pair of her underpants when headlights from a car pulling into the driveway swept across one of the bedroom walls. Then he climbed back out the window and ran away. The most startling aspect, for Mary, of this story had been her realization that she knew people who did things like that.

Eric set the remote control down and sat forward, having spotted the phone bill. He picked it up and looked at it. "Damn," he said.

Dean let out something that sounded like a giggle. He had already seen the phone bill, as had Mary. "You pay all that money and, man, you get laid like once every three months and then you also have to buy a *plane* ticket to fucking *England* to even get that."

With his elbows resting on his knees, Eric turned his head to the side to look at Dean. Without malice, he said, "You don't really get it, Dean, do you?" Then he caught Mary's eye, briefly. "See, Mary gets it," he said.

"What?" said Mary, blinking—innocently, she hoped.

———

Her last class of that day was an evening one, and afterward she decided to take a detour on her way home. She did this sometimes. She exited the freeway at Army Street and went east toward the bay instead of west toward the Mission District, where she lived. There were times she wanted to be reminded of certain places—rather, there was a clarity she had experienced in certain places that she wanted to be reminded of.

She had spent one night with Kenny that summer before he left, in the converted warehouse where he'd been living on the outskirts of the city. The warehouse was on a lot at the water's edge, next door to some kind of factory. It was a jumble of cranelike machinery and metal boxes; rusting-yellow towerlike structures climbing into the sky, emerging out of a confusion of chutes and pipes and crisscrossing iron bars. At the very top a span of ironwork extended like a plank bridge between the two tallest towerlike structures. The warehouse nearby was low-slung and subtle in comparison: it hid its working parts.

Driving down Third Street at night, she kept her doors locked and her windows rolled up. Third Street ran from the Embarcadero downtown into the industrial section of the city, right alongside the bay. It seemed to her that not many other cars traveled on that street at night. Buildings slid by smoothly and dimly, beaming an occasional lonely, lit window or doorway in her direction as she drove by. Streetlamps made ruddy pools of yellow light on the asphalt. All this ran as backdrop to her thoughts of Kenny and gave her the mysterious feeling that these sights—the warehouse where he had lived, the factory next door—should be able to explain things to her. The longing to have it all explained was acute. She felt like she missed him yet knew she had little to go on, really, in regard to him and his place in her life. She had a factory tower reaching toward the sky and a warehouse unit by the bay, not much more. She suspected it was undeserved, the amount of emotion she felt for him in relation to how well they had actually known each other. This incongruity begged to be explained.

She could take the events of that night apart and look at them piece by piece, and sometimes she did. She had come to his warehouse close to 1 a.m. that night, after first going out dancing at a club with some girlfriends.

She was dressed for her night out—thigh-high black suede boots and hot pants and a clingy black top. She was aware of the smell of perfumed smoke still caught in her hair, as she cut the motor and stepped out of her car in the empty gravel lot. The night was clear and dark and vivid to her senses; a breeze came off the water, and she could hear it lapping against the nearby pilings. The stars above appeared bright, thick. Her car door stuck when she closed it—it was an old car, and the doors had been jamming on and off that summer—and she had to go around to the passenger side then to retrieve the extra clothes she'd decided at the last moment (she could not face him in her dancing clothes, she'd realized) to put on.

Shielded by the open door, standing on one leg and then the other, over her nightclub outfit she pulled on a pair of oversized jeans and a sweater.

They went for a walk later that night, and he suggested they sneak into the factory lot next door. *You want to climb up there?* He had pointed. *Sure,* Mary replied, hoping he would notice she had not hesitated. Had he done this before? She thought it might tell her something about the two of them, maybe, to know whether this was a routine adventure or a new one for him.

He had not, he said. He'd thought about it before, though.

"I thought about it a little," were his actual words.

They crawled through a hole in the fence and began to walk across the asphalt. They could hear the low buzzing of the overhead streetlamps and an occasional, labored, metallic shifting of machinery from inside somewhere. In the pockets of his black overcoat, Kenny was carrying several cans of beer. His sneakers made no sound on the pavement, but Mary's boots did. Her heels echoed rather sharply against the asphalt.

"I don't know if this is possible," he spoke so slowly and carefully that she thought maybe he was on the verge of confessing something personal, "but do you think you can make your boots make less noise?"

She lifted her heels so that she was walking on only her soles. It wasn't a comfortable way to walk, but Kenny said, "that's better," so she kept walking like that. Once they got to the ladder at the base of the towers, it was easier. You didn't need your heels to climb a ladder, she found.

They came up the ladder into a boxlike chamber at the top of one of the towers and then walked across the metal plankway to the next tower, which reached farther out over the water. They sat cross-legged on the gratelike floor of the structure and opened the cans of beer Kenny had brought. A framework of crisscrossing iron poles, yellow paint chipped and rusting in spots, rose up around them like the metal skeletons of walls not even trying to encase them. Sometimes a gust of wind hit the structure, and they felt it actually reverberating, sending mini-shudders through the iron-gridded floor beneath them.

"My father, when I got caught shoplifting last year, he told me I should try hang-gliding instead. Then he took me to Fort Funston to watch the hang-gliders," Mary said this flippantly, spontaneously, at one point: she was grasping for the most dramatic information about herself that she could find to tell him.

"That's a pretty unusual reaction for a parent," was Kenny's response. "Is it because your father's Vietnamese, do you think?"

"He's not, though—he's American. But he's not my real father, either. Him and my mom met here, when we first came over. He was a volunteer at the refugee camp. I call him my father, though, because he's the only father I've known."

"Do you have brothers and sisters?"

"One of each, both younger than me. We're all only weirdly related, though." Mary shrugged. "Like, my sister is adopted—my mom took her in from another woman who didn't want her, basically, or couldn't keep her. My brother was born here; our dad now is his real dad. But *my* real dad was someone else. When we escaped from Vietnam in 1978, *he* fell off the boat in the middle of the night and drowned. I was only two so I hardly remember it. Maybe if I remembered him it would, like, haunt me more or something, but it just doesn't, you know?"

Usually when she relayed this information to people, they made energetic, disbelieving remarks about how hard her childhood must've been or about how special or amazing a person her real father must've been, while Mary suppressed her urges to remark on how she didn't see what was so amazing about falling off a boat. Why did death suddenly elevate people to the status of deserving reverence? For some reason that bothered her more than the fact of her father's death. Kenny's response was hard to read. He said nothing right away, only looked at her, then took a slow sip of his beer and let his eyes slide away from her. For a moment she thought maybe she had spoken foolishly; maybe he thought she was lying or, worse, fishing for sympathy. When he did respond it was in his usual measured way:

"You don't really look like someone who'd be a shop-lifter."

A sidestep, it felt like, a gentle evasion, but of what? She still didn't know.

Now, here she was pulling her car over on the gravel shoulder of the road between the warehouse where he had lived and the factory lot. Here she was turning off her engine and getting out of her car. All this—she chastised herself—was sentimental and futile behavior. You could eke meaning out of memory however you saw fit, but it still did not mean anything for sure. The night outside her car was very quiet, was not the same as it was inside, with the music and sooth-ing electric-green lights of the radio. She looked up at the tower structures standing out against the dark blue sky. She looked at the black water of the bay with its small glimpses of silver flashing on the ripples of waves. How does someone fall, unnoticed, off a boat? she wondered. She did not often give thought to the details of her father's drowning; she had continuously been told by her mother that the night was too dark and the ocean too big, that there was a storm, and that was why he had not been rescuable.

People leave—sometimes it is not a surprise.

And what did any of this have to do with Kenny, except that some things are a net that other things get caught in, she thought.

Mary left her car door open and walked a few steps away, hearing the gravel crunch beneath her shoes, and she recalled him asking her to walk more quietly. She remembered feeling out of place (too glossy, too vain) next to him in his soft-soled, worn-out sneakers—there had been nothing trying or vain about his clothes, as there had been about hers. She also remembered the entire three hours they'd sat up in the factory tower talking, he did not try to touch her even once, and she had known he wouldn't. It was only later, after they came back to his room in the warehouse, that he asked, rather politely and remotely, already unfolding a blanket onto the floor for himself, if she wanted to sleep together or, and she answered "yes" before he could finish his question. She was still wearing her dance-club clothes under her other clothes, and he teased her about it, when it got to the point of removing their clothing. *You've got on a few layers.*

The following morning when they said goodbye, she wrote her address on a scrap of paper and he put it in his pocket, smiling. The sun was shining on the bay, turning the water into a crystal surface, a buoyant, shimmering, multi-faceted plain. White triangular sails drifted on silver-capped waves. They laughed at her jammed car doors, and he unstuck the driver's side door for her by fidgeting with something inside it. Everything she looked at that morning seemed bathed in white light.

But the night now was very quiet, and she felt frightened. Of what, she couldn't say. She felt around her presences she couldn't see and knew probably did not exist, but still. She felt foolish, then. She turned around and got back in her car, turned up the radio, and drove home.

Eric and three of his friends were sitting around the living room in front of a movie (two in wheelchairs, the other two on the couch) when Mary came down the hall. It took her a second to recognize what they were watching—it was her copy of *Barton Fink*.

Eric glanced up as she entered the room. The pleasure on his face caught her off guard. "This is a really good movie," he said, in an uncharacteristically jovial tone of voice. "This might be the best movie I've ever seen."

Mary looked at the screen and saw that the movie was at the part where John Goodman bellows "A life of the mind!" over and over as he chases John Turturro, playing the part of a screenwriter struggling with writer's block, down a hallway of a dilapidated hotel. "It's just *totally* fucked up," said Eric, laughing.

Mary took in the room, the coffee table, their hands, as quickly and tactfully as she could. She saw no plates of cocaine, no razor blades, no signs of marijuana even, only a paper wrapper with a half-eaten hamburger on it.

"And I'm not even stoned, man, but I feel like I am," said one of the friends, the one called Hector. He was skinny and sharp-featured, half-Mexican and half-Italian, she'd heard him mention before. The expression on his face was stricken, and he did not look away from the TV screen.

Mary hesitated and then said, "Yeah, this is one of my favorites, too." She was aware of sounding pedantic. To lessen the weight of that she added, lightly, "Not that I actually get it or anything." She took a seat at the end of the couch, and sat through the rest of the movie with the boys.

At one point Eric began to stutter. "Sometimes there's things—sometimes the things—" Looking his way, she couldn't believe he was not stoned; she felt both intensely sad and irritated, suddenly, for just a second. She saw him coming into Dean's room to retrieve his panicking bird from the corner, all of the room's objects bathed in filtered blue light, all of it somehow *her* doing, her disregard, and she felt only sad then. He finished, "I swear I *know* how that feels," and laughed.

————————

When the three of them, Mary and Eric and Dean, were all in residence at the same time, the apartment felt like a potentially happening place, Mary thought. She normally did not allow herself to use this kind of terminology, however, and never out loud.

The phone rang often. Random boys she'd never seen before (and some she saw around campus every now and then) came in and out, passing glances through her doorway as they sauntered by on their way down the hall. Mostly, they were Dean's friends. Sometimes they stood out on the sidewalk and hollered "Hey, Dean!" or "Hey, dipshit!" at the windows. Then they came inside, laughing and clomping, casting about their oblivious and self-satisfied boys' energies. Mary got small inside herself waiting for them to pass her room, even if they were not the kind of boys that generally interested her—which, with Dean's friends (they were all business and political science majors), they usually were not.

She was also aware that her presence helped to make her roommates—or at least Dean—look good. Mary could recall, in her first week of meeting Dean in the dorms the previous semester, how he had talked her into coming along with him on various errands: to the bank, to buy ecstasy from an old buddy in Concord, to some other houseful of boys for no apparent reason at all other than for the boys to stand around Dean's convertible MG in the driveway. These boys seemed to have not much to say to each other, except to curse under their breaths that they had to call so-and-so or that so-and-so had better call them. It finally dawned on Mary that she was being used by Dean, slightly. She was being used to sit in the passenger seat of his MG, saying nothing, wearing her mirrored sunglasses and with her hair looking appropriately wind-blown. "Your hair looks good blowing in the wind," Dean had told her on the freeway, grinning in his uncontrollable way. Mary had thought it all fairly stupid but had been willing to go along with it because she was bored at the time and thought Dean was harmless. He was harmless, but he had a car, which she did not at the time.

She had gotten her own car, finally, at the start of the summer. A used Celica passed on to her from a cousin in San Jose.

"Hey, roommate," Dean would say upon entering with his friends. "Hey, you've met my roommate Mary before, right?" he would turn and say to his friends who, like him, would be staring at her with amused, seemingly expectant expressions on their faces.

She liked and did not like it, this form of attention. Any acknowledgment by Dean of her attractiveness was, and had been from the very start, purely impersonal, she felt—and they both seemed to know it. It was something complicit between them, almost like a business contract. She felt a brotherly familiarity with Dean, similar to the way she felt toward her boy cousins; it had something to do with them both being Asian. She felt the same toward Eric but not quite; she wasn't sure why. Dean would invite her out to clubs and rave parties with him. She would go, and she would be nice to his friends and let Dean pay for things if he was in the mood to. She would go because she wanted to dance (she told herself) and to look at people. In truth she harbored vague hopes of going out to these places and meeting someone—among the throngs of good-looking people who were always there—who was also interesting enough to fulfill what she knew were her contradictory standards: she wanted a guy with a nice body who didn't care that he had a nice body, a guy who had good taste in movies and music but was not overly serious or condescending, a guy who would remain desirable and interesting to her without becoming evasive. At the same time she knew the whole ritual of searching in these circumstances to be pointless.

Once, uncharacteristically, she accepted a tab of ecstasy from someone handing them out and ended up going home with one of Dean's friends whom she'd seen a couple times before around the apartment. His name was Carl. He was big and stocky, an extremely clean-cut white boy, not in the least bit her type. Guys like that, there was nothing imaginative about their looks, she thought, even if there was nothing amiss about them either. He was a business major and an ex-wrestler. She did not have sex with Carl that night but took off her clothes and let him rub her back and felt him get an erection against the back of her leg, which she ignored. She thought that he, like Dean, was a buffoon, but the kind that was good to be around sometimes. It was practically guaranteed that—as a girl—you would at least receive some attention from guys like them.

But something turned over in her that night. By morning she was crying in Carl's bed, and he was not the kind of person in whose presence she would've ever expected to be acting this way. What had allowed it? He had a mustache; he wore his shirt half-unbuttoned to show off his chest muscles and his vulgar swirls of chest hair—at least that is how she saw him. He wore pungent cologne and a gold cross necklace.

"Now I know what Dean feels like!" she declared, sobbing and laughing simultaneously. She was unable to articulate what she really meant by that, though—in her mind it had something to do with the notion of Dean as a jester.

She straightened up afterward and said, "You can't count on anything I say at night, really."

Carl was sitting in a chair next to the bed, watching her, his hands clasped beneath his chin and his elbows on his knees. He had been sitting there for hours, she realized, as the color of objects in the room began to return to their normal, more muted tones.

"I bet you've never let anyone really love you before," he said.

Mary thought but did not say the words "How useless"—being told that by someone who would never be more than a passerby in her life.

———

It was not the last time love was spoken of to her in a useless way that year.

Another nightclub or warehouse, throbbing lights, a cold concrete floor. How many cold floors had she sat upon, hoping to be rescued by some dancing boy or another? Mary thought you could read the true skillfulness, the acumen, of people in the way they danced; that night, she'd been watching one shirtless, slim, brown-haired boy in particular whom she thought had the posture of a warrior, a graceful fighter. Dean was in an emotional state and sat beside her, having asked to hold her hand. "Mary, I love you, you know that," he was telling her. A minute would go by, and he would say it again. "You're a beautiful person, I'm not shitting you." Dean was not a warrior. He was hopeless, and she did not even *want* to help him, was all Mary could think. But still she held his hand. She patted his hair when he laid his head on her shoulder.

Later, they walked out of the club into a graying, misty city. It was 6 a.m., easily. What were these streets? She didn't recognize any of them. They walked for half an hour, searching for Mary's car. It was parked a lifetime away, it seemed, the distance between night and day. Since that summer, her sense of time had turned confusing yet profound. She felt as if she were walking through a maze of heightened moments, trying to stay on the track of only heightened moments, but she had to use her senses, her *acumen*, in order to avoid turning down a dull stretch. She might feel it impending if she sat too long in front of the TV in the afternoon. While waiting at a bus stop, an inexplicable sense of danger could arise in her gut. Portent could be attached to insignificant things: the mention of the same fact in two separate conversations, minor premonitions that proved true. There were other things, too, that seemed to happen twice. Sometimes she saw two or three car accidents in a day. Now it was the dancing boy she'd been watching inside the club. He was standing on a street corner in a loose group of boys and girls, and now he was noticing her. He even turned to keep his gaze on Mary as she and Dean went by. His look was nonsexual but piercing, almost adoring. She did not understand it.

"Are you Sue? Are you Sue?" she heard him say, but she did not stop. Sue was her mother's name, to some people, but of course she knew he hadn't meant that. It wasn't until they were well past that it dawned on Mary—he had meant Sioux.

———

Some weeks after Ping's history notes visit, their professor showed them an experimental film by Chris Marker. It told the story of a man traveling through time.

The film was told all in photographic stills fading one into the next. A man was in a chair, with wires connected to his head and chest, and other men stood around him. Mary was vaguely disturbed by the images of the wired man with the others standing over and watching him, though at the same time she could dismiss it all as hokey—impressionistic sci-fi, she thought. But something about the images also brought to mind, for just a second, a glimpse of herself in Ping's room, that night months ago when the two of them had lain on opposite dorm beds and she had distracted herself by studying the Clint Eastwood drawing above his bed as he talked on about how he'd tried to kill himself. Or, maybe it was just the day itself that was unnerving, a shift in the weather, springtime getting close; she was not sure how to account for her mood at seeing these images. She remembered not quite believing Ping when he told her about his suicide attempt. There were many people she did not quite believe, it occurred to her. Dean, too.

Other images in the film consisted of the man meeting the same woman in different locations for seemingly brief periods of time. The idea seemed to be that the man was not in control of his travels—he seemed to want to stay with the woman but would then get transported back to the room where he sat in the chair, connected to wires, with the men standing around him again. These men were scientists of some kind, was Mary's impression, and because of that they were a little heartless; they did not seem to care that the man had loved this woman or that it caused him pain to come and go from her presence so erratically. It wasn't clear what the scientists wanted or expected to find through this man, but whatever they needed from him— from his travels, in effect—had made them impervious to empathy. Mary disliked them for that. In the end, though, the implication was that the man had simply been traveling through a series of memories involving this woman, who had died. The film was, in short, a metaphor for his being haunted by his loss; the roomful of image-probing scientists (it could be interpreted) just a representation of the mechanics of grief.

Only one moment in the film, lasting about ten seconds, was not a photographic still but was instead a moving image of the woman—a close-up of her face as she woke—blinking her eyes, once.

"Can anyone tell us why that moment in the film is so affecting?" asked the professor after the classroom lights had gone back up.

Mary couldn't. She had been more preoccupied with the heartlessness of the scientists and had, admittedly, begun to nod off a little by the point in the film that the professor was now mentioning. (She noticed, by the blank, startled look on his face as the lights came up, that Ping, a couple seats across from her, had likely been dozing, too.) It was a boy sitting several desks behind them who spoke up, the classmate who had once called her Machiavellian. He was wearing a yellow shirt.

"Because it's the only moment in the film that's in live action. It pulls you in because it's juxtaposed next to only frozen images. It's intimate," he said, with what sounded like reverence, or like reverence being played down, really.

Mary turned in her seat and looked at this boy.

———

A sea quiet. But the sea is not really quiet.

4. *Meetings, Again*

Nine years later, she thinks the mechanics of an experience are malleable. In the editing room this is what she feels she is dealing with, over and over, and she understands her work better these days. She is a good editor, she finds, because she is unsentimental and tactical. She does not linger on dramatic moments, preferring to cut her shots and scenes in a rather economic, minimalist style, so that viewers are left a little wanting—she will do no interpreting for them, though neither will she withhold elements in a scene. The fact that emotional impact depends on the number of frames she decides to let a shot run is a mechanism she is comfortable with.

Kenny, by this time, is someone she is accustomed to hearing from once every other year or so. Postcards from Thailand, Japan, Russia, one letter from a tent in northern Spain, then Los Angeles: California-bound again, she thinks. Letters from Los Angeles. She was living in New York City for much of the time he spent traveling. She would write him back when she had places to go herself. She would write her letters on pieces of grid paper torn out of notepads she used for work, while sitting on trains and airplanes, in transit between jobs. She would try to make whatever she was doing and wherever she was going sound interesting or at least whimsical. One letter she wrote from a Buddhist retreat she attended in northern Vermont. Romantic longing, she thinks, must be able to be quenched by means other than actual romance: she has by this time learned to replace him, to otherwise fill the space in her heart he tended to occupy. He is just someone she thinks of fondly now, an old friend who has for whatever reasons (she is appreciative of this, she will say) stayed in touch over the years.

In this time they have almost seen each other again only once, passing through San Francisco, but ended up missing one another's phone calls.

Then came a span of two and a half years in which she didn't hear from him at all. In that time she moved from New York City to St. Louis, Missouri, following a boyfriend who had just accepted a teaching position at a state university film department. When Kenny's next letter found her, she wrote back about the details of her new life with a mixed feeling of resignation and satisfaction, both. She had just gotten married. She wrote about the house they had purchased (a deal they could never have gotten in New York) and about the pleasant surprise she felt at seeing the color of the leaves in the Missouri fall; she said she found the Midwest "actually okay" and that she was "getting used to the slower pace."

In these ways she neither lied nor told too much about how she really felt at hearing from Kenny again. The portrait she meant to draw of her life (and it was out of a form of politeness, to all involved, that she did this) was of a calm and happy, understated one. She kept the tone of her affections decidedly light and happenstance: *It's a nice surprise to hear from you again. I've sometimes wondered what you might be up to.* He wrote back shortly afterward about a trip he'd made to the Yukon Territory, working on a documentary, where the film crew's canoe hit choppy waters trying to cross a river. He had fallen out of the canoe and almost drowned. He had had to let go of the camera, and all their footage had been lost. These are some of the latest letters they've exchanged. She has been married going on three years now.

Mary is not in charge of gathering the footage she works with. As an editor she comes on the scene later and waits for the footage to arrive—canisters of film—so she can take it with her into the enclosed darkened rooms in which she does her work. She is an assembler. She has a talent for juxtaposition; she is good at creating cohesion out of the jumble of information (not always chronological) that is passed on to her by those who work directly behind the camera; and she prefers to work alone. She has an excellent memory for images and details.

The person she has married is also a film editor, along with being a professor. His name is Joseph, but he goes by his middle name, Marcus—so as to distinguish himself from his father and the long line of Josephs before him—his is a background of tradition. Though they didn't know each other very well then, they went to college together. He is the boy who once called her Machiavellian.

She remembers not really taking notice of him until that day he spoke up in class about the Chris Marker film; he was wearing a yellow shirt that day, a faded sports jersey of some kind. He had a manner of wearing thrift-store-type clothing that made the clothing seem new and strangely clean, she had noticed. He was rather scrubbed and clean-cut himself. She had thought this must be because he wasn't from California; she already knew then that he was from the Midwest.

They did not start dating in college, but two or so years later, after running into each other again in New York City.

Living in Missouri, they don't see the ocean that often these days. Every now and then they return to California, and when they arrive Mary is struck by the swiftness and tenuousness of California. Such a magical, dangerous place! The freeways seem surreal to her after the stolidness of roads and the gravity of weather in Missouri. The freeways of California are like open veins of surging metal energy. That people live in this place and actually dare to believe the ideas that occur to them while living there disturbs Mary in a way she can't quite explain. The ocean now seems to her like a vast, beautiful, dead place. She cannot look at it without feeling its pull, which has something like oblivion behind it. Being on the cliffs above the Pacific Ocean, she feels things coming to a head inside her in a way that suggests a deep yet unrooted truth she doesn't know what to do with. The skies above northern California are charged with something she could follow or choose not to follow, and sometimes she thinks that might be her life's primary choice—that there is a kind of tug-of-war inside her. Here is Missouri, the place where her life has so far coalesced, and there is California. Standing on those cliffs above the Pacific, she can feel the very Earth trembling. In so many ways, it seems to her, California is vying to get loose and will get back to the ocean sooner or later, and sometimes she thinks maybe it is safer to avoid it.

She keeps these ideas to herself for the most part, however, having through experience learned to identify when she is in safe company for the revealing of such ideas and when she is not. Some people she can look at and see in their eyes that they see what she does, and explaining is not necessary then. But most people are embroiled in the known way of looking at things, is how she generally feels. In her soul and in the intuitive parts of her mind, she *knows* that California is trembling and scheming and that she wants no

further part of it, but who can she really tell that to? Not
her husband. "California isn't a good place for me," she has
said, but she cites the apparent issues (media, congestion,
commercialization, superficiality) and says she would not
want any children of her own to grow up there. She does
not say that she thinks California is a place of an ethereal
nature and that she is already too much a person of an ethereal nature—that she does not *need* it, in short. She can't
emphasize enough the danger it really seems to be to her.
Her husband agrees with her on the apparent issues; most
non-Californians do, she finds. So they live where they are
more landlocked and where people, it is rumored, more
consistently do what they say, say what they mean.

Still, there are many things her husband doesn't see. He
cannot abide vagueness. For example, she would like to, but
cannot, say things to him like "It's all the negative ions in the
air," even as a joke.

Today, Mary is logging interview footage for a documentary about emigrants from countries in Eastern Europe. The
documentarian is a young man who grew up in the States;
he is documenting his elderly parents' decision to return
to their homeland after having lived in the States for forty
years. "Ending their forty-year sojourn in New Jersey," says
a talking-heads shot of the documentarian, standing in the
middle of what appears to be an old village with stone buildings and dirt streets.

Mary thinks: *Sojourn? Well, of course.*

And it happens on some days—like this one—that, for
no identifiable reason, a thought of Kenny will appear at
the forefront of her mind, quite abruptly. Maybe it has to

do with looking at footage of countries she has never been to before; or maybe it is something finer, some barely discernable frequency her mind is attuning itself to at just that moment, a frequency along which rides some revelation about distance and witness, she thinks; or maybe it *is* him, actually, psychically, trying to contact her. It is at this moment that the phone rings. It is Marcus. His calling now seems to her, almost uncannily, a disguised way of retrieving her back to whatever is the contract of their life together, like a father catching the string of his child's balloon just in time to stop it from floating off into the sky. He does it instinctually and pragmatically, not even aware of the timeliness of his intervention, and never pausing to imagine his child might want anything different than for his balloon to be kept hold of.

The reason for his call is, "Hey, I was thinking of taking the chicken out of the freezer."

"Okay," she says, as it occurs to her that the deepest ironies of her life will never be seen by anyone but herself.

"Should we broil it or stir-fry it?"

"Whatever, I can't really think about food right now." She feels unreasonably pressured by this question, and the ensuing brief pause from him tells her he has picked up on this.

"How's work going?"

"It's work," she replies, with a sigh. "What do you think of the word *sojourn*? I mean, can people sojourn in a place like New Jersey, do you think?"

"Sure they could. If they're not from New Jersey, I don't see why not," replies Marcus, "though it does sound like something people did in the Middle Ages more than now, for some reason. But I gotta run right now. Call me when you're on your way home, okay?"

"All right."

They exchange *I love you*s and then she hangs up, returns to gazing at the stilled image on her editing room viewing screen. And who is Kenny, wherever he is now? Mary used to trust in her imagination—used to rely on it, like a faith—but doesn't anymore.

———

Toward the end of that year (the year of living with her intermittent roommates Eric and Dean) she, like many of her classmates, was busy trying to finish her senior thesis film project. For Mary, it was all she thought about at the time. It was as if there was an abyss she could keep her back turned on as long as she kept working on her film. Other classmates, too, spoke about the withdrawal—as if filmmaking were a racy addiction—they felt at nearing the end of making their films.

During this time she often crossed paths with other classmates during editing shift changes at the lab downtown that students used when the one on campus wasn't available. Some shifts at the downtown lab began as late as two in the morning. Mary would stop at a corner gas station for a cup of coffee, feeling as if she were embarking on a secret mission. The doors to the editing rooms were mostly always closed, the activity inside dark: she had the impression of other souls quietly, complicatedly at work, each of them hashing out memory and sequence and the importance of one image over another. Sometimes, when she needed a break, Mary would loiter in the hallway drinking coffee and nibbling on a blueberry muffin or other snack, and she would wait—hopefully—for another soul to come out of one of the other rooms; she would hope it might be someone she knew. If someone she didn't know came out and left the door ajar, she would peek into the room to get a glimpse of what their footage looked like. She was curious to know what kinds of pictures kept other people up at these late hours.

Sometimes there were excuses for joining others in their dark rooms, to sit or lean nearby and peer with them at the tiny screen, watch the frames flicker past, and make quiet comments. There was something intimate in sharing the endeavor of editing, even if they were all working on separate projects. At least they shared the physical facts of the endeavor—that of using tiny squares of transparent tape to connect one fraction of movement to the next and thereby turn a string of frozen images into one moving shot. Taking care to lop off just the right number of frames in order to make one shot meet with the next in a manner that would create the illusion of natural, continuous motion. Payoff, pacing, tension, flow—these were the kinds of terms they used to talk about what effects they were trying to achieve.

Mary did not eat or sleep much during these months, nor did she spend time with any friends who weren't also film people. Nor did she really have a love life, just random incidents and temporary interests. Kenny stayed at the back of her mind throughout it all. The thought of him could override every present desire, if she allowed it to, but since she knew there was nothing she could do but wait, she decided she should not wait. Still she checked her mail, each day.

———

One night she ran into Ping at the lab downtown. "Hey, what are you working on?" she asked, stopping in the doorway of his editing room.

"You can come in if you want," he said, and after she had taken a seat next to him in front of the viewing monitor: "It's about homelessness."

Mary didn't respond right away, as this was one of the student film subjects she felt was cliché. Kids living in the city for the first time, feeling like they were onto something daring and profound by filming homeless people—it disgusted her a little. But maybe that was because she knew she could not do such a thing with sincerity herself.

"Kenny helped me shoot some of this footage," said Ping. "We walked all over the city for, like, sixteen hours straight. There was this family—they were from some kind of indigenous tribe. In Vietnam, I think, actually. Don't they have indigenous tribes there?"

"I don't know," said Mary. She looked more intently at the footage on the screen now, wondering if she would be able to spot Kenny's hand in it.

"Actually it was a mom and her son, but he wasn't really her son, she just thought of him that way or something. Like, she'd adopted him on the street. He was weird. When he first started talking to us, he just seemed like a regular street kid, like me or you, you know? I don't mean like *we* are street kids, but I mean like he was Asian but totally Americanized, too. Then he just all of a sudden switched over and started talking in this other language and acting all paranoid and, like, primitive."

She looked at Ping as he spoke. He kept his gaze forward, on the screen, and his hands seemed calm resting atop the levers that moved and stopped and controlled the speed of the reels. She could see the shape of his Adam's apple in his profile. His face still had the hapless, slightly dumbfounded expression it usually had, but he looked comfortable here in front of the editing equipment, it occurred to her, which gave her a feeling of camaraderie with him. She remembered him pushing his way into that party in the dorm room that night, his head bobbing in the crowd, leaving her behind in the hallway with the other stragglers, Kenny and his friend Jim. If it were not for Ping's invitation that night, she never would've made whatever contact she'd made with Kenny. And it struck her how people like herself and Kenny might go through life missing boats—or were they ports?—were it not for people like Ping.

"He told us he'd been born in the mountains in Vietnam but was taken away from there when he was a little kid—like, taken out of the bushes, you know. Then he got adopted and grew up in the States pretty much since he was four or something like that." Ping was still looking at the screen as he talked. "But then something happened, like, when he turned thirteen. He'd been in all these different foster homes, and I guess it was just traumatic. One day he took off all his clothes and climbed up into a tree and wouldn't come down. He was, like, eating bugs and leaves and stuff, like reverting back to his indigenous behavior or something, is what his foster family and the social workers all thought. He wouldn't speak English anymore, and they had to call the fire department to get him down. Then he went into a mental health institution. They let him out 'cause he could be normal some of the time, I guess. But for the most part I think a lot of the time he's just kind of out there, you know?

"Of course, he told us all this about himself when he wasn't all freaking out, when he was in his normal American boy state, as he called it."

"That's weird," said Mary, cautiously. She wasn't sure how she felt about the story or if she even believed it. She thought perhaps Ping was just gullible. The kid on the viewing screen was dressed in baggy shorts and a flannel shirt over a skateboard insignia T-shirt. He had a profusion of bracelets—the plastic kind that adolescent girls wore, mixed in with a few chain-link ones—going from his wrist up to the middle of his forearm. He had a happy face, the same kind of dopily smiling face that Ping had, but with a more angular jawline. His skin was rather dark and his eyes small with a bright, mischievous light to them. He looked to be not much younger than Mary. He was talking and pointing and kept bouncing and turning around as he walked. The camera was following him: they were moving through the Civic Center Plaza downtown; Mary recognized it. She thought (aside from the fact that he was living on the street) that this boy looked fairly normal. He wasn't bad-looking, in a way.

Mary wasn't one to keep her skepticism to herself. "Maybe he was lying to you," she said.

A smirk broke at the corner of Ping's mouth as he turned his face toward her. "I knew you would say that."

Just then, an image of Ping himself walked onto the screen and stood conversing with the boy, laughing and gesturing. "There you are," said Mary.

"Oh yeah, Kenny shot this roll."

Ping onscreen glanced the camera's way and grinned, once. He wore a baseball cap and had his hands in the front pockets of his jeans; he looked comfortable and somehow more ordinary—more American—than the street kid did. The boy was the subject here, it occurred to Mary, and Ping (whom she'd never thought of in this role) was the chronicler.

"Whoa, hey," said Ping, leaning forward suddenly to peer closer. His fingers moved fluidly; he pushed the lever to stop the film and then reverse it: they watched the footage go backwards, slow, then stop and start again, at just about the point when Ping turned and grinned at the camera. "Hey, you see that?"

"See what?" Mary asked, wishing the screen would show her Kenny. But, like Ping, he was the context, not the content here, she realized.

Ping was not looking at himself or even at the boy anymore. He was looking at an even smaller figure on the screen, someone standing in the background next to a graffitied wall beyond Ping and the boy. Another street person, it looked like. An older man, white, bearded, in a torn ski jacket.

Ping nodded. "That man there, look—that man is crying," he said.

———

When finally a letter did come for her from a foreign country, it wasn't from the country she had been expecting—hoping—it would be from.

Dearest Daughter, the letter began (so that Mary thought it must be a hoax of some kind), *you don't know me, but I have looking for you long time. I think by now maybe you have belief I was dead, so have many friends told me this is the news of me they hear, but I am not.*

5. *The Ocean, Again*

Mary didn't know she had a father living in Australia. He had escaped from Vietnam in 1986 (when Mary was ten), and he would have found her earlier had he known where she was. He was sorry he had not found her earlier, said his letter.

He had gotten her address in a roundabout way—he had managed to contact a friend of Mary's mother who had gotten the address without letting on to Mary's mother who it was for. *I try to write you in 1983 and 1984, but I think your mother want to protect you. You should not be angry for her if she do that. I understand she reason.*

I live in Sydney, Australia, now. I come as political prisoner in 1986, and here I have my wife, your Ma Shen, and your two little brothers, Tu and Tuan. I wish you could know well all your family. We all miss you so much and have wonder about you time to time. You not know how much we all wonder, but your poor father most. In my life, some years while I was in prison, I have nothing but time to do but wonder and about you are one of these thing I wonder a lot. Even I dream of the day to meet you again. The last time I meet you was in 1978, but you probably could not remember that. My wish is only to you will read this and so know me now, at last.

Her father had not married her mother when she became pregnant with Mary, because her mother was already married to another man at the time (the one who would a couple years later fall out of the boat into the South China Sea). Her father had known her mother even prior to her marriage; they had known one another since high school, in fact. *I love your mother but never can marry her, for she think I only bring her trouble. She is right, maybe. In Vietnam before 1975, I was a painter. I have little money, many enemies.* By the time Mary was born, her real father had been sent to a reeducation camp—his paintings were thought to have political implications. Mary had met him only once when she was a baby, through a fence: her mother had made one visit to him after he was imprisoned. *Your mother, I wonder, do she still paint now?*

Mary had never known her mother to be a painter.

Now, in Sydney, the man claiming to be Mary's father did not paint anymore, had too long ago lost the fire for it, said his letter. Now he and his family ran a dry-cleaning business.

As he put it: he had looked death closely enough in the face during the weeks of his trying to escape from Vietnam. After that, how could something like painting feel important to him anymore? It should have, but it just didn't. Another method of survival had replaced it.

Her father's escape. The image of the ocean this conjured in Mary's mind was fantastical: it was how she pictured the Apocalypse. A night at the end of the world, ocean and sky reflecting each other over parallel platforms of seemingly endless, almost-black space. Except there was a moon in the platform above, and the silver points of light lying upon the platform below were slightly less fixed than the ones above— they shuddered a little. On the night he finally broke out of the jungle onto the beach, the beach gravel glowed eerily white. He had been running, hiding, climbing, and wading through jungle foliage and swamps for a fortnight or more, not knowing, just praying that he was moving in the direction of the sea. The sound of the waves was both the quietest and loudest sound he had ever heard. Like a mother's womb to her baby, you might think. But the ocean was male, her father had decided, a lustful and heavy-bodied entity, like a glistening black bull or other potent creature you could not trust to control itself—he was hallucinating by this time in his journey and had been seeing many things, speaking to many ghosts and other kinds of spirits. *Do you believe in spirits? Vietnamese people do, but maybe in America you have already grow up without this kind of culture anymore. I come to understand this happen in the West after I speak to many Australians too.*

———

Do you want to meet him? It would be hard for you to meet him, you understand.

Do you not want me to meet him?

My friends tell me he's still very, very stubborn man. Maybe his letter to you show another side of him, so you think. But I don't know, is up to you, said Mary's mother.

Mary's answer came out of her with surprising ease— easing them both, Mary was aware. I guess I don't need to, she said.

———

A letter came from Kenny eventually, too, before the end of that school year. He was in Nagoya, Japan, having a picnic on a cliff above the sea while watching "Japanese people flying these really cool-looking kites around in the sky," he wrote. The letter went on to describe things about Japan and the odd jobs he was doing to make money. The Japanese girls were pretty, both he and the American friend he was traveling with thought so, but they couldn't speak to them much since they didn't know Japanese. He would be flying to Bangkok soon, from where he would start traveling across Asia by trains and buses and hitchhiking, probably, he wrote. He was excited to go to Tibet. Only at the end of his letter were there a couple lines directed more personally at Mary:

> *It was nice we got to spend a little time together before I left, though I guess there wasn't much of a chance of us getting close, I realize. I hope you are well, though, and that life in SF treats you all right. You seemed sometimes melancholy there as I did a lot of the time I was there. I don't know exactly where I am going any more certainly now, but it feels right to me to be traveling like this. I keep thinking of that Beatles song, you know the one? "Oh that magic feeling, nowhere to go . . ." or something like that. Oh well, maybe we'll see each other again someday on one continent or another.*
>
> *Your friend, Kenny*

Mary thought, But what does he mean by that? For no matter how hard she tried to understand it, no matter how many ways she looked at it or how many times she re-read the words, she could not manage to fathom—how there could be anything magic about having no place to go.

6. *What Was Left Behind*

The last she would see of Eric and Dean—ever, in fact—
would be the day they all moved out of the apartment. Dean
was moving into a houseful of boys in Daly City, closer to
campus, while Eric had taken a studio apartment downtown, just himself alone. Mary was moving into a sublet in
the Inner Sunset District with a film classmate, Andrea, who
was older than Mary and with whom she'd worked on several projects, including the one in which they had used Eric's
bird and Dean's room. Mary was expecting to graduate in a
few months. She was already making plans to move to New
York City as soon as the semester was over.

The things that none of them wanted to take with them
they left on the sidewalk. They included the pieces of lum-
ber for the loft in Dean's bedroom that never got made; the
couch that they all thought was ugly and too big to bother
with; several boxes of clothes and odds and ends; and one
of the wheelchairs that had broken. Mary climbed onto a
bucket balanced on the porch railing in order to peel off
the pieces of tape that spelled "TRUST" on the transom
window. She felt a little bit nostalgic as she did this, which
she also thought was a slightly comical and silly way to
feel. She took her timing belt in its plastic bag down from
the living room wall and actually thought twice before casting it, finally, into one of the boxes of junk to leave on the
sidewalk.

Dean, looking at Mary's timing belt as they stood on the
sidewalk, said, "Mary, you have the weirdest stuff of any girl
I've ever met."

"Speaking of belts," said Mary, suddenly remembering the belt she was wearing had come from Dean's room. She pulled it out of her belt loops and tossed it at him.

Dean caught it, and jumped up and down. "Striptease on Bartlett Street!" he yelled.

"Mary's not a weird girl," said Eric, who was taking a break from the moving and was sitting now on the couch, looking out at the street. "She's just got a lot going on in her head."

A few months later, Mary ran into one of Dean's friends on campus—the one named Carl with whom she'd spent that one errant night—and she heard from him that Eric had had a heart attack, after which he'd left San Francisco and moved back to Concord. His family and his doctor had decided perhaps the city was too exciting for him.

"Not to mention all the other great things he was doing for his body and his mind," said Carl with a sardonic laugh, as Mary pictured Eric padding slowly through the thickly carpeted rooms and hallways of his parents' large, quiet house.

Then, because it was a chance to say it and because she didn't want to make the mistake, again, of revealing too much of herself to someone like Carl, Mary said, "Oh, Eric didn't really have a heart."

7. Sifting, Again

Still now, though, sometimes she recalls traitorous things she has said or done, things that she said or did in the course of that year especially. For instance. On that night that Ping

came to borrow her history notes and lay stretched out on
her couch, staring at the ceiling, as he spoke about things like
the underwear he had coveted, and the sadness of sex, and his
own disadvantages as an Asian male, and his Catholic guilt;
all the while she watched him and listened while privately she
was criticizing his shoes in the same light as she did his candor,
his painful-to-watch innocence, his unfortunate haircut; and
all the while she was not realizing—*was not understanding*—
that when someone lies on his back before you like that and
speaks toward the ceiling, that he is entreating you with something and that he might not even know that you are failing
him, if you are, and he might not at the time quite recognize
what is happening, and what then is your responsibility, if
you do recognize it but you keep throwing flowers instead of
stones? Who is she really betraying? It is a biblical parable she
read once that she is thinking of now, about an alleged heretic
in Jerusalem who was being stoned by a mob and how one
man in the mob, not wanting to admit he knows the heretic
and not wanting either to be spotted throwing nothing, thus
throws a flower instead of a stone.

Flowers instead of stones, she thinks, isn't that just how
some girls are?

2. Walruses

I.

There was a time when Darcy believed all she needed to stay satisfied in life was music. The practical aspects of life—money, foremost—would fall into place as long as first she took care of music, she told herself, the music inside herself. Her *art*, that was.

Darcy was, it had been said of her before, a bit of a dreamer.

Yet, her love for the cracked, trembling voices of singers like Ralph Stanley and Hazel Dickens was true and heartfelt. She had recently uncovered what she believed was a significant understanding of the frequencies created by the stringed instruments and high, careening vocal harmonies of old American music. They were tremulous, ethereal. But Darcy was not comfortable using the word *musician* or *songwriter* to describe herself, for she believed to label would be to defile. She did not want to define or even acknowledge the extent of her efforts. Also, she liked to say that she was unconcerned with societal measures of success. But that wasn't completely true.

She awoke in the middle of one night during this time to the dark shape of a man reaching toward her in her bed (which was not her bed, in fact, but the bed belonging to the person whose two-room garage apartment she was subleasing). This man was naked, wiry, and tall. It took her a moment to realize there was another presence in the room when there shouldn't have been. She sat up quickly. He stumbled and fell to the floor. Maybe he was drunk, she thought. He fell close to where her guitar leaned on the desk next to the bed. The moonlight shone through the room's one window onto the instrument's wood finish. The rest of the room was dim.

"Tom?" she said, and the voice that answered, "Yeah," was not Tom's, but because he had answered in the affirmative, for one fleeting moment she accepted it. She was loosely dating someone named Tom, though he was in AA and should not be stumbling drunk into her apartment late at night. And she'd known another Tom, but she'd not seen or heard from him in months and likely wouldn't. She scooted back across her pillows and pushed herself up to standing with her back against the wall.

She reached over and switched on the bedside lamp. The man was a stranger. The thought that she should be afraid occurred to her, but not the sensation of fear itself.

"Who are you?" She tried to summon the appropriate indignation into her voice.

"I'm Don's son, and that's my bed," the man replied, with equally feigned defensiveness.

"No. This is my bed right now," said Darcy. "How did you get in here?"

"I'm Don's son," he said again, standing now with his legs pressed together, forearms across his genitals. His body was long and skinny. His face was small and angular and heavily lined, with large, almost-bulging eyes and thick, chapped lips. "I didn't see you too clear," he went on, "I thought you were the woman upstairs and I've slept in a bed with her before, so I was just going to climb on in."

Darcy only slightly knew the woman who lived in the apartment upstairs. Sometimes they spoke to each other, only briefly and in passing. Once, the woman had told Darcy she was studying to be a lawyer, and that was as much as Darcy had determined about her. Now her imagination raced. Who knew what complicities existed in the relationships of a building's tenants?

"I'll go out to the garage, though. I didn't mean to scare you." The man extended his forearm, still holding it low, and made an apologetic gesture with one hand as if trying to wave. His tone became confidential. "Usually when my dad's not here, I just come in and stay. He says he doesn't want me to, but I know he doesn't really mean that. You're a nice girl. Please don't scream. I am sorry." He moved toward the bathroom as he spoke, and Darcy, standing on the bed with her back against the wall, followed him with her eyes. "Funny though, isn't it? I'm a musician, too," he said, nodding over his shoulder toward the far side of the room. This comment was conversational and uncanny, as if he were answering a question plucked out of the air. There seemed an element of truth to it. Had he said this because his father was a musician (Don's piano was by the window) or because he had seen her guitar? "I'm a really good musician, too. My name's Tracey," he added with a quick smile, as he stepped into the bathroom. He closed the door.

Darcy looked around. There was her guitar, near the place where his face would've been when he fell on the carpet. So yes, he had seen it. She felt wary but not afraid anymore—information had fallen into place. He was just Don's son. An alarming approach, but maybe it had been an honest mistake. Maybe it could be something laughable. Don had made some mention of him, that his son sometimes stayed with him but would not be coming around while the apartment was Darcy's. She thought maybe he hadn't understood, maybe Don hadn't made it completely clear. Darcy decided she wouldn't mind his presence as long as he left soon, for she was—she liked to think—a person willing to help people out, even dubious characters. From the foot of the bed, Don's cat, Kenji, looked up at her calmly, blinking. That told her the cat was familiar with Don's son, too. Darcy started to relax. The cat had been a plus for her on taking the sublet. She adored cats, all kinds, unconditionally and indiscriminately. Don had told her he didn't allow the cat to sleep with him, but if she wanted to let him, she could. Her first night in the apartment, Darcy picked Kenji up from the chair in the kitchen and carried him to the bed.

She heard the toilet flush, and Don's son came out of the bathroom. He was wearing one of her towels around his waist. She stared at him, waiting for action. She was half-sitting, half-kneeling on the pillows at the head of the bed, near the lamp. He made a motion with the towel. "I hope you don't mind. I'm on my way to the garage now." He was trying to reassure her. On his way out, he shook his head at the cat. "Bad Kenji on the bed," he said.

He knows the rules, thought Darcy.

———

She had come back to California this time slimmer than that state had ever allowed her to become before. Her jeans hung satisfyingly slack on her hips, and her arms did not jiggle. There was nothing unnecessary on her; she felt capable and contained. She had only as much money as she needed and no desire to spend more. She had no boyfriend. She ate small meals. Everything she owned fit in the back of her truck.

She had come back because she had no better plan, and for the first time in her adult life that felt okay. All the times before, she had been returning out of desperation or debt or a broken heart. But now she had nothing important or specific to do, and she didn't feel pressured, guilty, or inferior about it. She was twenty-three. She did not have a college degree. Her work in the world, she had decided, was of the invisible kind. Was not of this world, in fact. Not many people understood that when she dared to say it, and those who did usually only did so when they were drunk.

She found a job as a cocktail waitress. At certain peaks in the course of an evening, she felt actual grace, she thought. Immense comprehension might be passed in a glance from a cute boy; a man might tell her, "Keep smiling, it makes the world a better place," and it would seem not generic but wholly, honestly, uniquely directed at her. For one second, something *would* be generated. Would rise and mingle in the air, then travel out into the night with the dispersing people and would thereby, yes, be making the world a better place, even if only in tiny increments. After a few drinks her belief in this theory solidified, and she walked through the crowd believing she could glean essential characteristics about people in a glance. She felt lucid and critical and sexy. The room was hers. Handing drinks off of precarious full trays to sympathetic, flirtatious, or oblivious customers, she experienced a feeling of satisfaction at being the one at work in the midst of others' leisure. This satisfaction was aided by the fact that she was also privy to some exclusives—free drinks, favorable attention from the musicians who played there, privileged passage through the crowd, the right to push. It was a position that made her feel known (people either avoided a waitress's gaze or sought it out) but exempt from social expectations. At the end of the night the overheads were switched on, and in that new stark glare she would gather and stack pint glasses with a kind of lowdown pride.

In this manner—she felt—she was reinventing herself.

———

The place Darcy had given up on was New York City. As she saw it, this was her biggest accomplishment to date: deciding she did *not* want to accomplish anything in particular there.

She had grown tired of being asked out on dates by ad executives and investment bankers who, after a few drinks, would admit their true desires to play in a band or move to Hawaii and become surfing instructors. She had also grown tired of performing grunt work for people not much older, but far more fast-minded and assertive, than she knew she could ever be. People like her sister Mary, for instance.

Mary had moved to New York a year or so earlier and did film editing work there. Darcy, too, had gone to college to study film. Mary, one year older, was the reason for this choice. For years, Darcy had followed in Mary's footsteps, not so much out of admiration but simply because she agreed with Mary's ideas about what was good and what was interesting in the world. Unlike Mary, however, Darcy spent one semester overseas, in Sweden, and then did not manage to graduate but dropped out during her junior year Christmas break. She ended up in New York City on Mary's offer to help her find work, although by that time Darcy's filmmaking ambitions had fizzled more than she cared to admit.

When she arrived, New York overwhelmed her at the same time it seemed to her rather transparent and deceptively (by this she meant politically) safe. The city was full of high-minded yet unenlightened young people. People like Mary, in fact, who scoffed at everybody who didn't see things in the same aesthetic and intellectual light as did she and her peers as being "regular." What a terrifying and humiliating thing it was to be "regular," Darcy was learning. Mary was *not* "regular," and neither were her friends and colleagues, who were all artists or filmmakers or producers of some kind or other. Mary and her friends were enviable, influential: they were those responsible for the creation, versus the passive enjoyment, of things to be looked at and listened to by—ironically enough—all the "regular" people in the world.

Darcy, for her part, spent a total of two years in Manhattan feeling stifled by its concrete canyons. She felt full of secret relief and pity whenever she went outside the city to the kinds of places where people didn't think twice about going to the mall and could shop at Target without making rambling discourse about it. Darcy, truthfully, longed for ordinary life—even for how disparaging it was. At the same time she knew she'd probably never survive it.

Then, one afternoon, while walking down a sidewalk in the East Village, she had spotted a shoebox of discarded cassette tapes. She took these home and listened to them. She hadn't really heard old country music before, and she thought the songs were humorous at the same time they were heartbreaking. The voices sounded raw and scary yet strangely familiar to her. She thought the song "Stand by Your Man" was appalling, yet it produced in her a rush of exhilaration when she heard it. She couldn't explain it. Her boyfriend at the time had been trying to teach her to play the guitar; she'd been only mildly interested at first. Later, she would think that box of tapes was like a marker on the side of the road, and she might have missed it. She might have missed the turnoff toward the change in her destiny. Not that *music* per se was her destiny, just that—if there was such a thing as destiny—then in her version there must have been programmed a moment of deviation in order for her to start moving toward it.

———

Don, the man whose apartment Darcy was subleasing, was a jazz pianist in his late fifties. He loitered in the afternoons— with a whole group of them, friendly, tousled-looking, middle-aged men, all musicians—at the neighborhood coffee shop where Darcy often spent hours at a time, trying to write lyrics. Since she had not been playing music for long, she was not particularly confident in her abilities. Music, she feared, might call for a kind of personality more direct and dynamic than her own.

Don and his friends spoke in gruff voices and had bad skin from years of smoking and drinking, and each had a sad story to tell: divorce, estranged sons and daughters, a perfect girlfriend who had died only a year ago, bad breaks in the music business. They were ingratiating and subtly flirtatious toward Darcy. They made quips and cast sidelong glances at one another in a manner that told Darcy that they—the men—were staying silent about what this situation really was to them. A slight contest and maybe a travesty, something to tease each other about later, regarding the much-younger girl at their table. But she also believed them to be sincere. They were honestly curious about her, and they seemed genuinely encouraging.

They offered her music lessons (she politely evaded accepting, not wanting to go alone to any of their homes). They gave her advice about having "soul" and "playing it your own way"; they assured her that technical competence did not necessarily equal "good" in terms of what really mattered in music. Darcy took their advice to heart even though it held its share of clichés. They were old and wizened to it, she told herself; they played jazz. She admired their commitment, their poverty, their good-naturedness about their poverty and even their anonymity—all things she believed might be requisite and consequent of a life dedicated to music. She liked how, with chagrin, Don told the others he'd been doing the Nordstrom's gig, which involved wearing a tuxedo while playing piano in the menswear department. They were humble about their talents and nonchalant in the face of the uncertainty of their careers. In contrast, all the young male musicians Darcy knew wanted to be rock stars. They believed themselves to be profound and misunderstood yet destined to be famous, no matter how adamantly they claimed they didn't want fame. They were all pop-culture conformists, thought Darcy. The men at the coffee shop were different—were the relief, the satisfaction, of resignation.

So when Don offered her his apartment for two months (he had gotten a few gigs in Seattle), she took it as another sign. Something provident connected to music. She could stay for free if she took care of his cat, Don said. The apartment-hunting process since her return to San Francisco had been, for her, ridiculous and trying. Rents were high, available rooms scarce. Current tenants held multiple rounds of interviews before selecting roommates. Darcy had gone to at least twenty of these interviews and been offered none of the available rooms. What did it mean that the only offer she received was from an old man with a needy cat? She told Don yes, she would do it.

"You'll get along fine with Kenji. You have a gentle soul," he assessed her when she came to meet the cat and see the apartment. She sat on Kenji's chair, and Kenji, a fat gray-brown tiger cat, settled on her lap, purring.

Don's apartment was at the back of a garage on Anza Street in the Outer Richmond District, twenty blocks from the ocean, five blocks from the park. The building was a three-story, pastel-pink, rectangular affair, one of those houses that slightly resembled a boat. To get to his front door, she had to walk down an alley at the side of the house and through the darkened garage that was full of the amorphous shapes of junk and cluttered shelves. The apartment was low-ceilinged and consisted of two rooms—kitchen and bedroom—separated by a short entrance hall. Both rooms were dim and somewhat dirty.

Don offered her a soda. She drank it and listened to him talk about Kenji. Kenji ate only tuna-flavored Friskies, two cans a day. Kenji liked to go out at 6 a.m. and usually came back in at 5 p.m. They went out to the small backyard, and Don showed her how to pull up a stalk of dry grass from the lawn and drag it around for Kenji to paw at and chase. They sat on the patio and played with the cat, and then Don asked if she would like to go to the ocean to watch the sun set.

"Oh, I have to be at work at seven," she told him, making her tone regretful. Inside, she chastised herself for having let things become weird. She believed it was probably *her* doing—whenever she let herself get comfortable in a man's presence, whenever she let herself get quiet and pensive, they took it as affection, or the shyness of interest. When all she had wanted, really, she told herself, was a little kindness. Maybe. And a place to stop, just stop, for a second.

The next time, when she came to pick up the keys, she brought along a friend, a girl named Tara who worked in the coffee shop. The two girls made bright, silly conversation and laughed at inside jokes in front of Don, who smiled and shook his head at them in such a fatherly way it made Darcy worry that, perhaps, the time before, she had been mistaken.

"I totally understand your wanting me along. Guys suck," said Tara, as they were walking away from Don's apartment, and Darcy felt a little guilty at allowing Tara to lump a sixty-year-old man into the same milieu of experience by which the girls condemned his younger counterparts. "But

at least you have your own place now." Darcy had been living intermittently on Tara's floor as well as on other friends'
couches. Tara was an old acquaintance. She and Darcy were
from the same hometown. In the foothills, about three hours
northeast of San Francisco.

———

Darcy heard the door that led back out to the garage close,
and she eventually drifted back to sleep. When she woke
again, it was still night. She didn't know what had woken
her until she spotted Tracey, Don's son, sitting in a chair,
Kenji's chair, in the kitchen. From the bed she had a perfect
view, through the bedroom doorway, across the entrance
hall, of that corner of the kitchen. He sat in the dark with
his legs crossed, smoking a cigarette, gazing into his lap with
an anguished expression. As far as she could tell, he was still
naked.

"Is something wrong with the garage?" She said this
flatly, not quite but almost warily.

He looked up. His face cracked into a smile. "Well, it's
cold in there. But really, I just—I can't sleep. I've got a lot of
things on my mind." His tone was grateful and confiding.
"So you're the one taking care of my dad's cat. I would've
taken care of Kenji. I love Kenji. You're young. Seventeen?"

"Twenty-three."

"Wow. You have a child's energy. A true innocent spirit,
really. What do you do? I see your guitar. I bet you're good."
He seemed genuinely taken, and Darcy—though she was
aware it was somewhat absurd—thought maybe this man,
odd as he was, was capable of seeing things other people did

not. She wanted to believe the definition of herself he was offering.

"I don't really play the guitar," she said. "I just play chords."

"No, I can tell you're good. Your guitar has good energy. So, are you a college student or something?"

"Not anymore. I studied film a little. I used to want to be a screenwriter." She meant this last statement to sound whimsical, ironic.

"Writer, huh, really? You must be some kind of genius." He seemed to be speaking without forethought, which made his words seem instinctual, uncalculated, she thought, at the same time she could still feel the manipulation behind them.

Don's son was fidgeting; he kept folding and unfolding his forearms. His legs still crossed, he splayed the fingers of both hands over one knee and stared at them for a drawn-out moment. Then he looked up and said, "Funny us meeting this way, though, huh? That'd be a good scene in a movie. Don't you think it'd be?" He grinned.

"Maybe."

Darcy actually hated it when people said things like that. She was not, anyhow, a real writer. Though she understood that writers stole from life all the time—their own as well as the lives of friends, family, even total strangers. They wrote down every bit of good dialogue they overheard at bus stops. The sheer, strange indecency of this was another reason Darcy wished she could be an aspiring musician instead of an aspiring filmmaker—if you had to be an aspiring anything, she thought, which, unfortunately, did seem unavoidable.

"Hey, maybe we should play together." Tracey motioned to her guitar again. "What's your name?" She told him, and he said, "We could be a duo. Tracey and Darcy. I bet we'd be good together."

Darcy actually entertained this for a moment: her Gram and Emmylou. *I am this desperate and naive*, she thought. But it could also be said, she believed, it was more about her willingness to let possibilities unfold.

"Why doesn't your father want you to come around here?" she asked.

He half-sighed, with a wry smile. He put a hand in his hair and looked to his lap, then up again at her with his face at a downcast angle. She saw the large whites of his eyes in the dim blue kitchen light. "He's just a grumpy old man, I guess. He likes to keep it all for himself, you know, all for himself. I'm his only son, I get in a spot sometimes—he tells me his life is hard enough as it is, and, you know, he stopped drinking six months ago. Good for you, I told him, so you're doing better for yourself, then you can help me out when I'm in a spot. But he's so angry with me all the time. He just won't give me a chance, you know?" He sighed, looking around. "You're a good girl. Don't tell him I came around here, okay? I'll stay out of your way, I promise. Most other girls, well. They would've screamed or called the cops or done something, you know, *uncool*, like that. You were so cool, though, you didn't even make a sound." He chuckled. "When you first turned on that light, I thought you were asking me, 'Are you a cop?' So I just said 'yeah.'" Darcy recalled the moment—what had she really said? Oh yes. She had said, *Tom?*

Don's son didn't seem concerned with what she'd really said. He went on, "Other people, they get all crazy so fast, they won't give a person a chance. I'm grateful to you, you know? You have a gracious soul." He brought his cigarette to his lips, and she saw his long spidery fingers trembling. Hadn't his father said something about her soul as well? She felt wary and sorry, both.

"Are you going to go back out to the garage?" she asked carefully.

"Does my nakedness bother you? These bodies—" She could see him squinting as he made a gesture at his torso, as if to wipe something off it, "—they're just bodies. Flowers. We're no different than flowers, see." His hands came up, showing long, flat, crooked palms. "But I'll go, I'll go. You're in charge here. I respect you, and I like you. You're a nice girl. I'm just a free spirit, see? Sometimes I'm not aware when I'm making someone else uncomfortable." He took the pillow from Kenji's chair with him as he stood, to cover his genitals. His legs were long and crooked like his fingers. "That cat sure does love you," he said more lightly, before he walked out.

Again she waited to hear the door close. Next to her on the pillow Kenji raised his head, his gaze comprehending her completely—she was sure of it—and in a language far surpassing English. He stared at her with what she took to be concern; then he blinked, and his gaze slipped just to the right of hers.

———

The next morning Darcy went to the coffee shop where Tara worked and told her about what had happened. She had gotten out of the apartment as gracefully as she could manage, but had had to lend Tracey a pair of socks in the process.

"You lent him a pair of socks?" said Tara with wild, delighted disbelief.

"There was just no way out of it," said Darcy. "He asked if I had a pair of socks I wasn't using right now, and of course I did. How could I say no to that? He said his car was broken down on the street, and he was waiting for a tow truck. He went outside or something, and that's when I left. Maybe he'll just be gone when I come back."

"Darcy, that freak is walking around in your socks right now," said Tara.

Tara was twenty-one and the kind of girl who found a certain confidence—social vindication, of a sort—in having friends to whom hilarious and troubling things happened. Darcy suspected this had to do with Tara being the kind of girl these things did not happen to, so she made up for it by being a ready audience for those to whom they did. Tara was not homely, just plain, with straight blond hair and eyeglasses, and she wore her plumpness under jeans and frilly-edged T-shirts, her colors subdued. But there was something deceptive in Tara's seeming magnanimity. In her relish of others' misfortunes there was almost, at times, a hint of malice. Darcy did not honestly feel that close to Tara.

"Well, he's a total drug addict. He was living in a crack house in the Tenderloin or something." Tara was claiming to know this about Don's son. "He comes around and harasses Don and steals his money. You should tell the woman upstairs."

"He said he slept with her," said Darcy, recalling this part.

"Really? I always knew there was something off about her," said Tara, shooting a quick wide-eyed look at Darcy, before moving down the counter to help another customer. When she came back, Darcy was squeezing honey into her cup of coffee. Tara said, incredulously, "So he offered you guitar lessons, too. Like, can he actually play?"

"Well, he did pick up my guitar this morning, and then he played 'I Will Survive' on it," said Darcy. This was true. It was also enough to make Tara double over laughing. Darcy, observing this reaction, decided she had better not mention how Tracey had also gotten her to sing along with him. She hadn't wanted to, but she hadn't seen any real harm in joining in either.

"Oh my god, Darcy," said Tara. "Are you going to call the police? Maybe you should call the police."

"Because he played 'I Will Survive' on my guitar or because he broke into my apartment?"

Tara laughed again. Darcy had known she would. Then, Darcy turned thoughtful. "I think I should call Don first," she said.

She took her coffee and the cordless phone from behind the counter and went to sit at a table in the corner. This early in the morning, Don's musician friends were not yet in the coffee shop; they usually didn't start rolling in until early afternoon. Darcy was glad not to have to face them today.

She dialed the phone and listened to it ring. She got Don's voicemail in Seattle, so she left a message. "I don't mean to bother you, but I'm not sure what else to do," was how she prefaced telling him about Tracey, though she left out the part about his being naked when he'd appeared at her bedside. When she finished and pushed the off button on the receiver, she glanced up to find that Eli, one of Don's friends, was watching her from a table across the room. She had not noticed he was there. Eli was somewhere in his forties. He had a waning, thin body that seemed lost in his clothes; he had gentle, sad eyes and the raw, scraped voice of a blues singer even when he talked. He was, in fact, quite a good blues musician. Darcy had gone a few times to see his weekly piano bar gig. He was lackadaisical and morose and heartworn without affectation. Anyone might guess, looking at him, that he had lived through enough not to have to try too hard when it came to the blues.

One evening Eli had managed to persuade Darcy to go out with him for ice cream. He then talked for two hours straight about the perfect five years he'd spent with his girl-friend prior to her dying of cancer. Her death had occurred a year earlier, and he was still grieving, he informed Darcy. She went home afterward feeling as if she were towing an-other ship's anchor, and was struck by the revelation that the blues up close was not the same as it was via music. You felt for Eli, even admired him, when you heard his sorrowful, weary fingerings on the piano, but in person, his weariness was more like lead. After that encounter, she found herself trying to avoid him. He had also taken to re-marking upon her special energy. Her "vibe," as he called it, which he described as open-hearted yet wiser than her years. "You're really aglow today," Eli would greet her. Some days he might make a simple declaration of "Wow" in her direc-tion. Darcy never knew quite how to receive this attention; she would smile and act shyly appreciative, even if she was beginning to feel annoyed. She did not see herself as being open-hearted.

Now Eli tipped his hat at her. An old man's fedora, she noted. He smiled with just the corner of his mouth and turned back to his newspaper.

Darcy looked out the window, quietly sipping her coffee. She was feeling unmoored again, she realized. She had been just starting to relax at Don's place. She had cleaned and scrubbed and even lit sage one night. She had bought a cheap rug to lay over the worn carpet by the bed: the first home decor item she'd purchased in months. Only, it was *not* her home. She didn't really have a home, and she was being made to face that yet again.

Tara was signaling to her. Darcy got up and went back to the counter.

"So where're you going now?" Tara asked, as Darcy handed the phone over to her.

Darcy shrugged. "I don't really feel like I can go home right now."

"That totally sucks. That's so not fair. That freak," said Tara.

Darcy sighed. She knew where she could go, though she also felt reluctant about it. She shrugged again. "Maybe I'll go hang out at Miller's place for a little."

"Oh yeah, he's always home right now. You should do that, that's a good idea." Tara spoke with vehement earnestness. At the same time she began to clean the espresso machine, banging the filter against the sink behind her to empty it of coffee grounds. Turning back to Darcy, she said, "Miller's *good* for you, Darcy. He is, really. Not like you with Kozak." She must be in one of her generous moods, thought Darcy, to be willing to mention that. "You and Kozak were like two birds, like too much the same, y'know? But Miller's like a nest, and he lets *you* be the bird."

Darcy felt slightly embarrassed. She set her coffee cup on the counter and glanced away from Tara. Spotting an empty cup and plate on a nearby table, she said, "Here, I'll make your job easier." She reached over and gathered the dishes and then slid them across the counter to Tara.

2.

Darcy's first two weeks back in California had been marked by a somewhat unexpected, brief romance with a childhood friend, Tom Kozak.

Tom, like Tara, was an old acquaintance Darcy had run into upon her return. She'd already heard from Tara that others from their hometown were also living in San Francisco now. As Darcy saw it: if you were from a small town, you fell into one of a few types. People like her and Mary (overambitious, high-principled, even a little prudish) made early escapes to impressive destinations. Then there was the kind who never left, who would claim no experience with dissatisfaction. The girls had a younger brother, Christian, who was like that; he was content and mellow. The next type were the ones who lingered but left eventually.

This type had left that town but liked to make claims of wanting to go back. Darcy had begun to notice this lately in some old friends from back home. Among them there was an almost collective attitude of lament, a shared feeling of self-satisfied displacement. They carried it around with them like a principle, a weakness to be proud of, this claim of being at times unable to bear life in the outside world and needing, every now and again, the reprieve of pine trees and rolling hills and a mountain river. They wore it like a style of haplessness they'd created.

Darcy, you could say, had fallen from the first group (where her sister Mary remained) back to this one: the group that had left but not really left.

She ran into Tom Kozak on her third day back in California, on Geary Boulevard, as she was coming out of a bar where she'd just dropped off a job application. They recognized each other and laughed. It had been at least four years since they'd last crossed paths. Tom had moved to the city only five months earlier. He thought the city was crazy, he said. He was having trouble finding a room to rent and had been living on people's floors and couches and also in his car, which he called "urban camping." Darcy had been doing the same, she told him. Their delight at finding this in common was buoyant, self-effacing. Tom was in a new band that he thought might actually go somewhere, which was why he'd moved to the city. Some nights he crashed in the band's rehearsal space, a windowless basement room under a pool hall in the Tenderloin District.

They decided to go for coffee. Morning soon spilled into afternoon, a good portion of which they spent roaming around an aquarium store, looking at fish. They drifted slowly from tank to tank through dim cool rooms, peering into the backlit blueness of the water and reading the name of each fish. It was as much about the fish as it was about their old friendship, Darcy felt, sensing in their lingering moments (in front of glass and murky water and quietly bubbling air filters) things between them taking a new, ambiguous shape, rising with poignancy this time, like something lost being drawn up out of an old well. The willingness on both their parts to become spontaneously absorbed in what was simple and present—the fish!—brought back to her the memory of their affinity as children: a connection that had always been about wonder and randomness and nature, she believed. She'd never thought romantically of Tom Kozak before, had even despised him on occasion over the years. Yet it took only that afternoon, a walk through the fish store, for Darcy to be convinced that she loved him. That they'd always loved each other and that she had come back, now, to San Francisco to find this.

The aquarium store's radio was playing soft-pop songs from the eighties and nineties. Perfect and awful, thought Darcy. She recognized "Fields of Gold," a song that used to put her in an insensibly dreamy mood when she was a teenager, and she soaked it in now, privately. They were looking into a tank of tiny black eels and paper-thin bright yellow fish. "They're amazing, huh?" said Tom, turning his face toward hers as she stood by his shoulder.

"The fish are good," she said, meeting his eyes. "This is a good place."

Tom nodded. "The music is good, too," he said.

So she was not alone, she knew then. He was feeling it, too. Though she still could not help noticing the few dead fish floating at the bottom of some tanks.

———

What was it about Tom Kozak? His looks were average, with one memorable tattoo (of the fox from the storybook *The Little Prince*) on the inside of his forearm. He was lanky and thin, with a boyish, slender chest, but good-looking, strong hands. Sometimes, actually often, he smelled as if he hadn't bathed in days. This nonchalance about hygiene extended to his belongings, his car, and his overall demeanor: he could make carelessness and forgetfulness seem like virtues.

When he picked up a guitar, however, the image of him came suddenly, inexplicably together. His concave chest made sense; it made room for his instrument. He had never needed more than this. Too, his soft stomach made the right cushion for a guitar to rest against.

Darcy had come to notice this quality in some men who played music. Even the men in the coffee shop displayed it. Apart from their instruments, they were just men with old faces and ordinary, time-drained bodies; they were like any other drunk or sad case you might look at and assume had not had the gumption to follow through on a dream. But once they strapped in or sat down and began to play, then you saw their acumen. You realized that the dimness in their eyes had only been guarding their true devotion. They had allowed life to take its toll on everything else in order that they could remain in touch with the instinct required by their devotion. Music wanted its attendants to stay humble, inconspicuous. So these men had spent years cultivating this quality: making their bodies unfit without their instruments.

Someone might wonder at Tom, what is the worth of someone like him? Why is that boy always leaning over and looking down like that? And Darcy would know the answer. He's just waiting for that thing in the middle to come through, she would say.

Whatever it is, whatever you wanted to call it.

———

She and Tom slept together just a handful of times, all told, in the two weeks following their sidewalk reunion and the visit to the fish store. These encounters happened in transitory locations, in his car outside a bar one night, once on the beach by the Presidio, once in the rehearsal space under the pool hall. Never in any of the apartments either of them was staying at, never in a bed. Urgent, surprisingly intimate exchanges that were also noncommittal—no declarations, no promises or interpretations, even, were made. Pleasure taken quietly and with gentle flippancy, some sarcasm and unspoken concessions. Darcy told herself it was a matter of integrity not to ask or discuss what sex meant between them. She believed she was strengthening herself.

As for the facts of the situation: Tom's cell phone rang often, and sometimes he walked around the corner to answer it; sometimes he ignored it. His bandmates—the few times she met them—were amiable yet remote toward her, and that told her they were probably used to seeing different girls come around. And, in public places, Tom was incapable of overlooking any woman. He made endearing small talk at coffee counters, easily established rapport with bartenders and waitresses; he held open doors and always turned to look at groups of girls going by. Also in public, his affection turned neutral and ambiguous. He laughed equally at both Darcy and Tara's stories, if the three hung out together. Tom, Darcy realized, could not resist trying to win every girl's favor. She hadn't noticed this side of him before, not even the potential for it, when they were younger.

In their childhood, Tom had been just one more of those boys who rode around on his motorbike and was not popular at school. Darcy ignored him in school; meanwhile, back in their neighborhood, he would throw rocks at her or try to scare her pony with his motorbike if he was with other boys. When it was just the two of them, things were different. Tom might be persuaded to play jump rope. Darcy might find satisfaction in stomping on insects. They might both declare themselves opposed to the usual order of things between girls and boys. Some days (summers and holidays were their best times) they might spend hours roaming about in the trees behind their two properties, lost in imaginary worlds.

Back then, there were some moments in Tom's presence when Darcy had felt a feeling she couldn't describe. It was like friendship but better—a sense of allegiance that went deeper than their shared interests and experiences. A moment could become crystallized, and she would know even as it was happening. Laughing at a joke, sitting side by side on the floor in one or the other of their bedrooms. Lingering on the road between their two houses when they were supposed to be saying goodbye, looking at the stars coming out, or crouching to watch a tarantula crawl across the gravel. Something about those moments resonated. If she had to say what, if anything, she missed about her childhood, it would have to be the feeling of moments like those. A pink-gray haze of dust and light, a soft stillness the sky was letting down on just them, only them.

Darcy remembered other things about Tom.

Some days he came to school without a lunch or books or even his book bag. She remembered his blank expression when the teacher questioned him on those days. The lost look on his face caused anxiety to rise inside Darcy as well, and eventually she began to watch for it, in order to brace herself. She would check to see if he was empty-handed or not coming off the bus in the mornings. She wanted to protect him; she had always counted on his fallibility.

Another thing she remembered: a yearbook photo of Tom Kozak, a candid shot, of him sitting on a floor with a guitar across his lap, circa 1990. They were in high school then. He was staring up at the camera with perfectly calculated, winning disdain. The caption under the photo read: "I AM the walrus."

———

So maybe she shouldn't have been as surprised or distressed as she was when he stopped calling. Once he, in effect, disappeared on her. Yet she went through it. A typical, torturous process she thought she'd outgrown by now: the domination of her heart and mind—her basic common sense—by memories that were, frankly, not too out of the ordinary. Not really, not when you got down to it.

"Tom Kozak goes around looking and looking for love, and then when you give it to him he just runs away. That's just how he is. Honestly, he was playing me and you both."

This statement came out of Tara's mouth late one night; cool and tight-lipped. It was the only direct mention of the sort she would ever make, and it came as a shock to Darcy. She'd had no clue of anything beyond friendship happening between Tara and Tom. Now, in Tara's expression, Darcy saw it. Tara had loved him even more desperately, perhaps even more unreasonably, than Darcy had.

———

In an art magazine once, Darcy read an interview with a Japanese woman photographer who was also an ex–fashion model. Many of her photographs were of an Asian woman in various states of undress: self-portraits. The photographer was quoted saying, "People ask why my photographs are so sad. It is because life in the world today makes people tired, I think. I have been very tired sometimes, and sometimes I feel like I need someone to protect me."

So who will protect me? Who are *my* angels? Darcy wondered. And did everyone who needed them have one?

Sometimes she experienced a vision of herself wandering through a garden or the hushed rooms of a big dark house, like a heroine in a Jane Austen or other nineteenth-century novel. There was something about it, this picture, of women all dressed up with nowhere to go, wandering the beautiful, quiet interiors of places that had been built, most probably, by men. Darcy secretly thought she could be good at that job—a quiet tending to things, an energetic maintenance of personhood. Not tangible work; not like the work of those thin, tidy, career women (Mary was one version of them) she'd seen so much of in New York City; and not like the ones who worked in clubs and bars either, with their sultry confidence and strategically placed tattoos. Darcy was tired of trying to live up to such austere and savvy surfaces. She was more like that Japanese woman, she thought, or like a Jane Austen heroine in and at odds with the modern world.

But you had to look at things realistically, too, she knew. In those old novels, the kinds of women who wandered hallways and gardens never had to worry about money. Even if they didn't marry, there was usually something to catch them, a rich relation they could stay with if needed. A benevolent widowed aunt or somebody. And, no matter what, it was a given that someone (another kind of woman entirely, another author's territory) would always be around to help in the kitchen.

Once, in New York City, Darcy had seen a man standing in the middle of the sidewalk on Forty-Second Street. He held an umbrella over his head though it was not raining and he wore headphones, the wires disappearing into his coat. He was pressing his finger to his lips, with an urgent, consternated expression on his face, as people streamed by him. Darcy was impressed. The audacity of this man. To be demanding silence of the rest of the world so he could better hear what was for his ears alone.

3.

She happened on the silver man one night while out driving along the beach. A foggy night. Through the mist she had caught sight of the bust perched under a street lamp at the edge of the sidewalk alongside the Great Highway. Immediately, she pulled a U-turn. It was a bust, like that of a mannequin's, made of some kind of hard foam, and the features of its face were chiseled, angular, plainly masculine. The object as a whole consisted of head and shoulders and a little bit of chest. Hair was etched in deep, gentle curves across his forehead and over his narrow, rounded skull. The bust was surprisingly light (she found when she hopped out of her idling truck to pick it up) and had been spray-painted entirely silver. Darcy delighted in it as a find and was even more delighted by the late hour, the fog, the random eerie circumstances under which the object had appeared to her. She thought it amusing and ominous that the bust of the silver man fit perfectly in the gap between and slightly behind the two seats in her truck cab, like a middle passenger. She thought it was funny.

Her companion, someone she called Miller, was more dubious. "You sure you want to pick that up? You know, they say old furniture that people put out on the street can have spider egg sacs in the cracks and stuff like that."

"This isn't furniture," Darcy replied.

———

This Miller person was, in fact, also named Tom. From the start Darcy and Tara had called him Miller. There had been no question about it—the differentiation had to be made.

Darcy had met Miller in the coffee shop where Tara worked, about a month before she found the bust of the silver man and about a month after everything with Tom Kozak had ended. Darcy had, in fact, done her best to avoid getting to know Miller because she found him annoying. But he had persisted in proving himself to be a decent, knowable person, who just happened to like her considerably. He was also a guitar player, a mediocre one, but willing to play with her. She thought maybe this was the reason he'd come into her life then, that it had to do with music.

Otherwise, Miller was not the kind of person Darcy would've ever expected to date. He was mostly a foolish person, or, at least, Darcy knew, it might be difficult for her to think otherwise of him in the long term. For instance. In the park, instead of sitting or lying in the grass if they were out on a sunny day, he insisted on removing his shirt and doing sets of one-handed push-ups. Anywhere there was a bar he could hang from, he would do pull-ups. He had a dopey, flirtatious appearance; he was short and stocky. He sat open-shirted in front of the coffee shop in the mornings, eyeing women unapologetically; he was a Gulf War veteran. He was not really even that good-looking, thought Darcy. She imagined it might have been sufficient—might have made it easier for her to feel her relationship with him was justifiable—had his dumbness and muscle been complemented by height and good looks and reticence, maybe. A charisma of sensuality, of nonverbalness. Like the dumb guy in certain movies whose simple-mindedness is redeemed by his turning out to be moral and stout-hearted and good in bed, at least. Darcy forced herself to look beyond Miller's surface, to his past. While he was in the service, he had been a bull-rider for the army's rodeo team and a bomb detonator. Because of his size and because he was mechanically inclined, he had been sent to crawl into tight spaces where bombs were located, to decipher and take apart wires. He'd also been through a divorce. This had led him to AA, where he had found God.

"He's had an interesting life, Darcy, he really has," Tara would remark when Darcy retold these details. "You should give him a chance." Darcy took only scant reassurance in Tara's acceptance of Miller. She still remained careful not to bring him around any of her more (as she categorized them) artistic-minded friends. Next to them, Darcy knew, she would only be reminded of how decidedly "regular" Miller was.

She and Miller lived on different planes, was how she saw it. When she brought up figurative or philosophical concepts with him, he said things like "I hear you, but I don't *hear* you hear you, you know?" When she spent the night, he would walk about his apartment wearing only black socks and a condom, utterly unselfconscious. He was indulgent about sex but was, to his credit, not creepy about it. He had a healthily dismissive attitude toward pornography, which gave him an air of sexual liberation that Darcy found almost attractive. He was, however, prone to initiating sex while the TV was on, no matter the programming. The blue light of his forty-inch screen filled his living room with an underlying static energy that could make Darcy feel mired, stir-crazy, and guilty at her own laziness. But it was an inward laziness, like a dulling of something inside herself, the loss of which was leading her toward a precipice of some sort, she knew it, yet had not the will to pull herself back, not yet; an inner laxity was lolling, sloshing, swelling inside her. But there *is* a rightness to this, to *us*, he *is* a good person, she tried to convince herself. He had integrity, even if he was not a purist about anything. Art or his career or love, even. Her nagging feelings persisted.

Once, Darcy tried to discuss it with Miller. "Maybe I'm just scared of getting involved, I don't know. Or maybe I'm not sure. I just don't feel sure. Nothing feels certain to me," she said. "I think I have a problem with reality."

To which Miller's brisk, flippant response was, "You're feeling fear. *F-E-A-R*. Future Events Appearing Real. That's all fear is." He was chewing gum, looking to the side. When he looked directly at her, she could read his exasperation with her. Later, it would be revealed that his statement was an adage from his AA meetings. He had a number of these. Packaged, proven, life-survival tips that were quick and easy to dispense. That was the kind of wisdom Miller possessed.

———

Miller's apartment building was two blocks from the coffee shop. After saying goodbye to Tara, Darcy soon found herself there. She stood below Miller's fifth-floor bay window and yelled "Miller!" up at the khaki-colored curtains that were visible flapping over the sill.

Miller stuck out his head. Curly, sandy-blond hair, big nose, oblong face. He was almost always shirtless, or open-shirted, if he could be. Even from this distance she saw the smiling dim light in his eyes. He left his window open because his doorbell was broken.

"Hey, I'll buzz you in. Two seconds." He ducked back inside. A moment later the door sounded. She pulled it open.

The apartment building had no elevator. She walked up five gradually spiraling flights of stairs. His front door was open when she reached it. Inside he sat in a tall-backed leather chair in front of his computer, which rested on a wide chrome-legged desk. She dropped her backpack on the floor and flopped down on his couch. The informality he encouraged of his guests, mixed with the apparent niceness of his furniture and belongings, was another thing she liked about him—that she gave him credit for.

"Lookit this, look what I found." He was grinning as he rolled his chair aside so she could see the computer screen. A graphic of a baby danced across the screen in a robotically rhythmic style. The baby had an unchanging cherubic expression on its face.

Darcy smiled only slightly. "It looks like there's something wrong with that baby."

"It's dancing," said Miller, happily.

Darcy sank back on his couch. She thought she would not tell him about the naked man; she would live in a self-withholding secrecy, like someone who didn't ever need to unburden herself. She finally couldn't resist, though. "I woke up in the middle of the night last night, and a naked man was trying to climb into my bed."

Miller said, "Oh yeah, that was me. In your dreams."

"It was Don's son. You know, the piano man."

"What?" Miller's overall opinion of the group of middle-aged musicians who hung around the coffee shop was that they were aging perverts. "Just how naked was this dude?"

"He was completely naked, and I woke up just as he was about to get in the bed with me. I turned on the light, then he pretended to be all surprised. He said he thought I was the lady upstairs and that he'd slept with her before."

"What, you mean Teresa?" Miller glanced away from Darcy with what struck her as false coolness. He was trying to appear unfazed, she realized.

"It was kind of freaky, but I didn't freak out about it," said Darcy, proudly. "I mean, that's the really weird part to me, anyway. Like, the normal reaction would've been to scream or something, don't you think? But I didn't. I kind of weirdly felt like I could trust him. I knew he wasn't going to hurt me."

Miller swiveled in his seat to face her, his mouth twisted in an expression of thought. He looked dumb and vulnerable, Darcy thought. His bare feet toed the hardwood floors. The hair on his legs was straight and flaxen.

"But I'm pretty sure he is sort of fucked up," Darcy went on. "I mean, I know Don doesn't want him around. Tara says he's like a heroin addict and steals from his dad and stuff like that. He was walking around the apartment naked the whole time I was there. I don't know if he came in naked or took his clothes off once he climbed through the window or what. I mean, I'm guessing he climbed through the window to get in. He had clothes on in the morning when I left, thank god."

A focus finally came into Miller's face. His brow tightened. He began to shake his head. "No, no, no. It's not right. This guy has no right. You don't just go around naked in front of someone you don't know somewhere you don't belong. No, no, this is making me start to feel really pissed off. Who does this guy think he is? Did you tell him to get out?"

"No," replied Darcy honestly.

"Maybe you should call the police. Is he still there?"

"I don't know." Darcy sat up slowly, curling her feet under her body. She lay her chin on her hands on the back of the couch. She looked at Miller, waiting, she didn't know for what.

"Teresa's a nice girl. I've met her before," said Miller, continuing to shake his head, "she wouldn't sleep with a drug addict, I don't think. Darcy," his expression now turning solicitous with concern, "I think that man was lying to you."

Darcy held back a strange, untimely urge to smile. Instead, she made her face stay still, and she glared down at Miller's sunlit floor. The wood, in this light, was the warm, shining color of honey. Darcy took a deep breath. "God, I'm tired," she sighed, as the air seeped out of her.

———

It was true that sometimes she came over to Miller's just to sleep. He had a high, firm bed with a white down comforter and many pillows. Too many pillows. The bed had wooden bedposts, like a bed in a children's movie from an unspecified past era—the bedposts looked like elongated chess pieces. Bishops. Darcy actually hated having sex on his bed, as it made her feel like she was being smothered. She enjoyed sleeping on the bed, though, and they tended to have sex in front of the TV more often than anywhere else in the apartment. When she stayed over, at some point they would move from the couch to the bed. Miller usually woke in the mornings before she did. She would hear him knocking about in the kitchen, or music playing, as she lay, feeling adrift, among his fat, soft pillows.

On many nights it was well past 2 a.m. when she stopped under his window, having walked the seven blocks from the bar where she worked to his building, hearing the echo of her own footsteps against the sidewalk, the night jarring and lucid to her in her state of postdrunkenness. Even this late, Miller's window was always open. The blue reflection of the TV screen shone upon the glass. He would stick out his sleepy face, nod down at her, then buzz her in.

Sometimes she woke to the sound of the front door banging open and then shut—the sound of Miller returning with a tray of coffee and juice and a bag of breakfast bialys. By this time, he knew how she wanted her coffee. Cream and honey. Almost beige in color. She could get used to this, she thought. She had lost all hope of having any holding power over boys, restless, volatile, angst-ridden creatures that they were. She had come to the conclusion that maybe she was the type of woman who needed a buffer against the world—like that Japanese photographer-model who needed someone to protect her. Maybe some women were just like that and maybe it was natural, if you were, to want a man to take care of certain things. Miller was a man, not a boy. He was thirty-two. He owned things, held business meetings, had tattoos he no longer believed in with conviction.

He once said to her, "You know that blond chick who comes into the coffee shop, Annabelle? Well, she's a songwriter, too. This drummer guy offered for her to live in his apartment rent-free, so she could just focus on writing songs. That's what you need, you know." He was not making a direct suggestion but, without question, always picked up the tab when they went somewhere together. And occasionally he handed her a fifty-dollar bill when he asked her to go get him a Coke from the corner store, then he would neglect to collect his change. He would act indifferent and surprised when she handed money back to him. "Oh yeah," he would say.

———

But Darcy was, in truth, trying *not* to hang out with Miller as much lately. There had been a number of tearful, angered conversations on the subject; there had been wavering on both their parts. Sometimes she wondered if she was just supposed to give in (he seemed to want her to), that this was just the way life went for some people. They had to be coaxed into staying in relationships because they were dreamers— and dreamers often didn't recognize when the person for them was standing right in front of them; dreamers were so much in the habit of looking off in the distance.

Also, sometimes she felt she just had no one else to turn to.

So she stood by, with wary resignation, as Miller checked the windows of her apartment and found that none of them locked. He would cut up a couple broom handles, he said, to brace the windows with. She drove him to the hardware store, where he also insisted on buying her a new deadbolt lock, which he would install for her. He bought a handsaw to cut the broom handles, saying he needed one anyway. He also bought a new doorbell that he meant to install at his own apartment.

They went back to Darcy's place, and she watched as Miller screwed the new lock in place on the front door. She watched as he laid the cut broom handle pieces diagonally in the window frames. She could've done these things herself, she decided, but he had gotten to them first. The apartment, in the pale midafternoon light, did not look like a place that had been broken into by a naked man, Darcy thought. Patches of sunlight played over the wood body of her guitar, and she recalled what Tracey had said, in the dark, in the middle of the night, from that chair in the corner of the kitchen where Kenji usually slept. *No, I bet you're good. Your guitar has good energy.* Secretly, she knew, this was the real reason she had not done anything to make sure he didn't come back.

Kenji was lying on the bed, a tiger-striped football of fur, gazing up at her through the narrowed yellow slits of his eyes.

Can you hear me?

Are you trying to tell me it's going to be okay?

You know it. It's going to be okay.

———

Darcy went to work that night. Two heavy-metal bands were on the bill. The club was mostly empty when the first band got onstage; most of the customers were in the downstairs portion of the bar. Evening sunlight was still coming in through the second-floor windows, shooting low dusty rays of light across tables and catching on the candleholders Darcy was setting new candles inside of. She felt fortified performing this task. She felt humble and dutiful.

When the singer began to sing, Darcy felt it before she really heard it.

The singer wailed and flung her hair and body about. She was very attractive, no doubt, but it was more than her looks that made people in the bar stop and stare, transfixed. She was svelte and leggy, clad in fishnet stockings, spike-heeled boots, a short leather skirt. When Darcy first saw her come in with the band, she had assumed the singer was just another pretty girl who relied on sex appeal for her stage presence. But when this woman opened her mouth, the sound that came out held no vanity. No prettiness could stand in its way. Her voice was primal and elastic and full of what sounded like an otherworldly pain. She clung to her microphone as if it were something she had expelled. A sound that raged into being with the intention of obliterating every molecule in the air that was not as intense and raw as itself. That was how this music worked.

The effect was somehow compounded by the fact that the singer was a girl, and a pretty one. It occurred to Darcy that sometimes softness existed just waiting to be rent, and that there was satisfaction—and fascination—for some in witnessing it.

People were coming up from the bar downstairs now, just to see. All of them men, Darcy could not help noticing. They poked their heads around the wall to look in at the stage. They were exchanging comments as they passed one another on the stairs—"You gotta see this"—impressed, stunned, amused.

After their set, the band occupied a booth at the back of the club. Night hung outside the windows. Darcy was busy now, hauling trays, counting money, smiling and glancing her way through the crowd. She could forget the naked man as she focused simply on being of service. She brought drinks to the band's table at one point. The men in the band dominated the conversation, while the woman sat looking demure again. The drummer was her boyfriend. Darcy knew this just by the way they sat close together, even though they were not touching. There was respectfulness between them, she thought. He could've been her brother; he was just as skinny, not much taller, with spiky hair and expressive, deerlike features. His demeanor was wary and cool: the kind of boy who had probably developed cleverness and instinct—in lieu of physical assertiveness—to keep himself out of harm's way. He sat next to the woman, looking calm but watchful.

"That could be you, Darcy. Oh, why isn't that you?" the bartender, a woman named Lisa, had joked with Darcy earlier. They stood at the bar watching the band. Lisa portrayed womanly strength in an Amazon-like fashion, in Darcy's opinion. She was tall, athletic, and vibrant. She was training to become a firefighter; she was the kind of woman who was unabashed about her strength and competence. Darcy looked from the singer to Lisa, aware that she was like neither of them. She would never be like Lisa either, she thought. No darkness ever came through Lisa. Darcy looked again toward the stage.

———

In order to avoid returning to her apartment and also to avoid seeking refuge with Miller, Darcy found herself going home that night with Jacob, the sound man—or sound boy, really, as she thought of him, since he was only nineteen.

Jacob lived in a corner of a living room in a flat in the Lower Haight. With seven other boys, all members of a band called Little Minds. Jacob's belongings were stashed in three boxes behind the foldout couch where he slept, and he kept his blankets folded neatly in an old wooden crate. Darcy was surprised by the order with which Jacob kept his space and his things. It betrayed a truth about him that his youth was disguising, she thought, when she saw this care.

Jacob had come up to Darcy as she stood at the bar counting her money at the end of her shift. By way of greeting, he laid his hand lightly on her back. His touch was familiar in an unassuming way. "Hey, I heard you got chased out of your apartment," he said.

She had already told the story to Lisa and the other wait-resses working that night. It had been received in much the same way Tara had received it, with hilarity and incredulity. They couldn't understand why Darcy hadn't called the police and then went on to spend the rest of the shift teasing her about being too nice. At one point Lisa even snuck up behind Darcy and grabbed her behind. When Darcy turned, rather calmly, Lisa taunted her, "I grabbed your butt, I grabbed your butt. You should've turned around and smacked me, sweetie. Not been all, 'Ooh, who is it?'" She batted her eyelids exag-geratedly at Darcy, and laughed. "We'll learn you yet, lady."

Darcy had lied. "But I knew it was you, Lisa."

Her story had gotten out to some of the bar customers as well. A regular waiting for his drink overheard the girls jok-ing and had to put in his two cents, "If you ask me, I think the scarier part is his playing 'I Will Survive' on your guitar."

Lisa offered for Darcy to crash at her place, and another of the waitresses offered to walk Darcy into her apartment ("it'll be two against one, he won't stand a chance"), but for some reason, at the end of the night, only Jacob's offer felt real to Darcy—felt reliable. He was leaning beside her with his elbows on the bar, and he spoke in a voice low and gentle in its concern.

"If you need somewhere else to go or if you don't want to be alone tonight, you can come hang out at my place for a bit."

The further implication in this did not bother Darcy. It was a given, she figured.

Darcy had left the bar with Jacob one time before, though at the invitation of another waitress, Jessica. Jessica had taken them both back to her room in a large Victorian house, also in the Lower Haight. Painted black walls, red-and-black shrouded canopy bed, candles, black lace and beads strung like curtains around the room. Two similarly slow-eyed, smiling women exchanged surreptitious glances with Jessica when she entered the house, Jacob and Darcy following. Previous to this, there hadn't been any indication of interest from either Jacob or Jessica, Darcy had thought, but that night, undressing her, Jessica sat back and looked at Darcy and said, "I am so lucky," as if it was a moment she'd been anticipating. Darcy felt the adoration to be slightly misled. Still, she let herself be flattered. Jessica talked about Darcy's energy, and Jacob agreed. He had noticed it, too.

"You have a really powerful, pure presence," Jessica said. "Are you aware of that? Do you feel it?"

"Sometimes I do, I guess," replied Darcy. She felt the situation—how she received this assessment and what was required in order to maintain it—was somewhat dependent on the appearance of her naïveté.

Jessica looked at her, seriously and sweetly. "Well, you *should* be aware of it, so we're telling you now."

Darcy was, in truth, drawn more to Jacob that night than to Jessica. He was not handsome; he was ill-kempt, unsmiling, with bad teeth and cool eyes. He wore his black hair in a ponytail. The way he wore his clothes, which were utilitarian and slightly grubby, seemed emblematic: he was a person, his manner said, pledged to the seedier side of life. But when he touched her, Darcy felt warmth and capability.

Jessica's body was deceptive—soft, compelling, and demanding all at once. It surprised Darcy to see how another woman acted sexually. Jessica was unselfconscious in her expressions of pleasure; she was provocative and assertive, with an underlying slyness. She seemed to take pride in being able to invoke pleasure as well, especially in Darcy, who felt her own manner to be more submissive and foolishly sincere. The difference between Jessica and herself seemed evident: a woman who was comfortable with and forthright about the demands of her own lust had unlocked a part of herself that was still, for Darcy, a complication. Darcy waited, serious and timid, for things to be initiated; Jessica was more playful and animated. Darcy also could not deny the comfort she took in a feeling of surrender to the male anatomy. She did not mind allowing men this, was the truth. Still, she left them both in Jessica's bed before dawn.

The three of them wouldn't get together like this again, but an odd camaraderie had been created. Things like: once, Darcy and Jessica exchanged tiny, knowing smiles in the bathroom mirror at work, while listening in on a group of college girls talking loudly in front of the stalls. One girl was declaring, "Those boys out there, they talk all this shit about wanting it, but I'll bet you anything they wouldn't know what to do if they ever *had* two women."

Another time, Darcy even allowed herself to mention Tom Kozak to Jessica. They were standing at the back of the club, and Darcy had leaned her head against Jessica's shoulder for a moment. "There's this guy I'm really messed up over, and he hasn't called me, and I'm starting to feel like he's not going to," said Darcy, guiltily aware that she was giving the story up in the most rote terms possible.

Jessica stroked Darcy's hair with her hand. "Love sucks," she said, adamantly.

So it was clear: whatever had occurred between the two of them did not run the danger of entering into *that* territory.

Now Darcy watched Jacob fold down the couch. She was swaying but still in control of herself, or so she felt. The apartment was quiet, a marked contrast from the liveliness and ease of the bar—quieter than she had expected. His roommates were out, he had said. Darcy found herself thinking it incongruous that the people she knew from the bar could also exist in such mundane spaces. But why wouldn't they? Because he was a boy, because he was the sound man, and due to everything she associated with boys and music, Darcy had somehow expected differently of Jacob.

"Where'd you learn sound stuff? Did you take classes or something?" she asked, probing slightly, for what she wasn't quite sure. It had to do with how young he was, and how neatly his blankets had been folded and tucked in their crate; it had to do with how ugly and brooding he was, yet how confident and warm she remembered his hands to be from that night with Jessica. She would admire him, she realized, if he said he hadn't taken classes, but she would feel relief, in a way, and more hope of a real friendship, if he said he had.

"I just picked it up from other guys," he said. "What I really want is to get work on a tour."

That will still do, she thought, *it will still do*.

She emptied the change from her pockets onto the TV set facing the couch. There was a guitar pick mixed in with her change, and she left that on the TV set, too, hoping Jacob might see it and ask if she played. When she turned around again, he was tossing a blanket across the folded-out couch bed.

Making love in a situation like this, she knew how to do. It was easy.

It was five in the morning by the hands of her watch (which she still wore though she wore nothing else) when she awoke to the dim, close light of the strange room, with corroded pipes visible traveling the length of the ceiling above her. She sensed immediately that he was awake, too, coiled against her back and the back of her legs. The sweetness in this was almost unbearable. An acute warmth that she momentarily wished could be lasting but knew it could not, not with him. She felt his breath against her shoulder. He had said something, she realized: "I think you're beautiful." The words were detached from his voice, from his entire persona. They were uttered, it seemed, inside her head, already. She closed her eyes to hear it better.

But when she got out of his bed, she did so with an attitude of nonchalance that she knew he would have to match: he was not going to bother with seeing her to the door. She pulled on her clothes and stumbled out to the hallway. Her boots echoed on the hardwood floors. The light coming through the transom window blurred its shape, made it a wavering, pale-yellow rectangle. She could sense it all waiting for her—the lulled, naked city streets outside, the strike of morning air, the crisp early-light hues of houses and storefronts and graffiti, even the trash on the streets. If she drove down to the ocean (which was what she wanted to do, and she wanted to do it alone) she would hear the gulls and see their black comma shapes sweeping the colored bands of the sky; she would see swaths of whitening pink, orange, royal blue, and purple lying atop the horizon; she would hear the soft-loud, soft-loud sweeping-and-crashing rhythm of the waves. She would see morning walkers on the beach with dogs, and surfers, slickly coated like seals, and would feel herself part of a secret society whose members did not acknowledge each other. A vivifying, strong society that occurred only in the early morning hours. She wanted to buy a cup of coffee and drink it sitting in the cab of her truck in front of the ocean, thinking about these things and feeling the possibility—a sad, rich burden—of making something out of them.

4.

He was in the kitchen when Darcy got back to the apartment. He was standing by the stove.

"I just now came in, I swear to God. I knocked and knocked, then I noticed it was open. I just wanted to make some eggs, that's all," he said in an apologetic rush.

Darcy set her backpack down just inside the kitchen doorway. She stood tensely. She was ready to run if she had to, she told herself. "I wish you wouldn't come in here when I'm not here," she said.

Tracey was fully clothed now, making the previous night's situation seem less formidable, more comic. He wore a pair of dirty, bleached jeans and a black muscle tee with the logo of some classic rock band on it. He was barefoot.

Today, she saw the real haggardness in his face. His skin was creased and pitted across his narrow cheeks and high forehead. He looked sallow. His big eyes looked troubled and hapless, like Eli's, she thought—the piano player whose girlfriend had died a year ago of cancer. Tracey had about him the same quality, as did his father and the other coffee shop musicians: his body appeared somehow incomplete.

"Are you hungry? Would you like an egg? And look, I have bagels, too."

Unfortunately, Darcy was hungry. It was all of a sudden as if hunger had been shot into her body with an arrow. How strange, she thought. She also knew that she had no food of her own in the apartment. One bagel would not hurt, would not mean she owed him anything, she told herself. She folded her arms and leaned her shoulder on the doorframe.

"Maybe I could eat something," she said.

Tracey grinned, catching her eye briefly. "I love to cook. I cooked all the time for my recent girlfriend." He was trying to appear a certain way—nurturing, more ordinary than he was—and she could allow him this, she thought. When he cracked a smile, she saw that his teeth were quite crooked and brown in spots. "She's thin, like you, and she eats a lot. But she stays thin. I like girls like that, you know? Girls who actually have an appetite."

"Recent?" Darcy was mildly curious, but weighing how much further conversation she should provoke. "Does that mean she's not your girlfriend anymore?"

"Well, no. I guess she's not." His reply was—almost—sheepish. "No, she doesn't want to be anymore, she told me so. I'm still a bit confused about it, I have to say. I thought

it was all great, you know? We were having a great time together, cooking and laughing and lots of love, plenty of love
in there. Then she went away for just one weekend, to Tahoe,
and she met someone there. She said when she met this person
it felt like, how did she put this? It felt like she'd *come home*,
she said. Now she's off on a honeymoon with him. They got
married, Jesus Christ. I've seen her once since then. She came
back to the hotel to get some of her stuff, the hotel where we
were living together, our *home* together. I just wanted to see
her and say hello, maybe talk about it in person a little. And
she went crazy, actually. She went and got a restraining order
out on me. I swear to God I never laid a hand on her. But
women have a lot of power in these kinds of situations. No
offense, but they do, trust me. I just wanted to talk, for god
sakes, and now there's a restraining order with *my* name on it.
I feel really hurt by that, you know, just really—" he shook his
head, once, with his eyelids pressed closed, even paused to put
his hand on his heart, "—*hurt*." This last word was like a big
plastic teardrop, like a gelatin bubble: it dropped through the
air and struck the floor, made a firm splash but did not break.

Darcy was edging toward the kitchen table, trying to
appear unfazed by his story yet not totally disinterested. Admittedly, she was thinking more about the bagels. Just one. If
he got angry with her, he would not share his food; it would
get awkward and complicated. Then she noticed a pair of
tennis shoes lying on the kitchen table. They were ugly and
cheap-looking, wrapped in a clear plastic bag, next to the
bag of bagels. A dim square of sunlight fell across the bagged
shoes.

Tracey said, "Oh yeah, I bought you a pair of shoes."

The shoes seemed to be suffocating beneath the plastic, the openings like mouths in midgasp. There were no tags on them. Just by looking, Darcy could tell the shoes were too large for her.

"Thanks, but those won't fit me," she said.

Tracey turned from the stove and, taking one long step across the kitchen floor, reached the table. Darcy wanted to step back but only leaned. He held the shoes up and looked at them. "Oh no! Are you sure, really? I guess I thought you were bigger. It was so dark and all when I first met you." He looked her up and down. "You are kind of a tiny thing, aren't you? I mean, I knew you were thin. Didn't realize just how tiny, though. I'm really sorry about that. I just, I get overeager sometimes. I love giving gifts, you see. I gave that to my dad." He pointed at a poster on the wall that said "Venice, Italy" under a typical scenario of a quaint-looking European city street. "He's had that up for a long time now."

Darcy felt them drifting away from some more central point and was vaguely aware that, of course, somehow he was doing this on purpose. The lucidity and focus she had felt, leaving Jacob's and sitting by the beach in her truck before coming back here, had by now dimmed. She knew what the words were that should lay in the air between her and this man—*Get out*—but could not seem to bring the conversation round to a place where her saying them would feel right. She was conscious of herself in last night's clothes and that she needed to take a shower. She would not be able to do this unless he went back out to the garage, it occurred to her. Maybe, she thought, if she ate some of his food, then he might leave her alone for a little while.

Darcy sat down and reached for the bagels. "So I can have one of these?"

"Oh, definitely, please! Please do." He lit up, grinning over his shoulder at her as he moved back to the stove. "Would you like some eggs, too, Darcy?"

"No thanks, really," said Darcy, and she broke the bagel in half, meaning to eat it simply as it was. The bagel was dry and doughy.

"So, how long have you been playing guitar, Darcy?" His back was to her now.

"A year or so."

"And what made you pick it up?"

Darcy thought about the box of tapes she'd found and brought home that day in New York. A small event now laced with tenuous significance. "I got into old country music when I was living in New York City, I guess that's when I first started wanting to play music. I like those female country singers' voices," said Darcy. "And I like old gospel harmonies. I think they sound kind of eerie. That kind of singing just appeals to me, I guess."

Tracey turned, holding the spatula aloft. "That's good stuff; you like good stuff. Good for you," he said, gruffly, sincerely, his earnestness making her both uncomfortable and curious. What did he mean by that? What did he know that she didn't, about this music? With a brightening look on his face, he went on, "Hey, I like the old hymns, too. I grew up singing in church, actually." He cleared his throat and began to hum, and Darcy watched him. Whatever she was looking to find was not there, though, she decided. "You know that one?"

"I don't know," said Darcy.

"Dad didn't so much go for the church music. He was more like the city man, y'know? It was my mother wanted me to go to church. I guess you could say that's one of the reasons they ended up divorced. He started playing blues and jazz in clubs, staying out late and such. But I don't go in for church so much myself anymore either, so I guess I can't blame him." He spoke pleasantly, amiably. "But, what do *you* want from music, Darcy? Why do you do it?"

Darcy wondered why he was asking this. No one had ever asked her this question before. She shrugged. "I don't want anything, really. I just like singing. I like singing 'cause it feels good to sing." This was the safe answer, she knew, and she did believe in it.

Tracey smiled. "I knew it. I knew you'd say that. That's good, real good. You're like me. You're on the path for the sake of the path. You should stay like that. Really, you should. You're young, and it's easy to be like this now, but it can get harder. But if you're starting out from here, I think that's a good sign." He nodded, as if affirming the idea with himself. "Everything I do, I do just to spread love. People don't always see that about me, but it's true. I'm not like my dad, you see. Dad's playing doesn't have the love in it. Not anymore it doesn't."

Just then, the phone rang, and Darcy promptly got up to answer it. The phone was in the bedroom. She recognized Don's voice immediately, and the combined relief and shame she felt at that surprised her.

"Darcy, is that you?" His old man's voice sounded strange saying her name.

"Yes, is this Don?"

"Is my son there?"

"Yeah, he's here right now. He's in the kitchen. Um," she said, then faltered. She wasn't sure where to go from there, as she didn't want to sound accusing in earshot of Tracey. "He's making eggs," she said.

"Let me talk to him," said Don.

Darcy walked back into the kitchen. "It's your dad," she told Tracey. Handing the phone over to him felt both natural and totally absurd.

"Thanks, Darcy," he said.

He did not change much when he took the receiver, Darcy noticed, which told her that Don would not really be able to help her in this situation: he had no real clue about or control over his son, after all. All Don could do was play the piano. Darcy realized that was how Tracey probably saw his father: all his efforts in life had always been intangible and added up to nothing that made an impact. All Don did was put fleeting, pleasant sounds into the air in places—dark rooms—that were not his home. These kinds of people—they had no real homes, no solidity to their histories. They were sad and broken but honest, full of lost, unrecognized feeling; they were drunk on the sorrows of their own falli-bility, masters only of a subtle, obsolete language. Barroom atmospherics. She pictured Don in a jazz club in Seattle, in his tuxedo, hunched dutifully over the piano keys, with his eyes that were lost in the deep wrinkles of his face, his head of grizzled, white hair. She pictured the club to be on a street where, in the distance, you could see pine-topped mountains, and you could actually feel the elevation was higher. She imagined the atmosphere inside the club would seem more faraway and clean than jazz clubs in San Francisco—she thought you could call this a more "northern" feel. That was how it occurred to her. She didn't know why. But she understood that whatever Don had going on up there, he could not stop or put aside just because of whatever complications had developed down here. A line from a gospel song appeared in her mind; she realized it was a song Tracey's humming had started to remind her of: *No I don't want to get adjusted to this world below.* There was an above and below to everything. And, she realized, Tracey understood that. He was a fence-walker, the kind of person who resided regularly in states of ambiguity: the fact that people like his father did not have the ability to set people like Tracey straight or to put them out in the cold, in fact helped to sustain him.

"No, Dad, no, I'm not going to stay, I promise. I'm going to get right out, right after breakfast. I just needed a reprieve—I just, I swear, I had nowhere else to go." *Reprieve*, thought Darcy, his use of that word striking her. She felt it betrayed something about him. She was reminded of a television interview she had seen once of some famous criminal in prison, where he had used the word *furtive* at one moment, and how Darcy's stepfather had responded to that: *Listen to how he talks. You can tell that's not an ordinary man. He's cunning.* Tracey was still speaking into the phone, "I just needed a day to get stuff in order, Dad, one day. I didn't know you had someone staying here, I swear I didn't. I thought it'd be okay. She's been really generous. I'm not getting in her way, I promise you." After another minute of this, he handed the phone back to Darcy.

Don's voice had a little more force to it now. He said, "If he's not out by today you just call the police, okay? Okay, Darcy? You can even tell him I told you to do it. Just call 911 and tell them there's an intruder." There was a sigh. "Listen.

I'm really sorry about this. My son and I, we just have this history." Another sigh. "This is really between me and him. Oh, geez. You're a nice girl. I truly am sorry."

———

Finally, Tracey went back out to the garage, and she decided to get in the shower. She waited until she had not heard anything more from him for a good five or ten minutes. Still, she made certain she had locked the bathroom door behind her.

So, when he walked in, the first thought to occur in her mind was, *That lock doesn't work.* All this time she had been thinking it did, but it didn't. All this time she had been harboring the illusion that a lock, just because it turned, worked—it did not occur to her (not until sometime later) that he could've picked the lock. She let out a shriek.

"Oh, I'm sorry, I'm sorry. I didn't know you were in there," came his voice through the fog and the sound of running water. Another lie she was willing herself to believe was not a lie—for he closed the door again, quickly.

After she got out of the shower and had dressed, she found him in the backyard watering Don's plants with a hose she hadn't seen back there before.

"You can't stay here," she said, "Your dad said."

Tracey was smoking; his cigarette hung precariously out of the corner of his mouth, between his sensuous, cracked lips. He was ugly, one of the ugliest, most life-weathered people she had ever seen up close. He was a person with layers and layers of personhood to him, and she could not fathom the truth about him, she realized. She was too innocent.

"I don't want to, but your dad said for me to call the police if you don't leave."

He glanced her way. She saw the sinewy veins in his tanned, wiry forearms. His large hands holding the hose. There was a deceptive guilelessness to his face—it contained no malice. Even though it seemed she should be afraid of him, when he looked at her she felt something closer to sympathy. She felt him to be sincerely troubled.

"My dad didn't ask you to water this tree at all, did he?" he said, looking suddenly consternated. "It figures. It's my tree. I had to leave it here 'cause the last time I moved, I moved into that hotel, and this is an outdoor plant, this one, as you can see. You know what I said the other night about us all being just like flowers? This is my tree; it's just another symbol of me. Everything inside us has its representative in the external world, y'know? And see how this tree's got these branches turning brown? Well, we're just having a little trouble getting by right now, we just need some healing time, y'know? Some sunlight, some water." He blew a thick stream of smoke out over his shoulder, glancing away from Darcy.

Darcy looked at the tree. She could not deny that what he was saying was fascinating to her; by this time she was beginning to understand he knew how to do this. Somehow he just did. It looked like a pine tree of a sort, but it was small; it fit in a five-gallon pot. It had a straggly trunk and did in fact resemble its owner (now that the theory had been put forth) in its shabbiness, its haggardness, the unextravagance of its foliage. The bark had a spiky, nubby texture. The branches were thin and ungraceful; the needles were dry-looking, dull green, exactly like long needles. Studying it, and becoming aware that it was the bottom branches of the tree that had turned brown, Darcy felt a sudden flash of fear—it was just like that, a flash—as it came clear in her mind with which section of his body that section of the tree might actually correlate.

He was still talking. She heard, "My dad. I'm more talented than him, y'know? I am. He even used to say so himself. I have the raw talent, and more soul than most musicians would even know what to do with. So what I'm not a conformist. So what I can't wear the tux and play all the notes on the page just 'cause they're on the page. So what I choose passion over perfection sometimes. Truthfully, y'know, I'm a gentle creature. I want everyone to be happy, everyone to just have a good time. In fact, I'll lose at things, I'll mess up on purpose, just to make sure other people are having a good time. Look at me. Look at the way I live. Doesn't that say enough? I have nothing, and I don't mind. I'm much more comfortable seeing others get the pie, and the gig, and the girl, so to speak. I play just to play, I don't play to prove anything. I don't play to win. I'm just not comfortable with winning, you see?"

Darcy looked at him when he said this. She looked to make sure someone else was not speaking out of him at that moment. Things like that were possible, she believed.

———

What it had reminded her of was a moment from one of those meandering evenings with Tom Kozak, when they had found themselves at the pool hall above Tom's band's rehearsal space.

The pool hall was on the second floor of a daunting, crummy building in the Tenderloin District, its windows looking out onto Market Street. The glowing neon sign of an old hotel flashed the word REGAL just outside the window by their pool table—this may even have been *his* hotel, she thought now. The marquee of a topless dance theater listed names like Tisha and Dmitri as attractions across the street. Neither Tom nor Darcy was especially good at shooting pool, but they had the ambition to be, and they joked about it.

"You need to put a right English on that shot," she told him.

"A right what?"

They both cracked up, laughing. The cocktail waitress brought them another round of drinks. Tom made gratuitous conversation with her about the band whose T-shirt she was wearing, and Darcy enjoyed observing this.

"That song, man, that one just tears my heart *out*. It's got policy, tragedy, irony," said Tom, fishing a twenty-dollar bill out of his wallet and dropping it on the waitress's tray.

"Thanks, you guys," said the waitress.

Darcy smiled at her brightly, warmly, as she tended to do to other females, especially when the boy she was with was being friendly to them. She knew what her smile was meant to say, even as she was denying to herself the innate hypocrisy in it. *I have no problem with you. I'm a woman too.*

Then she remembered something she'd once heard somebody say about pool. "Pool is all about style," said Darcy, "have you noticed that? It's all about looking good. It's all about faking it and intimidating your opponent. I could be a good faker, I think, but something gets in the way. I'm not sure what."

"I could be a good faker, but I have a psychological block against winning," said Tom. "I'm just not comfortable with winning, you know what I mean? I'm more concerned with seeing other people have a good time. I'll lose on purpose sometimes, just so I don't have to feel guilty about winning."

Darcy looked at him then with love and surprise. "I know what you mean!" she exclaimed.

The thirteen ball was proving repetitively hard to shoot into any pocket; they had been chasing that ball around the table for a number of turns.

"Thirteen," announced Darcy, "it's a number of conflict. But it's also a number of wholeness, though most people aren't aware of that. But Jesus was the thirteenth disciple, you know? He was the—" she tripped over this word, "—amalgamation of all the twelve other elements, the other disciples." She liked how when she said this, Tom laughed.

When it was his turn again, though, something had shifted. "But eventually at some point you have to stop losing, you know what I mean? I mean, someone has to win. Sometimes it just comes to a point when you have to win," he said ironically, as he made the last three shots of the game, all in a row.

Darcy had thought, *Not fair*, but she didn't say so out loud.

Now, this phrase occurred to her: *In the true vicinity of one another*. What was true vicinity? She saw herself that evening with Tom, how they'd made a bed out of their sweaters and jackets on the threadbare carpet of the rehearsal space and how, laughing, they'd kicked over the drummer's high hat and it had clanged loudly as it fell. Herself on the floor amid all the equipment she would never actually see put into action, though she'd hoped somehow to get to be a part of it. How foolish, she thought, as this picture gave way to another.

She saw the three of them—her, Tom, and Tracey—in a room stripped bare of furniture, stripped bare even of its walls. It was a room without solid features, in a building of only energetic substance. Where, what was this place? It was the ghost of a building, and hence their bodies must be ghosts, too, she thought. It was them stripped of their bodies, in fact, and standing naked and pure against the night sky beside one another. There was no way of hiding from one another, and in that there was no need for communication, really, either. So what was all this talk and push and pull they were engaging in, all this pretend fear, pretend lust, and angst and ambition? It was just foss, she realized, the word *foss* occurring to her in much the same kind of atmosphere as the word *reprieve* had appeared when Tracey had used it on the phone with his father. There was no question (when she felt rather than thought it, and it didn't even seem uncanny anymore) that they would all be culling material from the same spaces. Like loom weavers gathering flax.

———

She ended up at Miller's apartment later that afternoon because once again she didn't know where else to go. She had wanted to spend the afternoon playing her guitar and singing in Don's backyard, but Tracey was still in the garage. He was packing up his stuff, he had said, and she felt self-conscious about his hearing her sing. She was also afraid he might try to join in. So, she had decided to leave.

When she went out, she passed through the garage as unobtrusively as she could. She could see part of his cot, and his big feet sticking off the end of it, toes pointed toward the ceiling. He was just lying there. She didn't know what he was doing, but he hardly seemed to be packing, she thought.

Miller was in the middle of installing his new buzzer. "Oh, good," he said when she showed up, "I need someone to help me. You can either ring the buzzer or tell me if it's ringing."

"What?" said Darcy.

Miller stood in the middle of his kitchen, holding a screwdriver in one hand and his cell phone in the other. With his screwdriver hand, he began awkwardly punching the numbers of his cell phone. Suddenly the phone in his apartment was ringing. It was ringing right in front of Darcy, in fact, who had just come in and sat down at his kitchen table. His phone was one of those space-age cordless deals, where the receiver stood upright in its cradle, as if it were an object being exalted. "Pick it up, pick it up now!" said Miller, too urgently for Darcy to comprehend. There was no stability in this place either, she thought.

She picked up the receiver and heard Miller's voice in weird amplification. He stood in front of her, talking in his natural voice; at the same time she heard the same words coming through in his telephone voice.

"I'm going down the stairs now," he said, "and when I get down there I'm going to try to ring the doorbell and you're going to tell me whether you hear it ringing up here or not, okay?"

"Okay," said Darcy. She sat back, keeping the phone to her ear, and watched Miller bound down the hall, out the door. He left the apartment door open. She looked out the window at the building across the street. A cat sat in one window, and the interior of the room behind it seemed dark and lonely. Darcy felt inexplicably depressed.

"Is it ringing? Is it ringing now?" she heard through the receiver.

The buzzer was not ringing. She told Miller that. He came back up the stairs, cussing and fuming. Darcy was glad when seven o'clock came round, and she could say she had to go to work.

———

Arriving at the bar that evening, Darcy passed a couple running out, in tears, as she started up the stairs. The man had his arm around the woman's shoulders, and the woman had her hands pressed to her face in clear anguish. The man also—it alarmed Darcy to see—was sobbing.

"It's the Breakthrough People," the bouncer at the head of the stairs informed Darcy, when he saw her confused look.

Jessica was the other waitress working. She looked rattled and tense. "Be warned," she said. "These things can be weirdly and totally unreasonably intense."

"They also don't tip because they don't exactly drink," injected Lisa, from behind the bar.

Jacob, who was working sound that night, was more indifferent: "It's an easy night for me." There was a house band, the same one for each Breakthrough Performance. Only the singers changed. Sound quality, as Jacob put it, was not their main concern.

The Breakthrough People were part of a New Age-oriented self-improvement program. The group had spent the past six weeks in workshops, seminars, and other types of therapy designed to culminate in a night of performance—a song each participant had personally selected to perform on-stage in a real nightclub. The idea was that each Breakthrough Performance was to be a transformative experience, an ave-nue for the performers to reinvent and empower themselves. When Darcy arrived, a very old woman was onstage, dressed in a leather miniskirt and sequined top, performing a ren-dition of "Bad Girls" by Donna Summer. It should've been hilarious, but people in the audience were looking on, teary-eyed, evidently moved; some looked stricken, even horrified. They were the family and friends of the performers. Watching, Darcy was immediately aware of something in the air. A re-ligious feeling, almost. Combined with the earnestness of the singer, it was both heartbreaking and endearing to witness.

Darcy stood at the back of the bar, quietly tying on her apron. When she finally started moving about the room, drink orders were given to her politely, seriously.

Next, a tragic-looking middle-aged woman got onstage. She wore a long green gown and sang "Somewhere over the Rainbow" off-key and with tears streaming down her face, smearing her makeup. Then, a curly-haired man in his thir-ties performed a sneering, open-shirted, energetic version of Billy Idol's "Rebel Yell," while several of the other perform-ers, females, knelt before him, pawing at his thighs. It went on like this, singer after singer, for some time. People watch-ing, and the performers, too, after they'd gotten off the stage, were laughing and crying simultaneously.

After a while Darcy decided she needed a break from the room. She walked down the stairs and leaned on the wall of the staircase, feeling—she could not have said why—close to tears herself. Briefly, she shut her eyes.

When she opened them again, she saw a baby. A woman was coming up the stairs, carrying a baby in her arms, and the baby was staring at Darcy. It was bald, with milky white skin and clear, depthless eyes; it was a sexless, cherubic creature, not even human, thought Darcy. The baby kept looking at Darcy as its mother carried it by.

Darcy straightened up and went the rest of the way down the stairs, to get some air, outside. The bouncer at the door was Thor, a large-framed, heavy-lidded black man with dreadlocks. He was usually kind to Darcy and struck her as being wise and philosophical. He was known for saying things like "Freedom is a state of mind" in response to others' barroom woes and, if a conversation began to descend into darker waters, would lightly evade engagement by saying, "That's a whole other topic, man. We'll talk about that next time." He was also known for watching out for his co-workers. Once, Darcy watched him steer a fellow bouncer, who was drunk, away from going home with one of the bar regulars, a middle-aged, alcoholic French woman. "It may look good to you now, my man, but trust me, it won't later."

"What's up, Darcy?" He addressed her only after she had stood on the sidewalk for a few moments, not saying anything.

Darcy turned, smiling slightly. "I just needed to get away for a minute. That stuff up there, it's just kind of crazy."

"Brings a good amount of dough in," said Thor, shrugging. "Think about it. They pay a thousand dollars to go through the program. Then they charge twelve dollars a head for each of their family and friends to come see them. Seems like kind of a racket, if you ask me. But if it's working for them and these people are the kind that have the money to spend . . . ," he trailed off, shrugging.

Darcy realized what was bothering her. "The music up there—" she looked Thor's way with gratuitous bewilderment, "—is *terrible*." Still, she had been roused by it, she knew. That was the confusing part. Things at that moment felt sharp and true, but in a way she could not put her finger on.

Someone was coming up the sidewalk. A feeling fired inside of Darcy, seeing this figure. The lanky frame, the ambling, already-defeated stride, hands in pockets, jeans loose around long thin legs. Could it really be him, out in the world? It occurred to her that she had never seen Tracey outside Don's apartment or the backyard. The figure passed by the darkened windows of a shop at the end of the block. The street behind him was spottily lit, a pool of yellow streetlamp spilling on the ruddy asphalt. A slight mist hung in the air, just enough so that Darcy thought she could see actual motes of fog drifting about in the pool of light. The figure got darker as it approached—the light from the streetlamp falling back, the lights of the bar not yet hitting his front side.

Another image occurred to Darcy just then: a thin blue ribbon of smoke marking a hollow between two hills, ragged trees rising out of a swamp. The old American music she liked—that was what it looked like in her mind. More lonesome figures, but these ones were white-skinned with dirt-blackened faces. Still, they were similar, in atmosphere, to the lone figure walking toward her now on the darkened San Francisco street, and they seemed somehow to be staring back at her out of the picture in her mind. In their arms they held instruments that looked tragically wooden, old, and unpolished; the silence in their faces reported how their sound had been stolen from them. *I have been here before.* The vision came at her incongruously aligned with her vision of the sidewalk where she presently stood and the figure walking toward her.

I have been here before.

But it was not Tracey, she saw now, as the figure came into the light. It was Eli, the piano player from Don's crowd. The one Darcy had had ice cream with that time, the one whose girlfriend had died of cancer. He looked harmless and sad and somewhat old, drifting up the sidewalk with his hands in his pockets. When he noticed Darcy, Eli lifted his head and opened his mouth in a half-grin. His mouth was large, which she hadn't noticed about him before. He had the same kind of lips that Tracey had—thick, cracked, rather ugly. He stopped on the sidewalk in front of the bar.

It was a neighborhood bar, so it was not a surprise to see Eli here. Even Thor knew him. The two men nodded amiably at one another.

"Hello, bluesman," said Thor, at the same moment Eli looked at Darcy and said, "Hi, sweetness."

———

That night Darcy finished her shift uncharacteristically sober. She attributed it to the energy of the Breakthrough People, which she'd finally concluded was too intense to be worth getting intoxicated for. She counted her money at the bar, untied her apron, tipped her share to the bartender, and then tucked the rest of her money into her jeans pockets. Then she waited around for Jacob, who had offered to walk her out to her truck. They said goodbye to the rest of the bar staff and then walked down the stairs, outside, together.

Jacob was easy to walk beside, a light presence, unprotective yet just solid enough, she felt. Temporary. She would enjoy it while it was here.

When they reached her truck and Darcy opened the door, she found herself noticing the bust of the silver man she'd picked up on the side of the Great Highway. It sat placidly between her two front seats, garbage collecting around its shoulders. She'd gotten so used to it being there, she had stopped noticing it. Tonight she saw it anew, though.

"I was meaning to ask you," said Jacob, "what the fuck is that?"

Darcy reached in and hauled it out from behind the seats. She walked it over to the curb, deciding to leave it there, next to some trash bags that had been set out in front of a nearby Chinese restaurant.

"I don't think I need it anymore," said Darcy.

5.

She would not hear from or see Tracey again. The next day or so, she would talk to the woman upstairs, who would immediately run down the stairs, through the garage, and, picking up the phone for her, would make Darcy call the police. That was the kind of woman you needed to be, sus-

picious, determined, and properly indignant, it would occur
to Darcy. One who took reason and reaction into her own
hands, one who kept up proper barriers. What was she,
Darcy, doing, just sitting around down there in the dark, for
days, next to an open window and easy-to-pick locks? The
woman would demand to know that of Darcy, who could
only reply that she didn't know why she had or had not
acted as she had. However, she did know that Tracey would
be gone by the time the police arrived, and he was. In the
end he could've been just a figment of her imagination. Only
Don and she and the cat had ever really witnessed any of it,
if you really thought about it.

Still, it had been enough for Darcy. Enough to get her
started.

Interlude:
View of Mother

I.

On summer mornings, after having served his breakfast and then padded, in her flat terry slippers and girlish white-blue nightgown, back down the hall to the bedroom to dress, she would reenter the kitchen with a swift, glowing quality that confused him. He could not understand why it had to be like that or what had become, so quickly, of the mother who had stood there just minutes before, sleepily frying bacon at the stove, wearing eyeglasses, black hair tumbling down her back in fat, lazy, silken curls. Returning, she broke the spell of the kitchen and his breakfast (refrigerator hum, clank of spoon against cereal bowl) with the harriedness of someone bursting in from outdoors— she was busy, magical, exuberant, contained, all at once! Her hair was swept back in a low ponytail, her eyeglasses were gone, her clothes showed the shape of her body just as her ponytail, gleaming black, now revealed the shape of her skull. From his spot on the cool vinyl floor, on the same brown curlicue-patterned diamond each morning, he saw, first, her bare feet and her legs up to her knees, and then the hem of her flared white wraparound skirt (less opaque than her skin, always this outfit, in his memory). She moved around him in porcelain, red and black flashes. Red lips, red blouse. Eggshell-white toes.

———

There were bamboo shades on the windows. Christian is certain this is an accurate memory. It was 1984; he would have been four years old. Their mother still dressed like she was in the 1970s, and the house, too, had a ragged, summery feel. Was this just the way of refugees? The first clothes they were handed, the first television shows they saw, froze in their minds, and, thus, in 1984, she was still wearing bell-bottoms and pointy-collared shirts. She was still wearing polyester and sporting a meek, willowy style of femininity, her prized long hair parted in the middle and falling, flowing, down around her ears. The girls, seven and eight, were already aware of their mother being anachronistic, but Christian was not. He felt something about her, though: danger could come to her. She would have to be protected; he knew it.

The sunlight filtered through the shades into the kitchen. The pattern of the bamboo slats played in bright shadow across his mother's face, her arms, the fabric of her shirt, striping her, as if threatening to slice her into sections. It alarmed him, to see the bands of light slide heedlessly across his mother. It felt disconcerting and perplexing in the way that things do when you are four and do not have the words to explain the phenomenon you are observing. Sometimes he would cry and thrust out his hands, palms forward, to ward off the light. But it would seem to his mother that he cried for no reason.

"I don't want the sun, I want the moon. The sun is stupid." It was the most powerful word he knew, this one.

"You no say stupid. Stupid not nice words." As she turned her face and raised her eyebrows at him, the thin bands of light transferred to her cheek, her right ear.

What the light could turn her into sometimes was startling and ugly.

————

"What is troubling you?" If she asked in Vietnamese, those were the words she used. If she asked the question in English, it came out, with a look of pain, "What wrong with you?"

"Nothing," Christian had learned to reply.

————

He spent a lot of his time watching her. She would notice this. Sometimes when he watched her, she had the sense that he knew things about her, that his young, worried gaze could actually see the former her: the young undedicated nurse she'd been before, forgetting certain duties and avoiding others; or, the wife in disguise she felt she was now. She suspected that somehow he knew, although she had howled, that she had not reached her arms out toward the water with sincerity, that night on the South China Sea when her previous husband fell over the side of the boat. He and another man had begun to fight on the boat—no more than a rowboat—and both went over the side. The water was viscous and black, the night dense and large. Nobody on the boat was willing to jump in after the lost men, and neither was there any rope or tools to recall them. That was in 1978. Death, at the time, was not unfamiliar to her; it was just day-to-day life, with a certain strangeness added. She had, in fact, developed a sense for death: some futures she simply couldn't picture. Her husband's, for instance. Though the thought hadn't exactly crystallized as such in her mind. Just that it was not a surprise, when his head slipped under the black water and then failed to resurface. Her two daughters, quite small then, had been with her on the boat. They showed no signs now of remembering the event. As far as she could see, they were not traumatized or impacted by it much at all. Ironically, it was under Christian's gaze, Christian who hadn't yet been conceived, that she felt the most guilt and solace both, regarding that night.

She would tell her children about the time before their emigration, gradually, eventually. Sure she would, of course she would. Yes, she thought they should know. But she didn't think they needed to know too much, honestly, and there were parts of it she would probably tell no one, ever. For instance: there had been a first husband; also a lover before and during her time with the second husband. The lover was her eldest daughter's real father: such were Su Heng's secrets. In the years to come she would adopt the habit of claiming she couldn't remember things, in order not to have to share too much. To her new husband—number three— the American social worker, Hammond, whom she would marry in 1979, she would lie quite a lot. Or at least omit key events. If pressed, she might snap at him and tersely relent one or two tragic, graphic details ("How he die, my cousin? He was shot in head, okay?") that would turn Hammond immediately tender and apologetic toward her. He hated to upset her; he understood completely how things might upset her. But he just wanted to help her and he wanted to *know* her, he would say. He had never known anyone else like her. Nowhere in his life was there any comparable experience. His life, it was nothing compared with hers, he would say.

And why should she deny him or anyone their tour of guilt? She wouldn't.

Let them think she had sacrificed, let them think she had mourned. Let them think she had cared enough to rage against grief. People who thought like this: they were too kind and simple, and had been too long protected, to be able to even begin to know what it felt like—what it entailed—to cease to care.

———————

He watched his mother wield a large knife over small pieces of fruits and vegetables. He watched as she pounded and sliced and peppered meat, wrapped it in cellophane, and placed it in a bowl, with grotesque, vacuous calm. He watched her sweep up fallen leaves from the potted plant in the corner, using a hand broom and small dustpan. Sometimes she spoke to him in a singsong voice, asking questions he didn't realize actually called for answers. Adults often spoke like that when they spoke to him, and he had come to understand that their questions were not serious. ("Christian, are you eating a yummy popsicle?" when it was plain that he was.) When his mother used this tone, he took the content of what she said to be of little consequence; he knew the only thing that mattered then was her love. It was there in her voice, and it bargained with him. *I will be this sweet if you, too, will be sweet.* Its cadence went, *My-boy, my-boy,* over and over and may have been saying only that, for all he cared. Her words to his ears were just like a lulling, unbroken stream of sound or a fog encircling him, following him through the world of their home, ensuring him always of her proximity. He did not go out of earshot of her, if he could help it.

As the day wore on, the morning light faded and softened. Afternoon came in, feeling very orange and shady and sleepy. At some point (right before or after naptimes, or after having come in from outdoors), his mother would take on a quality similar to her early morning self. In the kitchen again, looking peaceful, pouring lemonade over chunky, misting squares of ice. Maybe, too, by now she would have let her hair down again. So hot and cold, she was.

And she would glance at him, her son, gazing up at her with his cheek pressed against his hands laid flat on the table. The emotion in his eyes looked so adult! A moment would pass between them, like a secret, surpassing their known, understood roles—the kind of small thing a mother keeps to herself, ultimately, regarding the mystery of her own children.

"I wub you, Mama," he would say, pronouncing the word just like this, both comical and plaintive.

2.

Nothing his sisters said or did felt soothing, however. Christian clung to their words with anxious longing to understand. They spoke fast and decisively, and their eyes sparkled with a light that was almost silver; it was whimsical and daunting.

"Gimme a five." Christian can remember the first time he tried this out on them.

"Gimme *a* five?" One sister had to call this out to the other sister. "Christian says 'gimme *a* five' instead of 'gimme five!'"

Also, at times, they took it upon themselves to offer and immediately deny him favors.

"Christian can't read, so we'll read to him. But first, Christian, you have to finish your milk," said one.

"But Christian didn't even finish his milk, so we can't read him his story. Oh well," said the other. "No Peter Rabbit, Christian."

"Yes, I can," replied Christian. It was always difficult, trying to decide which parts of their sentences needed a reply.

"You don't even make sense, Christian. You have to drink your milk or no Peter Rabbit. Do you want to hear Peter Rabbit or not?"

"Peter Rabbit hit Mr. McGregor," said Christian, sincerely indignant and sorrowful.

His slowness would cause them to sigh and show their teeth or to stick out their lower lips and roll their eyeballs and blow their bangs upward. Sometimes they let out little screams of frustration and jumped up and down in front of him. Christian might laugh when it went this far. He believed it meant they were sharing something, a wild, harmonious moment. Rising in him would be a feeling of fright and excitement mingled. This feeling was not unlike how the promise of ice cream or a cookie or a chase could make him feel.

Sometimes they laughed with him. Sometimes they screamed or sighed yet again, and stomped away.

On occasion he hid his sisters' dolls in their father's shoes. The shoes were laid out in scattered rows, along with the rest of the family's footwear, on the rust-colored Mexican tiles just inside the front door. His father's shoes were the likeliest ones to fill because they were the biggest and darkest, inside and out; they beckoned like caverns. The place where the shoes were was like a mini–mountain range to Christian. Or a bumpy swamp he felt compelled to plunge into. Afterward, he stayed silent while his sisters ran about yelling "Where's my Lori?" or "Where's my Tina?" More often than not, though, he had completely forgotten having hid the dolls by the time his sisters got around to searching for them, and he was truthfully ignorant when they tried to interrogate him.

Only his mother could save him from his sisters' cattiness and bullying. In her presence, Christian's sisters' powers became diminished and merely petulant. She could control them with her hands. He would watch as she brushed and braided their hair, loving the skillful way she held bobby pins and barrettes between her lips and drew patterns through their hair with a comb. She drew and lines appeared, like grass parting in a windy field. He watched as his sisters whined and squirmed beneath his mother's hands; he watched the swift, efficient way she turned their bodies around to zip their dresses up in the back.

"Ouch, you're hurting me!" said one sister, as her hair was being put in pigtails.

"If you don't stay still, you turn out crooked," said their mother, meaning the girl's hair—and they all understood this without quite realizing, either, the mistakes in her language.

Their father, passing through the living room with a briefcase in one hand and a coffee mug in the other on his way out the front door, intoned, "Not '*you* will turn out crooked' but '*your ponytails* will turn out crooked.' There's a difference, now." Though Christian was the only one who was his biologically, all three of them called him Dad. He was large and infrequently there. When he was there, he gave the house a different feel, somehow—day was defined by his absence (Christian and mother and sisters wandering lightly around, like interlopers) and night by his presence (the house became warm, yellow, glowing, with all its spaces and objects properly utilized).

"Not ponytails, Dad, *pig*tails!" his sisters scrambled to correct him. "Ponytails is for when there's only one, pigtails is for when there's two."

The secret goal of this family—already, intuitively, Christian understood it—was to make one another perfect and impenetrable to the outside world.

———

The outside world, as far as they knew, was a place covered by pavement and symmetrical, flat arrangements of concrete. Lego pieces made more sense than Lincoln Logs out here, noted Christian, when they rode in the car to run errands. Their mother drove slowly, though they were all too young to realize just how slowly, or that she drove with immense trepidation, hugging the shoulder of the road with their small green Honda, itself like a diminutive bug next to the elongated, boxier vehicles that easily passed theirs by. In parking lots, she chose distant spaces because she could not always get the car between the white lines.

They crawled over the back of the front seats to get out of the backseat, and then he walked between his sisters, each holding one of his hands, across a blazing hot platform of black ground. It was summertime. When he looked far across the parking lot, he saw the world start to shimmer and blur at the point where the black ground met the bottom edge of the white-blue sky. Looking down, Christian saw cracks and graying gum stains beneath his feet.

"Somebody you have to fix it," he said.

"You can't fix it, it's the ground, the *ground*," groaned Darcy, who was the younger (and, equally, both sweeter and meaner) of his two sisters.

The grocery store greeted them—a fluorescent, rectangular haven. Everything in places like this appeared smooth, metallic, and crisp. In their shopping cart they rolled down gleaming aisles full of boxes, cans, and bags, an intricate spectrum of color. Christian squeezed his eyes shut. He liked how, when he opened them again, the colors zinged about in front of him for a moment before the world came back into focus. When he looked up, the ceiling was high and complicated. Then, in the canned goods aisle, his mother dropped a bottle of vinegar and the pungent odor of the spilled liquid filled the air around them. He and his sisters waited, with noses pinched, as their mother squatted to pick up the pieces of glass. It was a painstaking task, but she was ardent and humble as she went at it. Until a man in a tan apron came toward them, with a mop and broom and dustpan, and he directed their mother to stop. He shook his head at her and pointed. Sheepishly she dropped her handful of broken glass into his dustpan. The spilled vinegar looked just like water, but even after the man swished his mop over it the odor remained, like something to mark them. Of this their mother seemed aware, and the children also sensed it. But the man smiled gently, encouragingly, at her. He had a kind, bearded face. They saw their mother blush.

The store was Albertsons.

For some time afterward "like the nice man at Albertsons" would become, for her and her children, a kind of measure.

The girls would use it whenever they encountered a stranger they liked: *He was like the man at Albertsons, huh, Mommy?* The incident stayed in Christian's mind because of this. They were always talking about this Albertsons man, and they were always seeking someone like him, and it mildly distressed Christian because he wanted them to be satisfied, his mother and sisters. He wanted them to be happy, and he wanted his sisters to stop jumping up and down and for the fierceness in their faces to stop, too. His mother would actually respond to his sisters' assessments: yes, that one was like the Albertsons man, or, no, that one was not, really. The kind man with the mop, who had taken the broken glass from his mother's hand, had made a lasting, quieting impression. Christian noticed that his father did not seem to have the same effect on them. Even though his father, too, would surely have taken the broken glass from his mother's hand, wouldn't he have? But, perhaps, he would not have *offered* to take it from her, so kindly and patiently; more likely, he might have demanded it from her in somewhat of a panic. Christian could picture it this way. And the two pictures—the imagined one of his father and the remembered one of the Albertsons man—existed in his mind for some time, though after a while he forgot entirely about the spilled vinegar and remembered only a vague significance attached to the name Albert or to the sons of somebody named

Albert. In his mind he was aware of the presence of a robust, benevolent masculine figure, undeniably Caucasian, somewhat like Santa Claus. Christian had little hope of becoming this man himself, yet he understood it as a goal of sorts: it had something to do with diligence, and manhood, and with easing other people's humiliations.

3.

Fourteen years later, they see each other only every now and then, during holidays and in the summers. That is when his sisters return home, filling his father's house with their quick new lightness and good-humored bickering, with whatever is their current style or politics or self-determined ideals. Darcy and Mary both live in New York City now. Christian still lives with his father. Their mother and father have been divorced going on three years now. Their father—the girls' stepfather—stayed in the house in the foothills town where the children spent most of their growing years, while their mother moved into an apartment complex in a Central Valley town where she'd found a job in a nursing home. She has returned to nursing. This is slightly ironic in light of how, toward the end of the marriage, their father would sometimes refer to her as "your mother the alleged nurse." Somewhere in this comment lay a clue, Christian thinks, as to why his father remarried the family pets' veterinarian.

Everyone, even their mother, is fairly certain there was no affair going on between their father and Sharon prior to the divorce. In the last year of their parents' marriage, two of the family dogs had to be put to sleep—one of old age, the other due to cancer. This, if anything, was the only intimacy their father and the vet shared: he had stood with her in the room, not just on one but two occasions, helping to hold the dogs on the table, stroking their coats, catching their last dog glances, as she administered the final shot.

"Dogs can get cancer?" was Christian's response when his father came home with the news about the last dog. His mother had stiffened only at the sight of the bill. She could not comprehend why they had to pay even for death. She wanted to simply live and prosper, not be reminded of what was inevitable anyway.

Their holiday conversations now, in the kitchen, where they tend to gather and loiter, are a grasping for blanket ends, an attempt to wield the amorphous, cumbersome shape of their collective past.

"You used to follow me around," says Mary, the older sister. They are recalling the first house they remember living in, a house in suburban Sacramento. "I used to trick you into following me into that closet with the two doors. I would tell you to close the one door behind us, then I would sneak out the other door when you weren't looking."

"You would lock me in the closet, you mean," says Christian.

"Never for that long. You just never gave me and Darcy a break. You cried at the tiniest thing, you couldn't take a joke." These days Mary is sleek and slim, her dark eyes nimble and penetrating.

"I did not cry that much," protests Christian. He is a slightly unaware, grinning, but secretive eighteen-year-old. He is charismatic without being overly friendly; he can speak personally without seeming to lose anything, least of all his composure. "Everything I remember in that house was happy," he says. "I honestly don't remember ever being locked in a closet by you." His easygoing nature has made him the kind of male that females will cajole but also rely on.

"Oh, but you cried when that damn fool across the street killed old Chinga with a slingshot," interjects his father from where he stands, sipping his coffee, leaning on the counter. "And so did I, nearly, for that matter, Christ!" And he laughs.

A vulnerability comes into their father's eyes now when he laughs—his eyes dart about, seeking contact. The old house, too, has undergone changes in the last two years: it has been repainted, each room has been refloored, the back wall knocked out, and a study added on, in which their father now does his writing—something he used to do before he became a social worker (which was how he met their mother) and then a high school counselor. He and Sharon have also combined all their animals, and the house has a happy zoolike atmosphere. Sharon is six years younger than their father; still, she is three years older than their mother. She is also considerably taller, as tall as their father. Lanky with a plain, clean beauty, an easy, confident air. She has lived in this part of California almost all her life and has never been infected by the kind of restlessness that carries people away from small towns. The few times the kids have been in the presence of their mother and father and Sharon, the three of them together, the sense of his mother as a perennial child in their midst has distinctly, painfully, occurred to Christian. It is better, he thinks, to just see her alone, one on one.

His father continues, "It was that fellow Guy Albertson, with the houseful of rowdy kids. Big, fat guy. What a ridiculous name, eh? *Guy.* He was a real low-brow character, too, never took his trash out on time, could be heard yelling at his kids in the middle of the night, obviously drunk. Neighbors like that—that was how I knew we couldn't stay in that area. I had to move you guys; I just did. Imagine you kids growing up next to kids with a father like that. And do you know what's there now? A shopping center right in back of our old backyard. They tore down all the houses that were behind ours."

"Albertson?" says Christian, "But I thought we liked the Albertsons."

"Oh no, no, we liked the *Fishers*, the neighbors on our other side," says his father, decisively.

4.

If it was raining or gloomy or too hot, they stayed inside, sprawled on the kitchen tiles in front of the sliding glass doors that looked out to the patio and backyard, and they played quietly indoors. But if the day was sunny, their mother would let them go out.

And if on those days Su Heng spied the Fisher woman in the neighboring backyard (separated from theirs by a hedge they could easily see through and then a fence), lounging in her swimsuit and sunglasses on a towel beside her swimming pool, and the heads of the Fisher children appeared and then disappeared above the fence as they bounced on their diving board; and if Su Heng heard the sounds of their splashing

and laughter as merry and felt infected enough by the sopor
of the summer afternoon—felt it as warm blessing and not
inertia, that is—and if her own children seemed contented
enough, then she might take out her drawing pad and sit on
the patio to sketch while they played.

Before she was a nurse in Vietnam, Su Heng had wanted
to be an artist. She had even for a time loved a man who
was a painter, a friend from her high school days. He had
encouraged her pursuit of art. That was, until his own paintings started to get attention. Then Su Heng had married, not
her artist friend, but someone else, the first husband, the first
ill-fated union. As for art, it became nothing more than a
hobby for her after that point.

She had sketched the woman on the other side of the
hedge a number of times. She had also sketched the neighbor
children's heads bobbing above the triangular wooden tips
of the fence slats. There was an atmosphere about the scene
she wished to capture. It felt vastly different from the life in
her own backyard, and she was mildly in awe of it. Their
joy, their crisp, perfect happiness. How could she bring forth
the quality of their laughter in lines and scratches on paper?
How could she depict the fluidity and the hum of peace that
seemed to emanate from their yard? She would try to capture
it by drawing the droplets of water that sprayed in an arc
through the air around the children's heads and limbs. But
the droplets of water were fast, catching the sunlight for a
millisecond only, dazzlingly; and she never felt like she was
successful at conveying this: the shining, swift motility of
stray water.

In her own backyard, they had only a kiddie pool to
splash around in. Once, shortly after they'd first moved in,

the Fisher girl had come over to play with Darcy and Mary. The Fisher girl was eight—Mary's age. She was blond and taller than Mary. Both Darcy and Mary had thrown such huge fits at the prospect of sharing their kiddie pool with the Fisher girl that she had to be sent away from their house. Su Heng had not known how else to deal with it. The Fisher girl was standing in the ankle-deep water, refusing to get out.

"Get out, get out! It's *ours*, it's not *yours*," Mary and Darcy were both screaming, their voices shrill, as the argument had been going on for several minutes now. Tears were streaming down their faces, and they were jumping up and down furiously, their fists clenched. They even clutched and pulled at one another, using each other's bodies as leverage.

Christian, observing, feared that something in them might break from their being so upset. They might even pop, like balloons, he marveled.

The Fisher girl spoke with resolute calmness. "Well, if you came over to my house, I would let you swim in my pool." She removed one foot, leaving the other in the water. "Look, I only have one foot in."

Even when Su Heng got out there, no amount of ordering or coaxing could persuade her daughters to share, so she, too, soon turned on the Fisher girl. "You have very big pool, your own pool. I sorry. You go, you go now. You tell your mom another day maybe."

The Fisher girl smiled proudly and lifted her chin higher. She sighed. She said, "Okay, bye," and extracted her foot from the kiddie pool. She stopped on her way out of the yard to pat Christian on the head as she passed by the patio where he stood watching.

"Gimme a five," said Christian, and the Fisher girl did.

———————

They had lived there almost a year, and Hammond had not yet done much to fix up the backyard. He was not that adept with his hands and was also quite busy at work, he claimed. He would get around to it soon, however.

The backyard was uncultivated, with rough patches of lawn and hard dirt, dug-up dirt all along the perimeters of the fence, and one strangely placed patch of tall, reedy plants that looked as if it belonged next to a pond, not in the middle of a suburban backyard. The reeds must've been deliberately transplanted, Hammond surmised, and then somehow they'd flourished. Maybe the previous owners of the house had been planning a fishpond but had left the project unfinished. The reeds grew on the far right side of the yard, along the fence line for a distance of about ten feet. The dogs went into the reeds to do their business, and the area stank, a murky, stagnant smell. The children sometimes went into it, too, pretending it was a jungle or forest. Once, Christian went into the reeds and emerged with dog mess in his hands, and carried it ceremoniously to the trash can. Su Heng and Hammond had laughed, witnessing this.

When Hammond was around, Su Heng's humor toward the children was generally better. It all seemed more of an adventure, more bearable—this odd new life she'd come to inhabit—when he was present.

But when he wasn't, the backyard felt too large and uninviting for her tastes. She stuck close to the house and made her children do so as well, if she could. She encouraged them to pretend the patio was an island.

The patio was a ten-foot square of ruddy gray concrete without which they might have sunk and drowned. The girls laid out towels, one next to the other, and rolled back and forth on them while their mother drew and Christian lay on his back on his own towel, pointing his fists at the sky, pretending to fly. The girls had their own games, ignoring Christian. They had one game called Steamroller in which they rolled, outstretched like logs, over one another's bodies, and another called Makeup in which they took turns drawing big-eyed faces on each other's backs and feet with washable markers. They read books and made tracks across their towels with their small dolls and toy animals. Then, they lay on their stomachs with their legs bent at the knees, feet twitching at the sky, black hair falling in a determined fashion over their small faces, and drew pictures on white typing paper. Christian also drew but tended to tire of it before his mother and sisters did. He would lie back and watch them instead.

Regarding their artwork, their mother was of the opinion that Darcy had talent and Mary did not. Mary drew pictures that tried to be faithful to reality. Noses and eyes in the right locations, careful attention to buttons and bows on dresses, semi–correctly proportioned bodies (they had necks, at least, while Darcy's did not). Su Heng thought there was something stiff and ordinary about Mary's pictures, especially for a child's work: already, this daughter appeared cautious and self-conscious. Her pictures did not leap off the page with the energy of wonder and implausibility that the figures in Darcy's drawings did. Darcy drew creatures—her versions of people—with noodley, preposterous long legs and arms;

and no torsos; the shapes and features of their faces were equally loopy and uncontrolled. When she drew them in chairs, they hovered, not quite fitting in their seats; even objects like coffee cups and television sets steamed and radiated and hovered above tabletops, as if energetically buoyed.

The irony did not escape Su Heng. That Mary, the less artistic one, was her biological offspring, and the other, whose imagination seemed freer, was not.

———

Another thing his mother seemed to like to sketch was bamboo, Christian remembers. She made many sketches of bamboos, some with people under them or beside them, people with lots of lines in their faces and wrinkles in their clothing, doing serious-seeming things, like passing cloth bundles or woven baskets between them as the wind blew their hair and lifted their robes and scarves. Lovers parting, the man often on horseback, the woman handing him small, bundled packages, bamboos swaying around them. Sometimes, too, the people were minuscule, pure black shapes that merged with the shapes of trees and other objects in the pictures. *This is what happens when the sun is going down*, he heard his mother explain to his sisters when they accused her of having forgotten to draw faces on the people in those drawings. His sisters, they were always so sharp, so intent on pointing out what was not, to their senses, precise. From his mother's explanation, however, Christian formed the notion that some people's faces could fade away with the daylight if they did not turn on lamps. In the dark, he pressed his hands against his face—his cheeks, his eyebrows—to hold things in place.

The information it would take her years to relay to her children (to the younger daughter in particular) went something like this: *I used to hear the girls fighting among each other; I heard and saw so many of them having their unwanted babies. The hospital where I worked was the place these kinds of girls were sent to. So you should never, never complain. And you should always expect things of men—even if you don't really love them, they are good for helping with some things at least. Why not! Your birth mother, she has probably suffered staying in that country; God knows what her fate has been. She was vain, I tell you, and troubled. She said many unrealistic things, that she used to live in a beautiful mansion by the ocean, with servants, that she was a woman who deserved to live among fancy things all the time. She refused to feed you if she was tired. I would walk into her room and find her lying on her bed, staring at the wall, while you screamed, hungry and wet. She was not so good at being a mother, I hate to tell you. And she had no regrets about her former profession; she said she knew how to please men. I did not respect her, but I liked her, and I felt sorry for her and for you. She'd already had one other child, in fact, with a GI—he came back and took the child but did not take her. So, how do you like that! I think she did the best thing for you, giving you to me because she knew I had found a way to leave. Even if it was only with a man I did not really love. No, the one I loved was the only one I never married.*

Oh, but the reeds, the reeds.

Once, Christian wandered into them and found what he thought were dinosaur bones, and he ran back out to tell his mother, excited. Hard, ridged, pale-brown woody stems curving in and out of the mucky, dark ground. Christian did not know that these were roots connected to new bamboo shoots nosing up among the reeds—his mother pointed them out to him. The bamboo shoots looked ugly and dangerous, like short stakes driven point-up into the ground, because the pale yellow-green fronds were still tightly folded in against the culms. But Su Heng was familiar with bamboo and knew that when these shoots unfolded, the fronds would become long, thin branches; they would lose their yellowness and become more and more green, and would reveal the trunk also to be very thin and long and pliable. The whole plant would bend and sway and eventually sprout a splayed-out mass of elegantly narrow, pointy leaves along each branch.

"In no time for all," she told Christian (daring to try out a colloquial phrase she believed she'd heard Americans use). "Very fast it grow up," she said.

5.

"No, Christian, you've got it wrong. There was never any bamboo growing in the backyard." His sisters insist that is the case.

What Christian thinks he remembers is he and his mother, peering into a hole in the ground, studying a muddied, convoluted network of roots that he somehow knows are the roots of bamboo trees. He has been here before, or some moment like this one, with his mother, he is sure of it.

"There was a bamboo plant in the house, only that first winter, though," says Mary. "It grew in a pot in the corner of the kitchen, but its leaves kept turning yellow and falling on the floor. So, eventually, Dad decided to try and replant it outside. Neither him or Mom were very good with plants—it was only later that Mom got really good with plants, but only indoor ones even then. But anyway, Mom had some kind of attachment to this plant. It reminded her a little of Vietnam, I think. Dad planted it in the ground— in the *front* yard, though—and it died that winter. It was too cold for it out."

Now, Christian does recall a potted bamboo plant. Something about the plant: the air was rankled around it. On some mornings he surely felt this, and it upset him in much the same way the sunlight did, when it came through the window and lay stripes upon his mother. How could he explain that to her? He knew the plant was unhappy, but he could not tell her about it. She must've felt somewhat the same, for she was always fussing over the plant. She loved it; she knew she was losing it. She loved that plant more than she liked the cats or dogs. Christian understood that, too. She would get angry and chase the cats around the house with a wooden spoon if she caught them chewing on the bamboo leaves. That was how the cats learned to run from his mother.

To his sisters, Christian says, "Maybe it didn't really die. Maybe it spread from the front yard and got into the backyard somehow."

"That is so like you, Christian, wanting to believe everything Mom tells you," says Mary.

Darcy says, skeptically but quietly, "This is California, Christian," as if that should explain everything.

―――――

"There are two types of men," says his father's new wife, Sharon. "There's the more traditional type, who believes he has to provide and protect, et cetera, all that old hat. Then there is the type who has gone through all that and let it go. There's a point at which, as an adult interacting with another adult, you simply have to get past all those gender delineations."

"You don't have to tell me that, *I* don't want a man to provide for me. Oh my god, that's so weak," protests Mary. "I would never, ever end up like that. Like my mom, really. You just end up fifty years old and at a loss with yourself and all bitter, because you thought a man was going to save you, and then—hello, news flash!—he doesn't."

A pause from Sharon; a restrained look. She has heard it before. "You girls are hard on your mother," she says, reproving but not condemning, exactly.

―――――

When he visits his mother now, Christian tries not to be saddened by the small, meticulously organized clutter of her second-floor apartment. The Central Valley town seems to him quite flat and depressing, with its strip malls and ungracious city people and its traffic that he, a country boy, simply cannot stand. The furniture in his mother's apartment is cheap and squishy (not so squishy for her, he guesses, since she does not weigh that much); in her kitchen, she uses only one set of dishes—coffee cup, plate, bowl, a spoon, a pair of chopsticks—washing them repeatedly. There is a fireplace, but she never uses that, either. Instead, she stores shoes in it, and all over the hearth are arranged her potted plants. His mother, who was never good with animals, has at last become good with plants.

Her plants are, as it goes, the strangest and most vibrant harbingers of life in her abode. Many are tropical: exotic strains purchased in Asian markets. Emanating a mute and alien stillness into the small, neat rooms, their beauty both confident and eerie, his mother's plants appear dignified yet resigned. It is as if they understand that beauty is required of them yet is also the thing that has trapped them. They bend their long stem-necks just so; they turn their flower-eyes gently toward the windows: Oh, the tragedy of houseplants, thinks Christian, who feels cramped himself in his mother's surroundings.

Sometimes, on his way in, he pauses to look at the framed photograph of his mother in the entrance hall. A picture from Vietnam, in her pre-nurse, pre-1975, pre-escape (even pre-imagining the need for escape) days. She says it was taken by one of her first boyfriends. In it, she is absolutely beautiful, seated on a terrace, with the golden ocean sparkling beyond her. Her features are delicate, and her face is innocent, her neck like that of a deer or other fragile-seeming animal. She is wearing a traditional silk dress. There is no hint of what Christian's father would end up claiming her to be, a woman "incapable of enjoying life."

Now, his mother tacks Post-it notes in various spots on her walls, notes to herself, written in Vietnamese. Milk crates of books, papers, odds and ends, line walls and stack up in the corners of the combined living and dining areas. Her couch is covered in plastic, as is her remote control and various other devices, to protect them from spills. His mother, like many older Asian people, contains her life and her belongings—her life within a small indoor space, her belongings within bags and boxes and other coverings—as if to show how the outside world is, to her, impending and chaotic, something to shield oneself from, its disasters and injustices not things one should have to be responsible to. This is how Christian sees it, and he sees it through his father's eyes. He agrees with Hammond's theory because he has had to accept the fact that he, too, prefers his father's house and his father's way of living—its reasonable comforts and open vistas; its open doors; the in-and-out animals and other guests; the stocked refrigerator and large, imperfect yet cozy, overstuffed furnishings. His mother's apartment, in contrast, is orderly and modest but also unreasonable, not a place where one can easily linger. She is fervent about keeping the interior as it is, while even just outside—her balcony—is unswept and littered with dead leaves and spider webs. She rarely opens that door because she is afraid of letting in insects, the noise of her neighbors' rap music, and (so she says, with a frown) barbecue smoke.

Christian opens the sliding glass door and sweeps her balcony for her when he visits. If he is there in the mornings, he will drink his coffee out there, wearing just his sweatpants and socks, while his mother makes excuses for why she must stay inside. To torment her just a little, he will lean on the balcony rail and call out to her joking warnings about the sunshine.

It is his duty, Christian will sometimes think, to watch the coarse-haired elderly woman his mother is now and to try to glimpse the younger one she once was, with her thin, graceful neck; desirable, lovable; the one who rules the kitchen of his early memories, with her hair tumbling down her back. He will think, too, of his sisters. And he will wish they could have all stayed a little longer, together, in his father's house. He also understands, he can see it in them, in their mistrustful, longing eyes, in the way they have learned to hide behind their curtains of dark hair, why it is they had to go.

3. Neighbors

Leena went to the party with Josie because it was the first night she was to be totally alone. Pearl had been picked up that afternoon by her grandmother and would be staying at her house in Dallas for the next four and a half days. No Trevor, no Pearl. Trevor's mother had a way of inviting Pearl, staking her loving claims on her granddaughter, while tactfully excluding Leena.

"And now you get some me time for Mom," Trevor's mother had said, with fake glee, on the driveway in front of Leena and Trevor's home. She said it in the manner of a woman who understood other women's needs for "me time" (but did not herself need it). Leena knelt in front of Pearl to tell her goodbye. Trevor's mother stood back politely, looking away. She was a small, immaculately dressed, red-haired woman who looked younger than her sixty years; her face was cold and tiny, and her eyes were unnaturally blue. Her paleness seemed almost a statement of some kind next to Leena's natural tanness. Pearl, who was a mostly quiet three-year-old, stared at the older woman holding a hand out to her and then took the older woman's hand, as if she had intuited whose will was stronger. Her own mother, Leena, was not a fortress, could not even decide most things for her. Pearl seemed already to know that. Leena felt stripped around Trevor's mother—an unwanted stepsister next to her own daughter.

After they had driven away, Leena went inside and took a pill. Anxiety was normal, she reminded herself. She had been having the anxiety spells ever since they'd moved to Texas, and recently Trevor had made her go see a psychiatrist who had told her that, given her circumstances, it was probably normal. The incident that had marked March and April of that year (those confused months, in Leena's memory) was not talked about, not explicitly. It was treated, rather, as a side effect of the prevailing circumstances: her displacement, and the not-unusual isolation of young mothers whose husbands were often away on business.

Medication, Leena had been assured, was a normal way for some women to cope, especially when one could not immediately change their circumstances. And Leena knew what that meant. She was going to have to get used to things as they were.

About her uneasiness with his mother, Leena never said anything to Trevor. Once at a family dinner, Trevor had pushed back his chair and stood suddenly to call his younger brother Davis aside after some disparaging remark Davis had made. About the steak their mother had prepared, Davis had said, "Is this cooked all the way through?" but he had said it with disgust, shaking his head, as if the situation were somehow representative of a greater, deeper disappointment. The stern manner with which Trevor pushed back his chair and stood only intensified this sense of things. Leena did not hear what Trevor said to his brother. Meanwhile, their mother sat looking ahead and eating as if nothing out of the ordinary was happening. "I don't care. I'll do it myself," Leena heard Davis say, as Trevor came back to the table. Leena at the time had admired Trevor's loyalty to his mother and thought Davis was ungrateful. Eventually, though, she had come to see how the dynamics between the brothers and their mother were more complex than this and how there were things maybe both men did not see about their mother.

But *women* saw these things, thought Leena.

———

The party was a pre-Christmas gathering in a part of the city Leena sometimes drove through and wondered about, but she had never been inside any of the houses. They reminded her of French colonial-style buildings back in Vietnam— two-story, rectangular structures with adobe walls and small, ornate balconies, glass-paned balcony doors, porticos framing front patios. The neighborhood was called French Place (Leena had read the name on a street sign and then recalled having seen or heard it before as the name of a part of the city). Many of the houses even seemed to be in the same dilapidated condition as buildings like these would be in Vietnam, with peeling paint and visible cracks in the outer walls. But some of the houses looked neat and well-kept, newly repainted, yards overflowing with plants and tod- dler toys. A few were painted absurdly, playfully—one was electric blue with sloppy-looking planets floating across its walls. Leena was mystified by the neighborhood. Her friend Josie explained that the area used to be military housing but was now mostly occupied by college students. She said the area was "still sketchy in a way." Leena wasn't familiar with the term but didn't bother to ask what Josie meant because she felt she understood just by looking.

"Some people are buying and fixing up here, though, I guess," said Josie, as they were parking the car.

The guests at the party (they went into one of the more neutral-looking houses on the street—it was not too neglected, but neither was it very clean) appeared to be about Leena's age or younger. They struck Leena as independent and probably intelligent but also immature and a little self-satisfied. There were no toddler toys in the yard of this house. The young women were well-groomed and attractive, but Leena still felt older and sexier.

She lost Josie somewhere in the crowded kitchen. She decided to get a drink for herself and then go look for Josie.

"There's Woodchuck cider. I recommend the cider," said a man standing next to the refrigerator.

"Excuse me?" said Leena.

"You're remarkable looking." He was the same height as Leena, a short, slightly balding man in his late twenties. "Where are you from?"

"Vietnam." She let him open the refrigerator for her, even though she knew that meant entitling him to more conversation.

"Pisces," he said, handing her a bottle, twisting off the cap. "Your sun or moon or rising, or all of it. I detect a lot of Pisces in you. Beautiful, just beautiful." He fixed his gaze on her, and Leena read his type: the kind who justified lust, baseness, by having a dignified manner.

Leena took the compliment as a warning of sorts. Men were noticing her again; she was inspiring them to say these kinds of things. "I have to go find my friend. Excuse me," she said. Then she left the bottle of cider on a table in the hallway, once she was out of the kitchen.

Leena found Josie out on the balcony.

"North Korea in the house," said Josie, gesturing to the young man who appeared to be the center of dialogue out there under the blue Christmas lights. It was cold out here, making Leena realize how warm it had been inside. The Korean man was wearing black slacks and a long black coat, and he sat with his legs crossed in a professional, comfortably nonmasculine manner. He wore wire-rimmed eyeglasses. He and Josie and Leena were the only people of color at that party, as far as Leena had seen. Still, he did not pause to acknowledge her when Leena said, "You are from North Korea?"

Leena wasn't sure if he had ignored her or just not heard her. She did not try to repeat herself. Josie made room on her seat, and Leena sat down. She noticed, as she did this, that both she and Josie were wearing tight pants that made creases above their thighs when they sat.

Besides Josie and the young man from Korea, there were two boys crowded on the small balcony. These two looked more like boys than men to Leena.

"You've got to hybridize," said one of the boys. He was in his late twenties and was not, in fact, wearing an Abercrombie and Fitch T-shirt, though Leena had initially thought he was. The logo on his shirt said "Pimpercrombie and Bitch" and in every other way resembled a perfectly ordinary, navy blue, Abercrombie and Fitch crewneck T-shirt with long sleeves. It took Leena some time to realize the boy's shirt was a joke, because he didn't look to her like an especially joking type of person; he had an innocent, clean-cut appearance, not bad-looking but young for her tastes, with short hair, babyish cheeks, sincere eyes. She didn't understand this kind of joke, really, either. Abercrombie and Fitch was a brand of clothing she liked—her husband bought from there often. "We know a free market economy is the way it *is*, but we're talking about the way it *should* be. We're saying a free market economy is what is at the root of the problem." His way of speaking, too, was slightly hesitant like a boy's.

"But that's a pointless exercise in speculation," said the one from North Korea. "It solves nothing. If you understand anything about military history and U.S. foreign policy, you know there is no way the powers that be will build 'one bomb less'"—he made quotation mark gestures with his fingers—"and then apply that one billion dollars of funding to healthcare or something more needed, as you say. It's a clichéd and futile argument for us to be having, frankly."

"I'm not saying that it will happen, just that *it should*."

At this last statement, the second boy chimed in with the Pimpercrombie one—they said "it should" in unison. The second one was Joel, a sardonic-looking blond boy, also with eyeglasses. Leena had met him before as a friend of Josie's, and he was the one who had told Josie about the party. He, too, had babyish white cheeks, though there was something sharper to his face: his lips were sensuous in shape and didn't come all the way together. This, paired with the watchful, amused light in his eyes, made his face uninviting to Leena. She thought Joel and Pimpercrombie seemed to be ganging up on the Korean man.

"Okay, sure, it should, it should, but it's not going to," said the one from Korea. "Take the Vietnam War. The real tragedy of that war was not our misunderstanding of what we were getting ourselves into. The real tragedy of that war was the debunking of the intellectuals, who were all along stridently and repeatedly informing the U.S. government that they were making the same mistakes France had made in 1954. But does the U.S. government listen? No. And it's impossible to expect that they will or can—it's a machine with too many cogs, and to expect one gear to stop turning just because an action seems morally wrong is a ludicrous presumption. America just can't do it. So we lost a war, technically, but what did we really lose? In the end who is thriving? *What* is thriving? Vietnam has her piddly independence, and we threw away a whole lot of money, sure, but a free market economy is *still* thriving—throughout all the better parts of the world, in fact. So something about it must be working."

Josie was looking at the Korean man, aghast. "But *what* are you *saying?*"

This was Josie: she was pretty in the same slight, feminine way as Leena, yet there was an entirely more modern and savvy demeanor about her once she started talking. Leena sat with her knees pressed together, while Josie sat with her knees apart, boyishly, carelessly. The two were sometimes mistaken for sisters, but Josie was a type of woman Leena knew she could never be. Josie had grown up in the States; Leena had been here six years. Josie could still speak some rudimentary Vietnamese, however, and that was a big part of the connection between them.

The others, too, looked restless and appalled at this latest statement from the Korean man.

"You can't just say something like that," said Joel. "You're disregarding so much when you say something

like that. Economics can't be the sole determining factor
of what's justifiable as successful, can it? We're dropping
bombs on Afghanistan now for reasons everyone knows are
false, but you're going to say that's okay because economic
dominance is inevitable?"

"You're a liberal, but I'm a historian, all right?" said
the Korean, a little defensively. "I understand your point of
view, but I'm speaking about facts, not moral issues. The
democratic free market economy has basically survived all
the challenges that've been made to it in the last two hundred years. What does that mean? How else can that possibly
be interpreted? It means we are headed into a future of no
further economic opposition, no two warring factions. The
ideals of socialism were not sustainable, and neither will
be dictatorships or anarchy or monarchies. There can be a
bright side to this, you know. With capitalism—and I know
this sounds extremist—but with capitalism at least there is
an objective means of determining who will be granted inclusion. I mean, in a pure capitalist circumstance, that is," the
Korean finished in a clipped, superior tone.

"Huh?" said Joel, and it made Leena think (despite the
fact that she was hardly following the conversation herself)
maybe Joel was not that smart after all.

The other boy seemed to be following it, though. He said,
"He's saying anyone who has money can purchase entry
into, say, a certain society, while in, say, a vegan society,
it's ideology that determines your right to enter—you have
to be a vegan or you'll be kicked out. He's saying it's better that something objective like money, that's theoretically
attainable by anybody, according to merit, be the medium
of exchange and not ideology, basically. But I think you're

wrong," to the Korean man now, "because the pursuit of wealth then becomes its own corrupt ideology that indulges in inhumane acts in order to keep its certain small exclusive club of people in power."

"In a *pure* capitalist circumstance, I said," argued the Korean man, "and again, I'm talking about facts, not morality."

Leena was accustomed to not always comprehending the conversations around her. That was often the case, especially when she witnessed discussions among men (it was always groups of men, here as well as in Vietnam, more than groups of women who sat around discussing such matters, it seemed to her). Like these boys, her husband and his friends would discuss world politics and economics, but their take on things—it was evident even to Leena—was different. They were businessmen. They laughed when they dropped the names of famous corporations; they had more bravado and verve than these college boys. Trevor's friends' conversations took place in well-furnished living rooms in large houses and in elegant bars, with food and drink flowing, music in the background, and an undercurrent of appreciation, of unabashed satisfaction, she thought, buoying everything. Her husband's friends—she hadn't been around them in a while now, but she remembered how it usually was—would nod and smile at her and say "Thank you, Leena" in low, pleasing tones when she handed one of them a fresh drink or passed them a napkin.

"But of course we're discussing morality," the Pimpercrombie T-shirt boy was saying, "and a free market economy has no moral concerns, that's the whole problem." He turned abruptly toward Leena. His eyes, it occurred to her, were afraid-looking even though his speech was confident. "You're from Vietnam somewhat recently, aren't you? Let's ask her about what has been done to her country in the name of capitalism."

Leena was startled. It took a moment for it to dawn on her that he actually expected her to answer. She replied unsteadily. "Under capitalism it's much better now, though you get in very much trouble still, I think, if you say so there."

The young man from Korea laughed, tossing his head back sharply. He uncrossed his legs and sat forward with his hands on his thighs. He was not at all her type, but at that moment Leena thought he was the most impressive of the males there. Her interest in any of them, she assured herself, was not personal.

———

Leena first met Josie one day in the park by the kiddie pool. Leena was there with Pearl, and Josie was a part-time nanny for a family in Westlake. Josie was three years younger than Leena, who had just turned thirty. Josie was the only other person of Vietnamese background Leena had met in her time in Texas.

Before Texas, Leena had lived in a loft apartment in Greenwich Village in New York City with her husband— new husband at the time. Leena had loved the glamour of New York and had learned the ropes quickly, she'd thought. She knew how to dress to go to certain restaurants, what drinks to order, what magazines to read, which celebrities to pay attention to, what brand names to trust. In New York her new American life had a wonderful gloss to it. She felt sophisticated, as if her beauty was an undeniable tool. People regarded her with fascination when she told them where she was from. Salesgirls—themselves as glamorous as the fashion models in magazines—would cater to Leena when she walked into certain upscale boutiques. But then, after the baby was born, her husband had decided they should move back to Texas, where he was from.

Leena did not feel the same in Texas as she had in New York. The salesladies were plainer looking here and regarded her with dull coolness when she came into a store pushing her stroller. The wives of her husband's Texas colleagues lived by rules of etiquette Leena couldn't yet grasp. She felt their eyes on her back, saw the insincerity in their smiles. They were well-groomed women who were not naturally pretty; they had to work at their beauty and thus wished to discount any woman who didn't have to do the same. Leena recognized that from experience—there were women like them everywhere—as being their chief motivation for disliking her. She would never say it out loud, though, of course. But she found herself more comfortable around Americans like Josie, who was slightly younger than these women, a little on the bohemian side, and confidently pretty in her own right. Josie was mixed (some Hawaiian, some Irish, along with her Vietnamese) and originally from Los Angeles: that also helped to explain why she was not like the Texas wives. Josie cared more about politics and other subjects, like movies and books, than she did shopping or clothes. She dressed rather sloppily, actually, in Leena's opinion.

For this reason, Leena also never worried about Trevor's attention straying too far if she brought Josie around to their home.

It *was* something one had to think about, as a woman, in regard to men. Leena believed in that, simply and without much angst about it. To her it was just a fact. Trevor was a man, after all, and it was an issue every woman should be aware of in regard to her man, even if she was the kind of woman who said she didn't care, she didn't worry, and even if she felt she could claim her man was not like other men. All men, Leena believed, *were* like other men, at least in this one way, when you really got down to it. And, in her experience, it was knowledge a woman shouldn't lose her awareness of, not if she wanted to stay safe.

———

Leena didn't like being alone in the big house, so Josie had promised to come back with her that night. Joel and the boy in the Pimpercrombie and Bitch shirt came too.

Leena didn't like her house much at all. It was too large and old and somber for her tastes, and the land around it far too quiet. The house had been built in 1901; Trevor had told her that was noteworthy, but for Leena it just emphasized that the house was old. She had always lived in cities and coveted new things, modern things. The idea of country living having a kind of charm to it mystified her, although by now she'd seen enough depictions of this idea in American movies and on TV to understand that it did have value to some people. It had value to Josie, for instance, who often said about the old house, "Leena, you're lucky. It's beautiful out here." Still, Leena couldn't shake the feeling of it being less of a life than she'd bargained for (had spent years conjuring, in fact) upon marrying a man who would bring her to the States.

New York had met with her expectations, she would say.

Josie and Joel stumbled around the kitchen, laughing, as they got out tumblers and mixed drinks for themselves. The other boy (whose name, Leena had learned by this time, was Kasey) went out to the porch and stood looking at the front yard for some time. Leena walked down the hall to her bedroom.

The house rested on several acres of land, the most accessible amount of that land being the front yard, a large rectangle of semi-rocky, sparsely grassy ground with no trees and no shrubs. A long, straight gravel driveway led directly up to the front of the house; two smaller country roads connected their driveway to the highway. To one side of their lot was what looked to Leena like a forest: thick-trunked cypress elms with sagging canopies of branches and foliage only at the very tops of their trunks, all leaning together in a staggered array. A creek wound beneath those trees. She knew that only because Trevor had taken her on walks over there and had shown it to her. After rainstorms the creek swelled far beyond its own banks and you could hear the sound of its waters running; in the summer the creek shrank down to mere puddles.

On the other side of their lot was a fenced-in field that held a couple horses and grubby-looking sheep and another house, much smaller than theirs, with walls that looked as if they'd been made out of old stones cemented sloppily together. This house was shaded by a smattering of clumpy oaks and a partial fence with ivy vines growing over it. At night Leena saw the lit windows of the house, so she knew people lived in it. There were also two rusted trailers on the property. Several older-looking cars were always parked to the side and in front of the stone house. Leena had the idea that the people who lived there (she had only ever seen them from a distance or passing by in one of their old cars) must be like everything else on the property—old, unkempt, somewhat grizzly. Sometimes Leena heard voices carrying across the field—men's voices, hooting, laughter, a woman's laughter; sometimes music too; sometimes occasional popping or thunking sounds, like something being thrown against a barn wall. Once, at dusk, she saw fireworks exploding in the sky above the neighboring house, and it was nowhere near the Fourth of July.

There had been an offer recently from a development company for the land on which Trevor and Leena's house stood. Within the past year, just down the road, a new neighborhood had sprouted. The houses were small, almost artificial-looking in their newness, set on immaculate little lawns, with a community park at the center. Leena had thought the development looked charming but quickly learned better than to say so, for her husband had been one of the people signing petitions and going to meetings to protest the developers moving in. Davis could have cared less and would have liked for Trevor to sell, for the money, of course. But Trevor was stubborn. He liked old things. One could say he made his living from the rescuing—the revaluing—of old things. He, along with two partners, ran a business that involved the searching for and reselling (at exorbitant prices) of old furniture and novelty items from remote corners of Asia.

The house had been in Trevor's family for some time, though no one had lived in it since Trevor and Davis's grandparents. Trevor and Davis used to visit the house when they were boys, on holidays and in the summers, and Trevor had always been fonder of the house than Davis was. Years ago, when he was still single, Trevor had begun fixing it up, bringing in his designer and architect friends, filling it with the artifacts of his travels. On the walls he mounted elephant tusks, masks from South America, and Buddhist-themed artwork he had bought in India and Nepal. He was a collector of baskets and blankets and pottery made by indigenous women in Third World countries—the designs and colors from Vietnam being among his favorites, he would claim. All this he had mixed with Eames chairs and coffee tables, Frank Lloyd Wright design–influenced window seats, and a well-stocked bar. He had had the kitchen renovated with retro-modern appliances. He had had the original pine floors refurbished until they shone like honey-blond wood. Entering the house for the first time, Leena felt oddly unnerved. It was then it dawned on her that all the places she had thus far lived with Trevor, in Vietnam and New York—places she had considered ports of arrival for herself—had been for him nothing more than way stations. He had always been meaning to come back here, to the house in Texas. She realized then that she did not truly know him.

And maybe, too (she sometimes thought), he had always intended to bring someone back here with him. He had never lived in the house with his first wife, who'd had her own career as a TV producer in California, where that marriage had both begun and ended.

Leena lay on the bed in her bedroom. It was a metal-framed canopy bed, imported from India, and it was positioned diagonally out from one corner of the room. Draped over the frame of its canopy were some long strips of sheer fabric she and Trevor had brought from Vietnam. These details were mostly Trevor's doing; he cared about such things—about what the view out the windows would be from their bed, about the room's color scheme being cool and dusky and earthy. The concrete floors were stained a slightly glossy umber. A wall of windows looked out over the backyard, which was not a yard so much as it was the underside of a cliff. A natural wall of limestone rose up very close behind their house, with plant growth and roots nosing through cracks in the rock, and the feeling created was of the house seeming to be braced against this backdrop: the mountain might collapse were it not for their house, marking the line between rock and grass. Everything back here was very gray-brown and sometimes made Leena feel as if she were in a cave. Sometimes she liked this feeling; sometimes it unsettled her, and she tended to spend more time at the front of the house.

Leena did not really understand the attraction to big houses that many Americans seemed to have. A clean, new city apartment with a good view seemed far more glamorous and adequate to her. But, especially in Texas, size seemed to mean something—it confirmed a sense of entitlement, of belonging. Big houses, big cars. Upon first arriving in Texas, Trevor had traded in their BMW convertible for a Toyota Land Cruiser, and he then required Leena to learn how to drive a stick shift. After that point she began noticing these big, boxy vehicles with women driving and children in car-seats gazing benignly out the back windows. Leena felt like an impostor, but of what she wasn't even sure. From where they lived, she had to drive at least twenty minutes to get into the city proper or even to the nearest shopping center.

On some days she dreaded leaving the house, having to brave the highways. Many days she went no farther than the front porch and sat there on the swing while Pearl played on the steps. They never ventured far into the front yard, especially if it was just the two of them at home, which it was more often than not. Leena might walk across the grass to the side of the house to turn on the water spigot and fill Pearl's kiddie pool with water, placing it close to the bottom of the steps, but she never walked out as far as the wooden playhouse and sandbox that stood (and had ever since Trevor and Davis's childhood) in the blazing, treeless middle of the yard. It was a place only the wildest and loneliest of children would ever want to play, thought Leena. She did not, in fact, like it at all when Pearl wanted to play outside. The sun baked down mercilessly, especially in the summer months, and the vastness and stillness of the surrounding land felt ominous and depressing to Leena. These feelings honestly scared her; she had never felt anything like them before.

Trevor would claim this was not actually the countryside, that they were still, in fact, within Austin city limits. Go shopping, make friends, take walks in the evening, were his first suggestions, before the medication. *I will not take a walk*, Leena had said, and that was as close to impertinent as she could ever get with him.

So, as much as she could, she kept her daughter inside the house, where her clothes stayed clean and where she, Leena, could busy herself with her own activities while her daughter played with her toys or watched videos. When Trevor was out of town and Pearl woke in the middle of the night, sometimes Leena would let her watch cartoons until four in the morning, just to calm her down. Leena made sure, however, to put the videos away, back up on the high shelf in Pearl's closet, before Trevor returned.

Tonight the moon was almost full. Leena could see it coming into view, rising beyond the rock bank behind the house, which meant, too, that the hour was late. She did not usually see the moon from her bedroom window unless she awoke in the middle of the night. Leena sighed, staring at the canopy poles above her. She was glad, at that moment, for the sounds of Josie and Joel's muffled conversation and their intermittent laughter, their uneven footsteps on the stairs. They were heading up to the guest bedroom. At least somebody was making use of the extra beds in this house, thought Leena, and she found herself easily imagining what Josie must be feeling just then. Sex, in Leena's experience, had always had an element of foreboding to it, especially when it was with someone new. The imminence of it, even when it didn't involve her, she could feel like a current in the air. Some aspects of it were almost always the same, she remembered. The way each occurrence offered up a new sense of possibility, even if just slightly, and how the feeling afterward would always be one of either uplift or letdown. She had always tended to feel one way or the other, even when the act had seemed routine. These things seemed far from her now, though. All those nights of men coming to her rescue or she to theirs, or so it had often seemed, and the washed-out mornings of feeble hysteria or heightened inexplicable emotion that followed some encounters—well, it all had to be over for her now; she understood that much. And something else had replaced it, something that took longer to get through and that Leena couldn't yet fathom the pattern of.

"You're quiet in here." Joel's friend, Kasey, was leaning in the doorway with his arms folded across his chest.

Leena startled, rising to her elbows. Seeing who it was, she laughed. "Oh, you," she said, "I forgot you were still here."

He glanced around the room in a resigned, remotely curious manner. The room was lit only by an indirect glow coming through the windows; the moon had risen beyond the window frame now. "So you have a daughter," he said. "Where is she tonight again?"

"Her grandparents in Dallas. It's not too far." Leena made her tone bright and appropriate. She sat up at the edge of the bed with her legs crossed.

"And your husband—he goes away on business a lot, is what Josie said." It was not completely a question or a statement. He was hovering in the doorway with his shoulders hunched upward, his neck sticking forward. He looked like a little boy, thought Leena. She recalled her impression of him at the party during the balcony conversation: a hesitant but opinionated boy-man, sincerely indignant at the injustices of the world.

She replied, "Yes," with a polite smile.

Again his eyes swept briefly over the room. "Looks like y'all are doing all right, I'd guess."

Leena never knew how to handle comments of this sort from Americans. She shrugged, still smiling. She said, "Are you from here, from Texas?"

"Born and raised right here in Austin." He lifted his eyebrows briefly, and Leena didn't know how to read that. The facial expressions of American boys—it was as if they were leaving out key pieces of information. Kasey unfolded his arms and stuck his hands in his pockets, shifting his body against the door frame. As he looked at her, an expression crossed his face: it was both dismissive and wanting, she realized. And it made her aware that she had not, in some time, interacted one-on-one with a man who was not her husband—not since April, in fact. Perhaps the strangeness of that radiated off of her, for suddenly he straightened up as if to leave. "But I should probably let you sleep," he said. "I'm just standing here bugging you and it's late."

Leena shook her head quickly. "No, no, not at all. You're not bugging me. I'm not tired." Impulsively, she patted the spot next to herself on the bed. She would invite him in, she thought; it was nothing. Just a holiday sense of liberty—or loneliness—in the air, and she should not shut it out. "Come, sit; we'll drink some wine. I'll get it from the kitchen. We can talk. I will like the company," she offered. "I'm not used to being so alone, you know. With my daughter away, I mean."

His eyebrows moved. "Okay." He said this rather remotely and benignly, as he started across the dark shining floor.

Leena got up from the bed as he approached it, and they crossed paths in the middle of the bedroom like strangers, she ducking her head and smiling as he met her eyes blankly, enigmatically. Leena continued down the hall to the kitchen. She found two green-tinted Mexican glass tumblers and an already open bottle of wine that she'd known would be there. She came back to the bedroom, smiling. She climbed onto the bed and sat cross-legged on the comforter. Her hair fell forward around her shoulders with this movement—she was aware of it, and of him noticing it, as she handed him a tumbler. He was sitting on the edge with his feet on the floor. He twisted his torso slightly to face her as she uncorked the wine.

"So tell me what you do for a living," she said. It was a question she had asked hundreds of times.

He rolled his eyes, turning his profile to her for a second. "I work at Dell," he said, somewhat sheepishly. "I work with Joel—you know, Josie's friend."

"But it's a good company, no?" said Leena, not understanding his chagrin.

He shrugged. "It's a job, not the rest of my life, hopefully."

"And how old are you?"

"Twenty-seven," he said, and his gaze dropped.

"I am one year older than you," declared Leena, energetically, because she thought it might make him feel more comfortable, though the truth was she was three years older than he was.

She poured wine into his tumbler and then into hers. At the back of his head a dull crest of moonlight appeared, shining in through the large window behind him, framing him. She saw the tips of his dark hair—cut close to his scalp— glowing pale blue, almost like frost. She kept smiling at him.

"So," he said, his brow wrinkling slightly, "how did you meet your husband? I mean, to end up in Texas, of all places."

"Texas is my husband's home state," replied Leena carefully. "Meanwhile, I was working in a hotel in Ho Chi Minh City," as she reached to place the wine bottle on the bedside table, "and my husband was working for some foreign companies throughout Asia, like he still do now. First time he came to Ho Chi Minh City, he came into the hotel where I worked and we talked at the bar that night. He was very polite and nice-looking, I thought so. He said he is going to Hong Kong, but he be back. Many men who travel and stay at our hotel, they say to the girls they will come back and then they don't. It is not surprise after a while. But my husband he came back, a couple weeks later. So that is how it began." She added, "But I am not what you think, what many traveling men think when first they come into that hotel, I know. We are just girls to dance with and talk to."

That was not the clear-cut truth about her experiences working in hotels and nightclubs, but she had long been in the habit of presenting herself as innocent. She had figured out, years ago, even before she'd met Trevor, that it was what most people preferred and were willing to believe (whether they were propositioning her or just trying to befriend her) when she first met them. Leena went on, rather lightly and proudly, "Then, after about four months, he ask me to marry him and I say yes. Not the first time I am asked, but the first time I say yes, that's with my husband."

"Oh," said Kasey, and he looked a little bit shocked. By what, she wondered, but she couldn't tell for sure. She thought, he is just a nice boy. Like a reflex, her hand reached out and placed itself on his leg.

But then she removed it. In her mind she counted the months since March: nine.

———

Trevor was not the first foreign boyfriend Leena had had, and she initially treated him as she had all the others, with equal parts remove and submission and occasional fits of passion. She had been doing this act for so long, in fact, that she believed in it each time just as wholeheartedly as she re-

lied on its passing and on her resilience: she would always be
ready to fall anew.

What she did back then was not an official form of pros-
titution, more like seduction, or role-playing, as she thought
of it. She showed interest, she feigned ignorance; she received
gifts and special allowances; in short, she got to enjoy herself. For a period of time, she had ensured her exemption
from government harassment by sleeping with certain policemen and municipal leaders under the pretext that she was
to find out things about them for certain other men in lead-
ership positions—some of whom she also slept with. Then
there were the businessmen from Korea and Japan, and then
came the travelers from Europe and eventually the States. She
counted on the transience and loneliness of these men and
found the ones from the West especially receptive to her and
often quite kind in a way that was new to her. She met her
first Western foreigner in 1990; Trevor came along in 1995.
By that time she had changed her name and had mastered
just the right combination of Orient (she had gleaned this
to be a romantic but inaccurate, and somewhat generalized,
vision of Asian cultures) and sophistication. The name Leena
she had taken from one of her earlier Western boyfriends, a
Swede, who had told her she looked like a Vietnamese Pau-
lina Porizkova. That was in 1991, before she had ever seen
a fashion magazine from the West. He was the one who had
left her a British *Vogue*, and she had found it—for many
months—to be very instructive.

The truth was Leena loved men. She always felt sympathy
for them. She saw their lust and even their violence in a vulnerable light, for she had seen how they would forsake much
in the pursuit of a little bit of pleasure; how even the stron-

gest could be swayed by characteristics that to her were just
a given: an appearance of softness, simple prettiness, the willingness to surrender. Men liked to be surrendered to. That
was, she believed, another unignorable fact of nature. This
need (she could spot it in most men who had it) could prompt
them to give her things and to give things up to her. And no
matter what they did in the rest of their lives, no matter what
significant positions they held in the outside world, no matter what they claimed, she went away with the knowledge
that she had known them in their starkness, in the beauty or
ugliness or pitifulness of their surrender to a moment totally
sensual and senseless. *Her* surrender was not a big deal: she
did it every day, and never, truly, lost anything by it. She did
not think about all this explicitly but felt it, in a way, to be a
justification of her particular talents in the world. But she was
sincere, too, and she made a point of treating all she received
and witnessed with care. She had an emotional conscience. It
required her to be present for whomever she was with.

    After she and Trevor met, she traveled several times with
him to other parts of Vietnam, and every now and then they
would pick up other travelers, inviting them back to their
hotel. Always, before getting married, they took separate
rooms at hotels, with Leena claiming to be his interpreter
or travel guide. They picked up men and women, usually
foreigners, young adventure-seeking types. The first time
it occurred, Leena had not been fully aware of what was
happening. They had been talking with a young Chinese-
American woman at a café, and Trevor was showing her a
lot of interest, but not in any manner that seemed licentious
to Leena. He was insisting she come see the view from the
rooftop of their hotel (a hotel in Hue, overlooking the Per-

fume River), and Leena had thought nothing of it, because it seemed to her that Trevor was kind and polite to everyone, had in him this streak of helpfulness and genuine concern— not about rescuing people from tragedy so much as wishing to ensure they have a good time. Like a bartender, Leena thought. They walked back to their hotel, the three of them, and it was only by the way the hotel clerks glared at them across the lobby that Leena became aware of there being another kind of energy in the air. She saw then what they saw: two Asian women going up the stairs with one well-dressed, slightly older American man—the type of man who could afford to pay for two rooms. That was new to her.

Trevor monitored pleasure like someone dealing cards, as if there was an unspoken etiquette to it that he wanted to be sure to respect. He was clearly the one in charge but was not forceful, not overexcited or even passionate; he asked if certain actions would be okay before he performed them. Leena relinquished herself to him totally, as if it were a competition between her and the other woman as to who could abandon herself more completely. She felt it to be a dark and tender act, whereas with other men tenderness was not something she had associated with submission. At moments Trevor sat back and just watched, everything in him seeming to be already sated. She understood then that he understood the nature of his own lust and inherent power, as a man and as a man with money, looks, and poise, and from this knowledge he had derived an attitude of seeming benevolence, of luxury even: he was confident that whatever he desired he could acquire.

Another time, on a boat in Ha Long Bay, with a group of other foreign businessmen and a few hired girls like herself, after much drinking and imbibing of other substances, Leena found herself at one point in a narrow passageway in the boat's hold, being fondled and pressed upon by two men. Trevor came down the ladder and looked at them. He said, "Not you," to one, and, with some prying, got him away from Leena. To the other one he said, as the man's hands went groping up her legs, "You let her touch you first." Leena felt strangely endeared to him at moments like these—for his being older than her, for his peculiar way of caring: how he would send her out into the thick of things yet still keep a firm hold on her, still give direction. She felt he protected her. And that loving him meant she must follow, looking only at the trail he made for them as they went, and not at anything else.

They married in Vietnam and then had to wait a year for Leena's paperwork to be processed. Trevor traveled frequently between Southeast Asia and the States during that time, and that impressed everyone Leena knew—family and friends. A man who could move so freely about the world was surely a prize. Leena believed it, too.

———

Leena did not meet Trevor's mother until nearly three years into the marriage, upon her and Trevor's announcement of their pregnancy. It was Leena's first visit to Dallas. When they arrived, Trevor's mother immediately offered to take Leena shopping.

She took her to an upscale boutique in Dallas and looked on encouragingly as Leena selected the simplest-looking gaudy top she could find, which still cost a hundred and fifty dollars. This seemed like a lot to Leena, even after her time in New York, and she didn't really like the top that much, but had felt obliged to choose something because she was afraid Trevor's mother might be offended if she didn't. At the cash register, however, Trevor's mother did not take out her wallet, as Leena had thought she was going to do. She stood by smiling instead, and Leena ended up having to apologize and say to the clerk that she didn't want the shirt after all. Trevor's mother's smile was the insipid but impenetrable smile of a well-mannered woman thinking thoughts she cannot verbalize—very much like what Leena was soon to encounter from the wives of Trevor's colleagues. It made Leena feel ashamed. After this shop they went to a department store in the mall, where suddenly Trevor's mother became less grim, more buoyant and flippant. She would look at a price tag and wave her wrist at it, saying, "It's a steal. Put it in the cart. Don't worry about it," as if it were a pleasure they were sharing. Leena thought things between them were on a better footing, until Trevor's mother ran into a woman she knew. The two women chatted, and Trevor's mother never introduced Leena, who waited behind her (Leena was well aware of this) looking little, dark, inexplicable, and pregnant.

In the midst of Trevor's divorce from his first wife, Trevor's father had died of a heart attack. That was about a year before Leena had met Trevor, who had decided after those bruising events that he needed to travel for a while. Trevor was his mother's favorite, she told Leena herself. His brother, Davis, was not so thoughtful a boy. *You know what I mean by thoughtful, don't you?* she said, looking at Leena piquedly. Leena did not know and just smiled politely and said again how wonderful she thought Trevor was. His mother patted Leena's knee with her cool, papery hand. *Good*, she said, *well of course he is*.

Trevor's mother had a big, prototypically Texan boyfriend whom Leena could not help being awed by at first. He was a businessman in cowboy boots and a white suit, with a large, solid belly and that manner of obvious entitlement that white men his size often seemed to possess. His attitude toward Leena was not much better than Trevor's mother's, though his veneer was one of inquisitiveness. He asked her questions, but as he listened to her replies his eyes took on a glassy quality. Beneath his jovial nodding and smiling was something hard and flat and mean, it occurred to Leena. She couldn't trust these people, could not even begin to comprehend them. The men were heavy and false, the women dangerously well-mannered and well-adorned. The women turned their men into bulwarks and raised their boys to be go-getters; they used the popular myth of their own softness and incapability to cultivate both lust and guilt in men, so that they would never be left high and dry. Leena was not blameless of such devices herself. Still, she disliked these tactics as she saw them put into play by Trevor's mother. Her own actions, in the case of Trevor at least, had always been heartfelt; her need always real, she thought.

Later, alone with Trevor, after that first shopping excursion, Leena was careful not to express her discomfort with his mother too vehemently. Instead, she stuck to expressing her bewilderment. "Did I misunderstand? I didn't even like the clothes in that store."

Trevor said, "She changed her mind at the last minute, she does that sometimes. She used to do it to my brother and me when we were kids. It just means she thought you wouldn't notice." This was a rare moment of plain honest analysis from him; he was usually close-mouthed about his family.

"She thinks I am a child?"

"It has more to do with what she thinks of me, really," said Trevor. He looked at Leena. "She was always hoping I wouldn't marry again and now it's even worse for her that it's you I married. You shouldn't take it to heart, though. She just doesn't understand you yet." He worked his mouth into a smile. "But I know she thinks you're beautiful, she said so."

———————

The boys left sometime in the night (more like early morning, right before dawn), and Josie and Leena stayed up, drinking coffee as the sun rose and filled the large windows of the house with orange. They sat in Leena's kitchen, on barstools pulled up to the center island.

They did not speak at all about the boys.

Josie had found a utensil in one of the kitchen drawers, and neither of them knew what it was for. Josie was making Leena laugh, as she banged the metal implement around.

"I think it's a spoon for eggs. Can this really be just a spoon for eggs?" Finally, she put it down. "Do you ever use this? Does Trevor ever use it?"

"I haven't seen him use it, no."

Josie said, as if to the room in general, "God, people have weird stuff. But I love your house. This house is amazing."

Leena poured them more coffee.

After a lull of silence: "Do you ever think maybe Trevor cheats on you, like when he's out of the country for a long time?" Josie turned to Leena and looked at her with a cool, almost calculating, honesty.

Leena met Josie's gaze simply and said, "Yes." Had it been normal daylight and had they not been up all night already, her reply, she knew, might've been more properly appalled, more demure.

After Josie had gone, Leena fell asleep on the couch. She was awakened sometime before noon by the phone ringing. She sat up in a flood of worry—that she had left Pearl unattended and then, remembering that Pearl wasn't there, that the phone call might be to tell her something had happened. But it was Patrice, Trevor's ex-wife. Leena sat at the edge of the couch, blinking, as she pressed the receiver to her ear. The light in the house was bright and ordinary now.

In the first couple of years with Trevor, when most of their time was spent in Vietnam, Leena had not given much thought to the ex-wife Trevor had told her he had or to whatever life he'd quit and left behind in America. Now, however, she was seeing the other side of things: the way it must've been for Patrice. She was seeing what had become, finally, unacceptable.

Some men would always need to be absent from somewhere. And, it seemed apparent, Leena was a part of Trevor's somewhere now, more than his somewhere else.

In a way she understood it. And she was willing to let him have it—that out-in-the-cold feeling, that devotion to courting peril. She was willing to let Trevor have it because she had been out there herself already and she knew well enough what it was like. Patrice, Leena suspected, had never known this kind of living. She had always been secure and determined. She was older than Trevor and had her own career; she was one of those women who prided herself on being strong. Women like that believed in sharing every-thing, thought Leena. They were hard to please.

Leena ran her hand through her hair, pulling it clear of her receiver ear, as she listened to Patrice. "I didn't know Trevor was out of the country *again*. You poor thing! But I know how it is, Lord do I know." Not more than a year ago, if Leena was the one who answered the phone, Patrice would hang up. Now at least she was civil and, if Trevor was away, would try to commiserate with Leena.

Leena didn't want to be friends with Patrice, though. No matter how hard she tried to feel all right about her, she never did. "I am not poor, I don't think. I understand he must work, and this is usually his busiest time of year."

"Oh, I'm sure you *do* understand. By now you've lived with him nearly as long as I did," said Patrice. "But, look, the real reason I called is to tell him some sad news. Larry died. It was a heart attack. I mean, I guess we all knew it was coming sooner rather than later. After all, he was at least eighty, in dog years." Larry was one of the dogs that stayed with Patrice after the divorce. They had had two large dogs, part Great Dane, brother and sister. Larry and Elise. Trevor and Patrice also had a son, Dominic, now eleven, who lived in California with Patrice. Dominic generally saw Trevor two or three times a year. "But Dominic is just devastated, of course."

Devastated, thought Leena. It was never quite as literal for Americans, she had come to understand, as her idea of it was. For most Americans, devastation occurred intangibly and was usually emotional and petty, rather than physical or large.

"Dominic is on vacation now, I mean for Christmas?" asked Leena. She had a slight headache. The wine, she reminded herself. Her memories of the night before had a bluish cast, like that of the blue Christmas lights on the balcony at the party they had gone to. She got up slowly and wandered toward the kitchen to get a glass of water, the cordless phone pressed to her ear.

"He's home for Christmas, yes. Our tree's theme this year is 'How would a pirate have decorated his tree?' and Dominic has been very imaginative about it. We're having fun. Except for this whole thing with Larry, of course. I woke up in the middle of the night yesterday and found him, just lying in the middle of the living room floor, gone already."

"How sad," said Leena. "If Trevor was here I'm sure he be very sorry to hear this news too." Glancing out the kitchen window as she picked a glass up from the drain board, Leena noticed someone coming down the driveway. It looked like a woman. For a few moments, with Patrice still talking in her ear, Leena watched this woman coming toward the house. "I have to go now, Patrice," she said finally. "I think someone is at the door."

"You tell Trevor," were Patrice's parting words.

"I'll tell Trevor," said Leena, and then hung up the phone.

———

The woman outside was not approaching in a straight line, Leena saw. She seemed to be looking, drifting from side to side as she walked, and her mouth was opening and closing: she was calling out something. To whom, it was not clear.

Leena crossed the kitchen floor and pushed open the nearest window. She heard, "Neigh-bor . . ." The woman was calling this out in singsong, stretching the word into two long syllables, "Neigh-bor . . ." Leena was not certain she was hearing this right. The woman was on their lawn now and seemed to be headed around the side of the house, was not coming to the front door after all. Quickly, Leena walked to the side door just off the kitchen. She opened it and stepped out onto the porch.

"Yes? I'm here?" she said, uncertainly but loudly enough to catch the woman's attention.

The woman looked to be in her forties and had about her a quality that was both youthful and haggard. Her hair was brown with playful streaks of platinum-gray, cut in a shaggy, energetic fashion. The woman's skin was very white, her face lined and angular, her eyes large. She showed her teeth when she looked at Leena, and it took Leena a moment to realize it was a smile. It was as if she were trying, though not very hard, to disguise a constant quiet state of laughter.

Now the woman took one startled step backward and doubled over slightly, bringing her hands to her mouth. She looked around, as if expecting there to be someone to laugh with her. "Oh—" she said, "Neighbor, it's, it's my dog. My dog's *name*. I'm looking for my dog. His name is Neighbor. And you thought—" Here, she bent over again, dissolving into soundless laughter. "I'm sorry," she said.

Leena, standing on the porch, folded her arms loosely, hands cupping her elbows. She didn't know what to make of this woman's laughter. The woman, from where she stood on the lawn below, had to look up in order to look at Leena, and it made Leena feel inappropriately and awk-

wardly elevated. She stared back at the woman and found
herself noticing the woman's sweater. It was bright white
and made of a soft, silky, woolen fabric with one red rose
embroidered down the left side. The white of the sweater
made it seem to glow, and that made the red of the rose
all the more red. The way the woman wore her clothes
made Leena think she must've been quite attractive in her
younger years.

"Are you from next door?" Leena asked finally.

"Am I from next door," said the woman, slowly. Her
tone seemed to suggest that Leena thought next door was
another country. "I am from next door, but I don't live in
the house. I don't have anything to do with the house. That's
all Pennyroyal and Terry's business, not mine. I live in the
trailer behind the house. Neighbor and I do." She put her
hand out to indicate the dog's height. "Has he been by here?
Big white dog? You wouldn't have missed him if he was."

Leena mutely shook her head no. For a moment, in her
mind, she found herself confusing this woman's dog with the
news of Patrice's dog, Larry, that she had just heard over the
phone. She had a flash of worry that this woman's dog was
dead, too.

The woman smiled suddenly. "Don't you have a little
girl? I think I've seen you out here with her before."

"Yes," said Leena, and felt an abrupt pang of missing
Pearl, and guilt, and the uncanny sense that this woman was
somehow aware of it all. "But she's visiting with her grandmother in Dallas right now."

The woman shifted her weight from one hip to the other
and struck a semi-seductive pose, raising her arms and lifting
her hair away from the back of her neck. She nodded know-

ingly, with her arms still up. When she moved, the furry tips of her sweater's woolly fabric seem to move too, almost as if its fibers still contained some of the life of the animal from whose body they'd been taken: she had this quality of something wild about her. "Oh, I see. Vacation time for Mom, too, huh?" Here, the woman grinned—a grin that scrunched up the skin on the bridge of her nose—and looked Leena right in the eye. Her expression struck Leena as being similar to what she sometimes saw pass between the wives of her husband's colleagues, only it was being directed at Leena now. "We saw those extra cars in your driveway last night," said the woman, sweetly, her grin unfaltering. "Not that we're keeping tabs on you or anything. Me and Pennyroyal are generally outside at night at some point or other; we like to stand out in the field and smoke, y'know?" Here she paused, as if what she'd said was actually meant to be a question. "So we couldn't help but notice last night when three cars drove up your driveway and you and your friends all got out. We were almost tempted to come over and crash the party, actually. Being neighbors and all, I guess we see you come and go quite often." She let her hands fall to her sides. "I guess you probably hear plenty of us, too. The way sound carries around here and all."

To all this, Leena could only offer her most honest reply. "I don't so much like to stay alone in the house when my husband and daughter are both away. It's so large, you know."

"I know exactly what you mean about large houses," said the woman. "I'm not a fan of them myself. Seems like so many people in this country take up so much more space than they really need to, you know? Me, what would I do with a big house? I always say that when people ask don't

I want a regular house of my own. I don't need any more space than my little trailer." Then she added, "But your friends are all gone now," lightly, cheerfully.

Leena shrugged. "They are more friends of Josie, who is my friend. She comes to stay with me sometime when my husband is away."

A slight silence followed, with the woman continuing to gaze and smile at Leena in her particular manner. Leena felt obliged to match the woman's solicitude. She thought it might be rude of her not to. She said, "I like your sweater. That rose is very pretty."

"Oh, *thank* you." The woman looked surprised. "Pennyroyal found it for me. In his grandmother's attic after she passed away last year. He thought it would suit me, he said." It was true that the white of the sweater set off the white streaks in the woman's hair.

"Who is Pennyroyal?" asked Leena.

"Oh," said the woman, and her "oh" was loaded with layered meaning and feeling, "just one of the people who lives in Terry's house. He's a sweetheart. We call him Pennyroyal 'cause that's his mother's maiden name. His real name is Jason. We won't talk about Jason's father, though." The woman rolled her eyes, her smile deepening again. "We all know everything about each other over there. I guess you could call it kind of a commune we've got going." Leena's incomprehension must've been apparent. "Don't you know what a commune is?"

Leena shook her head no.

"Well, it's where a group of people share a living situation even if they're not all related family members. Like us all there—it's Terry's house and Terry's property—Terry and I are just old, old friends. And the boys are friends of friends or friends' sons, that sort of thing. It's a good place over there, lots of years of friendship between us all, y'know? Sometimes people come to Terry's place because they have nowhere else to turn. That's how come I came there initially, and I've stayed for, five, six years now? And there's one more trailer besides mine on the property right now, where Clara and Renny live." She had stopped smiling, though the amused light in her eyes remained. She went on, "People think it's just a throwback thing from the sixties, but the truth is the concept of the commune goes all the way back to Europe in the Middle Ages. Not to mention here on this very land with the Native Americans and their concept of tribal living. I mean, living in small communities has been done for ages. It's the nuclear family that's the new, strange development now, *I* think. But I'm not so much the historian as those boys are." Each time she uttered the word "boys," Leena noticed, it came out floated on an extra pop of air, and hung in the space between them longer than any of her other words did.

"Terry and I call Calvin 'The Student,' in fact. Calvin is Pennyroyal's best friend and he just returned from studying in Egypt." She smiled again. "You really should come over and meet everyone sometime."

Leena realized she still didn't know the woman's name. "My name is Leena, by the way," she said, pointing to herself.

"Oh, I'm so sorry, how rude of me! I'm Dalva. Which isn't the name I was born with, but it's the name I've given myself. It's my most rightful name," said the woman, firmly and pleasantly. "It's so nice to meet you, Leena. You really should stop by sometime. Bring your little girl. We're a nice bunch, really. And we love kids."

Leena returned the woman's smile. "Yes, I will," she
said, meaning it but not seeing a plausible way it was actually going to happen.

"Well, I really have lost my dog," said the woman. "I
bet he went down the street to those new houses maybe."
She crinkled her nose. "Those houses are so ugly. I can't believe it, can you?" She began taking steps backward across
the lawn. "But come by, okay? It was really nice talking to
you, honey." Then she turned and walked off back up the
driveway.

———

Leena hated more than anything how it felt when the house
filled with the particular silence of Pearl being gone. Like a
cloud it moved through rooms and snaked down hallways,
spiraled up to the high ceilings, drew invisible shades down
over the windows.

For the remainder of that day and into the next, she
worked to keep herself busy. She turned on the TV, made
food in the kitchen, did laundry, vacuumed and cleaned. It
felt like a pretend life, though, to do these routine household tasks, especially to pick up Pearl's toys and straighten
her room, when Pearl was not around. Leena sometimes
felt as if the quiet were attacking her. Medicated or not, she
could be struck by it. A panic would rise inside her, and her
mind would race with thoughts both worrisome and desir-
ous. Desiring anything, it made Leena realize, always led to
the worry that you wouldn't get it or that you would lose
it. Sometimes in the midst of these panics, she felt as if the
moment at hand was, in truth, everything, and that the rest
of her life as she thought she knew it (life with her child,

her husband, any state of domestic happiness or safety she
had ever dared to enjoy) were lost already. Meanwhile, everything on the outside stayed utterly ordinary. She did not
know why she should feel this way. She had to stop herself
from picking up the phone to call to check on Pearl: she had
learned from previous experience that Trevor's mother didn't
like Leena to call too often. She had also learned to wait for
Trevor's overseas calls to her.

Sometime in the midafternoon of her second day without
Pearl, Leena got up from the couch and made herself switch
off the television.

She went into the bedroom and lay on the bed, pulling
a magazine off the nightstand and opening it at random. *A
truly beautiful woman will look stunning in either all black
or all white*, said the caption under a full-page spread of an
exquisite-looking African woman in a flowing white gown.
Her skin was a gleaming chocolate brown hue, her large eyes
ringed soulfully with black eye makeup. She stood on the
marble-columned veranda of what looked like a villa beside
the ocean. The next picture was of the same model, at dusk,
on the same veranda, now in a sleek black gown. Leena decided she would go to the mall and look for a white dress
(she had plenty of black ones already), even though it was
still the middle of winter. Winters here were mild anyhow.

———

It was amazing how well it worked. Trying on new clothes
with expensive price tags, and the diffused, warm lighting of
those stores, their neutral, cool colors, those shining floors—
these settings always gave Leena a restored sense of self. She
felt womanly and refined; she felt like somebody with money

and a place in society. These were important, lucky things to be able to do and buy. Not everyone was as lucky as she was, she reminded herself.

She saw other women walking around the mall, too. In fact, it appeared to be mostly women, wandering alone from store to store. Leena wondered, how many of them had come here, like her, to escape quiet houses? How many had come looking for brightness or levity or some form of assurance? When she compared herself to these other women, Leena placed herself in a league with the ones she thought were the classiest-looking. They were the apparently attractive ones, the ones she thought looked like they belonged in shops like Ann Taylor and Banana Republic. They sifted through racks of dresses and sweaters and shirts with reserved, peaceful expressions on their faces that did not change even if they saw an item they liked. Leena understood that. Meanwhile, inside each woman's head visions were surely churning, were rapidly, constantly coalescing and dissolving, and they did not reveal excitement or hope over such things (the hope that a piece of clothing, once donned, might change you) because, too, most women were familiar with the fact that hope was fragile, also possibly foolish, and that visions often didn't match up with realities. But still, one had to hope.

———

When she returned from the mall in the evening, Davis's pickup truck was in the driveway. Davis himself was sitting on the porch steps.

"Trevor said he was afraid those developer guys might be trying to survey the land again. He wanted me to drop by and check on things," said Davis, standing as Leena got out of her car.

Things, thought Leena. She looked back at Davis carefully, not wanting to reply right away.

Davis and Trevor might've been the light and dark versions of the same person, respectively. Davis was blond, his hair shorn to his scalp; he always wore old clothes; and he had a restless look about him that contrasted with Trevor's dark-haired, stately demeanor. Davis, like Trevor, also traveled frequently for his work, though his jobs came on an expedition-by-expedition basis—he was an adventure travel guide who sometimes didn't work for months at a time.

Leena reached into the backseat of the Land Cruiser, and emerged again with a shopping bag from Banana Republic on her arm. She gave each car door a firm push shut. The doors made a blunt, reverberating sound in the still evening air. She walked across the driveway toward the porch steps.

"I haven't seen anyone," she said. She didn't believe Trevor had sent him, she realized. It had to have been their mother. Some luridly voiced skepticism at Leena being left alone and to her own devices.

But her being left alone was not, in Leena's mind, what had caused what had happened in March to happen. Leena felt a flash of disgust.

She would not blame Davis, though, she told herself.

He seemed aware of all this—she felt it from him more than saw it in anything he said or did. This was the other thing about Davis; he seemed able to read her, though she couldn't decide if the way he looked at her was sympathetic or dutiful or, even, hateful. "Yeah, I told Trevor he was probably just being paranoid. I don't think they're going to be around all that much, seeing as how it's the holidays and all," said Davis. He had one hand in his pocket. He knocked the other fist gently, distractedly, against his leg.

Leena had reached the bottom of the porch, where she paused on the step below where Davis was standing.

He nodded at her bag. "What'd you get?"

"Just a dress."

There was a pause as Davis glanced aside then back at her, more firmly now. "You hanging in here all right without the baby to keep you company and all?" The way he asked this made something inside Leena quickly narrow itself, like a camera's aperture being closed down to let in less light. It was as if he expected her not to be doing all right, as if in his mind it was a simple fact of nature: women were not, and should not be, okay away from their children.

"Doing all right," said Leena, with a shrug. She and Davis were looking at each other, she realized. To break the strain of this, she smiled abruptly, then rolled her eyes, declaring, "Boy, I'm tired. All the traffic, the mall was so packed. I better go inside now." She was not, she had already decided, going to invite him in.

Davis shifted his feet about in their scuffed work boots, and then he hopped lightly off the porch steps to the gravel, easily clearing the step where Leena stood. She twisted slightly to follow the motion of his body, his clothes, brushing by her. He nodded over his shoulder at Leena. "Well, nice seeing you, Leena. Merry Christmas. Be careful," he said, as he turned away.

Be careful and *Be good*—Leena had noticed these were phrases Texan men used when telling a woman goodbye. Trevor had been away from Texas long enough to not have

such phrases in his vocabulary anymore, so it had surprised
Leena when she first encountered men who used them. The
closest Trevor ever got was *Take care*—which to her always
sounded as if the person was genuinely concerned about
your ability to take care of yourself, yet could still be lenient.
Be careful, meanwhile, left you no room for slipups.

————

When Trevor was gone last March and April, it was Josie
to whom Leena had turned. Josie helped her find where to
go, though it was Davis she had to ask for the money. She
had done this because initially, after much consideration, she
had planned to keep it all secret from Trevor, which meant it
also had to be kept from the other person involved—as this
person knew Trevor (was one of his business friends, in fact)
and might have felt in some way the need to inform Trevor
of it himself. Leena and Josie talked at length about it and at
last decided that Davis was the best bet.

As it turned out, it all came apart anyhow. Leena was
far more emotional about the matter than she had thought
she would be, and when Trevor returned in May, he seemed
already to know there was some news she was waiting to
tell him. On his first night back, after Pearl had gone to
bed, they stayed up late, and Leena, sitting on their bed
and staring at her hands in her lap as he stood a few feet
from her in the bathroom doorway, had said, "I don't know
how to tell you this," and then told him everything. Who
it was, and that Davis had helped her, and how much it
had cost, and that Jerry—undeniably the name of a weak
man, Leena could not help but think this of him now—still
did not know but was still calling her despite her wishes to

the contrary, which she'd expressed to him. The whole incident could so easily have not happened, she told Trevor
this too. It had been only one night. (It had been normal,
at that time, for Trevor's colleagues to check in on Leena
on occasion when Trevor was gone and to invite her places,
too, sometimes with their wives or girlfriends, sometimes
not; Leena was younger than most of them, so it had seemed
watchful, obligatory, even.) Technically, if you wanted to
get detailed about it, her finding out three weeks later that
she was pregnant should *not* have happened—was a complete fluke, really.

Trevor stayed standing in the doorway, shoulder against
the door frame, the whole time she talked. Every few moments
he took his hands out of his pockets and pinched his fingers
together in front of him, slowly, methodically. But he did not
look away from her for a second.

"Leena," he said finally when she had finished, "Oh,
Leena, Leena."

And so they had gotten through it. Though it did not
stay a secret, in the end, from anybody. The truth about
Leena was out, was how it seemed. At one point, there was
even a meeting—Jerry came over to confront Trevor and
write him a check, which Trevor would give to Davis, and
Leena stood in the corner watching Jerry cry because he was
forty-six and had become suddenly confused about his life.
Trevor was amazing in his tolerance; she experienced the vision, then, of his being made of something like gold encased
in a thick layer of ice. No one, she realized, would ever be
able to take her from him, or him from her. They belonged
together; or she belonged to him. Leena met Jerry's gaze only
once during this meeting, and it was so pitiful that she made

a point not to look at him again. He was still crying in the kitchen when she left the room because Pearl was calling to her from upstairs.

———

The white dress was simple, the hem resting just above her knees, with no sleeves and no collar, a thin silver chain belt slung loosely around the waist. She wore it with no bra. The thin, soft fabric of the dress pressed against her small breasts, but still they shifted about, giving her a sensual feeling.

She had put the dress on after eating some leftovers for dinner, and poured herself some wine.

She was still wearing the dress, walking about the house barefoot with the stereo turned up loud, when the doorbell rang. It was nearly 10 p.m.

Leena peeked through the keyhole. Davis, coming back for some reason? No, it was the woman from the neighbors' property. Leena opened the door.

"Hi there," said Dalva, not acknowledging either the late hour or the unexpectedness of her visit. "We're having a little get-together, I wanted to come tell you. I know you said your daughter's away, and I thought you might be a little bit lonely. It's just kind of a spontaneous get-together, some friends of the boys are bringing their instruments over. And Calvin has just made the most incredible curry soup. We're celebrating New Year's, we've decided. I know it's not really the New Year yet, but we like to celebrate things when we feel like it, y'know? And we'd love to have you join us."

It occurred to Leena as she stood facing the woman, who was wearing her same white sweater with the embroidered rose, that her own dress was also of a slightly furry white material. She must've had this woman's sweater in mind, without knowing it, while she was shopping that afternoon.

"Oh," said Leena, feeling put on the spot, "how nice of you."

"Or were you already on your way out somewhere?" Leena became aware that she looked like she was, probably. "You look good." Dalva said this with a clear appreciation in her voice. It was not the tone of a woman older than Leena giving her a compliment, but more like that of one woman making a concession to another whom she considered her equal. And she was not just meaning Leena's new dress, it seemed, but the whole of her at that moment. Dalva leaned in slightly. "Those earrings are such a great shade of green on you."

"They're onyx," said Leena, simply.

"I've never seen green onyx before. I guess I thought they were jade. Are you going out somewhere special?" She smiled—that sheepish but secretive grin.

Leena blushed when she had to admit she'd been just trying on the dress for fun. She shrugged, throwing her hands up in an uncalculated gesture. "I have nothing else much to do, and I just bought it today," she said.

"Well, you're dressed for a party, you should come over to ours then," said Dalva, warmly.

Leena weighed her options. If she closed the door, if she went back inside and said "no, thank you" to the night and all of its possible promises, she would be left to deal with the house's ghosts and its cloud of quiet and with herself by herself, for the remaining hours of the night. While from across the grass would come the sounds of laughing and talking, and their music, all of it rising into the big sky like one small, slightly visible dome of celebration and community, against the encroaching dark heavens above.

"All right," replied Leena, "Maybe I will go for a little while."

———

She thought of Trevor as she went to get her coat from her bedroom closet. She saw him plainly, like a video feed broadcast into her brain. He was sitting in a bar, placing money on a dirty table, and all around him, dimly, were the sounds of ice cubes clinking seductively in glasses, and low music, and the town he was passing through waiting just beyond the bar's perimeters. He was thinking of her, she thought, and of Pearl; she felt the subtle pressure of these thoughts landing inside her, knowingly and subtly, ordering that they be protected.

Sometimes, she felt, they communicated in this manner.

And that you could, with your mind, feel a person in their absence and gauge whether they were keeping their place with you or not. She sent her own message back to Trevor now—that she was here, as she should be.

Then she chose an old coat (a thrift store find, yellow) and turned off the music and went out to the porch where Dalva was waiting.

———

Leena followed Dalva across the grass, over the split-rail fence dividing their two properties, and down a gentle slope toward the little stone house. She was conscious of the night air blowing coolly against her face as she took long strides to keep up with Dalva. There was a fire in the fire pit off to the side of the house, and music and voices and laughter rose with the flames. A big white dog bounded toward them, not barking, its tongue flying out the side of its mouth. Dalva said, "Down, Neighbor! Down!" when she saw Leena flinch, the dog jumping up and down around them.

An old man turned away from the fire and greeted them first. He held a beer bottle and a cigarette in the same hand, and his fingers were long and knuckly. He looked quite old, thought Leena. He was dressed in a powder blue suit with a sprig of holly pinned to his lapel, and he had tufty white hair and a snow-white moustache. His appearance was both comical and angelic.

"Jeremiah is my ex-husband. He lives here sometimes, too," said Dalva.

"Just sometimes," said Jeremiah, gruffly, but chuckling.

"Oh," said Leena.

"Jeremiah and I are old soul mates. We've stayed good friends over the years, even after we couldn't be married to each other anymore. We were very young when we met, you see, and we just got it wrong initially. We'd been married in past lifetimes, but it wasn't the right kind of relationship for us to have in this one, is all," explained Dalva, in a gracious, measured tone, as Jeremiah, nodding and patting Leena on the shoulder, moved past them and went on up the steps into the stone house. He looked back only to say, "Come on, Neighbor, come on, boy," and the dog panted and made some jumping motions in Dalva's direction and then turned and ran after Jeremiah.

Next, one of the people laughing and playing music broke from the circle around the fire and came over to them, first setting his instrument down on a log. He was extremely tall, lanky but not too thin, and awkwardly handsome. He had a schoolboy's haircut, parted on one side, neatly combed, a simple shade of brown. He wrapped his arm around Dalva's shoulders and kissed her forehead in greeting, and Leena knew immediately that this had to be the one who'd given her the sweater, the one she called Pennyroyal. It occurred to Leena that she was being given a quick history: Dalva's loves—old and new. Pennyroyal had to be at least twenty years younger than Dalva.

"This is Pennyroyal, one of my guardian angels if I have any," said Dalva, and she was glowing, smiling, by the light of the bonfire.

Pennyroyal held his hand out to Leena. "Don't believe anything she tells you about us. Most certainly not about me, especially if she tells you I've done anything worth anything at all in my, what, twenty-four years of life." He shook Leena's hand with a loose gentle grip, as if he feared her hand might break.

Dalva took Leena by the arm. "Come inside the house with me," she said.

The stone house, though small on the outside, revealed high ceilings and more rooms than Leena had expected. The house was not very clean. It had a mossy, cluttered feeling. There seemed to be as much dust inside as there was on the ground outside. The floors were of hardwood, worn absolutely smooth in spots, water-stained in others. The wallpaper, too, was water-stained and peeling in places, and all the furniture looked very old and dull. Even the brighter-colored items—a maroon armchair, a floral-patterned couch—had an ancient, muted appearance.

Dalva leading, they walked down a dim hallway. Many of the rooms Leena glanced into did not have windows. Something about them struck her as being places where animals might feel safe.

She recalled the exterior of the house, mismatched stones cemented together, like colors dug up out of the earth, coated haphazardly in vines.

Leena and Dalva eventually settled in the kitchen, where they came upon Jeremiah seated in the corner by the kitchen table, nodding off over his beer bottle, already drunk. Neighbor lay at his feet, lethargically lapping soup out of a bowl set between his paws. The kitchen was filled with the smell of curry and spices.

"Sometimes he's belligerent. It's better when he's sleepy," said Dalva, nodding in Jeremiah's direction. "Let's have some wine."

They sat on stools pulled up to a makeshift plywood counter and drank their wine from coffee mugs.

"He sleepwalks through his life," said Dalva. "You can't stay married to someone like that for too long. You think they're going to come alive and that you might help them, but then they just don't, you know? Have you ever been married before? Before now, I mean?"

"No," replied Leena.

"I've been married twice. The second time was even worse. Like I said, they're better sleepy than belligerent." Dalva got down from her stool abruptly. She leaned forward and began clapping her hands excitedly against her legs. "Neighbor, c'mere, boy, c'mere!" She did this until the dog finally, begrudgingly, got up from his soup bowl and came over to her, tail and tongue wagging, as if relenting to the fact of affection as his duty.

"My ex-husband—not Jeremiah, the other one— sometimes he still comes around here." She laid her face on

Neighbor's neck as she spoke. "He thinks I'm sleeping with every man on this piece of property. He hides in the bushes, and the boys have to come out and chase him away. That's a laugh. Not so much when it's happening, of course, but later it is, when you think about it, y'know?"

———

They talked politics at this party, too, but not in quite the same way as had been going on at the party with Josie's friends. Here, everyone—Dalva's friends—seemed to be of like mind and quite cheerful, even in their disparaging comments.

"Just so long as this campaign is as successful as the war on poverty was. Oops, we won; the poor lost!" A man about Trevor's age, with eyeglasses and a goatee, made his entrance into the stone house kitchen exclaiming this to another, younger man with him. Both were laughing. Pennyroyal came in just behind them.

Spotting Leena, the man with the goatee stepped forward and held out his hand. Leena was still seated on her stool; Dalva was nearby at the stove now, stirring the pot of soup. When Leena offered her hand, the man with the goatee bent forward and kissed it instead of shaking it.

"You must be Leena from next door," he said. "I'm Terry." He looked her up and down, admiringly. "I admit we've all been rather curious about you. Especially since Dalva's report the other day."

The second man, the younger one, hung back. He wore an old black suit and was very thin and a little pale, with dark brown hair that hung in straggly curls around his

cheekbones. He was about the same age as Pennyroyal—
early twenties. His face was angular and effeminate, and he
looked at Leena with a reserved curiosity.

"Calvin," declared Dalva, with satisfaction, as she
reached over and laid her hands on his arms, pulling him
across the kitchen floor. "Here's our traveling scholar. We
call him 'The Student.' He knows everything you'd ever want
to know about ancient Mesopotamian culture—"

"What kind of Indian are you?" asked Calvin, leaning in
to shake Leena's hand with the same tentative grip Pennyroyal had used.

"Indian?" said Leena. "No, I'm not Indian."

"Oh, we're all Indian," he said, and smiled judiciously.

Leena didn't know what he meant by that. No one else
in the room seemed puzzled by it, though. Terry nodded and
said, "True, true," and Dalva kept smiling.

Pennyroyal crossed to the dining nook and dropped himself into the chair across from Jeremiah, who was still dozing
with his chin against his chest, his hand curled around his
beer bottle. Pennyroyal stretched out his long legs and held
his cigarette away from the table, down near the floor. He
looked relaxed, lucid.

Calvin spoke, as if picking up a thread from a previous
conversation. "But really, what I want to know is what's going
to happen to the private sphere then, if we are moving toward
an age where women enter the public sphere more and more."

"The private sphere, the public sphere. For a philosopher
you talk a lot like a politician," said Terry. His manner of
challenge had a teasing element to it, though.

Calvin said, "Well, I think we have to imagine that the
public sphere, what rules it has and whatever we consider

normal and predominant now, is going to change—especially with women coming more into positions of influence. I think we *can't* imagine how it's going to change, though. I think it might be beyond our present imagining capabilities. Because it means a new paradigm is coming into existence. I *hope.*"

Dalva spoke in a confidential tone to Leena, coming over and resting her hand on Leena's shoulder: "See what I mean? See how lucky I am—you, too? These are the kinds of men who truly *care* about the plight of women, you know? They will work by *our sides.* Do you know what I mean?"

Leena didn't exactly. But she felt something precious and careful in the atmosphere in general, so she smiled and nodded. "Everyone is very nice here," she said softly.

"But the raising of children. How can that possibly ever change? How can it *not* require what it requires of women?" Someone—it was Terry—was remarking this with animated bewilderment.

"But of course it can change. How can you say that?" said Calvin. "Women live in such a state of alienation these days. They are fed such stultifying crap by the media, by men, even by other women—they think there's only this one way of going about being women, but they don't *need* to be like this. They don't. They have just been socially conditioned to worry, and caretake, and preen, really. But they don't have to do those things. They can do other things, if they would just decide to."

Pennyroyal gestured languidly toward Dalva and Leena's corner of the kitchen. "Here we are talking. Why don't we ask the women who are actually present how their days are spent? Well, we know what Dalva does with her days; she does Dalva things." He smiled, catching Dalva's eye.

"I gathered a lot of your firewood today. Neighbor and I did," said Dalva.

Pennyroyal looked toward Leena now. "And what did you do today, Leena?"

Here, as in her first conversation with Dalva, Leena had only honesty to fall back on. Even in her incomprehension of their conversation, she still knew this answer would somehow not do. "Today? I went to the mall."

"The mall?" said Pennyroyal, her response warranting him to sit forward.

And Terry said, "No, not the mall."

Calvin's look was pained and sympathetic, as if it had just been announced that Leena had lost something valuable. "You see?" he said, somewhat meekly, though.

"Jeremiah prefers the unlocked doors down the road over the mall," said Pennyroyal, and they all looked in Jeremiah's direction and laughed then, for Jeremiah had heard nothing, was still snoring softly into his own chest.

Dalva said, in way of explanation, "Jeremiah has been caught wandering into people's houses on occasion. Namely those new houses down the road. He said he was just curious and he thought they weren't being lived in yet. He walked into one of them and used the bathroom. A woman called the police on him and ran after him down the street with a bottle of aerosol hairspray."

"Speaking of police," said Pennyroyal, and he raised his eyebrows at Terry.

Terry's hands came up. "Nope, no more restraining order; that's all over now. She saw the light."

"So we can go back to business?"

"We can go back to business soon." And Terry nodded.

Listening to this exchange, Leena suddenly recalled something—one of the rooms they'd passed when they first entered the house. A room that looked like a little girl's room, but from some past era: a narrow, frilly, lavender bed, child-sized wooden furniture, a few doe-eyed toy dolls, walls covered in wallpaper of an intricate and prudish, antiquated floral design. When Leena asked, Dalva had said that was Terry's daughter's bedroom, and that Terry's daughter was eleven.

Leena fixed her attention on Terry. She was genuinely curious now. "What is your business?" she asked.

Hesitant laughter went through the room. This group— they seemed to think so many things were funny, thought Leena. Were they ever serious about anything? Then Terry said, "I guess you could say I'm a historian of sorts. If you believe in my sort of history, that is."

———

Outside, five or six boys were playing instruments and singing around the fire. Pennyroyal had rejoined them. He played the fiddle. When he paused his fiddling to sing, he lowered his bow to his side and tapped it against his leg. Leena did not think he sounded like a good singer, because his voice seemed to crack and warble a lot, but she recognized that he sang as if he really meant it. All of them, in fact, seemed to play their instruments furiously but with much joy—sometimes they looked round at each other and laughed right in the middle of their playing. Leena thought the whole scene had the flavor of a circus to it. Something decadent and celebratory, yet also innocent and simply playful. It was like a children's party for adults; it was like no gathering she would've ever arrived at in Trevor's company.

She sat on a stump before the fire, holding her coffee mug of wine with both hands, and watched the festivities. Dalva and Calvin sat on a log to one side of Leena's stump.

Dalva was saying, "I don't want to kill the ants, you understand. I just want them to leave."

"It's the grass around your trailer. You just need one of us to come over and mow it, like a moat," said Calvin.

"But they're dropping in from the trees above, I think."

"Burdock, no, pennyroyal!" declared Calvin, snapping his fingers. "The herb, I mean. It'll keep the ants away. You sprinkle it around the perimeter of all the doors and windows. Native Americans used pennyroyal, god, for so many things. It's very potent. They used it when women wanted abortions."

When Leena looked toward Calvin as she heard him say this, she suddenly felt as if she were seeing him and Dalva through a telescope. They seemed close, but Leena was far away, slipping further away even as she sat a couple feet from them. It was as if his words were an echo of words already existing in her mind, but of which she'd not been aware until she heard them spoken externally, by him.

There was something women in Vietnam took to induce abortion, too, she remembered, though she did not know the word for it in English. Maybe it was the same thing here as there. Thinking this had an effect on her. She felt an invisible weight in her gut. Back in Vietnam, she had seen—or heard, rather—the occasional session involving a girl in her line of work writhing and moaning in a dark backroom. Because, if you chose this method, it took a while. The older women who attended these girls were aggressive and pragmatic in their caretaking and could sometimes be heard belittling the girls, saying things like "Crying does not help your hurting." Leena, too, had been more repulsed by the crudeness of their suffering than she had ever been sympathetic.

But, too, there had been births. Leena remembered the hallways of a hospital when she was a young girl, a place she had been brought to with her mother, who was pregnant at the time. It was all women in this place, some very young, some older, like Leena's mother. The women sat big-stomached in courtyards, waiting, fighting, laughing, chatting. Leena would see the same women being helped down the tiled corridors of the hospital, bent over, gasping, some days or weeks later. She remembered playing in the hallways to the sounds of their laboring and nurses rushing in and out of rooms. The nurses were discernible from the women in this place only by their uniforms; even some of the nurses, too, were pregnant. The only men in the place had been the occasional doctors.

And what would someone like this boy, Calvin, do in the presence of such suffering? Leena saw him plainly: his stricken, gentle eyes; his trembling, pale fingers—had she seen fingers like these somewhere or somehow before? She could picture them trying to hold on to something but fumbling; she could imagine a feeling of panicked helplessness pouring off him. But, no. Maybe that wouldn't be the case at all. Looking at him now, she could also picture him as kindly effectual and unflinching, a quiet nurse, a healer of sorts. Leena experienced a sorrowful sensation along with these images. She did not understand it. Her own abortion—she had never thought it worth self-pity, and she did not believe in God or unborn children's souls, she had told herself. Yes, she had felt sad and unmoored in the weeks following the

abortion, largely due to the consequences that had followed
the event, but that had all been dealt with by now, hadn't it?

To distract herself, she decided to get up and dance. She
wanted to look sexy and feel revived.

She stood up and began to sway and shift her hips. She
kicked off her shoes and let her feet settle in their full flatness
against the warm, dry dirt around the fire. She held up her
cup and raised her other arm too and began to swing her
hair about in front of her face, the way she'd seen girls in
the audience at rock concerts on television do. The others
laughed and cheered her on appreciatively.

Then someone brought out a bag with fireworks in it,
and, one by one, the musicians put down their instruments.
A couple of the boys lit sparklers and began chasing one another with them, running off beyond the circle of light cast
by the bonfire so that sometimes all that was visible were the
thin shoots of light sizzling and moving erratically through
the dark. There were the shadowy shapes of animals out in
the dark, too, Leena saw—four or five sheep, the old horse,
and Neighbor, like a blur of dim white bounding after the
sparklers. The larger fireworks, when they began setting
them off, made long whooshes as they went up, echoing
clapboard pops as they splintered into neon sprays of light in
the sky. The way the firework explosions echoed gave Leena
the impression that the sky was not just open space after all
but was instead strangely tiered and solid, a thousand invisible planes of some kind of substance, haphazardly arranged
up there, like the crooked walls of a maze.

Somewhere in the midst of these antics, Jeremiah stumbled away from the fire and did not return. Leena soon
forgot about him. Terry got up and stood close to the fire

with his arms raised. What was he doing? He looked like a priest, the way the wide sleeves of his loose linen shirt hung down below his arms, or like a bat, thought Leena, a white bat.

Then, Dalva came over and put her arm around Leena and said, "Let's trade your coat for my sweater," in her conspiratorial manner. Fireworks were going off all around them, and everyone was happy, and it was almost midnight—their prearranged New Year's moment—besides. So Leena could not refuse. Dalva put on Leena's yellow coat and it suited her. Leena slipped her arms into the soft white sleeves of the furry, embroidered-rose sweater and smiled, trying to match Dalva's quality of intimate exuberance.

————

They had taken her into a room off the kitchen a little earlier, before they all moved outside to the fire. It was a small, cluttered room, with high ceilings like the rest of the house, and one long, narrow, filthy window surrounded by tall bookcases. There was an old green couch, a low coffee table, and two red-cushioned armchairs with beautiful, carved wooden armrests. Piles of books and newspapers and dried candle wax covered the coffee table. Terry opened one of these books and began flipping through pages until he found what he was looking for.

"There," he said, pushing the book over to Leena, who sat across from him on the couch.

He had stopped on a page of old black-and-white photographs that appeared to be from the Old West era. Leena saw grainy, brown-tinted images of busty, hard-eyed white women, hair piled severely on top of their heads. They wore stiff-waisted dresses with full skirts and high lacy collars, standing in front of falling-down wooden storefronts and slanting porches. In the photograph Terry had indicated, there was a brown-skinned woman with rather austere facial features, dressed in the same manner as the white women, seated, holding an open umbrella over her shoulder even though she appeared to be indoors. The woman gazed at the camera expressionlessly.

"Something like that, I'd say, is the situation I think we've known you in before," said Terry. "That's my feeling about it."

Leena looked at him, and waited quietly for him to explain.

"I work intuitively, you see—some people use hypnosis; I'm more for sense impressions, really. Then I tell what I see, and the others act it out, like a play. We're like a spiritual improv group, you could say. We travel around the country doing this—that's our business. It sounds far-fetched, but it can actually serve as quite a healing process for many people. When they see the actors acting out some past life event they may've already repeated in this life or are on the verge of repeating, then they become aware of the circumstances of their karma. It can be a quite wrenching experience. Because in becoming aware of karma, you also become aware of choice, I believe. Now that you know, you don't have to repeat the same circumstances again. Destiny is not inevitable, you see." His gaze held hers as if, through this, he meant to pass his information into her. Leena found she could not look away from him.

"Many things were taken from you in that lifetime before, I think—your land, your culture, even loved ones dear to you. You were forced to leave, I believe, and to live under obligation to people like us. Well, some of us, anyway. Some of us were Indian like you, too. Calvin was, and Pennyroyal was. Dalva and I have always been more like interlopers. But now you've come back."

Leena looked at the picture again and thought that the woman in it looked very sad and somewhat ugly. How could these people think she was beautiful if they thought she looked like this woman? She saw a different vision of herself then, in her new white dress, walking through a house that was not this house and was not her own house, either. The carpet was very thick and white and new; she was walking barefoot, coming to stand at a window. White sunlight cascaded through the windows. It was one of those new development homes down the street—it dawned on Leena—that she saw herself wandering through.

"I don't believe in ghosts," said Leena. "Many people do, where I come from, but I never do."

Terry smiled at her. "Interesting," he said then, and sat back slightly.

———

She hadn't meant to fall asleep at the neighbors' house, but when she woke she was lying on the lavender bed in the room that looked like a little girl's.

Through her disorientation, she recalled having come into the room just to sit; something had drawn her in. She could still hear their voices and the festivities from outside. She could hear the whoosh and pop of the fireworks. The wall lamps in the little room cast indefinite shadows across the walls and bedspread. Leena had felt the strangest sensation then, as if the beginning of the day in her own house, and yesterday, too, were years in the past. Time had stretched out in this way since she'd come to the neighbors' party: her previous reality had escaped, somehow. And she felt as if it would be a long road back, that nothing would ever be the same again as it had been yesterday.

But what a silly, unfounded thought; she had just had too much to drink, and she was disoriented and lonely, she tried to tell herself. It was just that she missed her daughter and she missed Trevor. Still, she saw herself taking in the details of this room acutely, as if these motions—her sitting down on the bed, moving her hands across the bedspread, noting the brass knobs of the dresser beside the bed—were motions overlaying motions she had already performed in some distant, inexact past, in this exact same pattern. Yes, there seemed to be a pattern to it, these movements. Though Leena did not believe in it, Terry's theory of past lives and parallel histories was still adrift in her thoughts, confusing her. Maybe different races' histories followed similar patterns, and it might explain why people could think a Vietnamese woman living in a house in Texas had some quality in common with a converted Native American woman. Or maybe all brown-skinned people *were* in some way the same, she thought. Then, like a dream, or like the dimly remembered plot of a movie she'd once seen, an imagined sense of being separated from her daughter for a long period of time, by circumstances not of Leena's own choosing, came to her. This had never happened to her with Pearl, but still she could imagine it. And when they found one another again, they would be totally different people, their ties to one another irrevocably changed.

But no, she told herself. This was just overdramatic worry, a mother's worries. When would this night end? She laid her head on the pillow, not meaning to close her eyes, but then—it seemed—she must have.

There was something happening, now. She realized it suddenly. Silence was all around her but it was not a complete silence; a clawing sense of activity was still out there somewhere. She got up quickly.

The glow hit the sky, like a grounded sun struggling to get free from where it had fallen. The light wanted to go back up to the sky, and the sky wanted to stay dark. It was still nighttime, though a little colder than earlier.

Leena realized then that the glow was not from the fire in the fire pit. That fire was here, as she stumbled down the stone house steps, and it was smoldering now, just embers. This other glow was larger and came from farther away. Now she heard voices, too, carrying across the grass, not laughing, shouting. She stayed frozen for a second, watching the light hit the sky, watching it seem to tremble and jump, as if it, too, were shouting up to the heavens and stars above (in its own language, though, the one they—people— could not hear). She began to run. She headed up the slope, toward the fence between the properties. A shape loomed at her from the side, from the dark side of the stone house, and she leaped away from it but did not scream. There was not time or space inside her for panic anymore. She landed like a cat, still on her feet. It was the old man, Jeremiah, who had come lumbering out of the dark, headed in the same direction she was. He looked wildly about, like a caricature of stealth, with his arms held out from his sides. Finally his eyes met hers.

"My house is on fire," said Leena. She had never before called it *my house*, she realized.

Jeremiah took a deep slow breath, then let it out. Behind him, soundlessly, the dim shape of a sheep plodded by, glancing mildly in their direction. "I was sleeping," said Jeremiah. "I was sleeping over there in the leaves. I woke up and I thought something was wrong. It felt like maybe an earthquake, I thought. Or maybe a storm coming." He rolled his eyes, looking befuddled, an old man with grass in his hair and dirt on his suit, a ridiculous and outdated suit, stinking of alcohol. And then Leena saw him—she saw all of them—for what they really were. They were people who had chosen to live like fools and paupers in the world. And they actually preferred that, and their insights were in some ways true and useful, but they were still just people with strange ideas that most other people wouldn't ever believe.

Without replying, Leena turned from Jeremiah and continued hurriedly across the field, knowing he was following right behind her. They reached the fence, where Leena saw it was not her house that was on fire after all. At first she couldn't place it—what *was* on fire? There was a blaze in her front yard, yes, and the silhouettes of people standing around, moving about, up and down, in slight frenzies. There was shouting, and there was also some stifled laughter. It was the playhouse that was on fire, she soon realized. It was just the playhouse.

Her own house, hulking at the back of this scene, was all lit up; she had left all the downstairs lights on. The windows of the top floor appeared like eyes, darkened though, to what was going on in the yard below.

Dalva came over to Leena. She looked wild-eyed, aghast, but she was also holding back her laughter. "Oh my god," she said this a number of times. "Oh my god, sweetheart. Oh my god, we're so sorry. Your poor little girl, her playhouse. Oh, it's so sad, I can't believe this."

Someone was shouting, "Where's the hose?" and then someone else was running toward the house, running back with the hose, but tripping along the way, making the others laugh again.

Their laughter. It made it so Leena did not feel like telling them Pearl never played in that playhouse anyhow. She would not ruin their fun, nor give them the satisfaction, she thought.

That was when the old man said, "Do you know if you dream your house is on fire it means you're in love?"

Leena said, "My house isn't on fire."

4. Husband, Wife

I.

They had been driving—for hours, it seemed—toward a distant whitish sketch of mountainous plateaus seeming to relay vague promise, at some point ahead, of breaking up the I–10 flatness. Finally, large jagged banks of rock rose above the highway, flanking their vehicle and filling their windows with a view of the striated textures of granite and limestone. Then the banks of rock fell away, dissolving again into the brown savannah-like landscape of West Texas.

Sage was driving, and they were listening to music she had selected. A mournful female country singer from the mid-1970s singing about making it back to Birmingham, Alabama, from Boulder, Colorado, though the man she was singing to had not made it back. Because he had died, presumably. The music sounded so beautiful, sorrowful and enriching, that Sage thought she felt the true danger of tears. She had always considered that an odd figure of speech, that crying should be a danger, odd in the same way that some people and books spoke of "surviving" the first weeks of life with a newborn (this terminology being not about how the baby would fare but about how the parents would). With the

highway flying by and the music playing, however, the sensation she experienced did indeed justify the word *danger:*
it was the danger of what could be summoned to surface in
a person, an emotional lucidity that threatened to unmoor
her. She could feel dislocated from the presumed stability
of a history between two people; self-honesty could mean
remoteness; her husband could have no inkling of her true
thoughts and feelings. Dalgleish was not really her husband,
not technically, but they lived together and had a four-year-
old son named Praxis. They had found it easier, in their
dealings with most people, to refer to each other by the
terms that provoked the least amount of curiosity or suspicion: *husband, wife.*

They stopped at a rest area about sixty miles before Fort
Stockton. Sage walked across the pavement to the public
restroom, leading Praxis by the hand, while Dalgleish wandered off to smoke by the picnic benches.

"Remember when these kinds of places used to have a
funny smell and no one ever seemed to take care of them?"
said a woman who appeared to be in her forties, as Sage and
she waited side by side against the tiled wall to enter the
bathroom stalls.

Sage did not remember; still, she smiled in agreement.
Then a stall freed, and the woman dashed into it. How old
did that woman think Sage was? She was accustomed to
women that age taking her to be not older than her early
twenties and looking askance at her, especially when they saw
her with a toddler and no wedding ring, especially in Texas,
and especially whenever they traveled outside Austin. She
was not used to them addressing her in the knowing, readily hospitable way that—as Sage perceived it—more *normal*

women addressed one another in public places. Normal *white* women, that was. Sage led Praxis into the next available stall, still puzzling over the woman's comment because, it seemed to Sage, the restroom *did* have a funny smell.

Sage's dark complexion, in Texas, was more often than not taken to be Mexican (this, with all its connotations of teenage mothers and illegitimate fathers, thought Sage) or, in the odd case, Native American. On the jogging trail around Lake Austin, men sometimes called out "Hola!" to her in passing. Even Mexican people approached and spoke to her in Spanish. Busboys in restaurants, matronly women in the grocery store, jewelry vendors in the mall, the hired help who worked under Dalgleish in the machine shop he managed. Sage's immediate response was usually an apology. She thought this ironic, apologizing to strangers—what did she feel guilty about?—for what she was not. But the fact that she was half-Vietnamese and knew next to nothing about that culture, was partnered but unwed to a Caucasian male, both of them two thousand miles from their home states, was somehow hard to explain. She made a constant effort to be agreeable toward strangers. She thought of it as trying to adopt a more southern demeanor, though she knew this, too, smacked of her habit of harboring preconceptions. She was a skeptical person, it was true, but that was really due to her skepticism about herself.

Just the night before, for instance, in a bar after playing a gig, a boy she knew had come up and tried to compliment her, and she had shot him down.

"But really, we sounded bad, too, huh?"

"What?" the boy had to yell back at her. She couldn't tell if this was a "what?" of disgust or of nonhearing.

Someone next to her, another boy she knew only slightly, said then, calmly and emphatically, "Darling, don't *do* that," and placed his hand lightly on her arm.

Both of these boys were twenty-seven. The first, Jet, was cute in a dark and cerebral way, a biology research fellow at the local university, a vegetarian though his body did not exude health, the lead singer of a local punk band. He was appealing to Sage mostly for his confidence in being ill-fitted for the status quo—he was a laughing, striking, rebellious figure in her mind, a little unclean, wholly untrustworthy, but possessing a germ of incongruous kindness. Also, he was covered head to toe in tattoos. His face and forearms were tiger-striped—thick, inky bands of black—while the rest of his body read like a hieroglyphic map. She was taken by the commitment it showed, and with the way the whites of his eyes stood out against his black face stripes; they made him look somehow exempt from age.

She had never thought of herself as the type of girl a guy with tiger stripes tattooed on his face would ever be interested in, until one night she had found herself at a party at some-body's house (she had come, rather innocently, with one of her bandmates), having her shirt unbuttoned by Jet against a pool table in the basement. The whole scene was so sordidly cliché, and seemed to hold no basis or consequence in reality for either of them. And, since there was no real affection in it, no real lust even, Sage had not thought it a significant enough matter to confess to Dalgleish. True, it was the first incidence of infidelity she'd had in her relationship with him and in her life as a mother, but it was not the first time she'd been un-faithful in a committed relationship. Not by far it wasn't. If she ever had to explain these events, she might claim herself to be simply the kind of person capable of living a dual existence or the type cursed to do so, perhaps. She was susceptible to present moments, given circumstances. She *had to* transcend moralistic conventions at times, she felt, to preserve some far-seeking aspect of her spirit. She believed there existed a core of goodness (or something of that nature) in every person, and that it was reachable, most readily through sex—a meeting of people's cores. It was reachable with nearly anyone, if she allowed it to be.

Yet she was also a believer in the idea that who you ended up with was a matter of destiny.

That something in her connection with Dalgleish had dimmed, she was willing to acknowledge, even to voice this to him, but they both attributed it to circumstances—baby, work, too many hours apart, too little money—and believed it would eventually work itself out. They thought it was a matter of tending to external factors first. Dalgleish actually enjoyed his job in the machine shop, and she had her creative goals. Romantic energy came from the same source as creative energy, which was why she didn't always have enough to go around: romance would just have to wait. She suspected that was how marriages went, along separate but together paths, undiscussed, unlamented. Theirs might be a form, albeit lesser, of that kind of love described in those famous letters by Rilke, in which lovers guarded one another's solitudes.

Sometimes, though, she had glimpses of the future. These came as shots of nervousness and portent running through her body like electrical waves, indicative of something, she was certain, though she could never decide exactly what. The feeling she'd just experienced while driving, for instance,

with the rock banks rising and falling outside her car windows and the music affecting her as it did—she had wanted
to hang on to that and follow it, but it had dimmed when
Dalgleish spoke, reminding her to pull in at the rest stop.

The next time Sage saw Jet, after the incident against
the pool table, they were at another party (this time she was
there with Dalgleish). She and Jet were both only able to turn
away from each other and laugh, and later they said "Nice
to see you again" when they bumped into one another trying
to cross a living room crowded with dancers. Her attraction to Jet had been, she knew, only a product of boredom
and projection. It didn't stand a chance outside the context of nighttime or alcohol or punk rock. More precisely,
that meant the atmosphere she felt was generated when she
listened to punk bands play live. The walls of noise they con-
structed, the fierceness and humor with which they did what
they did. It made her feel as if she were in a cave, and residence in this cave came via a righteously, and painstakingly,
maintained stance of integrity; the residents had carved this
place out for themselves, and if they did not keep digging and
fighting the world above them, the walls might collapse in on
them. You wanted to stay there, to commit to a lifestyle of
substance-enhanced nighttime allegiances, to hold out against
the hypocrisies required by day. But she was also wise enough
to know that there were other ways, more feasible ways, of
maintaining one's sense of integrity.

The second boy was different. More a part of her day-
time existence as well as her nighttime one. He was a teacher
at her son's preschool, and he was also a musician, a guitar
player connected to bands she saw in clubs and bars around

town. He was blond and tan and wispy with a gentle, enthusiastic smile; he often wore yellow; and his hair was never
combed. His whole being projected warmth and playfulness
and good judgment, all melded together. Her son miscalled
him Kevin, though his name was really Cyrus.

At work with the kids, Cyrus had a way of bending down
to talk to them that was mesmerizing and personal. He never
overreacted to any crisis, a Cheerio up a toddler's nose or
blood after a fall from the swing set. All the teachers at the
preschool were like this, Sage had observed. They were like
svelte, plodding creatures, warm-blooded but slow-moving,
with a kind of primal grace. They meandered among the
children without much comment, with vacant but watchful
expressions. The girls were loose-limbed and flat-bellied with
gentle, pert, pretty faces; many were pierced and had dyed
hair. The boys, too, were dreadlocked and earringed and ef-
feminately gorgeous, with older-seeming eyes looking out of
baby faces. Most of them were college-age or a little older.
Among them there seemed to be an unspoken history of inti-
macies. Sage envied that.

Cyrus's independence, though, also intrigued Sage. He
had no apparent girlfriends or longings and lived by himself in a tiny cabin on the heavily wooded piece of property
where the schoolhouse was located, ten or so miles outside
town. On occasional mornings she saw him coming up the
hill from his cabin with his hair wet and his T-shirt sticking
to his body, a towel flung over one shoulder, having started
his day with a swim in the creek at the bottom of the hill
behind the school. And one time—the first time, really, that
she'd felt him noticing her as something more than just an-

other of his students' parents—she was singing to herself as she walked back to her car, past his cabin, and had not noticed him standing on his porch.

She was singing, of all songs, "Amazing Grace." He smiled at her with what seemed like genuine appreciation.

Sometime after that incident it occurred to her that she looked forward to the ritual of dropping Praxis off in the mornings. (She was always the one to take him to and from school; Dalgleish never did.) Cyrus said hello to her warmly and attentively each morning, and though she observed him doing this with nearly every parent, still it resounded inside her, sending her into the rest of her day—random errands, guitar lessons, voice lessons, the occasional waitressing shift—buoyed by a feeling of goodwill. Part of her believed that one day she would look back on Cyrus as someone who had indirectly helped her get through a stagnant period, that in her memory she would regard him as a compelling temporary presence, a beacon of sorts, a gentle pressure on her heart. Another part of her believed that something more real might be waiting—a tangible connection, lasting consequences—to explain the growing affection she was feeling.

He was young, though, and seemed too carefree. He did not strike her as the kind of person foolish or desperate enough to complicate his life with unwise entanglements. Not that that was what she was looking for. She just liked wondering, she would tell herself. She liked trying to imagine the kind of woman he might one day commit himself to. She imagined this woman would have to be as independent and capable as he was to hold his interest and that he was the type who might stay single well into his thirties, or longer, even. She imagined there would be plenty of chances, plenty of willing women for someone like him, but that the search would still be a difficult one; he would be an idealist in love as well as in life. How did she know all this about him? She didn't. Yet she was sure it was true.

"Hang on, Prax," Sage said, catching him by his shirt as he was trying to crawl on his knees out of the bathroom stall, under the door. "Stand up, stand up. Let's walk, okay, honey?" She turned his body to face hers in the cramped space. She knelt and buttoned his pants, straightened his shirt, then opened the door and gently pushed him out of the stall in front of her.

At the sink she washed her own and Praxis's hands at the same time, glancing at the older boy who stood by the hand dryer machine waiting for his mother. Sage assumed she must be the woman who was saying from inside one of the stalls, "And I think Courtney would really appreciate it if we did that, don't you?"

The boy didn't respond until Sage and Praxis had started to leave. Behind them she heard, "Mom, you always say that—."

The bar Sage and her bandmates had gone to the previous night had no windows. It was a tight little smoke-box decorated with neon signs and red Christmas lights. An unfrivolous bar. No cute waitresses in tank tops, no absurd art on the walls, which were the color of salmon. A Wednesday night and the place was packed. The rampant energies of all the people inside swirled and zinged about, invisibly striking walls and pinball machines and body parts, all of it gathering and gathering momentum with no way of release until each current had rebounded so many times as to have dissipated itself. That, she believed, was why, when you were in bars like this, you felt like everyone in it could be your friend, in some temporarily vital way. But perhaps, too, they were just drunk.

She was with two other mothers from the school and two of her bandmates. All of them were around the same age—somewhere in their thirties. That was significant to Sage; it had to do with the different kinds of woman you could be at that age. Both her bandmates were single; one had a boyfriend, but the other didn't. Andrea, the one who had a boyfriend and played drums, was the kind of woman whose boyfriend complained she didn't pay enough attention to him, was too caught up in her own activities: she would go home early that night, for instance, because she was training for a marathon and had to get up early the next morning to run. Sheila, who played the bass guitar, wore vintage dresses from the 1950s and claimed to be bisexual. Sage envied the lively, removed way Sheila had of conducting herself around men. Yet, she also thought, there was a vulnerability to Sheila—she actually cared a lot about how men reacted to her. The two mothers were Brenda and Karen: Brenda was a massage therapist, and Karen was a culinary student. Karen's husband worked in a restaurant, and Brenda's husband worked in a high-tech company (it wasn't clear to Sage exactly what he did). All three of them were the mothers of four-year-old boys. The differences between them Sage saw to be a spectrum that went: herself, Karen, then Brenda. This because she'd had her baby completely unplanned, with someone she'd been with only a very short time, and they were still not married; and Karen, too, had had her baby unplanned, though she'd been with her boyfriend for several years previous, and they had married when they got pregnant; and then there was Brenda and her husband, who had been married for some time and had actually decided to get pregnant when they did.

"Whatever you're doing, ladies, keep on doing it," the bouncer who checked their IDs at the door had said, and the women walked into the bar feeling good about themselves, feeling their exceptionality (women who didn't look old enough, or boring enough, to be mothers), with Cyrus in tow.

He was their audience for the evening. He shook his head and smiled as they made loud, sarcastic remarks and jostled other people on their way up to the bar. They were doubling over exaggeratedly when they laughed. They wanted to be seen laughing. That was plain to Sage even as she was indulging in it. And she was letting parts of herself brush against Cyrus's arm, his leg, while making brash, magnanimous declarations like, "I think women should always show their stomachs, whatever kind of stomachs they have." She was saying this because the others were teasing her about having worn a shirt that bared her midriff. She was now even going as far as saying she believed in naturalness and that she liked it when she saw women with some fat on their stomachs. A man standing next to them in the crowd, overhearing this, turned and looked straight at Sage's midriff and said, in a tone almost accusatory, "You're not fat."

"I dress this way for myself," declared Sage, loudly because the bar was loud. "It's not vanity. It's more like I'm trying *not* to be vain, really. I have to feel like I'm not trying to hide any parts of my body, you know?"

"What did you say?" the other mothers yelled, and Sage yelled back, "I said I have nothing to hide!"

Sheila and Andrea stood back through this, nursing their drinks. Sheila had already remarked that it looked like they needed to get out more often—she meant the three who were mothers. Andrea kept glancing at her watch and, after finishing her beer, said she had to go.

Cyrus, meanwhile, was laughing generously at their antics and buying them more drinks. He was holding Sage's bag because she had flung it aside, not caring, and he was concerned she would forget it. They were, it seemed, attracting attention. Or maybe it was just the atmosphere of the bar. Everybody was listening in on everybody else. Everything seemed to be flowing and swift and clever.

Brenda was making Sheila clink beer bottles with her in an elaborate pattern that looked something like patty-cake but involved taking swigs of beer at certain points. Sheila looked reluctant, but she was doing it anyway.

"That," said a boy in a baseball cap, "is crazy. That is some awesome shit." He wanted to learn the beer-bottle-clinking routine, too, so Brenda began teaching it to him.

Sage was still defending her midriff: "I've got stretch marks, you know."

"I love my stretch marks. I *love* them." This from Karen, whose body was voluptuous and strong-looking. Karen was pretty. "I want to lose about thirty pounds," she would say, matter-of-factly, "when I can find the time." She said things like that yet seemed unperturbed by vanity. Sage liked her a lot for that reason. "Look," said Karen, lifting her shirt and pulling back the waistband of her pants.

Soon, all three mothers were lifting their shirts and showing their stomachs.

Sheila decided to leave then. That was also the moment when Jet came up to compliment Sage about the show, and Cyrus laid his hand on her arm, as if to stay her.

To Jet, he said, "Do you ever wake up some mornings and wish you weren't a tiger?"

"I guess I'm past all that," replied Jet, shrugging amiably, and for a second Sage saw his stripes anew and the incongruous kindness in him. His stripes were not meant to prove or disprove anything, she thought.

How there could be nights like this, and then came morning.

She had woken slightly hung over. That caused her and Dalgleish to start out on their trip to Big Bend later than they'd originally planned, but it was all right, they decided. It gave Praxis a little time to play before having to endure the long car ride. They had been planning the trip since January, waiting for the spring blooms to start. It was late March now. Over coffee Dalgleish asked her who all had gone out with them after their show last night. Scenes from the bar lingered in her head masked in a pink fog: it felt special, full of vitality, and segregated from the dangerous, deadening rest of reality. It also felt a little silly. She did not think her reply gave her away when she said, as lightly as she could, "Cyrus came along. That was kind of fun, actually."

———

Sage and Praxis rejoined Dalgleish at a picnic bench in one of the rest area's limestone brick alcoves. None of them wanted to get back in the car just yet. Sage took off her shoes, stretched her arms over her head. Then she did a few hand-

stands falling over into backbends and a few slow-motion
walkovers on the warm concrete, while Praxis laughed
at Dalgleish's fumbling imitations of Sage's acrobatics.
Dalgleish had some tricks of his own from his skateboarding
days, however. He could push up into a handstand from a
cross-legged sitting position and was unafraid of falling—he
handled his body with a controlled recklessness. Sage, on the
other hand, had always been timid and flexible. She practiced
yoga regularly, used to take dance classes, cared (though not
too much, she thought) about appearing graceful. An elderly
couple sat at a table in the next alcove over, and Sage thought
she could feel them watching her. But maybe this was her
problem, assuming people were watching her and that what
she was doing could be construed as inappropriate behavior
for a woman who was a mother. She didn't care. At that moment she trusted the pliability of her body over the hardness
of the concrete.

They got back in the car, and Dalgleish drove. The late
afternoon light was just beginning as they turned onto a
southward highway and the landscape became undeniably
prettier: rolling yellow plains, mountain ranges in the distance looking like shadows behind a low-lying cloud cover.
Soon, the Chisos came into plain, stark view. They were nearing Big Bend National Park. A low-flying biplane flanked
them in the sky for a short distance, and then turned east
and disappeared. They were listening to Dalgleish's music
selection now, a band called Sparklehorse—this music was
mostly slow and atmospheric and inarticulate, lending itself
well to the slanting light that glinted maize-yellow off tufts
of grass in the fields. Between the two of them, Dalgleish was

always the one who looked for and spotted signs of cactus first.

———

She had fallen in love with Dalgleish for his name. Partially, that is, in the beginning, she was drawn to its unusual coolness and the medieval aura of its syllables. She had liked the fact that his friends called him Dag and liked the idea of herself paired with someone who could abide under a name like that; it had a ring of persona to it. Now he no longer had a name to her; he was mostly just "honey," or there was no need for an address at all.

The child had not been planned. Maybe cosmically planned, she would say, for in the months preceding her pregnancy, preceding even her meeting Dalgleish, she had felt—looming, promising, like a beautiful premonition—the most singular feeling of certainty she had ever experienced in her life. She had walked around with this feeling enshrouding her like a visible light. Strangers told her she was beautiful and asked with determined curiosity (as if the answer to this question would explain everything) where she was from; they thanked her for things as inconsequential as her smile. The most mundane exchanges seemed dazzling and holy. Drunk at her cocktail-waitressing job, she walked about the bar through the crowd feeling so *sharp*, how could she even describe it, and critically lucid and empowered—by something that was like sexual knowledge but deeper, and profoundly feminine. Men spoke to her. "What is someone like you doing working here?" or "You're studying to be something big, I can tell, something special, a doctor, a lawyer." Musicians came up after their shows and gave her tips, thanking her "for your vibe." And in the glow of her feeling of secret knowledge, these did not seem like generic or silly compliments but like intense and allusive observations of something on her horizon that she knew was coming but that she hadn't yet concretely fathomed. There was no such thing as a steady reality, she thought. Her bar job felt like a tenuous home, the other bar girls so pretty and tough and herself among them, shrewdly dodging the spears of men's compliments and their common lust. She wanted to radiate the tenuous beauty of vulnerability she saw in some moments: the pretty dark-haired waitress who was an art student by day standing on the stairs in her short skirt counting her money; or the rosy pinkness of the light from the stage and herself standing alone at the back of a crowd, feeling strangely grateful in her intoxication. Men named Mario put their hands on her, gave her shoulder rubs that had the potential of real affection in them. How easy it could be! The barback brought her a bottle of water when she hadn't asked for one, and she took gestures like that to be compliments.

Dalgleish appeared to her somewhere in the midst of this, not in the bar, but one morning in a coffee shop.

A morning of aftermath, it had felt like. She was reading a book on ancient mythologies of "the Orient" when a black man in his late thirties whom she saw regularly in the coffee shop stopped to talk to her. There was a modern Egypt worth reading about, too, he had told her once before, and now he handed her an article about a militant Islamic uprising outside Cairo. "I saw you earlier this week on the street," he said. "You were sitting with a young man. You were," his pause was excruciatingly calm, "distraught." Sage had, in fact, been sitting on a sidewalk earlier in the week, crying during a messy encounter with an ex-boyfriend.

"A man shouldn't be making you distraught," said the one who had given her the article on Egypt, "he should be making you laugh. He should be making that face of yours light all up."

Dalgleish was sitting nearby, listening, and she had noticed he was listening. He had black hair and a slight beard and intense blue eyes. A dirty gray backpack leaned on the floor next to his feet; a skateboard leaned on the backpack. After the black man moved on, Dalgleish held up his own book. Its title suggested his book was of a similar topic as hers; his was called *Unforgetting the Mysteries of the East.* At that she gave him an unsurprised smile.

———————

Texas was new to both of them. They had met in Portland, Oregon, had for some months debated relocating, had considered New Mexico, Washington, Minnesota—but then went, suddenly, a last-minute decision, to Austin, less than a year after Praxis's birth. This trip to Big Bend was only the second camping trip they had attempted with Praxis along. They were not *really* camping, though: they had made a reservation at a place called the Terlingua Ranch Resort.

Dalgleish, it had turned out, had few long-term or close friends in his life and seemed to have less need than Sage for community. At first, she had admired him for this. His self-containment, his stalwartness, she thought of it. He was from a third-generation Norwegian-Midwestern family that had retained little of their Nordic beginnings, save for a story about Dalgleish's paternal grandfather's emigration from

Norway to the United States in his early adulthood, in order
to escape (it was suspected but not clearly known) either a
hurtful family past or something shadier, like a crime. No
ties to the old continent remained, and no family was left for
them to visit in Minnesota, where Dalgleish had spent his
childhood. His parents had been killed in a car wreck some
years ago. Dalgleish had been an only child.

His parents' car accident had occurred when he was an
undergraduate in college in Minneapolis. He then dropped
out of school and rode around the States for a year or so
with a group of people who sold audio equipment out of the
back of a van—and eventually ended up in Oregon. Sage believed he contained the mystery of that and other adventures
deep within him. She emphasized that when she first told her
father about Dalgleish, having also to tell him in the same
conversation that she was pregnant. She had hoped that the
knowledge of Dag's self-sufficiency and adventurousness, the
fact that he had known tragedy, would reassure her father.
Sage, too, was an only child. Her father alone had raised her,
and she had no memory of her mother, whom her father had
known (Sage had been frankly informed) only as a prostitute
in Vietnam during the war. When the mother had written
him asking, initially, for abortion money, Sage's father had
felt something inside him click. He knew he had to save his
baby, bring her back with him to the States. So, he would
say, that is what he did. Sage's mother had agreed to the plan
for a certain sum of money; that was the plain, if not painful,
truth that Sage had had to accept, growing up. When she became unexpectedly pregnant herself, there was no question
of choice in her mind. Her father cried when she first told
him but said he also understood.

Now, her father regularly sent checks and care packages from his home in Southern California, where Sage had grown up. In their one-on-one conversations he would remind Sage she could always come back, with Praxis, if she ever needed to.

Sage and Dag had been waiting a long time to see the desert. Both were drawn to notions of remoteness and open spaces; they talked about it often, as if it defined them, it set them apart from other people. Dag's was both a scientific and aesthetic preoccupation with nature, while Sage's was purely aesthetic. Dag knew the names of many plants and could draw conclusions as to why certain vegetation grew on the sides of some slopes and not others; he could expostulate on the dynamics of plants that grew at the bases of other plants. Plants had a living intelligence, survival tactics. The lives of different species of plants, seemingly separate, were radically entwined. It was an obvious epiphany, Sage thought, and it pertained to the whole world. She knew that, even if she could not give specific examples of it the way Dag could.

They drove up to the Chisos Mountains scenic overlook through a fantastical landscape: at the point where the desert plateau met the base of the mountain range, the differing vegetation of the two terrains made a surreal meeting. Spindly-armed ocotillos mingled with enormous fat-branched flowering cacti. Yucca flowers rose like long-necked alien heads above the tentacle-like rest of their plant bodies. They saw all this in the early twilight. They took several short hikes where Praxis could run along the dusty path and shout out the names of the plants Dag had taught him to identify. They sat on big rocks and looked at the desert. Even before the sun reached the horizon, the moon became visible in the sky, a blue sky. She saw it as a small, pockmarked white circle high above her son's head.

It was dark by the time they reached the cabin, sixteen miles out on a badly rutted gravel road, twenty or so miles outside the national park boundaries.

————

It was morning now. They had pulled chairs out to the little front porch of their cabin and were sitting looking at a view of the desert stretching off to the south. The cabin was no more remarkable than a cheap motel room, but without a TV. Sage was reading a book; Dag was sipping his coffee. The children of a family in another cabin were racing around the narrow dirt roads of the Terlingua Ranch Resort on motorbikes. One of the children—this was surprising—looked only slightly older than Praxis.

"There's no way," said Sage, setting her book on her lap. "I guess some of us are just not as destined or equipped or whatever to lead really physical lives. Like, from the start, some kids are simply more at ease in their bodies than others. And the ones like us who aren't as at ease are the ones who don't live in places like this, huh?"

At four, Praxis had just recently begun to use the pedals on his tricycle. He was, in regard to the physical life, an extremely cautious child. He was not completely disinterested; he was just not the kind of child, as other boys seemed to be, who threw himself into things. He crawled on all fours across unfamiliar playscapes until he became familiar with them; he did not like to go high on the swings; and he had a pattern of refusing to participate in most group activities until at some point he decided for himself that he had watched and understood well enough what was going on. This was ironic to Sage and Dag only because the name Praxis meant action. The name had been Dag's idea; he had not wanted his boy to be lazy or ordinary or easily scared. His greatest hope for any child was a life of adventure: a happily accepted restless nature. (This is what he used to say before the reality of his son's true personality had showed itself.)

"No, I think we could live out here," said Dag. "It's just a matter of finding something to do. I think you have to be a hunter to really appreciate it out here. I think this is a place where people who like to hunt come, or something."

This was a habit of theirs, to speculate about living in places they happened to be passing through. They became united in these momentary excursions into worlds different than the one—it seemed agreed—they were now only temporarily inhabiting, their life in Austin with the child. There was an unacknowledged understanding between them that their circumstances must soon change; their proverbial ship would come in. But no thought-out particulars accompanied this feeling, and the only thing their speculations really affirmed was a shared attitude of being noncommittal toward nearly everything.

She pictured it: they could live in a trailer on a patch of desert with the sun beating down. She could become one of those women, passing herself off as Native American or Mexican (they would be border town people here), deeply brown, with laugh lines around her eyes and wild, long hair. Their son could grow up rafting on the Rio Grande; he could be a desert rat, dark-haired and dusty-skinned, riding around helmetless on a dirt bike, communing with lizards and large insects. Dag would build them a rock wall made out of pieces of shale and limestone collected from the desert. They would renounce all the givens of a liberal urban lifestyle—coffee shops that served lattes with soy milk, video stores that divided movies according to directors and languages, a multiple choice of yoga schools, a multiple choice of vegetarian Mexican restaurants—and reestablish themselves as the recluse-aesthetes of their new desert community.

Dag took a sip of his coffee. His coffee was in a styrofoam cup and had come from the instant mix in the cabin. He didn't mind mediocre coffee, but Sage was longing for a hot cup of a certain brand of tea. "That kid must be closer to five, I'd say," said Dag. "Maybe he's just little for his age."

Praxis was playing with his Batman action figures on a blanket Sage had spread out on the porch. He had four of them, two different versions; he had wanted two each of the same ones. Sage leaned forward now and tossed the novel she'd been reading—*Love Invents Us*—onto the blanket.

Sometimes she liked to do this, to abruptly throw aside a book she'd been reading, in midsentence and without having bothered to mark the page. Lately she read books slowly, starting many and getting through few. It was not only because she was a mother of a toddler and too busy to read. Sometimes she was just so full of an excited, convoluted feeling that she couldn't concentrate on anything. She had recently attempted reading *A Death in the Family* but had had to stop because of such feelings. The book's heightened attention to detail and mood, and the highly stylized, unearthly glow the author's language cast around scenes like the boy's evening walk through a neighborhood with his father, how all of that was in fact a map, on some precise spiritual level, of what-may-happen-in-one's-life directly preceding a death: that is what the book seemed to be pointing to. She couldn't read it without being flooded with fear—fear of loss or harm regarding her son most of all. The house they lived in seemed hopeless and confining, the nature of reality, of domesticity, just a long road of fightless acceptance. And the thought that it could be known—that loss or tragedy was coming—*could* it be known? Could it be read in the details of one's daily goings-on? Did it mean death was coming when suddenly the minutiae of life became enhanced by an acute, delicate light? she wondered. Rather than thinking further along these lines, she preferred to say she thought reading was boring; that literature fell short of the immediacy, the immediate *impact*, of other art forms like, say, music.

Music was a far more effective healer, she thought. Music was a salve that eased the pain of living in the world, yet it still kept you in your body and in the world more than words on paper ever could.

She had also recently read some Rudolf Steiner essays about the evolution of the human race. The larynx was the most important and advanced human organ, spiritually speaking, these lectures said, and in the future of the human race (it could be eons, *millennia* from now) human beings would have the power to physically manifest—thoughts, ideas, and eventually new bodies as well—via this organ. The larynx would become the future human's reproductive organ. Thus would come about a time when, as had been stated in the Bible, humans would be capable of "speaking forth" more humans into being, as fluidly as they did their thoughts and feelings. The human voice in this era, and the chemistry of the human body, would be other than it was now. Made up of elements not even known to science in this era. You had to think with your soul and not your mind, said Rudolf Steiner, in order to grasp the truth of these concepts.

That is why music, she thought, *but what about why I think so much about love?*

She nodded now at *Love Invents Us* as she simultaneously reached behind her for her guitar—it was leaning in the cabin's doorway—and drew it onto her lap. "I don't know if I buy that story. That book I'm reading. I don't know if it's convincing enough for me, you know?" she said.

"I don't know if you don't explain it to me. I'm not the one reading it," said Dag reasonably.

"Well, it's a love story, sort of, a few love stories. Unrequited love. It starts in high school; they get separated; years later they see each other again—it's all good prose and funny details, but then what's annoying to me is that years later the characters are still obsessing over the same details about each other that they were obsessing about in the beginning. And it's like, you'd think life would've intruded more by that point and given them other experiences to obsess about, you know? And I guess the other thing that gets me is how the memories that linger, what motivates their experiences of love, has mainly to do with sexual details. I guess I don't buy that. I just don't understand defining love in that way."

"Well, what would you say is the way you define it, then?"

"I don't know. An undercurrent. Not the physical person, I mean not their physical self. Not foremost." She picked at her guitar for a moment, then came to a revelation. "It's a *male* writer thing, that's what I think. Writing about the mystery of attraction as sexual, as having mainly to do with the body, you know? It's boring, frankly. But the thing is, this book, this one is written by a woman. I guess I find that a little disappointing or something." She didn't know why, but she sometimes needed to downplay the significance of sex. She liked to envision herself, svelte and chaste, later in life, joining a Buddhist monastery or traveling to India to become a hardcore yoga devotee.

Dag sipped his coffee, sitting forward with his elbows on his spread-apart knees. Frequently, increasingly frequently, in fact, he seemed to think it unnecessary to respond to her. She watched him; she stared at the side of his face, calculatingly. Then he stood, arching his back to stretch and yawn. He looked her way.

"Are you going to get ready? I mean, we should get going before it gets too hot."

"It's because of my tea," she said. "I really need my tea. That would help me feel happier about moving."

———

They had to ask the waitress in the ranch resort restaurant if she would warm up Sage's tea, but when the travel mug Sage always carried was finally handed back to her, the tea was still only lukewarm.

"Our microwave is a little busted," said the waitress.

Sage sometimes wondered if she relied too much on drinking tea (morning and afternoon) to ensure the stability of her moods. But wasn't there that Chinese proverb, something about how it was good to go without food some days but that one should never go a day without tea? *My food is my country*, thought Sage. Road trips were a challenge now because she had become a strict vegetarian after Praxis's birth—it had taken a life outside her own to make her care about health, was how she saw it. Soy milk versus dairy, honey versus sugar. Dag was a flexible vegetarian. He could survive on diner eggs and cheese, and sometimes, yes, he broke down and ate a hamburger if that was all that was available. He acted cynical but unapologetic about it whenever he did make a decision like that.

Dag paid for their bagels and his second cup of coffee while Sage went to collect Praxis from where he was banging open and shut the screen door that connected the lobby to the dining area. There was only one customer in the dining area, a man in his forties, scruffy and dusty-looking, probably the driver of the mud-splattered Ford pickup that was parked outside next to Dag's 4Runner. He was hunched over a mug of coffee with a blank expression on his face.

"Prax, it's time to say bye-bye to the door," said Sage. The screen door was making a lot of noise, and the man wasn't looking at Praxis. She smiled in the man's direction, but barely, because she didn't feel any degree of welcome from him. Toward her son she cast her energy in a fun and indifferent manner, a tactic she often used to get him to follow her without a fuss. It worked well with animals, too, she had found. "Let's go, let's go," she said lightly, turning her back.

Praxis said, "Oh, all right," and raced after her.

Sometimes it worked; sometimes it did not.

They stayed mostly on the western side of the park that day. They took several hikes down mile-long dusty paths, passing monstrous palm trees, mission ruins. They stopped at unspectacular warm patches of river water. They crossed one stagnant strip of river by rowboat and paid $6 per person for a mile-long ride down a bumpy dirt road into Boquillas, Mexico, in a pickup truck driven by a driver who spoke no English. The whole escapade was sad and hot and silent. In a café they drank Cokes while Praxis crawled around the concrete patio pretending to be a cat, and a toothless, wrinkled, elderly Mexican man tried to play with Praxis by tickling him. To this Praxis took great offense and called the man "stupid" and "bad guy." The other Americans in the café were complaining about the price of their boat ride and the ride into Boquillas. Because of how they sounded, petulant and ungracious, Sage decided *she* would not complain. On the dusty street, a one-armed man tried to finagle them into paying him to take their photograph. The town was desolate and utterly unremarkable. Some people got romantic about the barrenness of the desert, and some people loathed it. Both types, Sage thought, lacked the same thing, which was an honest acquaintance with their own inner starkness. Or something.

They recrossed the border and drove southwest. The highlight of their day, they had decided, would be the hike down to the Rio Grande. Praxis was tired and easily distracted, so the two-mile walk took them nearly an hour. Before they started up the canyon part of the trail, Praxis had to stop and sit down in the middle of the path six or seven times to scoop handfuls of dirt onto his legs. And he didn't want to be carried. Sage tried pointing out lizards to him, to keep him moving, but the lizards dashed by too fast. He also stopped if he thought there were rocks in his shoes.

"I have a shoe in my rock," he would say.

At the first part of the Rio Grande they reached, they watched another family—the child was older than Praxis, ten maybe—push a canoe onto the water. Both parents were obese. Sage couldn't help but wonder how far down the river they would go, and whether or not the woman would row, too. She wasn't sure why it mattered to her, but it did. She lacked faith in the fat woman, she realized. Unfair a prejudice as it was, she could not picture that woman helping with the rowing.

As they walked on the steep path that ran up and then down alongside the canyon wall on one side of the Rio Grande, Sage and Dag took turns holding Praxis. The sun was high by this time. Upon reaching the water's edge, they leaned on one side of a large, smooth boulder and gazed up at the sheer vertical faces of orange-and-brown rock enclosing the serene green band of the river. Sage had the impression that these rock walls, with their hushed, ancient energy, sat counsel over the rest of the landscape. She spotted some plants growing out of crooks in the rock faces.

"Why on earth would a plant choose to grow there?" she let herself wonder aloud, willing to let Dag elaborate.

"They're just prickly pears. Those'll grow anywhere," he said.

Then, a group of middle-aged women came off the path and gathered around a boulder a few yards from Sage, Dag, and Praxis. The women were dressed in light-colored shorts and white sneakers. They all had gray or white or graying short hair. They talked while fanning themselves with their hands and wiping sweat from their brows with bandanas they'd had knotted around their necks as scarves. They did not seem to have a long history of friendship, for they were telling one another things close friends would've already known.

"I have four sons, yes, but my eldest is passed away."
The woman who said this was the healthiest-looking of the
bunch. She was white-haired with a tall, rectangular frame;
her face did not look pinched or frivolous, as a few of the
other women's faces did; hers looked gallantly lined. She had
clear, small eyes and had smiled in Praxis's direction when
the women first walked past.

"Oh, I guess I did know that," said the woman with
whom she was speaking. This one had salt-and-pepper
hair and a pear-shaped body, not the type of woman Sage
would've expected to see on a trail next to the Rio Grande.
But then she hadn't expected obese people pushing onto the
river in a canoe, either.

"He was in the air force," said the white-haired woman.
She appeared to be going into a history. Her son's ambition
since high school to be a pilot, his tour in the Gulf War,
certain accolades. He had always been a superb athlete, a
competitive swimmer. Sage tried to only half-listen, out of
a semblance of discretion. The son had married, there were
two grandchildren, and his death had occurred not while
flying but in some other kind of accident. A motorcycle accident. "He was living in Arizona at the time, and we were
still living here. We got on a plane for Phoenix that very afternoon," said the woman. The way she was speaking, with
willingness and a calm distance, made Sage think her son's
death must not have been recent. How did one get to that
stage, Sage wondered, where one looked back on the events
of upheaval in one's life with such benign composure?

Now she felt a disquieting flutter of knowledge in her
chest, a feeling of herself as profoundly *herself*—dangerously
strong and, hence, dangerously alone. She did and did not

want to be this way. She looked toward Dag. He was sitting at the top of the rock, trying to discourage Praxis from climbing it, too.

"Are you listening?" she asked surreptitiously, but Dag was not. Louder, she said, "But what do you expect? When you're up there yourself."

————————

That night, tired and dusty, they came back to the cabin with carry-out meals from a roadside Mexican café. The desert, as they had driven through it at sunset, was pink-white, rising and falling in undulating lumps to either side of their vehicle, and the memory of it stayed in Sage's mind with a rhythm like the sound of the sea. Now, the sky was dark and big and alight with stars. The air was warm. Sage and Praxis lay on a blanket spread out on the porch, and Praxis pointed out the lights of planes passing overhead, high and silent. Dag sat in a nearby chair, strumming on the guitar. They could hear, dimly, the sounds of the family in the cabin opposite theirs. Eventually, Sage drifted off. She awoke with a start and found Dag looking at her. Praxis was asleep beside her; the cabin across the way was now dark and quiet.

"Are you okay?" said Dag. "You were having a bad dream."

She had been dreaming that she was in a trailer and when she looked outside, the tops of trees overhead were bending, with a tremendous screeching, grinding sound like steel being crushed. It was the sky coming down. She ran outside, and people in a panic were trying to crawl away on their stomachs, while someone else—a woman—threw a machete like a boomerang. Sage saw it slice one of the people in half.

The lightness. These words appeared now in her dream, as if being projected onto a screen. *The lightness is killing me.* Still, it occurred to her to smile. "Just the story of Chicken Little," she said.

———

If Sage were to attribute a color to the young teachers at Praxis's school, it would be indigo. That glowing deep shade between blue and violet.

In her first year of motherhood, Sage sought out books to explain what it was she was experiencing. She wanted literature that spoke of motherhood in the cosmic scheme of things, not just month-to-month guides and how-tos. She wanted the world of women explained in mystical, soul-satisfying terms; she wanted the isolation of mothers and babies, especially as it occurred in modern societies, explained as both spiritual necessity *and* aberration of nature. Was it? A few books used Greek goddesses to explain various parts of the female psyche; many books talked about God or (annoying gentleness, she thought) the metaphor of Mother Earth as a nurturer and how women had only to reclaim their connection with nature. Another book daringly posited that maternal instinct was not, in fact, an innate female tendency. Sage took all these ideas in.

In one book, the author claimed many young people presently living and being born on the planet had auras that were indigo in color. The author called them "indigo children." Auras could be divided into three types: physical, mental, and emotional, indigo being one of the latter. Physical colors were becoming extinct, what with the approach of the new millennium and the advent of technology eradicating the need for physical labor. A refined, super-technological—in fact, a more cerebral and spiritual—age was coming. New aura colors were evolving; the human race was evolving, said the book. The author, an expert at divining auras, had encountered her first indigo aura in 1972. Sage had been born in 1973. It struck her that she could fit into this group as well as Praxis might. Indigo people were hypersensitive, creative but impractical, likely to be uncomfortable with aspects of the physical world. They cried often and easily as babies. They might be socially awkward but were good with children and animals. They were the dreamers and innocents. To those who didn't understand them, they might appear simply inept, or irresponsible. It was in the nature of indigo persons to live according to an intuitive knowledge foremost, one that was heedless of the outer world's generally accepted rules and rites. Indigos could not conform even if they wanted to, said the book.

> Our indigo children with their great potential for gentleness have arrived to guide us into a wiser view of tomorrow. We must learn that while the material world is unreliable, touch is never inconsequential; we must, in effect, learn to tread more lightly.

But hadn't the potential for gentleness been brought into the world by children throughout all time? wondered Sage.

Also, in that first year of motherhood, she had searched for friendships with other mothers. She even went as far as signing up with an online service. The profiles of other Austin mothers said things like: "Thirty-three years old chasing around rambunctious two-year-old boy and still sixty-five pounds over my target weight—HELP!!" Similar conversations were to be had in parks, in the children's museum, and at the Gymboree play program, where playing, it seemed, had to involve a soundtrack, a bubble machine, and a play instructor who spoke to every child in the same impersonal, endearing, high-pitched manner. The state of modern motherhood seemed quite hopeless and depressing to Sage. Until she found this school, where the teachers were young and bohemian-looking and the other parents were, like her, less easily classifiable. Lesbian couples and gay single fathers, jazz musicians and PhD students, even one moderately famous science fiction writer. The school was located west of the city proper, on ten acres of privately owned hill country land, and the schoolhouse was a straw-bale construction that recycled rainwater in an underground cistern. At this school, the children knew what solstices and Native Americans were; they were not permitted to eat sugary foods at lunch; they were not allowed to play gun games. There was an organic vegetable garden as well as a small corn patch on the school property. The children caught ladybugs and released them in the garden. They played fearlessly among daddy longlegs and beetles and other insects.

The first time Praxis saw a line of six or seven daddy longlegs moving swiftly, gracefully, on their hairline-fine legs down the schoolhouse steps, looking impossibly light, he had screamed and took off running. (Sage, too, was unnerved at the sight of them, though she pretended to be fine with it.) Witnessing Praxis's reaction, Cyrus and another of the teachers began picking up the daddy longlegs and placing them on their arms. They said "Look, look, Praxis, it's all right" as they let the spiders climb all over their arms and up to their shoulders.

Details like the rainwater cistern and the organic garden and an adherence to a Native American perspective on history, even if it was all a little precious, could make Sage feel as if she were aligning herself—and her son—on the *better* side (for lack of a better way to put it) of a battle being waged between invisible forces in the world. But perhaps they were not so invisible, these forces, she thought, for there was, now, an actual war pending. The debate whether or not to send U.S. forces into Iraq had been going on for some months; the virtues of things Eastern, religious, and veiled being pitted against those of things Western, secular, and supposedly forthright. The advocates of forthrightness were in favor of invading, while an acceptance of ambiguity seemed to be the platform of those against. In her mind, Sage saw how her idea of opposing cosmic forces had a parallel in this opposition between liberals and conservatives. The liberal versus conservative battle was no longer just a matter of differences in lifestyle and politics: it had become a matter of light versus dark, with each side believing theirs was the side of light.

The teachers at Praxis's school were, without exception, on the liberal side of things. They could be overheard saying to the children things like, "Hey, ants are not bad," if they were caught squashing ants. And when the kids would not quit squashing the ants, "Hey, okay, it's your karma." The collective style of these young teachers was a combination of neo-hippie and hip-hop. Among them, Cyrus stood out like a herald of their kind. The first time she met him had been at the school's Halloween carnival after Praxis had just started attending. This had been her first impression of Cyrus, before she knew him also as a person who lived alone in a cabin at the back of the school's property (and before that small, pivotal moment when he looked at her as she'd walked past singing "Amazing Grace"): at the Halloween carnival, he had jumped aboard the grounded wooden ship in the playground where Sage was standing, talking with another parent, and he had exclaimed, "Who am I!" He was dressed in a painted-green thermal shirt, cutoff green khakis, and a cape made of tissue paper streamers. He had twigs and leaves in his hair and green marker smeared on his face and hands. Sage thought it was obvious.

"You're Pan," she said, and he pointed a stick at her and said, "Wrong! I'm *green*."

The next time she saw him, he was wearing a bright blue T-shirt with white V-neck ribbing and orange sweatpants. He looked dauntingly sloppy. His hair was almost hay-yellow. He was talking with some other parents, and he appeared serious and cheerful. He struck her as the kind of boy who would never be interested in someone like her; *she* was far too dark and closed, she thought. The mystery of his lightness and his color, that was what got to her.

When recently Praxis came home saying, "Kevin wouldn't let me go on the hike today," Sage knew immediately, somehow, that he meant Cyrus when he said Kevin. She knew because the mention of this name, even though it was the wrong one, sent a dull shock through her body.

She didn't bother to correct Praxis's mistake, though. "What do you mean Kevin wouldn't let you go on the hike?" She often repeated Praxis's misnomers and mispronunciations; she considered it a way of respecting his perception, which—she thought—was vital and innocent; vitally absurd, as well. For instance, he called macaroni and cheese "spicy" and toy trucks "saucers," and so did she, on a regular basis. "I'm sure Kevin would've let you go on the hike, Prax. Maybe you were just too busy with something else. Did you miss the hike because you were busy playing with something else, maybe?"

Praxis said, "I was playing with the black paper, that's what I did today."

"Who's Kevin?" asked Dag. They were having dinner around the coffee table in their living room, where they usually ate because they had no dining table. Their couch, a hand-me-down from a couple they'd associated with briefly, was bulky, green, and somewhat ugly.

"Cyrus, he means Cyrus. The blond one. That really nice one, you know. The one who lives in that cabin below the school."

"That guy? He seems kind of cocky to me," said Dag. "I like Lisbeth better, personally." Lisbeth was a willowy, dark girl, one of the female teachers, who was quiet and ethereal and whom the children followed around the schoolyard as kittens trailed after a mother cat, stumbling and club-footed in the wake of her grace. "She's so quiet it's almost unnerving, but it's appropriate too," said Dag. "Like, it makes sense that people like that work with kids. They're not that good with adults, but it makes sense they're good with kids, you know?" He looked at Sage as if from a distance for a second. "I guess you're a little bit like that, too, actually."

Sage said, "You think? I don't know," and found she couldn't look him in the eye saying that.

2.

Inevitably, they ended up fighting at some point during their road trip. Sage always entertained ideas of leaving, taking Praxis with her. A new life of self-containment and gentle attention between mother and son, something purer and larger, could be waiting for her. A clear, sharp newness seemed plausible. Being on the road energized her, made her believe she had the strength to do all this—leave, start over—and more.

What had they been arguing about? She couldn't remember anymore. Or, yes she could, she just didn't want to. She had been the one to get upset, because she'd felt he was not joining in enthusiastically enough in her speculation of a life in the Chihuahua Desert. They were driving along a scenic route through the southernmost section of the park, and she had been feeling particularly awestruck by the landscape: gray-white lumps that were almost hills; distant cracks like veins crisscrossing the dusty pale desert basin. It looked Martian, formidable, unearthly—she imagined living out there might be the closest one could come to experiencing what it would be like to live on another planet. She had begun to imagine a scenario in which they built an eco-efficient home on forty acres of rocky, bone-white desert; it would be one of those super-modern, minimalist designs with some kind of consciousness-enhancing aspect—like dome or yurt living was purported to have. They would spend winters here, spring and fall in Austin, summers elsewhere. You could buy land for as little as two or three thousand dollars an acre, a local had told them.

Dag had shot her down, or so it had felt to her. "Who lives in the desert, really?" he said. "I don't think the desert is a place one goes to by choice or in order to seek community. If you want to participate in the world in a connected, recognizable way, the desert is not where you build your home. Generally, figures throughout history have been *exiled* to the desert. Think Jesus, think Moses, the mystics. Think Mongolian nomads and Bedouin tribes. Think Rapunzel, even—in the unedited version of the fairytale, that is. You don't build the hub of a civilization out in the desert. I mean, sure, there's Las Vegas, but that's a totally unnatural occurrence, it's a place sustained, in its own strange way, by the sort of magic that's possible only in the desert. The desert is like a go-between place. I think out here you can get in closer touch with living on a nonmaterial plane, but probably it makes it really hard for you to live with other people if you stay out here too long, you know?"

Sometimes when he got talking, he did not stop. She used to tell herself it just showed his enthusiasm for ideas; now, more often, she felt resistant to giving him too much attention once he got going.

"Nowadays, I think you can come out to the desert to seek spiritual refinement or rejuvenation for a temporary time—if you *choose* to stay out here, that's another story entirely," he went on. "The kind of people who stay in the desert, they do it in renunciation of the rest of the world. But you can't renounce society without accepting that society then *must*, in fact, be a continuing thing, you know?"

All this, thought Sage, was just theory and made no move, really, toward a true appreciation of the scenery outside their windows. She had wanted, just for a little while, to *entertain* the idea of escape.

"Humor me," she could've said, but she said something more to the effect of "You're hurting me." In this way their intellectual speculations turned into arguments. Soon, everything was being taken personally, and she was admitting to being able to picture a future without him, while he was launching into "how I see myself at forty-five, where I would like to be a wholly realized individual whether I'm with or without a life partner."

"Honestly, whether I stay or go comes down to the same choice," said Dag, "that it *is* a matter of choice. Do I want to live my life alone? Not necessarily. But could I survive without you? Yes, I'm certain I could. I've never wanted a love founded on habit." He had spoken like this many times before.

"Well, neither have I." Sage had to match his indifference. Dag, for his part, never tried to coax explanations from her tight, small rebuttals or her nos. If she didn't have it in her to tell him fully what was on her mind, he wasn't about to ask. And she respected him for that, his refusal to grovel. She felt satisfied herself when she managed to gaze out the window and stay silent for miles at a time. It felt Zen-like. Phrases like *emotional mastery* and *spiritual discipline* played through her mind. The thought that she could be released from need—of conversation, of affection, of *him*—gave her a focused, gratifying sensation.

Human flight could only be temporary, however, she would realize.

"Why're you stopping?" At first she thought (she almost hoped and feared) a form of anguish was making him pull the car over.

"I have to pee," he said.

They stopped at the base of a rock promontory that overlooked a scattering of low, cactus-pocked hills. Wooden stakes marked the heads of several hiking trails. She watched Dag go off down one of these trails, and he did not immediately return. In fact, he seemed to be taking an inordinate amount of time if all he was doing was peeing. Praxis began complaining in the backseat, so she got out of the car and got him out, too. He wanted to have a picnic sitting on the tailgate and he wanted butter crackers, he said. Sage reached into the back and dragged the cooler across the open tailgate. She couldn't find what Praxis was asking for, though.

"You ate them all already," she said. Words like *already* had to be used so meticulously with a toddler. Praxis was refusing to understand. She felt like throwing up her hands, or worse. "Are you listening? Are you listening to my words? There are *no more*. No more butter crackers. All gone."

It was not that he didn't believe her; it was that he thought the situation should be instantly reparable because— she realized in fury and amazement—she was the designated mender of his world. These two emotions mixed together turned to something like sorrow, finally; they always did. The future—that high-flying nervousness and anticipation she rode on so much of the time lately—was not visible from these depths.

"You can have cheese, or you can have apples." She laid out these choices, sternly.

After another five minutes, Dag reappeared (Praxis was now contentedly nibbling on a piece of string cheese) carrying a large rock in the crook of one arm. An act of retaliation and self-appeasement, both, thought Sage: the way he displayed it, this coveting of an object from nature, but would not, she knew, offer up why.

She asked, "What's that?"

He replied, "What's it look like?"

He swiped at a lock of his black bangs with the back of his hand, leaving a mark of pale-gray dust on his forehead, lightening a corner of one eyebrow. Perhaps it was a glimpse of his older self, turning white, frail and incandescent. Like her as an Asian person with large eyes and olive skin, he, too, was an anomaly—a man of Scandinavian descent who was dark-haired and slender. What place in the world would Praxis inherit, then, coming from two such similar extremes?

She turned away from him and began packing up the cooler.

"Look at this, Praxis. Lookit what Dad found." Dag laid the rock, jagged and gray, on Praxis's lap.

"It's a ocotillo!" exclaimed Praxis, for *ocotillo* was the word they'd been having him say every time they aimed the camera at him.

"No, it's a rock. It's a rock, and it's special 'cause it's from the Chihuahua Desert. And we're going to take it home with us," said Dag, "but we're only going to take just this one."

————

Some semblance of reality (whatever that was) felt reinstated when they happened upon a natural foods café in the tiny town of Terlingua, just outside the national park boundaries. Her fits of depression and wildness, it seemed, could be as

easily controlled by food and drink as they could by dras-
tic measures and empty threats. These were silly comforts,
but here she could get a cup of chai tea with soy milk and a
smoothie. Normalcy regained through consumption.

The man behind the counter of the café smiled warmly,
readily, as they entered. Sage wanted to reciprocate the
openness he was radiating at them (it meant something
when strangers did this to you, and on simple faith, no less)
but realized she was too tired. The arguing had worn her
out. She disliked herself when she fell into her antisocial
moods, but she couldn't help it. She was just too fragile,
she decided. Sometimes she needed to retreat, to not have
to continue to uphold herself among the multitudes. Like
that book said about indigo people. The more sensitive you
were, the more easily you absorbed the energies of others.
And there were so many of them—other people—walking
about, each engulfed in an amorphous energy field, each of
those fields pulsating at its own discordant and jarring rates,
so unsynchronized with her own. When she pictured things
in this way, the term *beautifully nervous* came to mind. She
saw the world as being full of bodies that were similarly,
beautifully (that meant innocently) nervous, as if people,
though their physical forms might appear calm and normal,
walked about, each outlined by a personalized cloud of roil-
ing, spasmic, wrenching movement: the truth would mean a
human population of unaddressed frenzy.

Sage absorbed herself in drinking her tea and her
smoothie, sitting on the floor playing with Praxis, who was
absorbed in the wood pieces of a Jenga game. Dag made
small talk with the man behind the counter. The man, who

looked to be in his late thirties, was originally from upstate New York. He had come to Big Bend as a tour guide one season, had fallen in love with the desert, had stayed. Five years ago now.

"So, you're a tour guide," said Dag. "Any places you'd highly recommend we see?"

The man said, "Oh, don't get me started," with a pleased laugh and shake of his head. "The old *tinaja*, have you gone out there? That's one of my personal favorites, if you've got the time and you're willing to face the road. God-awful gravel road that I swear the county has said it was going to fix, but they haven't spent a penny on it, of course. I'll admit, every time I'm in the van on that road I swear to myself I'm never going out there again. But once I get out there, it's well worth it. It's where the old mineral quarry once was, see, they used to mine salt from there. All this used to be under an ocean, of course. But there is this natural formation in the rocks out there, a bowl of sorts. It's known as the *tinaja*, or watering hole. And it's the perfect watering hole because it's so deep, it never dries up, even in the middle of the summer. The water is crystal blue and the inside walls of the hole are just these amazing sheer, smooth, white rock faces. The quality of the rock out there is just astounding, amazing. I can't say it enough. It's otherworldly, really." Here, he paused, and his eyes took on a sparkle. "If you've got some rope and at least two people, you can jump in and go for a swim. Gotta go with someone you trust, though, 'cause to get out you need the other person to throw the rope down to you, then pull you out."

"So you can enter, but you cannot exit," said Dag, with mock portent.

"By yourself, no. Animals fall in there and drown a lot, actually. We've fished out javelina, coyotes, even a horse one time."

"Really? That's wild." Dag could be good at the casual but cheerful conversational tone, when he wanted to be. "This is a nice store you've got," he added, after a moment.

"My partner and I opened it—well, it's *her* store, actually," said the man. "We were longing to have these kinds of products available for ourselves, really. My partner, she's extremely health-conscious. She's been a vegetarian for nearly thirty years, a real chemical-free conscious person." He glanced toward Sage here, as if he expected it to appeal to her in particular. "It's just a delight, really it is, to be able to live out here and still have these choices available to us."

Feeling as if she was giving him what he wanted to hear, Sage said, "It is nice to find a place to buy soy milk out here. I guess I wasn't expecting it."

The man looked at her directly now. "There's a lot of forward thinkers out here, though it may not seem like there would be. You know, we've even had people come in here and tell us we carry things they can't find in organic foods stores in their cities. Now, that's a good feeling."

"Really? Wow," said Sage. Dag, by then, was flipping through a book of photographs of Marlon Brando he had pulled from the shelf next to the café table where he was seated. Sage asked the man, "What's it like living out here?"

"I love it," said the man, with a quick nod and a lift of his eyebrows, "and I've lived in big cities most all my life. I honestly don't feel anything lacking out here. It's remote, certainly, but I guess that's what I like about it. The rest of the world, the rest of you all can have it, I say. Especially with things as they are now."

Sage said, "Oh sure. God, I know."

"We just count our blessings that we're our own bosses out here, and, to be quite honest, our overhead is rather low," said the man.

A woman entered from the patio outside. She wore a sleeveless summer dress of what looked like an ethnic-African kind of fabric, and work gloves. Her blond hair was short and styled in semi-spikey layers. She was tall, big-boned; she appeared to be older than the man. She did not acknowledge Sage and Dag as customers, nor did she smile in Praxis's direction. Her voice had a slight British accent.

"That filter is the wrong size. Now I'm going to have to go into town and pick up another one," she said to the man. Her tone suggested she knew she was being observed but wanted her observers to know she didn't care.

The man answered her in a lower voice, "I was just there earlier, Ray. If you'd told me, I could've picked one up."

"Did I know earlier? What did I just tell you? I *just* tried it." She pulled off her gloves, began to vigorously wash her hands in the sink. Then she crossed to the cash register and began punching buttons with assured brusqueness. Sage felt an instant dislike for this woman—and sympathy for the man. Men like these, she believed, really wanted kinder women; they just didn't know it. Or maybe they did but chose to do nothing about it, for reasons only they knew.

The man, standing to the woman's right, was now having a problem with a fly buzzing in front of his face. He took a step sideways, awkwardly. He reached for a fly swatter hanging from a nail on the wall but then hesitated, casting a glance in Sage's direction. "Wait, are you a pacifist?"

Here, the woman, too, raised her gaze from the cash register and, chin lifted, looked squarely at Sage.

I have been playing a part, it occurred to her then.

Because—truth be told—Sage was not that much of a pacifist, and she knew it. She just appeared to be that kind of person, with her tea and her juices and her praise of soy milk, with her expression of consternation at the mention of current events. Sitting tolerantly beside her son on the floor as he repeatedly stacked and knocked down pieces of the Jenga puzzle, making a mess. The man had already assured them "that's what that stuff is there for" with a firm, admiring smile in Sage's direction: it was the kind of smile frequently bestowed on young mothers by men who did not have children of their own. Sage had come to recognize it. And she had smiled back, playing the part of earthy young mother, patiently admonishing her child while paying quiet attention to his game. In this pose, she passed judgment on all other parents who did not commune with their children's spirits; she passed judgment on all other women who were not nurturers, who were not self-sacrificers, who were, in short, not mothers.

Sage laughed a little. "No, it's all right."

The man went after the fly with the swatter, somewhat noisily.

Dag, glancing furtively at this exchange, slowly closed the Marlon Brando book and replaced it on the shelf. As he reached for his wallet, he looked at Sage. She felt, as she sometimes did, the steady, beating darkness of a message carried between them in his gaze. He saw everything she did, and still he let her be.

3.

Praxis's school was run by a husband-and-wife team, a couple in their late thirties. Her name was Kitty; his was Brian. They had started the school nine years earlier, as business partners, and then somewhere along the way had gotten married.

Kitty and Brian had no kids of their own. Sage knew, though, from hearsay, that Kitty had stepchildren from a first marriage to a man quite a bit older, and the stepchildren still sometimes visited her. Sage disliked Kitty, or, perhaps more truthfully, she was intimidated by Kitty and had been looking for reasons to dislike her; she wasn't sure why. Brian was tall, well-built, and genial-looking. You could almost call him dopey, with his heavy southern drawl and his aged innocence. In general, he did more talking than Kitty, though Sage had a suspicion (it had to do with Kitty's dark, self-assured good looks) that Kitty did more of the talking in private.

While Kitty stayed upstairs in the school's office handling most of the administrative matters, Brian was usually outside. Arriving to pick up Praxis in the afternoons, Sage would see Brian, tool belt heavy around his hips, carrying supplies in from his truck or standing on the roof handing fallen branches, stray toys, or overthrown balls down to Cyrus or another of the teachers on the playground. On occasion, she had seen Brian rigging elaborate contraptions out of PVC pipe for the children to play with. Despite the seem-

ing separateness of their roles, Kitty and Brian had appeared
to Sage to be a happy couple, a "good" couple, until one
night at a campout on the school's property.

She had noticed before that Kitty was aloof toward other
women, that she smiled at them but seldom stopped to talk.
And she engaged in playing with the kids only if, in doing so,
she was interacting with one of the young male teachers at
the same time. There was something suggestive and exclusive
in her body language toward men, especially younger ones—
Sage had noted this with a feeling of satisfaction tinged with
envy. Kitty looked at least ten years younger than her thirty-
eight years. She still had freckles, a brunette cuteness, with
laugh lines just starting to deepen around her eyes and at the
corners of her mouth. She had tanned, muscular arms and
a flat chest. She was slim and small but strong and sharp-
looking, too.

Perhaps what Sage really disliked about Kitty was the
sense that there was something the two of them had in common, or that she and Dag had in common with Kitty and
Brian, maybe. His stoicism and the ability he had to immerse
himself in purely physical tasks. Her secret watchfulness and
not entirely well-meaning reserve.

The campout took place sometime around Halloween.

There was a spot on the school's acreage that the children called the Fairy Meadows, a clearing amid the scraggly
cedar elms that dominated the hillsides. A campfire was
blazing; marshmallows were being roasted. Parents gossiped
with one another and sang songs with the kids and told them
stories. They let them play with flashlights, shining them up
at the sky and trees while they lay sprawled out on blankets
laid over the hard ground. There was alcohol around the fire;

there was—not even that discreetly—marijuana, too. Parents had set up tents on the outer edges of the clearing. There were maybe eight parents present and five teachers, along with some outside friends and partners. Cyrus was there. To this number of adults there were about a dozen kids.

Earlier, before the sun had gone down, Sage had walked into the schoolhouse kitchen to get a cup of water for Praxis, and there she had seen Cyrus and Kitty, standing in the doorway of the pantry, not embracing but certainly kissing. He stood with his arms raised, hands hooked on the edges of the doorframe; she leaned in toward him with her hands loosely clasped behind her back. Something about their intimacy did not seem real or even truly intimate, was the strange part, and neither was it in the least bit discreet. Sage didn't know how to interpret what she had seen. Perhaps she didn't understand all the nuances and complicities that existed amid this group of people. As quietly as she had walked in, she turned around and walked out.

That night, Sage and Dag, both mildly drunk, went for a walk through the trees with Praxis and a couple of the other parents and their kids. They laughed and called out after the kids, while indulging in banal but heartfelt exchanges about the division of labor in their households, funny things their kids had said, and the prices of items in certain stores.

"We've finally closed down the dairy farm, but he still has to hang on to them in order to fall asleep. Num-nums, he calls them."

There was this kind of frankness and humor. Even the men were matter-of-fact and sincere on the subject.

"At first I felt envious about it, yes, I admit. I even considered, you know, this advertisement I saw on TV once for fake breasts that men can wear. The milk is siphoned through tubes. Really. You can order them online."

"I know it's nontoxic and I know the philosophy here is permissiveness, but I wish they'd do just a little something some of the time to stop Sophie from eating paint."

"We're very pragmatic about it now, what can I say? Love-making is a weekend event only."

Sage and Dag remained slightly on the outside of this, too, though. Dag wandered ahead, seeking out a route with a couple of the older kids, while Sage walked along holding Praxis's hand on one side and the hand of someone else's child, a red-haired girl named Medea, on her other side. She felt glad to be in the midst of all this talk, even though she had nothing to add to it. She did not voice worries about the darkness or express doubts about the safety of the trail, as some of the other mothers were now doing. A few wanted to turn back, and finally they decided to.

"Who wants to go back to the campfire now and roast some marshmallows?" This directed, in hearty tones, to both children and adults.

"Me, me," went the children's voices, followed by a couple deep, mocking men's voices as well, "Me, me."

The few who went on were Dag and Sage and Praxis, a young hippie-ish couple (who were the parents of Medea and her twin, a boy named Hunter), and a quiet single father, named Grant, with a daughter called Fortuna. There was a feeling walking in the dark under the trees, stumbling over roots and jutting-out rocks. The image of Cyrus and Kitty kissing was still in Sage's mind, but she would not acknowledge this as any sign of abandon or licentiousness that was to come with this night. What she felt was a loaded feeling, a pleasurable, restless weight, as if something were about to take flight from within her, something was going to push its way out and expand. She wanted to sink back, to watch and feel with these others around her but not privy to her thoughts. She wanted to remain here, grateful and quiet, walking along holding Praxis's hand and this other child's hand. And no, she had not smoked anything tonight, she mused.

Through the overhead branches she saw a full moon in the murky blue sky. "Hey, do you guys see the moon?" she asked the kids.

"I see the moon! I see it!" exclaimed Praxis. "The moon is *white*!"

"That's right," said Sage.

The red-haired girl on her other hand said, rather pensively, "When you can't see the moon at night, it's because it's hiding behind the sun."

"Is that true?" Sage thought it sounded possible.

Now they were walking up a hill. Praxis let out a sigh. "Earth has many big hills," he said.

———

In the middle of the night, after the campfire had died down, Sage awoke and took her flashlight and crawled out of the tent, leaving Dag and Praxis sleeping. She headed through the trees and down the hill to the schoolhouse to use the bathroom. At one moment another flashlight beam bobbed toward her across the grass. It was Brian. He smiled and said "hello there." Sage smiled back and said "hi" as they skirted one another on the path. The whites of his eyes glowed in the dimness. Their whole fleeting exchange felt, to her, permeated by the warm glowing look of his eyes. It was not an invitation to stop or say more, though it was an acknowledgment of a sort, a delicate passing of one another in the dark, she felt. The whole evening had become saturated with this peculiar feeling, in fact—a feeling of kindness and fragility having to do with community—and she did not think it was her sensitivity alone creating it.

She reached the schoolyard, opened the gate. She crossed the playground. The empty sandbox and scattered toys, the wooden structure of the playscape rising toward the stars, the moonlight shining dully down on the metal of the slide. The lingering vapors of the children's energies seemed to emanate from these objects, lucid and eerie. Then she heard voices, noises from the side of the schoolhouse.

Two bodies were hoisting themselves onto the roof, jumping from the deck railing onto a low part of the roof, then scrambling up higher. One of the shapes was Cyrus's, she could see, and she assumed then that maybe the other one was Kitty, but it was a man's shape. She could hear two male voices. They were laughing and talking low. Then one of them pointed a flashlight beam down at her.

"Who goes there?"

She stopped. She turned her own flashlight up at the figures on the roof. "I'm not sleepwalking," she said, as if this were the accusation she expected them to put to her.

Cyrus was the one shining the light on her. He gestured melodramatically with his other arm. "Nonsleepwalker, come join us on the roof! We're looking at stars as well as houses on the hills!"

The other one leaned against Cyrus and said, "And we're drinking bourbon." She saw the bottle held up against the sky.

"I'm just here to pee," she said, deciding to play it cool. Then she continued on her way into the schoolhouse.

The moonlight shone in through the big windows. The branches of trees outside cast faint, swaying shadows on the wood floors inside. The wood floors gleamed. Shelves of toys, low tables, little chairs, piles of books of all different sizes and thicknesses stared back at Sage, blue and silent and waiting. She fumbled through the darkness of the kitchen to the bathroom.

On her way back out, she lingered in front of a wall of paintings until she found Praxis's name under dried blotches of green paint. At the sight of this, she felt a surge of affection that was strangely heartbreaking. A feeling of lightness bloomed in her chest. Moisture blurred her eyes.

Outside again, she let herself be persuaded to climb onto the roof. Cyrus reached his hand out to help her. She tried to refuse. "You don't have to."

But he was being playfully chivalrous and insistent. "C'mon, take my hand, just take it." Gripping her by the forearm, he pulled her up.

The other person on the roof was the quiet single father, Fortuna's dad, Grant. He immediately offered Sage a plastic cup in which he served her a small amount of bourbon.

"Are you kidding? I can't drink this," she said.

"Sure you can," said Grant, affably. His instant comfort with her caught her off guard. Here was somebody she'd never looked at closely, and when now she did she saw a reserved-looking man in his mid- to late thirties who had more complexity and mirth to him than his soft, plain looks belied. "Have some Coke with it," he offered, reaching into a small cooler at his feet and pulling out a liter bottle of soda.

Why were they being so inviting toward her? She would not make too much of it, she decided. She would try, rather, to remain calm and indifferent and to ignore the feelings of anticipation their attention stirred in her, for she did not want to be one of those mothers who read too far into things (things with men, that was) just because of their own state of isolation: she had noticed mothers of small children got like this. They blushed when strange men smiled at their children in the grocery store; they applied too much sincerity when telling the man behind the deli counter which thickness they wanted their ham slices to be and too much sweetness when thanking him. Sage knew because she had done things like this herself, too. At a birthday party once, a mother had leaned over and said to Sage, "That man is winking at me," meaning Dag. The woman hadn't known Dag was with Sage, who knew, with certainty, that Dag was not winking at anyone. Sage said, "You mean my husband?" and the woman laughed, embarrassed: "Oh, it must be *you* he's winking at then!"

Now, she was trying to act oblivious toward Cyrus, after what she had seen of him with Kitty that afternoon. It was on the tip of her tongue to ask where Kitty was, but she did not. The secret knowledge of what she had seen, and her own—unwarranted, she knew—slightly crushed hopes, required her, now, to ignore him. She was not intimidated by Kitty as a sexual rival; in fact, she thought she had just as much to offer. None of these were concrete thoughts in Sage's head, however. Energetically, she made an alluring fortress out of herself, laughing while retreating, opening herself toward Grant instead of Cyrus, and when he spoke, she did not look his way immediately but lingered on other things and then looked, as if she had only just noticed he was talking.

"See that?" said Cyrus, coming to stand next to her and pointing. "That's the governor's house. The governor who was in the car with Kennedy when he was assassinated. That really modern-looking thing. He liked to cook so they made the kitchen be on the third floor, for the view—" She could not deny there was a feeling of ease standing next to him.

"No, man, you got it wrong," said Grant. "That modern-looking house is *above* the governor's house. You can't see the governor's house from here when it's all dark like this."

Sage looked to where Cyrus was pointing. She could see night-blackened treetops and lights on distant hills. She had walked through one of the hill homes once (Dag's company was doing a repair job there) and had been surprised by how safe and light and comfortable the place had felt; she was surprised, really, by how comfortable *she* had felt in such a place. All that attention to detail and beauty, all that care taken to make their home a haven—good views, top-of-the-line appliances, comfort to spare. It struck Sage that people like this (people with money, that was) intentionally fashioned their homes to be cushions against reality: of course they did, and how could you blame them? If you *could* do such a thing, why not do it? The house Cyrus was pointing to now was, from here, a garish rectangular silhouette jutting out from the side of one of the facing hills.

"If it were the current governor who lived there and I had a high-powered slingshot," said Cyrus, extending one arm and pulling back with the other, pretending to take aim.

"Did you hear the kids at the gate this morning? They were all sitting there waiting to go out for a hike, and they were all chanting, 'We want out, we want out.' You know what I said to Ellen?" He turned and looked at Grant as he asked this. Ellen, Sage knew, was one of the other teachers.

"What'd you say?" said Grant.

"I told her, 'You need to stop pushing your liberal propaganda on these kids.'" Cyrus grinned.

Grant gave a laugh. "That's a good one, that's a good thing to say to her."

"I am only concerned with the truth!" Cyrus downed the rest of his drink, then looked Grant's way again. "But no, really, like I was saying earlier, I went to that meeting with Ellen and it was a little bit disappointing. I mean, I agree the patriarchal system is to blame for a lot of the imbalance of power that exists in the world, but I don't think we need to take it so literally, you know? I mean, men suffer under expectations placed on them by the patriarchy, too. Not all men want to be patriarchs or are even capable of it, but they're *expected* to be capable. I just don't think we're arriving at a healthy solution when women try to place all the responsibility on men."

Sage said, meaning it good-humoredly, "Oh no, what did I just walk into?" She was already feeling the bourbon.

Grant caught her eye. "Sorry we got you up here, aren't you?" The affection in his remark, as if he were confident she would enjoy it, caught her attention. Tonight was a gift, she thought. Bourbon on a rooftop, always a gift.

"Women are powerful. They don't even realize the extent of their power, I think. It's no wonder a patriarchal system arose to try and contain that power, you know?" said Cyrus.

"I've been trying to figure out what in a man's experience is equal to the woman's experience of bearing children. Of bearing life, you know."

"Why don't you ask—" Grant looked at her. "I know you're Praxis's mom but I realize I don't know your name."

"Sage, her name is Sage." Cyrus reached his arm around her suddenly, placing his hands firmly on her shoulders. She accepted this with a frozen, surrendering grin.

"I know which kids belong to which adults, I know their faces, and I know all the *kids'* names," said Grant, shaking his head and speaking into his cup.

Sage said, "It's understandable, really. I think it's easier to just be so-and-so's parent—to know each other as so-and-so's parents rather than by all our names, that is. It's like a mask or something. You don't have to be yourself. You can just be your child's parent." She shrugged. "At least I've noticed I feel like that."

Cyrus still had his arm around her. She could take that any number of ways, it occurred to her. Something in his physical affection was, yet, chaste and nonselective. The image of him and Kitty kissing occurred to Sage again, like an image hovering against the night sky right in front of them; how could they not all see it?

"The quiet one speaks at last," said Cyrus. He gave her shoulders a firm squeeze and released her, raising his cup toward hers.

Grant said, "Bearing the child is not all there is to it, though, Cyrus."

"Of course not. But by the dictates of nature the mother is still the primary nurturer—"

"I think as humans we also have the ability and choice to defy nature, though. And sometimes that in itself is still a response that is true to nature—individual natures, perhaps."

"I know who you're talking about, and I will give you that," responded Cyrus.

"There was no way that woman could've stayed around to nurture her daughter, nature or not. No way." Grant made quotation marks with his fingers around the word *nurture*. Then he looked at Sage and explained. She did not even have to ask. Fortuna's mother was, according to both Grant and Cyrus, the kind of woman who could have been dangerous to her child. Not that she was a bad person, just not the kind that was good with children. She had a fierce ambition; she was a little bit wild. It was what he had fallen in love with, in fact, once upon a time. There had been drugs involved, sex, the music scene—she was a singer. Not here, but in New Orleans.

"I can understand women not wanting to fit the mold, I guess," said Sage, carefully. "I see a lot of dissatisfied mothers out there. I wouldn't want to give up my own ambitions, either."

Some silence followed. Sage looked at the stars. The men went on talking. When she tuned in again, Cyrus was talking about a trip he had taken to Holland in college, how he had gone to visit the actual attic where Anne Frank and her family lived during the Nazi occupation. "Speaking of rooftops," Cyrus was saying.

Sage finished her drink. They had been sitting in a loose semicircle, and now she got up to leave.

"So tell us, Sage, where is your man right now?" said Cyrus, as if Dag's absence had just occurred to him.

"My man's asleep with my child." Sage felt the words come out of her mouth slyly, in a style that was not her own. She did not know where she had stolen it from. They were looking at her, she was aware. She didn't know what she was saying now. "It's just better that way," she said.

Later she would think, *it started that night.* Like a seed. Nothing concrete to ensure it existed beyond her imagination. Just a feeling that was barely a whisper: a question mark at the end of, not a question, but just a fragment of a sentence.

―――――

Still, things went on as they normally had. Except for the wakened feeling in her chest that seemed to come and go without clear reason of why or what it was to be associated with, she went about her days that fall and winter in the usual fashion. She was busy, Dag was busy, and sometimes they were not busy. Sometimes the days were long, and their activities were frivolous. Dag worked in the yard; she framed photographs and hung them on the walls. Together, they painted Praxis's room blue and theirs a dark red. In the news there was continuing talk of war or no war with Iraq. When she went out to play music she saw guitar players with "Attack Iraq? No!" stickers on their instrument cases next to their "South Austin: We're All Here 'Cause We're Not All There" stickers. She did not have a fully formed opinion on the matter herself. She was basically a supporter of the liberal side of things, but what were politics, really? She could not get over the sense of their false value in the deeper scheme of life as she saw it. At one music show she heard a singer say, "Fuck politics, let's just get right with God first," and felt that perhaps she agreed with this sentiment over most others she'd heard.

But, too, it could be said that her brain did not retain factual information well. She could glean essence but could not remember names, dates, relationships. Even when she made an effort, she could not quite follow the news—the details of events failed to penetrate more than the surface of her mind. She felt foolish admitting this, so she usually didn't. On the Internet one night she happened on an anarchist's website that said something to the effect of "why not let the kind of people who are dumb enough to go to war go," and that after all those people had been killed off and the structure of modern industrialized society had basically crumbled, the ones left behind would rebuild the world in a better way— more grassroots, smaller communities, that sort of thing. She knew that too was an imperfect theory but still found she couldn't entirely disagree with it, either. She was like a sponge; she could absorb nearly any viewpoint. And she tended to understand details better when they were filtered through the passions and opinions—or even ridicule—of others. She cared more about people than politics, was what it came down to.

Another truth for her was: sometimes one just wanted to be selfish. Sometimes one just wanted to be concerned with the esoteric matters of one's own life.

Three days a week she drove Praxis to and from school. Each encounter with Cyrus was now laced with a sense of watchfulness for her. She thought she felt something growing between them; she also thought it might just be her own flight of fancy. So, she watched this feeling to see how long it would stay and what made it stay or go and what made it seem to grow. It did not occur to her to try to approach Cyrus and communicate any of this to him. She even told herself maybe the feeling didn't really have to do with him at all, that maybe she had just fixed it upon him when, actually, it had only to do with a process that was happening inside herself. At times the feeling seemed to hang in the air around her like a general, encompassing grace. Like a short-wave frequency that was available to (but not meant to be received by) everybody. She also thought perhaps it had simply to do with being in the presence of the children and that she connected him somehow with the innocence and wonder she felt inspired in her by the children. She would have convinced herself of this, that her fascination with him was only a projection—but then would come a morning when, as she stepped through the gate, he separated himself from someone else he was talking to on the other side of the playground and walked over to hug her and say hello. In this gesture, she would again be engulfed by the feeling of white lightness.

This, she was aware, could be what was meant by phrases like *on another plane* and *blowing things out of proportion*.

When she went along on Praxis's field trips, these events, too, became beautifully laced with a sensation of lightness possibly leading her to somewhere new and better, a freer state of being. She wanted to get to the other side of it. She feared she might not get there, to that point of one day looking back (older and wiser) at even the most calamitous events of her life with gratitude.

At the field trip to the fire station, the firefighter donned all his gear on the lawn in front of the station, so that the kids would know what a firefighter in full gear looked like

and that they should not be afraid of him. He did look formidable. He got down on his hands and knees and crawled
around, to show the children what he might look like coming
toward them through the smoke if one day there happened
to be a fire in any of their homes or any other kind of emergency. Praxis did not seem interested in this presentation in
the same way the other kids were (he was standing up when
the rest of them were sitting down, he was walking around,
he was picking up sticks and leaves), while Sage was thinking
of how they would never need to use this lesson—somehow
she was sure of it. They did not live in the kind of place
where Praxis would ever be trapped alone in a room if there
was a fire; the house they lived in was small, all the rooms
opened onto one another, and Praxis rarely slept alone as it
was. But more than that, she simply knew it was not in their
fates to deal with that kind of emergency: the less definitive
emergencies were the ones that would be a test for people
like herself and Dag. The firefighter was advising them all to
have exit plans for their homes. It was the word *home* that
made her feel as if his speech didn't really concern them; she
didn't think of where they lived now as her home. She felt,
somehow, exempt from the concept of home and the respon-
sibilities of having one. Thinking this made her worry she
was just being immature as well, though.

In the middle of Firefighter Dennis's speech, Praxis
walked up to him and pointed at his jacket and said,
"There's a bug on you." All the adults found this amusing.
It also gave Sage the impression that her son took things in
much like she did, in pieces, not paying as much attention to
the foremost content of things as he was to his own private

measure of what order should be. This, too, told her something, she thought.

What worked for others might not work for them.

At the field trip to Bull Creek Preserve, she watched the
sunlight make everyone's skin glow and give the heads of
the children haloes, and she watched the water plunge and
eddy around the rocks. At lunchtime she sat at the picnic
bench Praxis chose (again, apart from the rest of the kids),
and Cyrus came and sat with them, and again there was
the feeling. The lightness. Within it everything felt magni-
fied. The morning was immensely beautiful and bright. The
children were the embodiment of purity, imbuing the adults
with their sense of wonder. Cyrus was drinking from a car-
ton of chocolate soy milk and spelling out the word *glass*
over his shoulder to another teacher: "I saw some *g-l-a-s-s*
over there, when they go back to the water we should move
them upstream a little probably." She liked the way he took
care of worrisome things without appearing worried. They
did not speak to each other, but they spoke to Praxis, while
in the air between them lay—what seemed like—a contract
of care and appreciation.

And at the field trip to the state capitol, she walked along
the sidewalk with the wind blowing her hair across her face.
This day was overcast and cool. The lightness was still there,
but it was different now, tinged too with poignancy. She was
leading a line of children toward the entrance doors. At the
top of the capitol dome was a statue of a woman in flowing
robes holding a tome in her arms.

"That's a goddess," said one of the children.

"No, it's a statue," corrected another of them.

"That's our Lady Justice," said one of the other mothers, quite cheerfully.

Again, for Sage, it was not the content but the sheer irony of being there, within the same moment as this other mother, but Sage was caught up in a feeling of the wind and a sense of there being a diagram to the moment, seeing it all as if from overhead—she was one X leading a line of smaller, linked x's toward the large domed circle that was the capitol; the other mother was another X, a little off to the side, leading only a few of the smaller x's. There were a number of them, these larger X's leading smaller x's, and between all of them there were slung tangential threads, creating in the spaces between all X's, big and little, a gigantic and complicated, parking-lot-sized web, each thread of which had its individual thickness and quality; she was linked more definitively to some than others. Sage knew there was a meaning to this view of things—if only she could learn *how* to read it! A frustration kicked inside her. It was like trying to read a billboard on the other side of a fogged-up window: it was large and should be plain to see, but for the fog.

Inside, the building was impressive, was spectacular, it was true. They walked from one immense, shining, circular foyer to the next. "Are there games in here?" Praxis asked, awed, and Sage understood that he had for some reason been made to think of a video game arcade.

"Well," she said, and Cyrus, walking just ahead of them, said, "There *are* games here, though I don't think they're the kind you're hoping for."

They gathered on a large star inlaid in the floor of the rotunda to listen to the tour guide, a young woman in her early twenties who looked like a college student.

"Where's the governor's heaven? Are we going to see the governor's heaven?" asked one of Praxis's classmates, the boy named Hunter, raising his hand.

The tour guide looked confused, and so did the other parents, but Sage understood immediately what Hunter was talking about; he meant the governor's mansion.

"Oh, the governor's *mansion*, of course!" said the tour guide. "No, sweetie, the governor comes *here*, to the capitol building, to do his work."

And that was how things would go for Sage from about the middle of the fall to the beginning of spring.

Mundane moments loaded with inexpressible sensation and meaning that she felt she must decipher. Cyrus on the periphery, sometimes closer to the center, weaving in and out among the clouds of her sad, wondrous stupor. A multitude of small graces striking her again and again. When would she wake up? When would she know more precisely what it was she was supposed to wake to?

Other times, it was her own son who told her everything she needed to know. From her bedroom she could see through the doorway into his room where he sat on his bed one afternoon, watching a video. In her mind the thought occurred, not even that strongly, *The boy he's growing up to be*. He didn't glance her way as he said, "Mom. I don't want to grow up."

4.

The lightness filled her chest like something palpable yet buoyant. It felt deliciously like love, or it felt sometimes like anxiety. It felt like it might sear a hole in her skin, or like it was making her skin thinner, or it felt like simple hunger. It was housed in moments and sights: a line of trees that faced her car as she came to a stop at the end of the road away from Praxis's school, each morning at the same hour. Tall, narrow, tangled trunks and branches making a phalanx on the other side of the highway, a mesh of textured brownness. The lightness made feeling itself feel somewhat dangerous, portentous—it would be too much to feel this way all the time. Some mornings she came home after taking Praxis to school and stood in the middle of the living room and cried for no reason she could clearly fathom.

The morning light poured through the windows, making bright patches on the hardwood floor, lighting up motes of dust swirling in midair, while in her mind she saw: the sunlight on his skin by the creek, the moon over the Mojave Desert that she and Dag drove across when they first started out for Texas, Dag's gray backpack and the skateboard that had leaned against it that day in the coffee shop where they'd first met. All these images struck her with a sharp sense of loss.

And: a pool of light under a parking lot lamp outside a bar one night after a gig. Who had been standing under that lamp? Some tattooed boy smoking a cigarette with lazy eyes, telling her, "You sounded real good tonight," in a southern drawl, and how that had made her think, was there a differ-

ence between "really good" and "real good," and would she
ever be able to call this place home, then?

She saw her son, too, his bright eyes and his smooth,
round, olive-skinned face. She saw him walk through the
gate of his school and glance back at her with a knowing, af-
fectionate look in his eyes. He wore a little backpack on his
shoulders, which were becoming square more than round,
already. When did it end, this habit of attaching love to every
movement a boy made?

The trees at the end of the road by Praxis's school quiv-
ered with green then yellowing leaves in October; they were
gray and leafless by January.

5.

Two weeks after the field trip to the capitol with Praxis's
school, she found herself there again, in early February, with
both Praxis and Dalgleish, this time for a peace rally.

The rally was to be the biggest of its kind so far in regard
to the pending war, and it was being purported that this was
the largest organized gathering of antiwar protesters since
the 1960s.

Dag, Sage, and Praxis parked a few blocks away and
walked through the downtown streets to the capitol. There
was a steady stream of others headed in the same direction.
A lot of people had children or dogs with them. It seemed
purposeful but not indulgent, not at all grave or radical. At
the last minute Sage had thought to bring along Praxis's toy
oxygen mask, and she was carrying it in her backpack. The

oxygen mask was part of a firefighter costume that Praxis
had received a few weeks earlier for his birthday. Bringing it
today was not entirely her idea; Praxis initiated it himself a
few days ago—he had insisted on wearing the oxygen mask
to the grocery store, and people had looked at them. Some
had smiled, and some had looked puzzled, even possibly offended. Sage was amused by their reaction. She imagined it
could be a movement. Toddlers in oxygen masks standing
in line with their parents at coffee shops, riding in shopping
carts down produce aisles, poring over picture books in the
bookstore. Whole playgrounds of children wearing oxygen
masks while the adults remained maskless.

Sage had to be talked into going to the peace rally, was
the truth. And her idea of toddlers in oxygen masks was more
satirical than it was a reflection of sincere concern about the
world. Dag was the one who had heard about the peace rally
and thought it would be worthwhile to go.

They walked across the rolling lawns, making their way
toward a statue of a man on horseback in the center of one
of the lawns. On the capitol steps somebody was speaking
behind a podium. Sage looked around at the crowd of protesters holding up signs and banners. They said things like
MAKE JOBS NOT WAR and ONE WORLD NO WAR, ONE
WAR NO WORLD and gave statistics about the percentage
of the Iraqi population that was children. Even a number
of the dogs wore signs, and theirs said things like LEASH
THE DOGS OF WAR! Most of the crowd were young, Sage
noticed. She saw smooth-faced boys in tie-dyed T-shirts and
sagging pants, groups of them, and wary, delicate-looking
girls sprinkled in their midst, all of them looking fashion-

ably disheveled and good-hearted. Many of them were barefoot. Looking at them, she could read their lives plainly, she felt, as if the emotional and sequential facts of all their histories and futures had taken solid yet unphysical shape—like thought bubbles—in the air around them. She saw the passion they felt for their experiences, and she saw that they had no real awareness of where their youth would lead them. She saw how this day's event would be just one more among a string of events that would someday add up to exactly that, their youth; though they didn't know it now. Some of them were sharper and wiser than others, though; she could see that, too. The sharper ones would know what to make of the experience of their youth leaving them when it did, while the others would probably struggle and fumble with it more, and would in consequence get old faster. There was, too, the distinct odor of marijuana smoke.

Sage wondered, was there a time like this for every generation? She suspected there was, in whatever context it occurred, and that what she was feeling was actually nothing new.

Praxis had put on his oxygen mask and was climbing on a bronzed cannon statue on the lawn. People were stopping to look at him; a few even took his picture. "*That*," someone remarked to the person beside them, pointing at Praxis, "is brilliant." A few people looked at Sage and smiled their approval, but many did not; they just looked at Praxis in his oxygen mask. She felt as if she had put her son on display. But she had not really meant anything by it, not wholeheartedly; for her it had been more of a sort of joke. There was no way of qualifying it now, however. Her

son in his oxygen mask spoke for itself, regardless of whatever the actual nuances of her intentions about it might
have been.

"Here, here," said a tousled-looking hippie man, wearing
no shirt, carrying a wooden sign on a stake that announced
his support of "subatomic particles for peace." He had a
hairy chest and a beer gut. He stopped beside the cannon
and struck a pose next to Praxis in his oxygen mask, and
someone snapped a picture of the two of them. Praxis had
recently developed a new way of smiling for the camera. His
mouth would stretch out in a thin line and his cheeks would
bunch up, making his eyes look like cheerfully narrowed
slits. He did this every time anyone asked him to smile for a
photograph.

Sage tried to listen to the speaker but kept having to
turn her attention back to Praxis, because she did not want
him to fall off the cannon. After a while she gave up listening to the speaker and focused instead on watching Praxis.
Dag, meanwhile, had moved up through the crowd to be
closer to the front, where he could hear better. Sage knew
he cared more about what was being said than she did. She
looked at the dogs wearing signs; she looked at the people's
faces. As she stood there taking things in, she saw Cyrus
approaching through the crowd with another of the male
teachers from the school, the handsome baby-faced one who
looked like a teenager but was actually twenty-five, and a
lanky red-haired boy Sage had never seen before, probably
one of Cyrus's friends. Neither Cyrus nor his companions
were toting signs or banners. They stood in the crowd, looking comfortable, looking forward, with their arms folded
across their chests.

Sage got Praxis down from the cannon and pointed out Cyrus to him. Then they made their way over to him. He stepped forward to greet her. The hug between them was warm. She realized (a slight realization, like tumbling into the bottom of a bowl that is not deep, that is safe) that tenderness was a possibility between them. Suddenly she was certain her life was about to drastically change—whether he had anything to do with it or not. She thought, *We are going to mistake the political for the personal*, or was it the other way around?

She half-waved at the other two, and they lifted their hands back at her in greeting. Timothy was the red-haired one; Hal was the baby-faced one.

Cyrus asked how her weekend was going, and she talked about a show she'd gone to see the previous evening. He had gone to see one, too. He said, "Just wild, decadent fun, you know." He had seen Reverend Horton Heat.

She had seen Neko Case. "This female singer I like a lot. Kind of country but not traditional country. She just has this presence. When she sings the whole place feels electric." At the end of the show the singer had urged the audience to go to the peace rally the next day. That had told Sage: there was a side to things presently happening in the world that people like herself—people who liked this music, that meant—were expected to be on.

Cyrus couldn't stand still as he spoke to her, she noticed. He bobbed back and forth from one foot to the other, like a younger, more boyish version of himself, while on the other side of him Hal, who was boyish, stood quite still, like a deer caught in the headlights of an oncoming car: in this case, the vehicle hurtling toward him (toward them all, really) was the ineffable might of the rally. It was as if this might were an actual entity, or substance, being blasted forth from the capitol dome. A map of their position in the crowd struck Sage; it was like the diagram of big X's and little x's she had seen in her mind on the day of the field trip to the capitol. The place seemed potent, and the circular shape of the dome had something to do with it. The sidewalks cutting across the lawns, leading in perfect diagonals away from the cap- itol building, were not unlike a depiction of the rays of the sun: that was the kind of place a capitol was, whether you wanted to believe in it or not. Cyrus was present now as he had been the day of the field trip; so was Praxis; so was she; so were others with their dogs and children. They had some part in this—this whatever-it-was—even if they were only molecules in the waves trying to beat at the concrete steps.

"It's really good to see you here." Cyrus was looking at her and saying that as if she had shown up at a party he was throwing. Glancing around at the crowd, he added, "It looks like there's been a good turnout. And it looks like the speak- ers are doing a good job motivating."

"Yeah, I think they are," agreed his red-haired friend, who was still looking toward the Capitol steps.

Sage swept her eyes over the crowd but only nodded, not wanting to admit she hadn't been listening to what the speakers were saying. "I think Praxis is more into the dogs than he is anything else here," she said, because now Praxis was pointing to a Dalmatian, the one wearing the LEASH THE DOGS OF WAR! sign on his back.

"Well, of course he would be. The dogs are super-cool," declared Cyrus, dropping to his knees in front of Praxis and trying to catch him in a hug. Praxis laughed and twisted away. Then Cyrus jumped to his feet abruptly, and Praxis screamed and turned and ran into the crowd. Cyrus went after him.

Hal, the baby-faced one, glanced Sage's way and said, slowly, "You can really feel it in the air today that people are trying to put out love, you know?" He was so soft and sincere, she had to take him seriously, although she knew a comment like that would make most people skeptical.

"Yeah, sure, it's encouraging to see this many people out here," she said.

"Sometimes I see things that are not physically here, you know?" He went on, "I feel like that most of the time, when things are just normally going on as they do. Traffic jams and people in line at stores and nobody looking honestly at anybody else. When I look at people I feel like I can see straight into their souls, and I see how they're *really* doing, you know? I can see that 'cause I have a lot of love inside of me, a lot of pain, though, too." His gaze shifted as he spoke; he furrowed his brow and stared into the crowd. "I'd like to try to record what I see in an honest way. I try to write it down, you know, but then I start to feel like I'm being egotistical, writing things down as if I'm someone who knows. So then I tear it up and throw it away." He was not smiling. "I tear it up and throw it away," he said again, with a slight pause.

This was the longest dialogue Sage had ever had with this boy; she thought it must be the mood of the rally. "Like tonight. I'll probably go home and try to write about the feeling in the air today, but then I'll get disgusted with myself and throw it all away," he said.

Were Jesus to be represented as a teen heartthrob, he might look like Hal, thought Sage. This boy's beauty was almost unfortunate, it occurred to her; because of it, she had not expected him to be a soulful person. A lock of sun-streaked hair curled perfectly above his left eyebrow, and his eyebrows were the color of honey with light shining through. His skin was warm and tan. She could not imagine this kind of boy ever growing up. What sort of man could a boy like this possibly become? He was better off as a boy, she decided, beautiful and soft and young-looking enough to attract others to care for him because he probably needed it. So it was with children, too.

Praxis came running back and slammed himself into her legs, wrapped his arms in a frenzy around her waist. He was laughing wildly. Cyrus wasn't far behind. He chased Praxis a little more, then stopped, feigning tiredness.

Dag came back through the crowd and spotted them. He and Cyrus shook hands in a hearty, enthusiastic way, while Sage looked for hints (of what—herself?) in the interaction between them. Hal sat down in the grass and kicked off his flip-flops, propped his elbows on his knees. Cyrus's friend, Tim, was also barefoot by this point. He sat cross-legged in the grass next to Hal and drummed his hands on his knees. He was wearing a South American parka and pants of a thin fabric. His hair was very frizzy and red. He was leaving the next day to backpack down the coast to Guatemala, because his father was down there traveling and they were going to meet up, he told them. He seemed proud yet cool about having a father he could meet up with backpacking in Guatemala. He and his father had had enough of America, he said.

"And to think this is also the home base of George W. Bush," remarked Cyrus.

"Where you have a large amount of liberalism you're bound to have an adverse amount of rigidity, and vice versa, I suppose," said Dag. "It's the law of opposing forces."

"It is," said Cyrus, looking at Dag as if just noticing something about him.

"When *we* were kids we all had hippie parents. Now kids have Dell parents," Tim spoke up from his seated position nearby them. He said this rather indignantly, almost maliciously.

Cyrus caught hold of Praxis and turned him upside down. "Except for this one here, of course. He's being raised in a corporate-free household, I think." Then he grinned in Sage's direction.

Eventually, the crowd began to disperse and move, in one collective motion, off the capitol grounds and onto the streets. The protesters were marching down Congress Avenue. Sage and Dag went with them, taking turns carrying Praxis on their backs. (Other parents who had planned better had their toddlers in jogging strollers, Sage noted, and they had water bottles and snacks.) They soon lost sight of Cyrus and his friends in the crowd and fell in step with a group of musicians, a couple of whom Sage slightly knew. The musicians were passing a guitar among them as they marched, and they were singing in call-and-response, the one holding the guitar leading and the others responding. It felt truly infectious and uplifting. The sun was shining, it was nearly seventy degrees in early February. Cars honked tempestuously at intersections. Policemen on foot and on horseback could be seen on the sidelines of the parade, some of them looking unwillingly stern and out of place. Strangers were smiling and talking at length with one another. They were moving south down the center of the city, it occurred to Sage, with the dome of the Capitol significantly visible behind them. She felt strongly that she was a part of something, so much so that she was suspicious of it. To be righteous about one's belief in how goodness is to come about: wasn't that dangerous even if it was only something as harmless as music that made you feel it? Melodramatic or not, the baby-faced boy had been right in saying there was a feeling in the air. If there was ever going to be somewhere she could call home, it occurred to her that this would be it. This gentle order of girls and boys. This parade of the lackadaisically middle class, the anonymous, the foolishly sincere; this parade of believers in the effectualness of art and in the virtues of barefootedness. Home would be a small circus and nothing more, nothing less.

———

At the end of Congress Avenue, where the protesters eventually reconvened and then dispersed for good, Dag and Sage and Praxis ran into Brian and Kitty and several others from the school, who told them there was going to be an after-rally party at Brian and Kitty's house. Kitty wrote down the directions and handed them to Dag, while Sage wrestled with Praxis's sweatshirt, which he wanted off and which was getting caught around his face. She pulled it free just as he was beginning to panic. A passerby smiled sympathetically, humorously, in her direction—a man with tattoos walking a large black-and-white husky with frost-blue eyes. This man had not made his dog wear a sign, Sage noted. She looked away from the man and his dog toward Brian and Kitty. With the hum and chatter of the crowd in her ears she saw, but did not quite hear, the words "Cyrus will be there" form on Brian's lips.

Dag went ahead of her to the party, taking Praxis with him. Sage went to the store to get beer and something for the grill.

Inside the grocery store, even the tinny-sounding bad pop music wafting down from the rafters seemed to her laden with an atmosphere both mystical and nostalgic. But she felt boundlessly good—selecting veggie burgers, cheap Mexican beer, one fat ripe avocado, tofu ice cream sandwiches for Praxis. She felt buoyed by the energy of the day. She smiled brightly at the checkout cashier, who was singing "Ramblin' Man" to himself in a low voice.

"I love Hank Williams," she said.

"A customer complained once about my singing, wrote a comment to my manager. She thought it was rude," said the checkout boy, rolling his eyes.

"Did they tell you to stop singing?"

"Hell, no. My manager's cool. It gets me through the day, standing here, you know? I mean, I'm not *not* doing my job just 'cause I'm singing. And I'm not even singing that loud."

"People are so weird sometimes," said Sage.

"People *are* weird sometimes," said the checkout boy. Then he told her "Peace" instead of "Have a nice day."

———

It was dark by the time she got to the party, and she saw the green lights before she saw anything else.

A bundle of green light on the lawn. She saw the silhouettes but not the features of people standing around on the driveway and on the lawn in front of the lighted house. She saw the lighted windows of the house and thought they looked like eyes. A fire glowed inside a half-barrel on the middle of the lawn. Approaching the house from where she'd parked her car across the street, for a moment she felt as if she were walking up to a stage—it felt portentous. There were butterflies in her stomach. The bundle of green light, she saw as she stepped onto the lawn, was her son tangled up in a long rope of plastic-encased Christmas lights. Another plastic-encased rope of lights, this one neon pink, lay strewn over the grass in a sloppy square to mark the perimeters of the party. Praxis, it appeared, had wrapped himself up in the neon-green rope of these lights and was turning round and round, tangling himself up further. His skin and hair glowed green—yes, that was her son, and somebody was asking if he was a Christmas tree. He was not answering, but there was a fixed smile on his face. He was basking in the green glow and in the attention, Sage could tell: the night was special, and he knew it, too.

And there were Brian and Kitty, the hosts, the two who had made this atmosphere possible, in their way. Brian tending to the grill, Kitty sitting by the fire with her legs crossed, her teeth white in the dim light as she laughed. They were all players in a production that had been leading up to this very moment in time. There was Hal. There was Lisbeth, the willowy dark girl who reminded Sage of a cat. There was Grant, the single father who had offered her bourbon that night on the schoolhouse roof. And there was Dag, standing beneath the eaves at the corner of the garage (which was open) listening to Grant, both of them holding beers, Dag nodding and then laughing in his harsh, self-pleased way. Cyrus was sitting on a chair not far from where Praxis was wrapped up in green lights on the lawn, and he appeared to be listening to Dag and Grant. They all turned their heads toward Sage as she approached, and she felt encased in light herself, felt around them all a sense of benevolence and warm celebration. She knelt beside her son who was bathed in the glow from the green lights—her son wrapped up in lights!— and immediately he flung his arms round her neck and gave her a kiss on the mouth.

"You're all green!" exclaimed Sage.

Praxis put his fat little hands firmly on either side of her face. "I love you, Mommy."

"I love you, too," she said.

Later, she and Cyrus crossed paths in the kitchen. The kitchen was upstairs in the house. The music—because the stereo was inside—was loud. Cyrus was reaching into the refrigerator. Without asking he handed her a can of beer and took one for himself, put another one in the pocket of his hooded sweatshirt.

"Let's have a talk someday," he said, "soon maybe. Maybe we can have coffee."

"Okay," she said.

There was no need to ask what there was to have a talk about. She smiled at him and turned away, wanting to preserve the integrity of the exchange. He went ahead of her back out to the party. She stopped in the living room and looked at the framed photographs on Brian and Kitty's walls. *Kitty and Brian, Brian and Kitty*, she thought. Something was missing.

"That's us last year in Vail."

It was the photograph of them standing in the snow, dressed in brightly colored ski gear, that Kitty meant.

Sage turned and looked at her. "Oh," she said, feeling as if a second conversation was going on between them, overlaying the words they were actually saying.

"My former stepson," said Kitty, indicating the teenaged boy in the photo. He was standing between Kitty and Brian.

But really she was saying, *I know what you're thinking, and I have been there already.*

"Do you need another?" Kitty held up her empty bottle.

"No thanks," said Sage.

Outside again, the partygoers were playing jump rope on the lawn with the string of green lights. Praxis must have relinquished them. But he was not jumping, in typical form contradicting his name. Instead he was helping— somewhat—to turn one end of the rope while Brian turned the other. Sage stopped at the edge of the driveway, before the lawn; she saw that Dag was watching from his place under the eaves of the garage. The other adults were laughing and ducking their heads as they took turns running into the swinging arc of light. Praxis was laughing, too, as he clasped the rope of lights with both hands and Brian turned it.

————

People come at you sometimes not as people but as instruction—or intersection. Some people you meet just long enough for them to deliver their particular message, and then they are gone. Some messages take longer to deliver than others; some people might be here to give you more than one message. And you may be doing the same for others and just not know it.

I have tried to look at you with love, she thought.

6.

"Minneapolis," said Dag, as if he were making an announcement. "I think Minneapolis." He had just come up the steps to the cabin, back from a walk by himself, and flung himself down on one of the chairs on the porch. He leaned back, arms dangling over the seat's backrest, legs stretched out before him. He tipped back in his chair.

Sage sat cross-legged on the other chair with her guitar across her lap. "You really think?" she said.

"I don't know about Texas anymore," said Dag. "It's hard to get inside of things here. I think it takes a long time. You know how we've both felt that way." He looked out at the desert as he spoke, and Sage had a flash of knowledge at that moment. She saw that if they stayed together, she and Dag, they would eventually leave this town and find another one to complain about and feel excluded from yet again, and it was likely they would continue to do this, moving on and forming their unit—Praxis cocooned within it—at odds with the world. It would always be "us" versus "them." But if they stayed in Austin and separated, she saw something else then. She saw no "them," not clearly, and no defined "us" either. The shape of their family would be a perpetually open, shifting one, with influences coming in and out of it.

Praxis would not know family life to be a form of insularity. This was, in fact, the main hope that came at her out of this vision. She saw him at that moment (did not have to look into their cabin to see him), asleep on the bed, flat on his back, arms laid straight along the sides of his little body, his legs straight, too. It was a waiting position, the way he slept, it struck her.

In front of the cabin next to theirs, the little boy who looked to be the same age as Praxis was riding around on his motorcycle. It made a high, zooming sound as he zipped back and forth along the strip of dirt road. Dust and pebbles kicked up behind him.

Dag went on, "I've been thinking that maybe eventually you have to go back to where you came from, you know?"

"But *I'm* not from Minnesota," said Sage, "I'm from California. And I haven't even *wanted* to go back there, and it's been almost fifteen years."

"Well, you can always go back to California, no matter how long away you spend. It's not as earned a citizenship as in other parts of the country, you know?" He turned and looked at her with this. Then he looked away. "But the reticence of the Midwest. I think I understand that."

Suddenly, she saw the boy's motorcycle fall over, and a small cloud of dust go up around him. The fall happened with only a slight change in the rhythm of the engine's sound. It was almost imperceptible. "Oh," said Sage, uncertainly. Dag stood up quicker than her and was down the steps, across the road, already. Sage removed her guitar from her lap and leaned it on her chair as she got up. She ran down the steps.

Dag was helping the boy to his feet. "He's okay, he's okay," she heard him say as he waved to the boy's parents, who were emerging from their cabin with hands over their mouths.

7.

On their last afternoon in the Chihuahuan Desert, it rained. Thunderclouds bloomed in the distance and billowed out over the desert like inflating parachutes. The air cooled. Lightning drew vivid, swift-vanishing lines across the clouds. The overcast grayness and flashes of lightning lit the desert in a subdued way. The reddish-brown hues of dirt and boulders and mesas deepened; their textures became more etched and visible. The sky had never looked so big to Sage. The dark gray clouds rolled and tumbled through it, as if they had been set loose out of some porthole on the other side of the horizon. Somewhere up there, she thought, it's still blue. Only down here, low enough to invade our vision, come these clouds.

They were watching the storm from under the eaves of the porch when—*it's a circus tiger breaking through a circus curtain*—a plane broke through the clouds.

It listed slightly and soundlessly, its engine's whir getting swallowed up in the sounds of the storm. The plane was the size of a thumbprint (if she held her hand up in front of her face) on the sky, but growing. It appeared to be coming from the north. Its wings seemed tilted, and it looked like it was bumping against the clouds, as if the clouds were of a firmer substance than they actually were. The plane was white with one blue stripe down its length.

It had propellers under its wings. Its nose and windshield windows looked like a robotic face. Seeing it bounce down out of the sky, Sage felt an odd surge of affection for the plane, as if it were, in fact, a kind of creature. She thought the windows might actually blink, in response to the impact, as the plane hit the ground on its belly and slid its chin across the desert floor.

"Holy crap," said Dag, standing up.

From a distance they watched flames go up around the plane. The tongues of flame seemed to sprout right out of the ground, and the rising clouds of dust mingled with the black smoke from the flames so you could not tell dust and smoke apart. Sage felt a wrenching in her gut. The hotness of tears welled up—a rush of fear and adrenaline—behind her eyes. She didn't know why, but that seemed to be her reflexive reaction to trauma, however near or far she was from it; she was a fount of sympathy and empathy but her body was frozen. *What use am I?* She could not make a single move in the world without asking this question. And the distance between their cabin and the desert floor looked deceptive. She would never be able to will herself across it without first constructing a map—a diagram of meaning connecting this event to previous and future ones. So it was fortunate that the world contained other kinds of people, people who were able to respond without meditation to the suddenness of accidents and the need for rescues.

The wind felt actually knocked out of her; a deep, sucking coldness entered her chest. *Let the injuries of whatever has happened to plane or people down there fill me*—this thought like a prayer; the total sincerity of witness. In a future world, a slower one, devoid of emergency and ruled by foresight, maybe there the kind of person she was might finally make more sense, she thought. Now: tiny figure of a truck plowing across the flat desert toward the plane; one, no two, people jumping out of the truck. Sage waited hopefully to see someone, anyone, emerge from the plane. It was hard to tell what was going on.

Dag was holding the keys to his truck. "Let's drive down there," he said.

In her mind she felt a slipping-away sensation. All of this, it was not real. The clouds had been spewed into the sky by a machine. She was almost certain of it. The lightning, too, would never strike anyone she knew closely. "No," she said, mortified. Then she added, "Praxis is *asleep*."

———

What else had she not told Dag about that night in the bar? There had been a young man with horns. They were more like little knobs, really, but they were under his skin, protruding from his forehead. Someone remarked they had been implanted. This man was mildly notorious, had been on a talk show or two, was a local character. Did he give an explanation for his desire to have horns implanted in his forehead? Sage wanted to know—she hoped the reason he gave might be something revelatory: that there was a new order of human being coming into the race and that he wished to represent it, something alien, something fantastical, that would put them in touch with realms the modern world tended to ignore. Or that his monstrous appearance was meant to be pointing a way back into an understanding of their oft-denied darkness. Or that his mutation was a symbolic representation of the devil in his person and, thus, in all people. Sage wanted to believe in the horned man's wisdom. Aberrations of nature must serve a purpose, she thought, perhaps they are meant to illustrate in shocking ways just how far off the track humans have gotten. The man's body was clothed in black jeans, a black T-shirt, a chain hanging off his belt, a dog-choker around his neck. She thought, *But his style is full of cliché.* Then she thought: how could any style of dress worn by someone with actual horns in his head *not* be construed as trying to make some kind of statement or other about our societal trappings?

The woman with him looked to be in her late teens. A girl, really. They were standing next to Sage, Cyrus, and the other mothers at the bar. The girl's shoulders looked like they had extra bones in them, just above her shoulder blades. Her skin was grotesquely taut around those bones. She looked over her shoulder and caught Sage staring at her. She bugged her eyes out.

"Hel-*lo*," she said.

———

"I had a dream and you were in it. There were lots of other people around, too, people who were our friends. There was something about our group—we were all very shiny. And we had been chosen to go on these missions. Where we lived was covered by a great big dome, we wore uniforms, like spacesuits without helmets, though, and we sat in these big auditorium meetings. You and I were in a room at one point in a big building, looking out a window. What we saw when we looked out was like an optical illusion, though—we were looking *up*, but it was as if we were looking *down* from even way up higher, like we were looking down on this spectacular view of the city, of tall, tall skyscrapers. Like, the view was just breathtaking. Then we had to say goodbye to each other 'cause we were going on these space missions. Each mission would take a whole lifetime to complete, and it was the building of space stations. One space station would create the material to make the next one, and they would alternate, all boys on one station, all girls on the next one. So it went boy one, girl one, boy one, girl one, reaching further and further out into space."

Cyrus laid his head down on his arms on the bartop as he was telling her this. Then he said, "I'm so tired. I could fall asleep right here, right now." Around them, the bar clinked and chattered, and music played from the jukebox, sounding as if it was coming out in chunks that were being tucked into all the nooks and crannies of the room. Chunks of music bursting and fading, invading every available space, like blooms of smoke, wedging into the spaces between bodies, between bodies and bar furniture, swirling around her head, making lights dance on the insides of her eyelids. She wished Cyrus would lift his head and look at her again; she wished the room would stop throbbing and flashing; she wished someone would have the sense to lead them out of this place so that they might talk where they could actually hear each other. Then she might say, *Well, I've had dreams with you in them, too.*

———

Dag was driving toward the wreckage. Sage stood on the porch of the cabin.

Acknowledgments

Thanks to my friends and all the "six o'clock" readers along the way: Kate Hill Cantrill, John Greenman, Elena Eidelberg, Sarah Johnson, Amy Lowrey, Arthur Lee, Alexander Parsons, Mike Yang, Amanda Eyre Ward, and Katherine Tanney.

Thanks to David Meeker for digging Nina Simone's song "Four Women" out of his record collection and playing it for me.

Thanks to the National Endowment for the Arts for much-needed and appreciated support.

Thanks to Jennifer Carlson and Megan Hustad for reading intuitively and taking the time to pay attention to subtle rhythms.

And thanks to my mother, again and always, for setting me on this path.

DAO STROM is the author of a bilingual poetry-art book, *You Will Always Be Someone from Somewhere Else*; an experimental memoir, *We Were Meant to Be a Gentle People*; a song cycle, *East/West*; and two books of fiction, *Grass Roof, Tin Roof* and *The Gentle Order of Girls and Boys*. She has received awards from the Creative Capital Foundation, RACC, the NEA, and others. She was born in Vietnam, grew up in the Sierra Nevada foothills of California, and is now based in Portland. Find out more at daostrom.com.

Printed in the United States
by Baker & Taylor Publisher Services